P9-DUK-084

The Rogue Mage Novels by Faith Hunter

BLOODRING
SERAPHS
HOST

Praise for
the Rogue Mage Novels

Seraphs

"The world [Hunter] has created is unique and bleak. . . .
[An] exciting science fiction thriller."
                                        —*Midwest Book Review*

"Continuing the story begun in *Bloodring*, Hunter expands on her darkly alluring vision of a future in which the armies of good and evil wage their eternal struggle in the world of flesh and blood. Strong characters and a compelling story."   —*Library Journal*

"This thrilling dark fantasy has elements of danger, adventure, and religious fanaticism, plus sexual overtones. Hunter's impressive narrative skills vividly describe a changed world, and she artfully weaves in social commentary. . . . A well-written, exciting novel." —*Romantic Times*

Bloodring

"A bold interpretation of the what-might-be. . . . With a delicate weaving of magic and scripture, Faith Hunter left me wondering: What's a woman to do when she falls in love with a seraph's child?"   —Kim Harrison

"Entertaining. . . . Outstanding supporting characters. . . . The strong cliff-hanger of an ending bodes well for future adventures."   —*Publishers Weekly*

"The cast is incredible. . . . Fans of postapocalypse fantasies will appreciate this superb interpretation of the endless end of days."   —*Midwest Book Review*

"Hunter's distinctive future vision offers a fresh though dark glimpse into a newly made postapocalyptic world. Bold and imaginative in approach, with appealing characters and a suspense-filled story, this belongs in most fantasy collections."   —*Library Journal*

continued . . .

"It's a pleasure to read this engaging tale about characters connected by strong bonds of friendship and family. Mixes romance, high fantasy, apocalyptic, and postapocalyptic adventure to good effect."   —*Kirkus Reviews*

"Hunter's very professionally executed, tasty blend of dark fantasy, mystery, and romance should please fans of all three genres."   —*Booklist*

"Entertaining. . . . A promising new series. . . . Steady pacing, dashes of humor, and a strong story line coupled with a great ending neatly setting up the next adventure make this take on the apocalypse worth checking out."

—*Monsters and Critics*

"Enjoyable . . . a tale of magic and secrets in a world gone mad."   —*Romantic Times*

Host

"Hunter's world continues to expand in this highly original fantasy with lively characters, where nothing can ever be taken for granted."   —*Publishers Weekly*

"Hunter has created a remarkable interpretation of the aftermath of Armageddon, in which angels and devils once again walk the earth, and humans struggle to find a place. Stylish storytelling and gripping drama make this a good addition to most fantasy collections."   —*Library Journal*

"Readers will admire [Thorn's] sacrifice placing others before herself. . . . Fans will enjoy reading about the continuing end of days."   —*Midwest Book Review*

"With fast-paced action and the possibility of more romance, this is an enjoyable read with an alluring magical touch."   —*Darque Reviews*

SERAPHS

A Rogue Mage Novel

FAITH HUNTER

A ROC BOOK

ROC
Published by New American Library, a division of
Penguin Group (USA) Inc., 375 Hudson Street,
New York, New York 10014, USA
Penguin Group (Canada), 90 Eglinton Avenue East, Suite 700, Toronto,
Ontario M4P 2Y3, Canada (a division of Pearson Penguin Canada Inc.)
Penguin Books Ltd., 80 Strand, London WC2R 0RL, England
Penguin Ireland, 25 St. Stephen's Green, Dublin 2,
Ireland (a division of Penguin Books Ltd.)
Penguin Group (Australia), 250 Camberwell Road, Camberwell, Victoria 3124,
Australia (a division of Pearson Australia Group Pty. Ltd.)
Penguin Books India Pvt. Ltd., 11 Community Centre, Panchsheel Park,
New Delhi - 110 017, India
Penguin Group (NZ), 67 Apollo Drive, Rosedale, North Shore 0632,
New Zealand (a division of Pearson New Zealand Ltd.)
Penguin Books (South Africa) (Pty.) Ltd., 24 Sturdee Avenue,
Rosebank, Johannesburg 2196, South Africa

Penguin Books Ltd., Registered Offices:
80 Strand, London WC2R 0RL, England

Published by Roc, an imprint of New American Library, a division of Penguin
Group (USA) Inc. Previously published in a Roc trade paperback edition.

First Roc Mass Market Printing, December 2008
10 9 8 7 6 5 4 3 2 1

Copyright © Faith Hunter, 2007
All rights reserved

 REGISTERED TRADEMARK—MARCA REGISTRADA

Printed in the United States of America

Without limiting the rights under copyright reserved above, no part of this publica-
tion may be reproduced, stored in or introduced into a retrieval system, or transmit-
ted, in any form, or by any means (electronic, mechanical, photocopying, recording,
or otherwise), without the prior written permission of both the copyright owner and
the above publisher of this book.

PUBLISHER'S NOTE
This is a work of fiction. Names, characters, places, and incidents either are the prod-
uct of the author's imagination or are used fictitiously, and any resemblance to ac-
tual persons, living or dead, business establishments, events, or locales is entirely
coincidental.
    The publisher does not have any control over and does not assume any responsi-
bility for author or third-party Web sites or their content.

If you purchased this book without a cover, you should be aware that this book is
stolen property. It was reported as "unsold and destroyed" to the publisher, and neither the author nor the publisher has received any payment for this "stripped book."

The scanning, uploading, and distribution of this book via the Internet or via any
other means without the permission of the publisher is illegal and punishable by law.
Please purchase only authorized electronic editions, and do not participate in or encourage electronic piracy of copyrighted materials. Your support of the author's
rights is appreciated.

To my Renaissance Man

Acknowledgments

Many thanks to:
  My Renaissance Man, for encouragement and for writing the
    songs.
  Kim, for support, for friendship, and for tea breaks.
  Tamar, for being there when I'm not strong.
  Kipper, for the stones.
  Ben, for the martial arts stuff.
  Matthew, for keeping my Enclave bearable.

  My agent, Lucienne Diver, for believing in me and for loving
    the world of the Enclave.

  Finally and profoundly, my editor, Liz Scheier, for making me
    think—and write—darker, faster, and leaner. And for put-
    ting up with me. This has been the *most* FUN!

Chapter 1

Claws gripped my throat, shutting off my air, and Raziel laughed against my mouth. It was a triumphant rumble, feral and heated, but the amusement had an unfamiliar edge, and fear gripped me. *"Yesss,"* he whispered, mind to mind, *"where are the wheels?"* The claws relaxed and I inhaled a scent, cloying and intoxicating, like lilacs and jasmine growing up from an open grave. *"Your heart beats with the fragrance of Amethyst and her wheels. Where are they?"*

I tried to open my eyes. *This isn't Raziel,* I thought, instinctively hiding the knowledge deep in my mind where the whisperer couldn't find it. And, *I'm trapped.* I struggled to make a fist, to grip the sword hilt, the metal cold in my unresponsive palm. In the distance, a predator cat called a warning, a portent. *A lynx.*

Distantly, an alarm sounded, muffled, flat tones. The door of my loft crashed open, followed by a bellow of rage. I opened my eyes. A Darkness recoiled, wrenched away, over my bed and was gone.

In a single movement, honed from weeks of sword practice, I gripped the handle of my walking stick and pulled the sword from its sheath, rolled from the bed, and attacked. Blade and sheath whirled in a frenzy, upward, together, and back out in the sleeping cat—a move that could disembowel an enemy. The sword and sheath, one in either hand, whispered along Audric's belly. His blades *shush*ed over my head as I pivoted. Coming fully awake, I dashed the tears from my eyes and glimpsed the bed, covers tossed to the floor, barely visible in the predawn light. The loft was icy, the frigid cold chilling my skin. I breathed the floral reek, and the sickly sweet scent of decay. *An incubus. An incubus had been in my bed.*

Audric, a half-breed warrior, rotated, and my sword met his with a ringing clang of steel on steel as I leaped high and cut down, placing my feet with precision when I landed. "Where is it?" he roared, ducking under my blade. With his superior strength, he beat me back, the flats of his blades slapping my sides, the hilts bruising my ribs. "*Seraph stones!* I smell it on you!"

Using his height and my own diminutive size, I danced under his arms and landed three blows with the sheath, any one of which would have been a mortal wound had I used a blade. His elbow impacted my jaw. I collided with the bed and rolled over the mattress with the momentum. The scent of old death billowed out of the cotton sheets and silk duvet. Behind me, the phone shrilled, ignored. My voice answered on the machine, the volume turned low, the greeting a murmur. I danced away from him. "Gone," I gasped.

Audric stepped back and crossed his swords, offering a respite. "Rape?" he asked, curt as all half-breeds are in battle. His eyes raked me, assessing. More formally, he said, "You are naked."

My breath heaved. I looked down. I *was* naked. My neo-mage attributes glowed along my skin with the rosy peach hue of mage-power, my scars blazing white like sunlight through quartz crystal. My amulets, which I had worn to bed, were missing. A fleeting look found them tangled with my pajamas, half beneath a pillow. "No," I said, catching my breath. "You got here in time." But my loft was icy, the smell of death rancid and choking. It shouldn't have been able to get in. My home, the shop downstairs, even the spring outside; all were conjured to keep me safe.

"The light is odd. Purple?" Audric scrutinized my loft, his weapons at rest, his face alight with hope. "You used the amethyst in the stockroom to fight the demon?"

I inspected the apartment, breath wheezing, heart hammering with exertion, ripped from dreams of arousal and sex to battle in a heartbeat. The loft was radiant, an irregular lavender thrumming in time to my pulse. Mage-sight focused, I sought the stone in its metal boxes one floor below. There was no answering flare of power, no might I could use to fight or conjure. There was nothing. A dull headache started over my temple as I tried to draw on the stone, throbbing with my pulse and with the lavender energies I could no longer use. "No," I said, hating the timbre of defeat in my voice. "It's still dead. If there's energy, it's residual."

Audric raised his weapons again, the blades still crossed. "And the incubus?" With his half-mage heritage, his skin glowed like mine, a dull peach sheen emanating from his dark skin.

"Got past my wards," I stated baldly, finally catching my breath. "I'll have to try something else. And yes, it still calls. It's getting creative."

"It will tempt you as long as it has your blood. Get dressed."

I sheathed the blade, knowing it was true. A Power of Darkness on the left peak of the Trine had my blood, having collected it during battle dire. Now it wanted all I had, all I was, all I knew. If I didn't get my blood back, I'd ultimately succumb to its lures, saddle my horse, and ride north, up the Trine, the tri-peaked mountain overlooking Mineral City, to my doom.

I turned on the overhead lights and, taking my cue from Audric's choice of attire, dressed in white practice dobok, a padded, form-fitting, martial-arts uniform adopted by the first neomages when they created savage-chi and savage-blade. Courteously, Audric kept his back to me, opening windows at the south and north sides of the loft. A frozen wind blew through, winter having returned with a vengeance, but the chill air took with it the smell of death, or froze it out. Before I was dressed, he made the same round, closing the windows. He knelt at the gas-log fireplaces, turning the flames of both on high. I could feel their heat instantly from behind the dressing screen across the room. Below the neomage glow, I was blue with cold, yet I could still smell my mage-heat, like cookies and almonds and blood. "Weapons?" I asked.

"Bamboo staves," he said, "lightweight." I heard a cloth-on-cloth abrasion and peeked around the screen to see Audric stripping my bed. When he caught my eye he said, "Stinks." Audric was typically laconic in battle mode, though he never lost the formality that marked his breed— the half-human, half-neomage second-unforeseen.

The sheets tied in a hobo's knot, he leaned against the front door to clear a wedge of snow, letting in another blast of cold air and the uncertain sound of sleet peppering the outside world. He tossed the sheets onto the porch and closed the door. The smell of the loft improved quickly, especially when he lit two scented candles, bayberry and fig. The big man surveyed the apartment and pushed aside the kitchen table.

I sighed. When he rearranged the furniture, I was in for a hard practice session and lots of bruises. It meant he was in a good mood and wanted to share, or was in a very bad mood and wanted to take it out on me. Either way, I would be sore. Still hidden behind the dressing screen, I slid to the bathroom and took two ibuprofen. I wasn't human, but the anti-inflammatory worked as well on me as it did on them. I'd also release the conjure stored in a healing amulet the moment practice was over. Though I was tempted, it would be cheating to release it now. I pulled on socks, two pairs, thick and warm, and slapped on soft-soled practice shoes.

While Audric busied himself making tea, I slid from the screen and approached on silent feet. "If you want a thorough drubbing," he said without turning around, "you'll strike when my back is turned. Otherwise, you'll wait until I'm ready."

"Snarky half-breed," I said, sotto voce.

"Indeed I am," he said, amused. Whipping bamboo staves from under his arm, he tossed a pair to me and slapped me twice before I could snatch them from the air. "You move with less grace than a ten-year-old, little mage," he said dryly, "and you're as slow as a human."

Mage-fast, I whipped around him and pricked him three times. "Dead, dead, dead," I said. "Now who's slow?"

"Look down," he said.

I flicked my eyes to see his left stave touching my side, angled to rip liver and kidney. Not so dead, dead, dead, after all. He slid into the swan and rapidly into the horse, almost as fast as a mage, bamboo staves slapping me rhythmically through the sequence. I leaped into the proper blocks and parries, warmth flowing into my chilled body as battle-lust wrestled with the cold of dreams and the touch of evil, as bloodlust replaced the mage-heat created by the incubus. Sweat glistened on my arms and trickled down my spine. I couldn't help what the incubus made me feel, but I could choose what I did about it. Battle was better than sex with an incorporeal Darkness. In fact, almost anything was better than sex with an incorporeal Darkness.

When I was warmed up, Audric slapped me across my butt, hard, like he might a child. "Fight, little mage. You move like a human this morning." I snarled at the affront. He chuckled. "You nearly let that thing seduce you, little girl. As if you were nothing more than a child." He slapped my backside again, playfully.

Audric was deftly moving me from one passion to another, from desire to anger. The fact that he had such control of my emotions made me even more furious. "You let a minor Power lie with you, in your bed. You are slow and lazy as a human. And you are a fool."

Insult piling on insult. But he was right. Evil had been in my loft. It had touched me. Moving as fast as my kind could, I cut, and cut, and cut, delivering deadly blows over his heart, over his left kidney, and over the artery feeding his liver. Three deadly strikes slid in under his guard. Audric knew it. "Better and better, little mage." He danced away. "Someday, if you dedicate yourself to battle and battle alone, you may defeat me. It isn't likely, but it is possible."

"I'd rather have you at my back, killing off spawn," I said. "And Dragons."

Audric missed a beat. I speared him fast, a single heart thrust. "Dead," I said.

"What do you know of Dragons?" he asked, closing on me, delivering a lung thrust.

I blocked and countered. "More than I want to," I said, still striking fast.

"Here?" he asked. And he slammed me in the left side.

I fell to the floor and he hit me twice more, blows that would have decapitated me from both left and right. Air erupted from my throat with a sound like "Uueeerpt." Audric laughed again, cruelly this time, finding humor in my pain. I skittered, reeling across the kitchen tile, seeing only a turquoise blur in the almost-dawn light. My teacher followed, lashing me. "You will tell me soon why this place on your left side causes you such pain."

"There's no pain," I lied. I had thought myself healed, but I could use the old wound as a weapon. Feigning injury with a gasp, I dropped flat and separated my weapons as if in surrender. He reacted; a minuscule hesitation, a millisecond delay. I brought up both bamboo staves, the practice weapons nonlethal, rounded, and blunt. Crossing them at the tips, I hit him just below his breastbone—a lethal strike had I wished. Even using the bamboo rods, the move was capable of rupturing the descending aorta.

The staves indented his chest, the tips shoving up under his ribs. Air whooshed from his lungs in a pained grunt. His knees buckled. Mage-fast, I whipped from beneath him and watched him fall, tumbling in an avalanche of joints and long bones and torso to the floor. And I heard myself laugh. "Die, mule," I said, insulting.

Audric looked up from the floor, his dark eyes meeting mine in horror. He splayed a hand over the spot where I'd struck him, fingers clenching. The bright glow of a deep bruise emanated from between his fingers. Fear snatched my breath. How hard had I hit him? Shock, sorrow, heartache, and disbelief bled from his eyes. *Little mage, what have you done? I am done for,* he seemed to say. Horrified, I fell to my knees. Audric bellowed, and lunged. "Gotcha!"

"Saints' balls," I cursed hoarsely, trying to block his practice staves from taking my heart. But the bamboo tips hit my chest, one digging in hard just below my sternum, the other below my left breast. The breath left my lungs. He rose from the floor and held me down, foot on my throat. I was finished.

"Never feel for the enemy," Audric said, a lesson from Battle Mage 101. "Never! And stop cursing. Your Darkness might hear you and come back to visit." His staves clacked together sharply. "Now get up. Try to do it right this time."

Mages have better night vision than humans, a better sense of smell, and are faster. But our musculature and skeletal frames are lighter, more brittle, and mock battle with a stronger opponent tires us fast. In Enclave—the gilded prisons where my kind are kept, separated from humans who hate us—such tiring helps control mage-heat, an out-of-control sexual arousal when in the presence of seraphs. In Enclave, almost everyone dances and practices the savage arts just as Audric forced me to. I knew that, if I refused, I'd end up with broken bones. Easier to give in.

An hour later, I was exhausted, sweating, my scarlet hair sticking in oily strands, my dobok damp and chilly, even with the temperature rising in the loft. I had bruises on my bruises and my right ankle was sore where I had twisted it, trying to replicate a move he'd shown me, an advanced horse, rising, walking, and prancing in a half circle all at once. When he had me thoroughly whipped, he let me rest. Well, sort of. He sat me at the kitchen table with a strong cup of tea and gave me a pop quiz on the history of the swan, and of the neomage who had created the flashy move.

In the midst of the testing, he questioned me again about the weak place on my side. I tried to sidestep the answer with humor, but he refused to rise to the bait, straddling a chair across from me, face serene but determined.

Finally, elbows on the table, hands clasped in front of me on the papers, I said, "I nearly died on the Trine, sitting in a conjuring circle, scrying beneath the ground into the hellhole of Darkness. I was spying, okay?" Trying to find Lucas ... trying to see what was down there.

"Thorn," he sighed.

"I know. It was stupid," I said, watching my scarred fingers flex. "And I don't really even know if everything I saw in the vision was real. But I got trapped in this reddish stuff, some kind of conjure, an enormous structure deep underground. And this"—I paused, not knowing what to call it—"this *thing*—half insect, half reptile—speared me with a claw or a barb." I touched my side, feeling the invisible bruise. "It wasn't real. It was all in my mind. But it felt real." *It still feels real.*

I didn't mention the creature I had found down there, the being called Mistress Amethyst, trapped in the structure. I didn't add that a seraph of the Most High had gone down there and hadn't come back out. I didn't know why I kept that part to myself, but I had. I also didn't add that I hadn't been able to get free from the trap by myself, and that if I hadn't had help from the surface, I would have suffocated in the midst of an incantation I hadn't been ready to try and should never have attempted alone. I had been lucky. Very lucky. And Audric didn't believe in luck.

My self-appointed teacher, his deep brown eyes trying to pierce the secrets I still held close, pointed to the *Book of Workings* on my shelf. "Study that. Learn what you did wrong. Then we'll talk about it. You missed proper training when you left Enclave. I *will* see you appropriately educated in all the mage arts."

At eight o'clock, he clicked his bamboo staves together and left, pausing once in the open door of the loft, a cold breeze blowing in from the stairwell. "You must strengthen your wards and find out why these are suddenly so ineffective."

"Gee, Audric, what a bright idea. Wonder why I didn't think of that?" I was feeling snarky.

He closed the door. I took two more ibuprofen and ate a breakfast of oatmeal, raisins, and almonds while soaking in a hot bath atop healing amulets on the porcelain tub's bottom. Underneath the neomage glow, I was a mass of welts, bruises, and new scars that crisscrossed and lumped over my older scars. I wasn't real pretty to look at, but then, if I didn't count the incubus who came by from time to time, I hadn't had a suitor, lover, or boyfriend in months, no one to see me naked. Audric didn't count. His preferences lay elsewhere.

I dropped a last healing amulet into the water, and let it

settle in the bottom of the old tub behind my back. It worked its conjure as I sipped my tea. The water in tea and bath was springwater, drawn from the conjured, shielded, and booby-trapped spring behind the shop. With the amulet, they would take most of the pain and a lot of the blood out of the bruises, making it easier to glamour them. The newer scars were harder to hide; they glowed hotter than the older ones, especially the ones on my left hand. I made a fist, testing the flexibility of the fingers and the ugly, ridged scars that pulled against tendons and bones. In mage-sight, the scars were a solid white glow across my hand. Even with a double dose of a glamour, there was still a muted radiance.

Not that I had to conceal what I was. Everyone in Mineral City now knew I was a mage, and that I had been in hiding among them for more than ten years. A lot of the townspeople didn't want me here, so I was keeping a low profile. No mage-clothes, no practicing savage-chi or savage-blade in the streets, no glowing, and certainly no display of my scars to remind them of the battle I had fought, the battle that had kept them safe for the last few weeks. There was nothing like demonstrating that people were beholden to you to make them hate you.

At nine, I braided my hair, dressed in beige overleggings and a tunic with boots, hid my amulets, and glamoured my skin down to the dullness of human flesh. The mirrors assured me I looked human, if not beautiful. The scars on my face resisted even my best conjures. Before leaving the apartment, I checked the messages, the red blinking light reminding me that a call had come through near dawn, just after Audric woke me with swordplay. No message, just the sound of breathing and a faint click as the caller hung up. Not a threat; not really anything. But there had been a lot of such calls recently. I figured it was disgruntled members of the orthodox, or maybe Jane Hilton, my ex-husband's alleged new wife. But I didn't know, and until someone made Caller ID technology cheap enough for the average investor, I had no way to find out. Like many such devices, the technology was available, but expensive since the end of the world.

I put back my shoulders, set aside my disquiet, and went to open Thorn's Gems, the jewelry and lapidary shop I owned with my two best friends. I would wear red brecciated jasper today to contrast with the brighter scarlet of my hair. And maybe today the townspeople would stop treating me like I had brought them a plague.

Chapter 2

⸸

Downstairs, I lit the gas logs to warm the shop, and opened the safe. By the time Audric and Rupert joined me, the dregs of an argument lingering in the air, display cases were filled with our wares, coffee was brewing, and water for tea was simmering. Rupert was close-mouthed, lips tight with denial. I knew what it meant. He was always like this when it was time for Audric to head back to work. Arguments always ruined their last few days together.

Audric was a dead-miner with a claim on the entire town of Sugar Grove. He had been in Mineral City, in the Appalachian Mountains, to sell his latest finds, visit among the humans he loved, and resupply. Now he had to go back to work. In late February, in a mini–ice age, work meant a grueling three- or four-day journey to his claim through snow-covered mountain trails, Then months of work uncovering more of the gold, silver, junkyards, china and crystal, and other treasures that had survived the town's destruction and abandonment.

Unless he sold the claim to a rich prospector or a big company that specialized in dead-mining, it would be months before he returned. There had been offers for the claim, which made this leave-taking even more bitter-sweet. I wanted to add my voice to Rupert's and beg Audric to stay. When he left, I'd be the only supernat for a hundred miles. Maybe more. But I knew better than to ask him to give up his claim. Few dead-miners ever located an entire town. Audric was famous for his discovery. The big half-breed had pride: pride in his find, pride in his claim, pride in his mining skills, pride in his fighting abilities. If he stuck around, he'd be less independent, and Audric could never countenance that. He had to make a fortune and a name for himself.

As they argued, covering ground they had scoured clean a hundred times before, I laid out a selection of emerald pieces, the stones extracted from the nearby hills. Mineral City was known all over the US for the quartz and feldspar dug from cliffs and scraped from strip mines. The two common minerals provided financial success for the town, but its gems were spectacular, calling to the speculator and the individual prospector, and the latest claims were making us famous for gemstones. The emeralds had been sold to Thorn's Gems by a local miner, and the deep green of the stones was spectacular. I had made a chunky necklace out of some B-grade portions, and added a faceted focal stone. The necklace was too pricey to interest the locals, but I'd listed it on the store's Web site. I was hoping for a quick sale at the asking price. Two comparable pieces had been sent to retail stores that showcased our jewelry in Atlanta and Mobile. Stores all over the country hoped to carry our designs, and we had to decide if we wanted to expand the line to satisfy the current demand, or stay exclusive. Expanding meant we needed to hire help or take in a new partner. Like Audric, who could buy in if he really wanted to. Which made these arguments even more difficult.

I was a lapidary, meaning I worked with raw stone, turning it into unique jewelry, statues, vases, and, now that I had been revealed as a mage, into amulets and charms for the customers who wanted them. Not all did. The sale of conjured items was a sore spot with some orthodox practitioners, both locally and out of state.

I set our pricey items in the center display case. The top glass was damaged, making it hard to see some of the merchandise, but the blemished site was probably the only reason Thorn's Gems hadn't been broken into, vandalized, and ransacked by a mob of the local extremists. Even in a town as small as Mineral City, there were plenty of those around. The flaw was a four-inch circle, created when a seraph, an angel of punishment, had dropped by to visit me—well, to judge me—and had removed his sigil of office, placing it on the display case. The antique, Pre-Ap glass had crazed and heated almost to the melting point under the powerful amulet, leaving the top permanently etched with a symbol of the Most High—the ring and its firelike lettering of the word Adonai. I polished the defect with a cloth.

If I had been taken away that day by the seraph, whose name was still unknown to us, there probably wouldn't have been two bricks still standing for my partners to divide. Now, I figured only the burned, cracked, partially melted ring of glass kept us safe. It was a reminder to the townspeople that I had permission from the High Host to be here. Lucky me.

I had hidden in plain sight, disguised as a human, for ten years, a blatant violation of the edicts set up by the High Host of the Seraphim. Any other mage would have been carted back to Enclave in disgrace or turned over to humans for judgment. For me, either punishment would have meant certain death, though the human execution would have been more bloody and violent than the mage-death. But I had been given permission to stay on in Mineral City. The reprieve was a two-edged sword. The townspeople treated me like I was a rogue tiger. Interesting, maybe even mesmerizing, but not something you wanted living next door.

I arranged the emeralds as my friends bickered and the townspeople strolled back from sunrise kirk services, many peering into the shop in curiosity, many more turning their heads away, as if the sight of me might contaminate them. It wasn't as if I flaunted being a neomage. I kept my skin blanked to human dullness and I dressed in human clothes, never displaying my amulets or weapons. With the exception of a few new scars, I didn't look any different from before the seraph had outed me, but now I sometimes felt like I had the words "Whore witchy-woman" tattooed on my forehead.

An elderly woman dressed in unrelieved orthodox black, from her dress to her boots and heavy overcoat, paused at the front window and deliberately turned to stare into the shop. When she caught my eye, I paused, holding a stunning turquoise necklace with silver beads that dangled. The woman lifted her hands and made a version of devil horns at me, thumbs and little fingers pointed up, the others folded under. The symbol had once meant other things. Now it was the sign of evil. My friends fell silent. Outside, the passersby seemed to stop, all watching. It was the most blatant reaction to me since the day the seraph had come. Up the street, two others dressed in orthodox black paused and gaped, their eyes gleaming, faces arrested in midconversation. My face flamed. The beads in my hands clattered.

A little farther, an elder also watched, his brown robes blowing in the frozen wind. Elder Jasper halted, his Bible in one hand, his crucifix dangling. Jasper, who had once been my friend. The elder looked censorious, not of me, but of the old woman.

The hateful woman dropped her hands and moved on, her boots crunching the frozen snow. Sleet wisped against the building and onto my porch over the front walk. The townspeople moved on, some clearly embarrassed, others openly gleeful. The hatred was now out in the open. On some level, I knew that things would change now. And they wouldn't be getting better.

Jacey, my other best friend, opened the door, the bells jingling cheerfully. Storming inside, she threw her walking stick into the umbrella stand and her cape over the coatrack all in one motion. The walking stick clattered. The coatrack wobbled. "Did you see her? The old bat. You just let Old Lady Vestis come by the shop again on a Monday when we're closed, needing a favor, a last-minute gift. That's the last time—" Jacey looked at me, standing unmoving behind the counter, still holding the turquoise necklace, and stopped speaking. She pointed a finger at me.

"You will not let that old harpy make you feel bad. You *will not*!" When I couldn't manage a smile, Jacey stomped over and took the necklace, setting it on the countertop

with a clank. Then she bent and hugged me tight, hard,
turning my face to her shoulder, before she pushed me
away and shook me like she might one of her many children and stepchildren. "You will *not* feel bad about her.
She's only one of a few—a very few—who feel that way.
Most people are excited at the thought of having a neomage living in town." She shook me again. "How many
people have come to the shop for a charm? Or a special
amulet? Lots!"

"After hours," I said. "Sneaking around, ashamed. People I've known since I came here, went to school with; people I liked." I remembered the faces, the shock, at the sight
of the old woman. A sudden realization hit me. "Or they're
afraid of me." I looked up at Jacey's brown eyes and
mussed brown hair, bangs tangled by the wind. "That's it,
isn't it? They're all afraid."

"Not of you," Rupert said softly from behind me. "Of
the orthodox."

"What's going on?" I asked. I tried to jerk away, but
Jacey held me firm, her strong hands gripping my shoulders, human muscle mass winning out against mage swiftness. "You promised you'd tell me if there was trouble
starting."

"There's been talk. A little," Jacey said. "But you know
we're standing up for you."

"Talk? About what? Strangulation? Drawing and quar-
tering? Hot pincers and knives? *Stones and blood.* I've put
all of you in danger, haven't I?"

To the left of the shop windows, the front door opened
again, bells jaunty. A cold wind skittered across the floor.
We all turned. Elder Jasper stood in the opening, his face
harsh, the crucifix dangling against his robes of office. His
Bible was tight in his hands, his knuckles white against the
dark leather. I knew he hadn't heard me curse—he'd still
been outside—but I clamped my mouth shut in fear.
Slowly, deliberately, he stepped inside.

Just as deliberately, Rupert, Audric, and Jacey flanked
me. Audric slid one hand into his sleeve. Jasper's eyes
tracked the movements and his forward motion halted. To
the side, the gas flames flogged the fake logs in a jittery,

hungry rhythm. Outside, sleet shushed down, the sound cutting off the rest of the world. Audric pivoted, clearing his target line. Violence wavered in the air between the elder and us. Tension constricted my throat. Faster than their eyes could track, I slipped to the side, around the display case, and up to Jasper.

"Thorn's Gems is honored to receive the kirk elder," I said, placing myself between Audric and Jasper.

Jasper's eyes widened, then tightened at my blatant use of mage-speed. His gaze moved from my face to the three beyond, taking in their taut postures, the locations of Audric's hands, the anger on the faces of my friends. Gently, he closed the door, so carefully that the bells didn't chime. "My blessing on your house," he said, the formal words an elder spoke when he came calling. But then he added, "And may you find absolution and forgiveness in the countenance of the Most High." Not casual words, but words of mercy, words uttered before judgment, when one has been called to trial for a crime worthy of punishment or death. *Seraph stones.* I was being called before the kirk.

Jasper was two years my senior, one of the few Cherokee to stay with the kirk rather than to withdraw his religious practices to the hills. He had dark eyes and black hair worn long and braided in a single thick plait. His hawklike eyes were black and piercing, his nose a commanding beak. At the moment, however, he looked anything but hawklike, his face creased with compassion. "I'm sorry, Thorn. I voted against this—I want you to know that."

"But?" Rupert said, black eyes belligerent. He elbowed his way between the elder and me, as if he would protect me with his body. And I knew he would. The thought warmed me. Maybe some in Mineral City hated and feared mages, but not my friends. I raised my head and watched the tableau, seeing through the storefront windows as two crowds gathered in the street, orthodox in one small group, progressives and reformed in another. Split fifty-fifty.

Jasper was still speaking. "I was able to help some, but Elders Perkins and Culpepper have a lot more clout than I do. They want you charged." He pulled a sheaf from his Bible, the pages sealed with the red wax of a kirk summons. "I want you to know I'm on your side. I always will be." He took a deep breath, gripped his Bible across his chest, and said, "Thorn St. Croix, you are officially served." He handed me the papers. So much for compassion, friendship, and the loyalty of old friends.

I held the legal summons as Jasper left, icy winter air again blowing across the shop floor, like a mistral of omens. The thick paper felt cold on my chapped skin as I cracked the wax seal, unfolded the pages, and smoothed them across the display glass. Rupert, Jacey, and Audric moved into a half circle behind me to read over my shoulder.

It was a legal writ, the paper signed by the Council of the Town Fathers—elected officials and kirk-appointed elders—who judged all things spiritual and most things legal in Mineral City. I read it twice before I understood the charges. I had been accused of practicing abominations. Meaning black magic or forbidden sexual practices. Fear raced up the back of my neck. The charge was a federal crime. If found guilty, judgment would be swift and lethal. My heart rate kicked up a notch. Fight or flight. Rupert cursed foully.

I held up a hand to stop him. There was something peculiar about the summons. Such a charge usually meant immediate arrest—shackles, leg irons, the witch-catcher: a special mask humans had created just for mages, with iron rods that were inserted between the teeth, holding the mouth open wide to keep a mage from chanting a defensive conjure. Maybe Jasper had more clout than he claimed he did. Or maybe I had more support than I feared.

I wasn't being summoned to the kirk, but to a meeting in the old Central Baptist Church building—the town hall—at ten today. That was both good and bad. Good, because it meant any judgment rendered would be secular, and would have to be ratified by a unanimous vote of town fathers rather than a few kirk elders in private. And confirmation of a guilty verdict would take time, time I could use to get away. It was bad for two reasons: because the whole town would be present, and because I wasn't being given time to prepare a legal defense. If the crowd turned to violence, a lynch mob taking the proceedings into its own hands, I'd be toast. Or I'd have to fight. Either outcome was bad.

As likely scenarios, tactics, plans, and possibilities ran through my mind, I refolded the writ and tucked it into my tunic. My hands, which had shaken so badly only moments before, were suddenly steady, as if my emotions had entered some kind of stasis, and the part of me that had studied as a battle mage in a different life had taken over. I looped the turquoise necklace over Jacey's neck, thinking while I tidied the rest of the display case.

"Is Zeddy available?" I asked the quiet room. Jacey nodded, her trembling fingers on my arm; tears glittered in her eyes. I patted her icy hand. "It's okay," I said, not certain if I was lying. "It'll be fine. But just in case, would you have him saddle Homer and gather supplies for a week in the mountains? If it looks like they're going to decide against me, I'll run. You guys need to be ready to take off too, or to defend the shop. I'll set a few wards—"

"Stop," Audric interrupted. "There will be no problem with Thorn's Gems. Concentrate on taking care of yourself." The big man pushed me between my partners and toward the stairs. "Go, little mage. You don't have much time to prepare. Jacey, call this number and tell the man who answers what has happened. Then call Zeddy. Have him saddle both the horses and put supplies for two on the mule, enough for ten days. What?" he asked when I looked at him, surprised. "You think they'll stop with you? If they find you guilty, they'll come for the rest of us. We've been planning for this. Now go change." Turning his back on me, Audric continued instructing Rupert in the defense of the shop. Jacey, taking a steadying breath, picked up the telephone and dialed the number Audric had written.

I turned and went up the stairs, my footsteps hollow on the cold, warped boards.

He fell, rolling across the nest of feathers to the rock wall on the far side of the cell. Pain and desire lanced through him, setting fire to the bones of his clipped wings, burning in his loins. Agony raced through him, and lust, and need.

He groaned. The cell door behind him closed, a ringing finality, the demon-iron scattering frost crystals with the vibration. He heard the shackles hit the ground on the hallway floor outside his cell.

"See you in twenty-four hours, Watcher," his captor said.

He moaned again, turning to lie facedown on the feathers. His feathers. The delicate bones of his severed wings gave beneath his weight. In an hour the new wounds would be clotted over, leaking a bit of thin, clear, serous fluid. Another hour, and that too would be gone; his flesh would heal over, his bones would start to regenerate, the agony would diminish. Shortly after his wounds healed and the bones began to redevelop, the lust would start to fade, unrelieved, unfulfilled.

In twenty-four hours his tormentors would return, shackle him in demon-iron, and take him back to the torture chamber. There, with human steel, they would again shear the new growth off his wings. Demon-iron would cause more pain, which they liked, but it would cauterize the damaged tissue with ice, and they wanted him bleeding. While he dripped blood and suffered, the pain weakening him, they would bring in a mage, likely one bred when he stimulated her captured mother into heat. He had been here long enough to be working on a second generation. Maybe a third.

He laughed silently, bitterly. Because of him, the Dark had hundreds of mages born in captivity. He was an aphrodisiac to mages. They were an aphrodisiac to him. Like today, this new offering would go into mage-heat, ovulating, as the species could do only in the presence of a seraph. And once again, he would refuse to mate. Refuse something he wanted almost more than forgiveness itself. Refuse to create kylen that could be used by the Lord of Darkness. When the mage was screaming and mindless with desire, their captors would take her away to breed with the being of their choice, to impregnate her, perhaps to create a new captive with special genetic traits. Half mage, half something Dark. But not half seraph. No.

Once they dragged her away, he would be tossed back into his cage to partially heal; twenty-four hours of recuperation until they came for him. Again. His laughter sounded half mad. When he sucked in a breath, the air reeked of his own misery and fear. Tears trickled across his flight feathers, mixing with his blood. A rich, iridescent green, the feathers threw back the dim light of the one candle they allowed him.

How long? How long imprisoned in the wretchedness of this river of time? How many times mutilated? Tortured. Tied to the earth, without flight. That was the worst of it. Was this the humans' concept of purgatory? The pain started to ease. His tears dried.

Watcher. Who are you?

"Go away," he said aloud, his voice a cracked bell trying to ring, speaking to the voice that no one else heard. It came when his pain was still fresh, but becoming bearable, a new temptation devised by his torturers. "Get thee behind me," he muttered. "There are no seraphs in the pit of Darkness, none but me. None."

Watcher. Who are you?

"Blood and feathers," he cursed. "I am no one. The Most High has so decreed. But if you wish to address me, you may call me Barak."

You who were once called Baraqyal? the voice belled, a startled tone. It was a seraphic intonation, the sound like gongs and the soughing of the wind.

Barak rolled swiftly to his feet. "Who are you?" he shouted.

Zadkiel. We are trapped. Help me. Help us.

His wild laughter roared, the sound more than mad, reverberating off the walls of his small cell. "Then we shall die together, O mighty one," he said. "For by decree of the Most High, I cannot transmogrify. And the Dark One has clipped my wings. I cannot fly."

Oh, a softer voice belled. *What have they done to us?*

Chapter 3

As I climbed, the dregs of my fear began to evolve into something leaner, sharper, and a lot more angry. The orthodox wanted me to be afraid. The toadies of two senior elders wanted to see me panicked, crawling and quaking in my silly little human boots, wanted me to cry and beg, to be submissive and weak, so they could protect the town from the evil magic-worker, a sexually promiscuous, wicked, licensed witchy-woman.

I stopped on the landing at the top of the unheated stairs, one hand on the knob. *Yeah. They want me afraid.* I pulled out the summons, fingering it in the dim light, tracing the broken seal. My skin tightened into tiny peaks of chill bumps. "Blow it out Gabriel's horn," I swore, and pushed open my door on the echo.

Inside, I ripped off the tunic, boots, and leggings and tossed them to the floor. Standing in my underleggings and long-sleeved, low-necked, silk tee, I opened my armoires and rummaged in their backs, between the clothes and linens. In the back of the third armoire, behind the dolls that smelled of my foster father, Uncle Lem, and my early years in Mineral City, I found what I wanted and tossed bags packed for a fast getaway on the stripped bed, abruptly fighting angry tears. A sob, a wretched sound like linen tearing, caught me by surprise and I stopped, shocked, as anger and grief welled up. I hadn't known tears were so close to the surface, and I was fiercely glad no one was here to see me cry.

For a long moment I gave myself over to misery, one hand on the armoire door, one holding a baby doll, its body soft, its porcelain face angelic. I had named her Asia, for her tilted eyes and blue-black hair. Tucking her under my chin, I stroked her hair, soft as seraph down. Her lace dress wavered in my tears.

When my breath came easier, I wiped my face and smoothed Asia's dress. Holding the doll close, I breathed in her scent. If I had to run, I wouldn't be able to take the dolls, and they were all I had left of Uncle Lem. They still carried his scent: old pipe smoke, stone dust, and after-shave. I put Asia on the shelf, straightening all the dolls, giving myself a moment of respite, a moment to grieve.

When I was forced to leave Enclave at age fourteen, I was brought to Uncle Lem, a human man who had no idea what he was harboring. Though he had wanted a son, he opened his home to an orphan, thinking me wholly human. For years, the taciturn, gruff old rock hound had given me beautiful dolls, which I adored, and he shared with me his love of stones, taking me into the hills looking for mineral specimens. I had grown to love him, and he me, until he died unexpectedly in my eighteenth year, leaving me to-tally alone.

Suddenly, I missed Uncle Lem with an ache that felt brand-new. Of the two loves, dolls and rocks, only the love of rocks had lasted. But I still kept the dolls. And now I might have to leave them all behind. Stroking Asia's hair, I closed her up with her friends.

More settled now that tears had come and gone, I held up the battle uniform I had worn in defense of the town, and the formal mage-clothes I hadn't put on in over ten years. I hung both sets of garments over the armoire doors and walked around them in my sock feet, studying. Dobok or formal attire? Acid-burned and talon-scored black mage-leather, or silk and lace? Battle dress or sex in silk?

I added items to the luggage as I considered what I might do and the impression I might make. The dobok would treble any guilt the orthodoxy felt about my fighting

Darkness on the Trine only a few weeks past. It would remind them that I was a warrior, and that I could kill six of
them before they even noticed. The fact that I fought for
the Light wouldn't occur to them.

The silks would have an entirely different effect. They'd
probably swallow their tongues. Not that I would be any
less deadly in the formal attire. Which reaction did I want?
Could I do this? I fingered the material of each outfit.
Yeah. I could.

Satisfied that I had the guts to follow through with the
role, I opened the stained-glass window at the back of
the loft and dropped the packed bags to the ground. At the
thump, Jacey's big, strapping stepson, Zeddy, stuck his
head out the barn door and waved up at me. "Morning to
you, Miss Thorn," he called. "Hope you live through it."

I waved back with sour amusement, shutting the window
and cutting out the cold. "Me too, kiddo," I said to the
apartment. Then I let down my hair, set my amulets aside,
and laid out my weapons.

On top of the underclothes I pulled a heavy silk mage-
blouse that followed the plunging neckline of the undershirt. The points of the long sleeves were navy lace; the
neckline was brightly embroidered, and sown with delicate stones to signify my status as a stone mage. I
smoothed the teal fabric to my waist and tightened the
stays at the front, pulling them out and pushing my small
breasts up against the lace and stones, tying the cords
under them. The blouse was part come-hither bustier, part
defensive weapon, its torso lined with thin, mage-
tempered steel laths that shaped me and provided a lim-
ber, mail-like corset.

The silk and lace would offer less protection against
sleet and snow than the dobok or even street clothes did.
Stone mages react badly to the touch of water that has
passed through air, elements that work better for water
mages, sea mages, and weather mages. A prime amulet
blunts the discomfort, and the fact that I have two primes,
one more than most mages, means that I seldom even
think about protection from the weather. A dunking, however, is torture, and with the thin clothes, I'd feel the patter

of snow or sleet. Not that I would change my plans because of minor pain.

I settled the copper and gold bracelet of my office over the sleeve, where it couldn't be missed. The bangle was too small to slide off over my hand, and had been equipped with a GPS locator device. It was inscribed with the words "106 Adonai." If I cut it off, the seraphs would know. If someone severed my hand to get it, the seraphs would know. If I died, the seraphs would know.

Presumably, if I needed seraph help, I could call them with it, but no one had bothered to tell me how, other than cutting off my hand, and Lolo, the Enclave priestess, had stopped receiving me when I tried to scry her. Maybe my constant questions had ticked her off. Or maybe she was still dealing with the fallout of a mage in hiding being found, going into battle, and being licensed after the fact by the seraphs. Couldn't be easy, explaining me away.

On my forearms I strapped my ceremonial weapon sheaths. I hadn't worn them in ten years, but they gripped my arms perfectly. I'd stopped growing taller at the age of twelve. I still looked pretty much the same now, slender, short, muscled, little body fat. The sheaths were tooled leather, dyed teal and fuchsia, and I slid long-bladed throwing knives into the casings, checking to see that I could pull them unimpeded. I missed my kris, its wavy blade catching the light as I fought, but I'd broken off the blade in the body of a Minor Darkness and damaged the hilt in the following battle. I figured my life was worth its loss.

I stepped into a Bohemian-style skirt, see-through silk gauze floating around my calves with the movement of the overhead fans. The fabric was studded with tiny rings and small copper and brass bells that chimed with each step. I shimmied mage-fast, the bells a warning or a paean of joy. It would all look perfect, if the ambient temperature of the meeting hall were warm enough to go without the under-leggings and undershirt, but the outfit looked pretty good even with extra layers.

On one thigh and the opposite calf I strapped standard weapon sheaths over the leggings and slid a knife in each.

A show of force was the mage way. Today, if I had a blade, I was wearing it. Setting the worn and tattered battle boots aside, I pulled out my only pair of dress mage-boots. They were constructed of tooled and dyed leather, conjured to resist burning, smoking, melting, or charring from the blood or spittle of Darkness. I tugged them over my feet and stamped hard to find that they still fit. The calf sheath peeked from the top of a boot, the decorative hilt set with rainbow fluorite in teal and ocean blue. There wasn't time to charge the stones sewn and embedded in the formal attire, but the humans wouldn't know that.

I looked at myself in the armoires' mirrors, turning and considering the effect of the clothes. I touched the prime amulet on the bed and let my mage-attributes shine out in full force, the scars earned in defense of the town blazing white through the soft, roseate sheen of my flesh. My cheek scars looked weird, white light shining in a crosshatch pattern that matched the mesh of the cage that had frozen to my face. Eventually it might heal. The scars still looked dangerous and would serve as reminder that the Administration of the ArchSeraph had kept me prisoner for a while. Only a while.

As I dressed, my heartbeat settled into a steady, fast rhythm. Grief firmly put away, battle-lust thrummed in my bloodstream, speeding my breathing. A flush lit my cheeks. Where my battle glove had torn, the blood of devil-spawn had left acid burns on my knuckles. The scars of my other hand glowed like a torch. A reminder, *A show of force.* Oh, yeah.

I braided my hair into a war-braid, the plait close to my head and turned under, the style exposing the tooth scars at the bottom of my neck and décolleté, revealing the mark left by a demon-iron sword. I strapped on the spine sheath and I secured the hilt of the battle blade in the queue of scarlet hair. It protected my neck from spawn teeth and from beheading. Its hilt was silver-plated forged steel set with garnets. The steel crossguard, silver, and stones glittered through my hair.

On my wrists went cuffs of Mokume Gane gold, studded with stones. Though I seldom wore rings, I placed one on every finger, different stones in each: some polished nuggets, some faceted, some charged with power. Into my ears I slid thick gold and copper hoops. Satisfied that I was wearing enough silk, lace, blades, precious metals, and stones to cause even the most hardened mage-watcher to gawp, I shook my hips, hearing the bells jingle. *Oh yeah.*

Over my head I settled my amulet necklace, in plain sight, to be worn in public for the first time in ten years. The prime amulet was a four-inch hoop composed of topaz, peridot, amethyst, citrine, and garnet in five inner layers, with a double helping of bloodstone sealing them at top and bottom; seven layers in all, a religious symbolism. The amulet had changed, however, from the conjured stone created by the mage prophetess at my birth. I had chipped it, then mended it, and the crack had filled with a fine, bloodred line like mortar, sealing it together. The center amethyst layer was subtly larger, thicker than the others, and it glowed, just a hint, with power that wasn't mine. I had been testing the altered prime to see what it would do but I still didn't know for sure. Today, perhaps reacting to my emotional state, the prime glowed hotly. I positioned it below my breasts, centered on my ribs within easy reach.

Beside it I settled my sigil of office, my visa, a ring of watermelon pink tourmaline, inscribed like the bracelet with "106 Adonai." One hundred six was the year my visa ran out, 106 Post-Apocalyptic Era. One year from now. If I lived that long. Adonai was a name of the Most High.

Lastly, I clipped on three stones from the time of the first neomages that were filled with wild-magic. The magic sometimes vibrated into my aura. I had little idea what they did, but I liked them. I had set each with a pendant cap and strung them onto my necklace. I added the newest amulets, a bloodstone cat and three damaged, half-repaired crucifixes, scorched and partially melted. The cat was an energy sink. I hoped. I had taken the incantation from the *Book of Workings,* modified it so I could draw on all the energy at my disposal at one time. A sort of a last-ditch conjure. I hoped I'd never need it. But today might be the day.

I looked again into the mirror. Shock settled its weight

across my shoulders. "Seraph stones," I whispered. Maybe I couldn't do this after all.

I had never seen the being looking back at me. Last time I had dressed in formal mage attire, I had been a teenager. Now I was a woman. I didn't look sexy. I didn't look good. I looked dangerous. Real dangerous. A mess-with-me-and-die woman who would still have every man in sight drooling. And some of the women too.

Well, that was my intention. To take the town fathers by storm.

I tossed the dobok out the window with the last of my supplies. Sleet fell in a heavy patter, dancing off the uniform when it landed on the ice. Zeddy stuck out his head a moment later and jerked with surprise. He stared at me, taking in the hair, the glowing skin and scars, and the exposed flesh. "Holy moly," he said, mouth and eyes wide, and then he looked around to make sure he hadn't been overheard. Dragging his eyes back to me, he said, "You sure you want to go like that?" When I nodded, he gave me a half salute and said, "Okay, then. Sorry I can't be there. Hope someone tapes the meeting for me." He shook his head. "Horses are ready, Miss Thorn, if you need 'em. Holy freaking moly," he said again, whispering the oath.

Not trusting myself to speak, I closed the window. I looked as outlandish as I thought. Outlandish as Enclave. For a moment, doubts eddied but I pushed them away. Strength, surprise, and the unexpected. It would save me or stun the elders long enough for me to run.

I pushed the kitchen table to the side and poured a salt ring on the deep turquoise tile, leaving six inches open. The salt wasn't sea salt, defiled by water and air, but had been mined from the earth, from deep underground. Earth salt for a stone mage. It had a faint bluish-green tint in some light, but in midmorning, even with sleet falling and a heavy cloud cover, it looked white. I entered the circle and sat yogi-fashion on the cold tile, bells tinkling. I closed my eyes and breathed deeply, feeling the pull on the amulets with which I had decorated myself. Once, it would have taken long minutes to calm my emotions and settle my body into the proper forms, but lately, though I didn't know why, it was easier. Much easier. Within moments, I sealed the circle with a final handful of salt.

As it closed, power seized me. Power from the beginning of time, heard as much as felt, tasted, and seen. It hummed through me, a drone, an echo of the first Word ever spoken, the first Word of Creation. The reverberation was captured in the core of the earth for me to draw upon, a constant, unvarying power of stone and mineral, the destructive potency of liquid rock and heat. Its vibrations rolled through my bones and pulsed into my flesh, the thrum of strength, the force, the raw, raging might of the earth, a molten mantle, seeking outlet. Finding me, rising within me.

I was a crucible for the incandescent energy—it was mine to use. *Mine.* I *was* the strength of the earth and stone, the might of the core, the power of creation. The prime amulet on my chest pulsed softly, harnessing the energies needed for the simple incantation. I needed only enough power to keep myself calm and focused during the coming town meeting.

Until recently, drawing on leftover creation force had been a dangerous moment of temptation. Only a few weeks past, I hadn't been able to begin such an incantation while wearing the amulets, but had to start without them and then place them around my neck at the right moment. Like my prime amulet, I was different. I didn't want to look too closely at the change in me, in my life. Maybe someday I'd have the leisure for introspection. Not now.

I breathed, calm just out of reach. The silence of the loft settled about me. I could hear the ticking of the black-pig clock over my shoulder, the sound becoming one with the stillness I sought. My heart rate slowed, decelerated to a methodical, slow pace. In mage-sight, my flesh was a roseate radiance lined with blood rushing through my veins and the bright, terrible tracery of scars down my legs and arms.

The loft pulsed with energy, a bower of neomage safety I had created in the humans' world. Stones were everywhere, at the tub and bed and gas fireplaces, in every window and doorway, on the floor. Even on the wood beams overhead. My home glowed with pale energy, subtle, harmonious shades of lavender, green, rose, yellow, and blood-red. Mage-sight saw what humans couldn't, the power beyond physical manifestations. Mage-sight saw the energy of creation in everything. Such power should have been protection enough to keep me safe from an incubus, but this particular beast had access to my blood, which gave it power over me. I shelved that worry, concentrating.

When I was centered and calm, I sent my senses scouring out, drawing power from every stone in the loft, pulling it into myself and my amulets, as I would before battle, in a slow, easy drawing of strength, not fast enough to interrupt the charmed circle, but enough to leach through and into me, like osmosis. As I drew it in, lavender energies misted out of the walls and floor, following the might I pulled from other stones. Startled, half disbelieving, I watched the mist as it moved for the first time in weeks.

As if scenting me, it coalesced into the shape of a cobra with glowing, dark blue eyes and a hint of yellow chatoyency, like blue tigereye stone. A pale hood expanded; its tongue tasted the air. My body tensed. Evil often took the form of a serpent, but this thing didn't glow with the energies of Darkness. It glittered with the brilliance of Light. Yet even Light could be dangerous to a charmed circle. If it tried to pierce the conjure, its energies would combine with mine, a fusion of wild-magic, the kind formed nearly a hundred years ago in the time of the first neomages. The union of disparate energies would discharge into a destructive explosion and splatter me all over the loft. Fire and death everywhere. If it was real.

I blinked. The serpent was still there, coiled on the floor in front of the salt, looking at me, a twenty-foot-long, lavender-and-purple-banded cobra of might. I blinked off my mage-sight and it was still there, a physical beast, but like nothing in nature. I knew that if I touched it, I would feel a real body, sinuous muscle beneath cool scales.

With a slow, hypnotic sway, it inspected the circle, tongue forking out, tasting the energies of the incantation. I sat frozen in the center, having no idea how to stop it from doing whatever it wanted. The serpent was a manifestation of the culled energies of the amethyst sealed in metal ammunition boxes stored below, in the stockroom. Stone that was empty, last time I looked: stones that had been so totally drained that I thought they were dead.

The cobra opened its mouth, exposing white tissue, devoid of life and blood. Hinged fangs lowered from its palate. It was hungry. It wanted in. It swayed, asking, begging. No words were exchanged, but I knew what it wanted; to join with me again.

Again? My mind found the only incantation I could remember, the first small conjure taught to every neomage, a nursery rhyme, almost the first words we spoke, later used as a conjure to calm and prepare, when a mage was afraid. Softly, I said, "Stone and fire, water and air, blood and kin prevail. Wings and shield, dagger and sword, blood and kin prevail."

It blinked once, hissed, and struck. I flinched, garbling the words of the verse. It pierced through the charmed circle, precisely, cleanly, without disrupting the incantation. There was no discharge of disruptive mage-power. No explosion. But now it was inside with me, writhing on the floor a foot away. Fear whispered through me, raising prickles on my flesh. I didn't know what to do except continue the incantation, my voice ragged.

The cobra grew more vivid, more intense, more *solid* with the ancient words. Once an incantation begins, a mage has to see it through, finish the verse, reach the end, close the purpose of the intent. I was breathing hard. My chest ached. As a trickle of sweat slithered down my back, I whispered the verse again, and then stopped, the last syllable fading away.

The serpent's hood swelled. I raised a hand as if to stop it, and it undulated, moving side to side, its eyes on me, its tongue tasting the air in front of my outstretched palm. *"I hear,"* it thought at me, hissing. I realized that in speaking an incantation meant to settle oneself before battle, to draw in energies for war against Darkness, I had called it, welcoming its power. And now I didn't know what to do with it, how to control it, or how to banish it.

"No," I said. "No."

The serpent slipped back against the salt of the circle, its hood brushing the circle wall, which should have shattered the conjure but didn't. "No," I said again, my fear swelling, thickening, my hand raised against it. The snake glittered, a coruscation of light and might. The elemental mist of its essence rippled, scales shifting, widening. Becoming eyes. A lavender snake with a body of purple eyes.

I was swaying in time with it. I blinked. It blinked. Mesmerizing. Asking. Begging. *"Take me. Use me. You made me yours. And I am lonely."*

"I didn't," I thought back.

"Yes. Yours."

I faltered. And the serpent struck, fangs buried in my palm.

My heart stuttered. In a single instant the snake saturated every amulet on me and overflowed, sloughing off the stones, splashing into a puddle of eyes on the tile. The floor heated beneath my thighs. The puddle expanded, splashing wetly against the walls of the conjure, soaking my skirt. But it didn't melt the salt, didn't feel like water against my skin; it tingled like electricity, like power. I could hear a soft resonance of bells as it rose in the circle, purple eyes rising like a flood.

My breath was rough, hoarse, my heartbeat fast, an erratic drumming of fear. "No," I whispered. It ignored me. A pressure like the deeps of the ocean pressed against me. I had never seen or heard of anything like this. The liquid eyes rose over my waist, up to my breasts. I needed to break the charmed circle, but if I did, what would happen to the energies gathered here? Would they explode? Burn? Kill half the town? Power shouldn't be able to gather, shape itself, and act on its own. The purple liquid that wasn't wet reached my chin, prickling, burning against my skin. I didn't know what to do. And I was going to drown in the stuff, whatever it was. A laugh tickled in the back of my throat, hysterical giggles of fear.

"Don't be afraid. I won't let them harm you," it promised.

The liquid energy eyes spilled over my lips and down my throat in a torrent. I gasped reflexively, and it flooded my lungs, pungent and sweet, suffocating me. It filled my sinuses, my ears, speeding to my stomach when I gagged and swallowed. My arms lifted, trying to swim, but the stuff was insubstantial, ethereal.

The energies, the *eyes,* sped into my bloodstream like cobra venom, reaching my heart in a rush. My heartbeat stuttered, a painful irregularity I could feel in my eyes and ears and throat, a heavy pressure in my chest. It swam into my bowels, filled my muscles and tendons, and moved deep into my bones and marrow. It electrified my nerves. Mouth open, no air to breathe, I was drowning. My vision telescoped into pinpoints of purple light. And was gone.

Chapter 4

I opened my eyes slowly, feeling the gummy texture of sleep in the corners. Turquoise glared in my field of vision. Slowly, it resolved itself into my kitchen floor. I was facedown on the tile, arms stretched out, my cold hands in salt. *Eyes.* I had been drowning in eyes. The purple snake was gone. The water-mist-eyes were gone.

I eased upright, supporting my weight on one hand. The circle was broken, my hands having dislodged the salt when I passed out. But there had been no explosion of wild energies, no fire, death, and destruction. The loft was unchanged, bed stripped, clothes hanging from the armoire doors. In mage-sight, I spotted one difference. There was a purple hue to every stone in the apartment. I lifted my amulets, seeing the same glow. It wasn't overpowering; it was, in fact, so faint a stranger might not notice.

I looked at my hand. "*Seraph stones,*" I cursed under my breath. Normally, mage flesh has a pearly peach sheen, even to human eyes. Mine was now slightly darker, vaguely purple. I wasn't sure what had happened, but it couldn't be good.

Skirt bells jingling, I stood and found my breath and my balance, and looked down at myself. I was dry and clean, and the salt was still in an almost perfect circle, broken in two narrow places where my hands had swept through it. But the salt was pale lavender. "Habbiel's pearly, scabrous, decayed, putrid toes!" I said, fury rising with each word.

"Thorn?" A knock sounded at the door.

"In a minute," I shouted. He didn't rap again, but he didn't go away, either. I could almost hear him breathing on the other side of the wood.

Movements jerky, I swept up the salt and put it in a fresh plastic bag, not wanting to contaminate the salt in the original container. I marked the bag with a big black X, and below it, in smaller letters, wrote, DANGER. PURPLE STUFF.

I looked at myself again, and realized that the purple didn't emanate strictly from my mage-flesh, but more from my scars; a pale, pulsing color where once had been pure, bleached-out white. I cursed so foully that I'd have been branded on both cheeks and forehead had a kirk elder heard.

"Thorn?" The voice was tentative, and I realized I was still shouting. I breathed deeply, pulling in the calm that had always been part of my home. The peace was still there, untainted by the lavender electricity I expected. I breathed several times, each breath slower than the last. When I felt like myself again, I looked down. The purple in my scars had faded to a barely perceptible glow. Even as I watched, it continued to dim. Whatever it was, it wasn't long-lasting. Maybe the remaining energy in the amethyst had now expended itself. With a final breath, I took my thick leather cloak and laid it over my arm, positioning it so I could pull a blade if needed.

The bells on my skirt jingled as I opened the door, to find Rupert standing there alone, black hair pulled back, dressed in unrelieved navy. Around his neck was a primitive necklace I had designed, tiny white pearls and silver beads interspersed between seven large, faceted blue tigereye stones and slivered white shells, like long teeth: like fangs. I stared at the shells and blue tigereye, remembering the serpent's eyes and wide-open mouth.

"Saints' balls," he breathed. "You look . . ." He didn't finish the sentence. Rupert had never seen me dressed as a mage, my neomage attributes radiating. Some of my fury abated at the pure wonder in his gaze.

I had been hiding in the human world because I knew— I believed—that no human would allow me to live. Until recently I hadn't even trusted my friends with my secret. Maybe I should have. Following his eyes, I looked down at my scarred knuckles. The tissue was white again, light spilling from them. "You ready?" I asked.

"Yeah." He lifted a finger and traced the crisscrossed scars on my cheek. "You're beautiful." I felt a flush rise. I would never be beautiful, but the compliment was nice. "Suggestion?" When I shrugged, Rupert took the cloak and draped it across my shoulders, securing it. "Keep all this hidden, even your skin, until the right moment."

"When will that be?"

"You'll know. Anyone who can wear this in public? You'll know." He waved his hands over mine and said, "Make that go away till then too. Okay? All at once, when the time's right, throw off the cloak with a flourish, like a bullfighter. And let your skin do this glow thing. It'll stop them in their tracks."

"Too bad you can't do it for me. You have a better sense of the dramatic than I do."

"No straight woman will ever have the style of a gay man, honeybunch," he said smugly. "And if you can get some mage-clothes my size, I'll start a new style that will take the human world by storm."

I rolled my eyes. "I'll see what I can do."

"If you two are finished with the mutual admiration society," Audric's voice came from the bottom of the stairs, "it's time to go."

Audric was not dressed for practice, but for war. A tight-fitting, black dobok was thickly padded against devil-spawn, his weapons secured in loops or fastened in place, his katana and wakizashi sheathed at his waist. Audric was a savage-chi and savage-blade master. A war ax was strapped across his back, the blade painted scarlet, feathers floating from the handle. Bombs dangled from a belt across his chest. Throwing blades were strapped in plain sight at wrists and calves. Smaller throwing weapons adorned his chest, hips, and upper thighs.

"Oh," Rupert breathed. It sounded like ecstasy. "Even if I were straight, I'd turn gay at the sight of you." I was pretty sure I moaned too. Nothing like a man in uniform.

"Are you sure you want to do this?" I asked. Audric had not revealed to the town that he was a half-breed. "There's no reason to."

"I am bound to Raziel, winged-warrior who fights with the ArchSeraph Michael. I have been charged with your protection." He bowed deeply, the formal obeisance of his training and heritage. I caught the sadness underlying his tone. Audric had never wanted to be bound to a seraph. He wasn't happy with his status, would never be happy serving another, not even a being of Light who would call him to battle. "It is my duty and my honor to protect the licensed mage my master has honored with his presence." When he raised upright, his sigil of office rested on his chest, and his skin was warm with the soft tones of the second-unforeseen. Not as bright as my own, but clearly displaying his half-neomage genes.

"Nice touch," I said, uncertain. "But don't risk it if you don't have to."

Audric laughed, the deep rumble echoing in the cold stairwell, his dark eyes hot with scorching brightness. "If the day is auspicious, the humans will attack and we will fight. Battle and glory call to me today," he said with all the formality of his kind. His hands rested on his swords. "The blood of humans is sweet when they trespass against the seraph's chosen."

"Hey. Human being standing here," Rupert said. "Enough of the blood and glory."

"If they attack, stay to Thorn's right," Audric commanded. He slung a scarred battle cloak over his shoulders and dobok. Tapping his lightning-bolt pendant, he damped his skin. I touched my prime amulet, blanking my neomage attributes, and checked my walking-stick blade. Eighteen inches of mage-tempered steel showed before I re-sheathed it.

"Okay," I said. "If you're sure."

When we reached the bottom of the stairs, Audric stepped into the uncertain light of the shop. From a chair in the waiting area of Thorn's Gems, he lifted a dark bundle and gave it a shake. Yards of velvet slinked down with a whisper of sound, taking the shape of a cloak. He held it to Rupert. "I bought it for your birthday, but it seems appropriate for today."

"*Sweet seraph.* It's wonderful." Rupert took the cloak, stroking the dark blue velvet, so fine it scattered the light. The lining was quilted scarlet silk. He shook the wrinkles from its folds, and tossed it over his shoulders. Assuming a rakish pose, he asked, "Well?"

"You look perfect," I said. "It brings a blue sheen to your eyes, and makes your hair look even darker." I'd have added it was lovely, except it wasn't; it somehow carried a sense of menace. The cloth fell to the floor, making his shoulders look broader, his form threatening.

"And there's this," Audric said. From the counter, he lifted a cloth-wrapped object and extended it to Rupert. A leather-wrapped hilt with a dark blue stone set into the pommel protruded from the end. "It's a bastard sword. It was specially made for you."

At the sight of the ornate navy-and-burgundy, tooled-leather sheath, Rupert made a soft sound, not quite a moan, not quite a groan, but way more than a sigh. The timbre brought a smile to Audric's face. "You're slower than a mage or a half-breed," he said, "but stronger. As your skills increase, that strength will make you a formidable opponent, even for me. The hand-and-a-half-length hilt is perfect to capitalize on that strength." Rupert pulled the blade from the sheath and set the leather to the side. Gripping the hilt in both hands, he swung the double-bladed, four-foot sword experimentally, getting the feel of its balance. "Don't start a swing that you aren't totally committed to, Rupert. It has its own weight. It won't be easy to stop in battle."

"Is it named?" he asked.

I stiffened at the question. Most sword masters—not sword owners, but *masters*—named their weapons, and that name often followed a blade from master to master. That name was part of the initiation rite when a savage-blade student was given his first battle-weapon. To a traditional swordsman, the blades he used were alive, with personalities and characters all their own. I had never named my own weapons, and had never been through the

ceremony that officially marked a mage reaching adult-
hood, thus I had never received my adult weapons. Maybe
I would feel differently about them if I had, but to me they
were tools, not toys or pets.

"No. Naming is your right, but only after you draw first
blood in battle." Audric handed him the sword sheath.
"Strap it on beneath your cloak. Today, it's for show. Most
likely." His voice was disappointed; there might not be
fighting and bloodletting in the streets.

"What are we today? Her escorts?"

Audric's mouth turned up, a mischievous twinkle in his
eyes. "Her champards."

I closed my eyes. The title was a formal one, established
by the first practitioners of savage-blade for the nonmage
companions of a mage—champions and partners who followed into battle, fought the same war, and wrestled
against a common enemy. Champards pledged themselves
and their fortunes to one mage-leader. And died by her
side. Cold scuttled up my spine on anxious feet. Rupert's
training in the arts of war had only begun when Audric
came into his life. He wasn't ready for his first battle blade.
He was good, very good, but was years away from being
skilled enough to fight in a real war. "I don't want anyone
to fight beside me. I never want anyone to die because of
me," I said.

"We took on your battles when we became partners in
Thorn's Gems, honeybunch," Rupert said, strapping the
sheath on his waist beneath his cloak. "When we first became friends. This was inevitable."

But he didn't know what he was saying, what he was
promising. He couldn't. Behind us, Jacey stepped through
the door with a blast of icy air, her boots on the wood floor
telling me who she was as surely as if she had announced
herself. It took a long moment for the door to close. "You
people look . . . wicked," she said, her voice muted. "Dreadful. And terrible. And exquisite. Like pure flame." It was
her trademark comment, flame having the power that pu-
rified gold and metal, and shaped glass. Her words fell like
an omen on my soul. I didn't want to look terrible, yet it
was the effect I had planned for. It was the exact impres-

sion I wanted to make. And with two armed champards at my side, I could look nothing else.

When I opened my eyes, I saw Jacey, wearing her finest, a scarlet velvet gown with long, full skirts, and a dark crimson cloak thrown back to reveal the dress. I was surprised she wore her best clothes. And then I wasn't. In her own way, Jacey, too, was declaring herself a champard. Her brown hair was braided, and she was wearing lipstick, something she seldom bothered with. I blinked back a sheen of tears. "Who's going to mind the store?" I asked.

"We're closing Thorn's Gems. It's been decided we need a show of force to combat the gossips, scandalmongers, and waggling tongues. Don't argue," she said as I was about to protest. "I need jewelry," she added. Going to the emerald display case, she lifted out the chunky emerald necklace made of locally mined stone and draped it over her head. The pendant nestled in the velvet and caught the light. "This emerald find made all the news. It won't hurt to remind the town fathers where a good bit of their tax base comes from." She dangled emeralds from her ears, and slid three emerald rings on her fingers. On her wrists went matching knitted cuffs, stitched with beads, which caught the light.

Calm, she looked us over, her gaze lingering on me, on the hem trailing from beneath my battered war-cloak. Her brows went up but she didn't comment. Instead she looked over the door to the loft, at the framed, embroidered proverb hanging there. It was my birth prophecy, the divination that claimed my twin and I would be great warriors against Darkness. *A Rose by any Other Name will still draw Blood.* The prophecy that could never come true because Rose was dead.

"You don't have a family," she said, "except us. And family doesn't desert family. Lock up, boys. Thorn. Big Zed and the kids are waiting." Regal, she floated through the room and out the door.

"You ever see her like that?" Audric asked.

"Yeah, with her kids," Rupert said morosely. "Best not to argue. She'll box our ears."

"Do tell. I'd like to see her try." Flipping his palm up and out, Audric said, "After you, little mage."

Dread tight in my chest, I followed Jacey into the sleet, my walking stick tapping for balance, the bloodstone handle-hilt of its hidden sword warm in my hand. With a deft movement, I freed my cloak's hood and pulled it over my head. Sleet had formed a brittle layer on top of the softer snow, and my boots cracked through, sinking to mid-shin. The town was quiet except for sleet landing with a secretive patter.

A snow-el-bile—a hybrid, battery-powered car modified with snowmobile sled runners—raced past, sliding and slipping. Another el-car, this one painted with the logo of the Satellite News Network and equipped with a rotating track like a bulldozer, churned toward us on the slick surface. Chasing a seraph sighting, reporters from SNN had been stranded in town when a blizzard hit and were desperate to find something to share with the nation before their superiors and fans forgot they existed. Or they could take the mule train back to civilization. Not a fun prospect. Oliver Winston had tried to interview the local mage, as had his companion reporter, Romona Benson. So far I had managed to avoid them.

From every building and storefront, town citizens emerged, locking up behind them. Some delivered surreptitious glances our way. Others turned away as if we didn't exist. Only a few acknowledged us, and I made note of them: Esmeralda Boyles—Miz Essie—who trudged across the street to join our little cavalcade; Sennabel Schwartz, who ran the local library; and her husband, whom I didn't know. A few others followed.

I smelled Thaddeus Bartholomew, a state police cop and Rupert's cousin, across the street before I saw him, his body throwing pheromones into the air like an advertisement for pure sex. Thadd was a walking come-hither machine, and I wasn't the only one to notice. Human women turned, finding him with their eyes without knowing why. His face was haggard, pain lines cutting through once-smooth flesh. Hiding among humans, half human, part seraph, part mage, his genetic heritage was jumbled. Stuck between forms, the change into third-generation kylen had halted. But the enzymes catalyzing his transformation were still active and, because I knew what to look for, I could see the slight humps on either side of his spine where infant seraph wings had begun to emerge.

"Can anyone join this parade, or is it only for the blood kin and the condemned?" a voice drawled. I cast Eli Walker a quick smile. The lithe, almost delicate man was leaning against the wall of the dry-goods store, his booted feet crossed at the ankles, partially blocking the walkway. I figured he was one of the people Audric had phoned when preparing for my trial.

Eli was part-time miner, part-time tracker, a great dancer, and a spiffy dresser. Today he was decked out in Post-Ap cowboy gear: jeans, hobnailed boots, cowboy hat, and fringed leather jacket. Around his neck was an old Indian necklace of dyed wood beads, glass beads, and porcupine quills on a woven, knotted jute thong. Eli liked me, and not for the jewelry I could make, the charms I might conjure, or my money, though he brought raw emeralds from his claim to Thorn's Gems and bartered high prices for them. Some of them hung around Jacey's neck, and I saw him glance at them before he looked back at me. His lips lifted in a slow smile, the kind that excluded everyone else present and spoke volumes to intent. He'd been trying to get me into bed for weeks.

"All help is welcome," Jacey said.

"Then you won't mind if I escort my mama into the meeting." Boots scratching across the ice as he stood upright, he intercepted Miz Essie and took her arm. "I imagine she's going to side with you. She always sides with the underdog, and that means trouble."

"You're a good boy," the older woman said, patting his face, "but you should have shaved. Shame on you, and you so pretty." A dark fuzz of beard grizzled his cheeks. It looked good below his odd amber-colored eyes. Very good.

"Yes, Mama, I am." He kissed the leather glove over her knuckles, his eyes on me as his lips touched. His expression said clearly that he'd like to kiss me, and wouldn't stop at the knuckles. I blushed hotly and Eli chuckled. It was dis-

concerting. "And you're a pot of trouble filled to the brim."
He still spoke to his mother, but I was his target. And when
he stood, I saw he was prepared for trouble of the worst
sort. Beneath the buckskin jacket he wore a white flannel
shirt with guns holstered beneath each arm. The hilt of a
baselard, a short sword with a two-foot-long blade, was
strapped across his back.

"No fighting," I said, my tone fervent. "Neomages never
start violence against humans. *Never.*"

"Don't reckon they do," Eli agreed. "But they damn sure
finish it when they're attacked." His mother gasped and
my flush deepened at his casual swearing, but he was right.
He'd seen me fight. And the history books confirmed his
claim. Unrepentant at his coarse language, Eli grinned at
me. "And I also reckon I don't much feel like being on the
losing side in this little internecine war some town fathers
and orthodox elders have cooked up."

"What have you heard?" Audric asked, his hands gripping the hilts of his weapons beneath his cloak. Two el-cars
skidded past us and disappeared. Silence settled on the
landscape, broken by footsteps and the rustle of people on
the move. Sleet peppered over my hood.

"Since Jacey called? Little here, little there. Enough to
know some folks got less sense than balls. Your pardon,
ladies." He tipped his hat as his mother swatted him. The
unmistakable affection between the two made me appreciate Eli, maybe more than I should. As if he knew what I
was thinking, he winked at me. "We should make an impression, though, when we all stomp in the room together.
Just hope it's enough of an impression to count for something. Make a few people think instead of getting all
heated up and mob-minded. The progressives and reformed are diddling about whether to intercede in her be-
half. Politics by committee sucks, but it'll suck more if the
three groups come to blows."

That was what I dreaded, a mob scene. Under my cloak,
I shivered and slid my fingers through the ring of my prime
amulet. With my other hand, I levered myself along, walking stick tapping. Its vibrant green-and-red bloodstone hilt
warmed my palm. It was also a prime amulet. Most mages

had only one prime. I had two. I hoped I wouldn't need to drain them both dry today just staying alive. And keeping my friends alive.

I should have been warmed and gratified by the supporters around me, should have been persuaded that numbers would make a difference to the future I feared. But I wasn't. Instead, I remembered the morning's dream and the cry of the lynx. My fingers found and worried the tiny release that allowed me to pull free the long blade. For fighting.

As we moved up the street, Eli stepped close. In a laconic tone he said, "Some of my boys been hearing rumors about a seraph trapped in the Trine." I whipped my head to him. "From when you went underground? Seven seraphs went in after you and only six came out."

I had no idea who his boys were or why he might mention that now, but I nodded stiffly. "Yes. One is still underground. Trapped."

"Hmm," he said. Which told me nothing. He pushed back the brim of his hat, allowing the weak sunlight to warm his amber eyes. "Let me know when you decide to go back after him. I'll tag along. Watch your back."

"I will never—*never*—go underground again," I said quickly, preventing a shiver of fear before it took me.

"I see," he said. "Fine. Sure. Whatever." And the miner fell behind me.

When we rounded the long curve and saw the former Central Baptist Church ahead, my hopes dwindled. The building was no longer used for religious services. It was now the town meeting hall. Out front of the old building a throng of people milled, split into two factions, an informal welcoming party to either side of the entry doors. The group with me faltered and nearly stopped. We would have to walk between the two crowds to gain entry. Well, in one way that was symbolic of what I had done to the town: Divided it utterly.

Murmuring voices raised on the cold air as black-clad orthodox and angry men in one group debated in loud voices with the smaller, more colorful progressive and reformed crowd. I figured it was the first time the orthodox and the rougher elements of Mineral City had ever agreed on anything. Too bad that agreement was to kill me. And too bad the other, smaller group looked so cowed. If I was attacked, they would probably run instead of coming to my defense.

I was so toast.

Chapter 5

B risk footsteps gained on us and I felt, more than saw, Audric whirl and half pull his short blade. I spun, ready for anything, but it was Elder Jasper and his pretty blond wife, Polly, who had been a half block behind us. "Morning, folks," the elder said, his gaze touching each of us, a warning conferred in his expression. "Hope you don't mind us slipping in front of you." His voice dropped, not carrying beyond our small troupe. "Seems some folk might need reminding that violence is punishable by kirk sanctions."

Jasper glanced at me as he passed, his eyes saying as clearly as his voice would have, *Wait!* Instantly he looked away, raising his arm. "Morning, Earl! Ephraim. Howard! How you boys doing today?" He and Polly pulled ahead of us. "I wanta thank you for showing up at widder-woman Henderson's yesterday. That ramp you boys put together for the old lady was the blessing of the year for her. Louis, missed you at kirk Sunday. Hope you're feeling better. Richard, good to see you again. Glad you're back in town. Joseph, hope that ulcer is better. Saw the new el-car. They call that color seraph blood, don't they? Florence, I see you're feeling better, making new friends, getting out some. I look forward to finding you back at jubilee this week."

I slowed, watching the effect of the elder's greetings. Louis looked away. Louis drank a bit. More likely he was hung over rather than sick. Richard ran an ongoing card game. Gambling kept him too busy to attend many services, and he stepped away, into the crowd, as his absence at religious events was commented upon. Gambling was punishable by branding.

Rumor had it that Joseph owned a still in the hills nearby, a still that made him rich and a lot of town men too drunk to worship or work. He too melted into the dissipating groups of troublemakers. Florence was a firm orthodox. A kirk elder placing her name in context with rabble-rousers made her flush.

"Mrs. Abernathy, no need to worry about Hannah Zelmack. That was all rumor. She isn't pregnant at all, let alone by a married man."

Mrs. Abernathy blanched. "I never said—"

"Of course you did. To all sorts of people. Let's get inside and seated, why don't we?" Elder Jasper said, shooing cowed people up the steps with his hands. "Otherwise this crowd'll disrupt the meeting. Thorn, Rupert, after you." He gestured us past the dispersing group and inside. Most of the crowd filed in behind us, boots scuffing, pews groaning as they sat. At the door, Jasper said, "I believe there's a special place for Thorn with the elders up on the—"

"Thorn will be sitting with us," Audric said. His tone brooked no disagreement, and Jasper smiled and took his wife's arm.

"Of course. This way, Polly, dear."

Audric maneuvered us to a pew midway down on the left and paused. The location was an odd choice until I saw the fire door set into the wall, a quick way out if needed. He leveled a gaze on the pew's occupants. I don't know what they saw in his expression, but all six people scrambled out the other side and into pews many rows back. The row behind took the hint and vacated as well.

Satisfied but dour, Audric held my arm when I would have gone in first, letting Rupert lead the way, trailed by Miz Essie and Eli, Jacey, Big Zed, and their brood. When they were all in place, he released my arm and shoved me down in the pew ahead, seating me in the aisle seat as if I were a mannequin he was positioning for display. Audric slid into the pew behind me and sat. No one sat beside me. It was the only empty seating in the full church.

A sour miasma rose, the collected odors of humans, damp mold, and old building. The Central Baptist Church had survived a battle on the Trine, the towering, three-peaked rock face that had risen two thousand feet during an underground war fought by seraphs and humans against minions of Darkness. Constructed of stone, the building's foundations rested on a single rock, making the church a place of power to me. Unknown to the elders, it was a conduit to the power of the deeps. I was lucky to have been brought here and not to the kirk. That building was set above a streambed, not stone.

A gavel banged, bringing a deeper quiet to the silent crowd. The town fathers were seated at a long table to the right of the stage, the table set at an angle to the audience so they could see and be seen, yet leave a wide space for proceedings. One of which would be me, I reminded myself. *Sweet seraph.*

Across the aisle to my right, Lucas slipped into a seat, Ciana beside him. My ex-husband inclined his head, his lips turning up. As always, my heart somersaulted. Lucas Stanhope was the most beautiful man I had ever seen, even when wasted from weeks of captivity. His cheeks were sharply defined, brow wide, nose a perfect line, blue eyes making every girl in town sigh. Too bad he was a lying, woman-chasing cheat.

His eight-year-old daughter from his first marriage, the child of my heart if not my body, waved, a bright smile on her face. Dismayed, I waggled my fingertips at her. She shouldn't be here, shouldn't see a town meeting. She should be safe, in school, where illusions about her world and the people in it wouldn't be shattered. Yet, even knowing that she should be carried away and protected, I was glad to see her, her bright eyes alight with hope and trust. Ciana's presence brought a measure of peace to me that I badly needed.

The girl was small for her age. She crawled into her father's lap, her back to his chest. Her legs were encased in thick leggings and kicked on either side of his, her arms

twined with his around her waist over her padded coat.
The seraph pin she always wore peeked out. The old
church had no heat and her breath puffed, tiny clouds joining the breath of the throng. Lucas leaned over and whispered, "She wouldn't go to school. Wouldn't take no for an
answer. Said she had to be here." He kissed Ciana's head
with a worried frown and sat back.

The gavel banged again. The chairman of the town fathers was Elder Shamus Waldroup, a baker and also the
senior judge over all civil and criminal disputes brought
before the district court. Shamus called out, speaking with
the thick mountain brogue of his generation. "The meetin'
of the town fathers of Mineral City will come to order. I
see we have quite a crowd for today's proceedings, and a
long docket. Let's get on with it. Court's in session."

The old man's dark-skinned balding head caught the
light as he peered from the dais into the seats of the condemned. "First item of business is the judgment on two
caught cursing. Their iniquitous words were heard by an
elder. Upon questioning at the last town meeting, they
confessed, sentences were pronounced, and will be carried
out posthaste."

The smell of smoke blew through the old sanctuary on a
gust of cold air as a brazier was carried into the room from
one of the doors at the front. Once upon a time, a choir
would have proceeded through, robed and singing praises.
Now it was five burly, brown-robed elders, all armed, acting as bailiffs. Two carried long poles with a portable brazier suspended between, the iron brazier glowing red-hot.
The others held Bibles and branding irons, all in the sign of
the cross.

Oh, *saints' balls,* they were going to do it right *now.* I
looked at Lucas in alarm but he was already turning Ciana
into the crook of his shoulder. "No. I wanna see," she said,
resisting, her shrill voice rising. Lucas quieted her with a
murmured word, and though she stopped fighting, she
hissed, stubbornly, "It's not fair."

The brazier was set on the stage and the five elders, all
young postulants, went to the pew set aside for the condemned. The clink of chains echoed in the still air. The

crowd leaned forward in anticipation. I stared at the cloak over my knees, the leather burned and scorched. I'd suffered a lot for this town, yet many wanted to see me brought forward in chains, a cross brand set aside for me.

Scuffling and cursing came from the dais, the words quickly muffled. Shamus said, "Now Mack, watch your mouth. You don't want to be punished twice in one day. Mack here is charged and found guilty for cursing, lewd speech, and propagandizing in front of a schoolyard and the kirk. Because this is a first offense, you have the right to address the assembled. If we take off the gag, you can even repent, which might cause this court to go easy on you, but if you cuss again, I'll have you duct-taped for the rest of the proceedings."

Mack started speaking as soon as the gag was removed. "I'm not being punished by the kirk because I cursed. I'm being punished to suppress the EIH." More scuffling ensued while Mack shouted, "You know it's true. The Most High isn't real. The seraphs came from another planet and took our world. It's a plot, a ruse to claim the Earth, to enslave us. We have to fight them—"

"That's enough of the conspiracy claims," Shamus interrupted, sounding tired.

The rest of Mack's words were muffled into grunts, unintelligible noises, and sounds of struggle. Vibrations thudded through the wood floor. "May you find absolution and forgiveness in the countenance of the Most High," Shamus said.

We were sitting close enough to hear his skin sizzle. I stared hard at my knees and managed not to quiver when Mack's half-stifled scream echoed dully off the church walls. The reek of burned human flesh combined with the sour stink of the room. My stomach rebelled. I pressed a fist hard into my midsection.

Two of the brown-robed elders dragged Mack by his shoulders off the platform and out, this time taking the aisle through the church, within inches of me. I couldn't help myself. I looked up. Mack was sagging between them and one of the men held him by the hair so the crowd could see his face. A two-inch cross had been burned into his left cheek, the top bar near the outer corner of his eye. The brand had pressed deep enough to sear bone, and the cross was blackened, flesh puckered and blistered.

Tears of Taharial. My fingers started tingling, my breath too fast. Unable to act, not permitted to fight, panic mode wrestled through my muscles. I closed my eyes.

Up front, another prisoner was brought forward, also a member of the EIH, a repeat offender. This wouldn't be his first punishment; his original brand had been poorly done, the flesh on the left side of his face drawing up, pulling his mouth into a leering half grin and permanently exposing his molars. Such men were outcasts, wearing rags, persecuted for speaking out against the High Host of the Seraphim, the ruling council of seraphs.

From the corner of my eye, I saw him struggle, cursing the elders, fighting. When the brand was applied, he whipped his body hard. The hot iron dug into his flesh as he wrenched away, tearing the cheek in a gush of blood. I wanted to gag.

I looked at Ciana. She had stopped struggling, her head buried in Lucas' shoulder. Thank God. She shouldn't see this—no one should—though the townsfolk were enjoying the show. I smelled moonshine, candy, and popcorn. My stomach rolled over again.

A woman's voice carried from the back of the room as the man was carted past, the words rapid-fire, without a space between for an answer. "Do you repent of the blasphemy? Do you have anything to say to our viewers? What does your family think about you joining the Earth Invasion Heretics?"

As one, the entire crowd craned around. Romona Benson, the television reporter, held a microphone to the injured man. Like he could talk with his face ripped half away. Behind her, a cameraman walked backward, getting video of the prisoner and the TV journalist. I guess brandings might qualify as news, but I doubted the Federal Satellite Broadcast Administration would allow the footage to air. Blood seldom got airtime.

And then it hit me. A licensed witchy-woman brought before the town fathers for an infraction would be news.

I would be something they could air, something sensational and scandalous. My trial would be breaking news, interrupting every soap, cartoon, commercial, movie, or weather update. *Seraph stones.* I was going to be on TV. And so were the orthodox town citizens who wanted all mages dead. If I had to fight my way out of here, the entire world would know that a neomage had spilled human blood. Those who hated and feared mages would rise up.

My trial had been orchestrated, placing me in position to polarize the human world against mages. It was a masterful move.

I groaned under my breath and dropped my head. Audric, leaning in from the pew behind, caught my shoulder in his fist, keeping me upright as if he thought I would bury my face in my lap. "You will not hide, Thorn," he said, for my ears only. "You will not."

I didn't need the threat. I knew now what I was up against. I sat straight, pushing away the sick feeling, and concentrated on the men sitting at the judgment bench. Once, there had been a pulpit, choir seats, a baptismal pool. Now, serving as the judges' bench, there was a long table with seats for seven town fathers behind it. To one side was a chair used as a witness stand, two rows of seats for the accused and witnesses, and places for the younger elders who acted as bailiffs and guards. All could be seen from any part of the old sanctuary, and were fully visible to the camera in the back.

The town fathers—kirk elders and elected officials—sat in the judgment seat. I knew only a few of them by name, and of them one was a friend of sorts, and one was an enemy. I bought my bread from Shamus Waldroup. Elder Culpepper, sitting beside him on the dais, was newly elected to the judgment seat. His eyes were on me, glowing with malice and satisfaction. It was a pretty good bet he had assisted with planning today's events. It was no secret that the elder and his son Derek hated all mages and were powerful men in Mineral City. The elder was orthodox; his son was reformed. Neither man liked me. I had spoiled a lucrative business deal when I melted the Trine's ice cap and made it needless for the town to move. Most people hadn't known I was responsible for that. Somehow, they had found out.

I should have worn the dobok, I thought irrelevantly. My hands were sweating and my breath came too fast. I steadied myself with deep breaths, listening as business matters came before the court—property disputes that dated back to the Last War, disagreements over who actually owned land that had changed hands during the times of disruption after the three plagues. A delinquent payment on a loan was presented. All were tabled for further fact-gathering, the gavel strident. Behind me, the TV camera whirred. Why hadn't I just run?

"Thorn St. Croix Stanhope, take the stand," the chairman called out.

Panic detonated through me, stealing my breath and leaving my heart thumping like a drum in the hands of a maniac. I couldn't do this. Not on national TV. The Enclave priestess would never forgive me once she heard. I'd be ruined. *After this, I could never go home to Enclave.*

The thought was a shock. Until now, I hadn't known I wanted to go to Enclave. I hadn't known some tiny part of me still thought Enclave *was* home. I shivered. What else didn't I know about myself?

Audric stood. From the far side of the aisle, Rupert stood. Both waited a beat until Audric moved up beside me and bent far down, placing his mouth at my ear, easing a hand beneath my arm, his lips by my face. "Showtime, little mage. Wimp out on me now and I'll beat you into a soft lump of modeling clay at our next practice."

A frenzied giggle burst from me and Audric clamped down on my arm so hard the giggle wheezed into silence. Pain helped clear my head. Slowly I stood, catching sight of Ciana's terrified face. My heart faltered, slammed a fierce beat into my chest and up my neck, settling into a fast, steady rhythm. Okay. For Ciana. I managed a smile. I glanced up at Audric and gestured forward. Showtime, the man said. Fine. What choice did I have now?

I threw back my head, took my walking stick in hand, and stepped into the passageway toward the dais. The three remaining brown-clad bailiffs were in a line against the wall to my left. Two wore guns at their hips; the other had a truncheon and Taser. All three held their hands at the ready, cupping the butt of guns or billy clubs. All three looked eager, a little too eager, to take on a mage before a national audience.

The last of my panic fled and battle tactics began to build in my mind. I had studied the strategy and tactics of war, training at Enclave until I was fourteen and had to flee or die. Lately, my training had begun again, every morning at Audric's hands. I looked around the room as I walked, studying it fully, as I should have when I first entered. I dismissed the guards. Rupert could handle the hillbillies with guns, even with the unfamiliar sword. The one with a Taser and stick I could stop with the throwing knives at my wrists. My breathing steadied as I analyzed. They might make two steps before their hearts stopped, say three seconds from throw till they hit the floor, but I doubted it.

Of course, if I killed them, I had better be ready to fight the entire town. And if they got my amulets away before I could mount a defense strong enough to save myself and my friends, I'd be toast. Worse than toast. Stripped, raped, flayed, beaten, butchered, and left to rot in the snow. Most humans didn't care much for mages. I smiled as I took the steps to the dais. I was pretty sure it wasn't a sweet smile.

Reason mulled over battle plans as I looked at the side door. A second alternative presented itself. I didn't like it, but it would be smarter. I could let Rupert and Audric take care of the bailiffs and hold off the crowd, and I could run. Yeah. Cowardice might save my friends, and me too. And there was a third way. I scanned the town fathers who would act as my judges, wondering which of the unknown ones were for me and which were against. I had risked my life to save this town, even if they hadn't been there to see it. I had lived in Mineral City for a decade and had hurt no one. Not once. Yet someone had decided I should face trial and die for an accident of birth that made me a neomage.

Holding my cloak closed over my mage-attire, moving slowly so my skirt bells didn't jingle, I took the seventh step, reaching the stage that used to be a holy place, mage-

boots silent on the scarred wood, walking stick clacking
softly. Flanking me, so much taller than I, Rupert and Audric climbed. I must have disappeared behind them, van-
ishing from the crowd. I felt my body drawing on the
amulets as we came to a stop in front of the judges' desk.

"What's this?" Waldroup asked. Without looking, I felt
the bailiffs step forward. Violence shimmered in the air.
"This won't do. We called a mage to speak, not you two."

As if they had rehearsed it, Rupert and Audric stepped
to either side, revealing my small frame to the audience behind us, and emerging in my peripheral vision. It was a
clever move with a two-pronged outcome: A triangle made
a good defensive fighting position if we had to draw
blades, and it made me look quite defenseless and helpless
before the judges. Mages are small, and behind the bulk of
my friends I probably looked like a young kid standing before the principal's desk.

"We are her champards," Audric announced into the silence, one eye on the slow-moving guards. At a gesture
from the bench, the bailiffs stopped, but I noted a slight
twitch beneath Audric's cloak. He had drawn weapons.

"What's a champard?" Waldroup asked the man on his
left, voices lowered as they conferred. Elder Culpepper
darted a glance at me, furious, hate-filled, and bobbed his
head down, realizing I had seen his reaction. He had plainly
hoped I'd be alone and unprotected. When no one at the
judgment bench seemed to know what a champard was,
Waldroup addressed me. "Well?" I stood silent, letting Audric handle my response. A champard's responsibilities included acting as a legal consultant, hauling firewood, acting
as a human shield, fighting to the death, and keeping his
charge warm at night, among other things that had been
known to include being sex slaves. If I survived this, I would
have ammunition to tease Audric unmercifully.

"You may think of it as a companion, a partner, and a
champion," Audric said.

"Oh? Well, the girl don't need neither. Sit down."

"We will not. It is a mage's legal right to have us beside
her. You may refer to the case of Masters vs. Tomlinson."
Which I had never heard of, but I wasn't going to argue.

Waldroup looked nonplussed but, after an even shorter
conference with the men to his left and right, he shrugged.
"Fine. Speak your name, title, and address, girl."

In a clear tone, I said, "I am Thorn St. Croix, residing
over Thorn's Gems on Upper Street." I gave the street
number.

"Not Stanhope?" he asked.

"No," I said, offering no explanation. Lucas had divorced me. I had seen no reason to keep his name, and I
saw no reason to tell the court my personal business unless
they asked officially. But I was aware of Ciana's distress at
my reply. I didn't understand how I knew what she was
feeling, but I could sense her unhappiness and growing
dread.

"I asked you for your title." Waldroup said, seeming to
understand that getting information from us was going to
be like pulling pig's teeth.

"Mages have no titles," Audric said.

Waldroup, a tiny, ancient black man, shook his head and
sighed. The wrinkles around his eyes tightened into an ag-
grieved weaving. "What kind of mage is she?"

"I'm a stone mage." I was other things too, having received training as a battle mage, but they didn't ask for
particulars, and likely they had no idea what differentiated
one mage from another anyway.

"It's come to our attention that you lived in Mineral
City for a time without presenting a visa. Mages have to
have visas and a GPS thing any time they leave, uh, one of
them Enclaves." When I didn't respond, he said, "Well?"

"When you ask a question, the mage will be happy to
reply," Audric said. The crowd tittered. I had a glimpse of
Ciana, pushing up in her father's lap so she could see better, her face pale and anxious.

"Do you have a visa and a locator band?" Waldroup
asked, eyes narrow, patience wearing thin.

"Yes," I said.

"When did you get them?"

"She refuses to answer," Audric said.

"On what grounds?" Culpepper asked, steepling his
hands in front of his mouth.

"Irrelevancy. The mage has a visa. According to international protocols, the moment someone asks for her visa, it will be presented as proof that she legally left the sovereign nation of the New Orleans Enclave, and her concurrent right to be in Mineral City." I hadn't been wearing it not so long ago when Durbarge, an investigator for the Administration of the ArchSeraph, arrested me. I just hoped no one present remembered it. I resisted the urge to look around at the thought of the AASI, *assey* to the insulting. Durbarge should be here, standing right beside me, glaring at me with his one good eye, and he wasn't. In its own way, that was more unsettling than anything else today.

"Let's see this visa," Culpepper said.

Stepping to the table, I displayed my left wrist, encircled by the bracelet containing my GPS locator device. From the folds of my cloak, I dangled the visa, carved of pink tourmaline, for inspection; it was similarly inscribed and softly glowing. At the revelation of a seraph-blessed object, two of the town fathers sat back. Culpepper, however, stared at the official stone visa and bracelet. His brown robe of office falling away from a bony wrist, he reached out, coveting them both and surely not aware that his desire showed so clearly on his face.

My first thought was to step back, but I stood my ground. He brushed the bracelet with a thumbnail, discarding it for the watermelon-colored tourmaline. Hesitantly at first, and then with inquisitive fingers, Culpepper stroked it like a cat. I knew that the flat, four-inch, ring-shaped stone would cause a faint, pleasurable tingle to a human. I had heard a visa could sometimes calm an angry man.

Unexpectedly, Culpepper made a fist around the visa and yanked. Surprised, I was pulled forward, nearly losing my balance. Faster than a pure-blooded human can move, Audric slammed his hand down on the elder's wrist, wedging his body between the desk and me. He compelled me back, off balance, forcing Culpepper to drop the visa. I heard the elder's wrist bones creak; his face flattened with fury. Wrenching his hand away from the bigger man's grip, Culpepper stood, toppling his chair with a crash. Instantly, the guards moved to surround us, weapons sliding from holsters.

Time dilated, expanded, decelerated. As if in slow motion, I saw Audric and Rupert throw back their cloaks, swords sliding free.

Chapter 6

Heart racing, I caught myself on the judgment desk,
drawing on my amulets. Unexpectedly, the tourmaline ring answered, saturating my system with unfamiliar
power. Battle-lust rose up, tempered by the strange energies of the ring-shaped visa. Tactics I hadn't considered
presented themselves to me, gifts of the ring of the seraphs, help I hadn't known was available. My mind separated out one strategy, a line of attack with myriad
possible outcomes. *Image.* Around me, men were still
drawing weapons.

Choosing the tactic almost at leisure, I dropped my
cloak to the floor with a shrug. Before it puddled at my
feet, before the bells on my skirt had time to sound, I drew
my blade and threw up a hand. I shouted, "No!" The word
roared, amplified, so loud it hammered the walls. My
mage-sight flared on, the room and everyone in it radiating with energy. My neomage attributes blazed, skin glowing. All movement stopped. The echo of my command
died. Every eye in the building was on me, my back to the
crowd, my sword extended.

My long blade was poised at Elder Culpepper's throat.
He grunted softly, his wide eyes ensnared by mine. Fear,
hatred, and fury merged there. I eased the blade tip back
an inch. My heart thudded in my ears. Slowly, I lowered the
hand that stretched to the ceiling, far overhead. I had
thought the stone ring was a dead political tool. I hadn't

known it possessed any strength except that of govern-
mental and legal protection. Hadn't known it was a diplomatic library and an amulet of power I could draw upon as
I had with my voice just now. Clearly I had a lot to learn,
but I didn't have time to think about all that. My skin was
blazing. And I was holding a sword to the throat of an
elder. *Oops.*

Stunned, Shamus Waldroup's eyes attracted mine. He
shook his head slightly. With one look, I gleaned that whatever had been set in motion today, it hadn't been planned
by the council. My eyes flicked back to Culpepper and my
lip curled. Not the *entire* council. I swallowed, throat dry
and burning in the aftermath of my shout. My fingers,
shaking and cold, brushed the donut-shaped talisman,
making certain it was still attached to the amulet necklace.
Following the basic strategy I had gleaned from it, I shifted
my sword to my left hand and turned, so my back was no
longer to the crowd, facing the audience, head high. Allowing the town to view a neomage, the way the plagues and
the sins of humans made us.

Speaking softly as I turned, I said to Waldroup, "I was
called here today to hear charges against me. Read them."

"Put away the weapon," he whispered, his eyes on my
hand and the blade. "Please."

The hilt, the prime amulet, was almost hot in my palm.
The skin of my hand was bright, white scars blistering, my
body luminous. Reacting to the strategy found in the tourmaline visa, I had drawn on every amulet I was wearing. In
the wash of their energies, I was shimmering, slightly drunk
on the mix of power swarming into my blood. I thought
about muting my attributes, but it was a bit late for that.
And maybe the gracious "please" was a start to rational
negotiations. With a decisive flourish, I sheathed my blade
in the walking stick, the motion jingling my skirt bells.

Relief flooded Waldroup's face and he banged the gavel.
"You guards get back over there against the wall. You two
champards put them swords away. We ain't gone have no violence here today." When no one moved, he banged the
gavel again. "You heard me. Do what I said, all a you, or
stand in contempt a court."

The guards holstered their guns and stepped back one pace. Audric and Rupert hesitated a long moment before resheathing their blades. The sound of steel on leather was supple, threatening. The guards retreated two more steps, widening a circle that had tightened around us. The testosterone was so thick I could taste it on the air.

As I repositioned, I caught sight of the TV camera at knee height on the edge of the platform. The news crew had mounted the dais. Fury still twisted Elder Culpepper's face. A quick look confirmed two others at the long table had been prepared for aggression. I thought there might be weapons beneath their jackets. I didn't know Culpepper's cronies, but I'd remember them, and so would the camera lens panning the bench. Of the remaining four judges, Shamus and one other were for me, it was clear. The other two had poker faces and were impossible to interpret. "Read the charges," I said again, hoping a return to procedure would restore the peace.

Shamus shook a sheet of paper, the rattle carrying in the too-quiet church. "It has been brought to the attention of a kirk elder that the licensed mage in Mineral City, Thorn St. Croix Stanhope, has indulged in debauchery, decadence, and dissipation, leading our town's human males into immoral and iniquitous behavior." The accusation seemed to bounce off the church walls, a bright, harsh sound.

"Thorn?" Jacey called from the crowd, disbelieving. The camera swiveled to focus on my friend as she stood with an expression of disbelief. In the sea of black clothing her red dress and emeralds shimmered. "*Our* Thorn?" The pronoun seemed to say several things at once: that I was one of them, that I was innocent, that I belonged to the town, that the accusation was ludicrous and everyone knew it, that I was a jewelry maker and a prosperous one at that. Jacey laughed, the sound infectious. Several others laughed with her. The level of antagonism in the room plunged. I could have kissed her.

"Sit down. When the judges want comments from the crowd, we'll ask for them," Waldroup said. Jacey sat, a confident smile on her face. I was pretty sure the camera loved it.

"When and with which men?" Audric asked. "What evidence is to be presented? And when can the defense question the accusers?"

Shamus scratched his head, gazing at the cameraman, who was repositioning to sight along the bench. I was sure he rued letting in the crew for the meeting. Mineral City was now hot news. If things got out of hand, the town fathers would have an image problem no matter which way things worked out. *Image,* the visa had suggested to me, a hypothesis and proposal with the greatest likelihood of success. Which meant the visa was an interactive amulet. If it had been alive it would have been purring with pride. As it was, I felt its distinct feeling of smug satisfaction. It was disconcerting. I wasn't sure I liked it.

"This ain't no big city court like they got in Raleigh or Atlanta or Mobile," Shamus said. "We mostly mediate minor stuff here." He was explaining for the media. Damage control. I took a breath, the first full one in minutes, and stopped a smile before it lit my face. "As to crimes, if someone's guilty, they confess and we punish them. Big crimes, federal stuff, goes to the district court in Asheville. We ain't had a federal crime in over twenty-five years. We just usually read the charges and talk it through."

"The licensed neomage has been called before a legal court," Audric said. "Specific charges? Witnesses?"

"That would be me," Culpepper said. His rage mutated into something colder as his gaze raked me, pausing at my breasts, pushed up by my mage-shirt. He thought he had me, and surely had my punishments designed and arranged, and he didn't care if the television camera saw it all on his face. My breathing sped up and I worked to appear unmoved, even as I slid my thumb across the release on my walking stick to make certain my blade was still free. Culpepper raised his voice. "I heard the confession of a twelve-year-old boy who was seduced by her wicked dancing and led into lewd and lascivious behavior."

"Who, where, and when?" Audric asked.

"He refused to say when. I didn't ask where. The accusation is enough for a kirk elder to charge a harlot. But let me remind you all," Culpepper said, his voice rising, looking past me at the crowd, "lest we doubt, the whole town saw her dance. At the last sun-day, the early thaw celebration, she wore *pants and boots,* dressed like a *man,* her body posed to entice. The mage danced before us all, a public spectacle. She moves like a harlot. We all saw!"

He was right. Well, sorta. Along with half the women present, I had worn jeans and boots to the town's early thaw gathering, where Audric and I had competed in the dancing, beating the band and winning a wager. The whole town knew that. It was fact, and one fact, even an unrelated one, added corroboration to accusations. Though there was no law against a woman in pants, and never had been, the observation was calculated to appeal to the orthodox.

"Will the accuser come forward for questioning?" Audric asked.

"No. I will not break the seal of the confessional for a mage and I'll not have him traumatized again. It's my right to bring charges and to testify for an underage youth."

Audric shrugged a huge shoulder, his cloak moving as if with a hard breeze. "We request that the charge be dismissed."

Culpepper darted a glance into the crowd and smiled, showing teeth. I really didn't like the look of that smile.

"What grounds?" Waldroup asked.

"The crime is hearsay. No dates for the alleged offense have been offered, no accusers have come forward." He looked at Culpepper. "The charge is gossip. And gossip is a sin," Audric said, "punishable by branding."

"He has a point," Waldroup said.

"As you wish. We have other accusers," Culpepper said, satisfied. The expression on his face said he wasn't surprised to have his first accusation thrown out. He had come prepared and had multiple legal assaults at the ready. I figured there was a witch-catcher under his chair too, for use if I was pronounced guilty. If humans took an unprepared mage, they would win, humans having much greater muscle mass than mages. But I wasn't unprepared. Culpepper didn't seem to know what that meant in terms of winning and losing a confrontation. Of course, if I fought, caught on camera, public opinion would crucify me. And not just me, but all mages. Even if I won, I lost. Maybe the elder was counting on that.

The elder slid a paper to Shamus. On it was a list of names. I would have bet the store that the accusers were orthodox. The orthodox wanted women in long wool dresses, unrelieved black, and ugly as sin. They wanted their women quiet and soft-spoken, chaste and dull, and to walk behind their men and masters. I wore slacks, leggings, and bright colors. I was a divorcée. And a mage.

"Call your witnesses," Audric said. He glared at a bailiff. "Get the accused a chair."

The bailiff looked at Culpepper, who inclined his head. The exchange was caught by Waldroup, who sat back, the shock on his face quickly masked. He stared at Culpepper for a long moment before turning his attention to the rest of the town fathers, as if contemplating a new reality. His gaze settled on the judges who were obviously siding with Culpepper. There had been a shift in the political climate and Shamus recognized he was on the outside.

I was offered a chair at the head of the platform, facing the assembly. I stepped over my cloak and approached the seat as if it were a throne offered to a queen. Before I sat, Rupert lifted my cloak from the floor and settled it with a flourish on the seat. The red silk lining picked up the radiance from my skin and glowed like a jewel. I let Rupert adjust the cloak for warmth in the unheated room and I rested the walking stick across my lap.

I could smell the assembled with both nose and that related mage-sense, the mind-skim. The human smells were sweat and the reek of unwashed bodies, leather, perfume, and moonshine. Beneath them seeped excitement and fear. Humans were beautiful in mage-sight, with the soft glow of life, the auras they carried—all except Audric, whose half-mage attributes rested beneath an oddly lifeless human glamour. I could pierce it if I wanted, and see him as he really was, but I didn't bother. As I watched, two more brown-robed bailiffs came in from the cold, bringing the total to five.

Rupert stood to my right, between the guards and my chair. Audric crossed the room and took up a stance beside the nearest bailiff. The guards didn't like that, but there wasn't much they could do if Waldroup allowed it. The tiny baker seemed disposed to allow the accused and her champards a lot of leniency at the moment.

Waldroup read the first name and called out, "Will Amos Ramps come forward and take the witness seat?"

An old man in black shambled forward, climbed the steps, and sat in a chair to the far right of the long table occupied by the fathers. "Swear him in, Tobitt," Waldroup directed the first bailiff.

Whispers swept the gathering and Amos' head came up fast. "Ain't no one said nothing about no swearing in. I was jist s'pposed to say my piece and go."

"I think we'll do this a bit more formal than usual. Swear him," Waldroup said. Culpepper's eyes narrowed and he sat back in his chair.

A look of alarm crossed Amos' face as Tobitt held a black leather-bound Bible to him. "Do you swear to tell the truth, the whole truth, and nothing but the truth, so help the Most High and all the seraphs?" the guard asked.

Amos looked from the Bible to the table of erstwhile judges and gulped, saying, "I do."

"What do you know regarding the charges brought against the neomage Thorn St. Croix?" Waldroup asked.

Amos tugged on his collar. "I heard—"

"Objection," Audric said.

"Sustained," Waldroup said. "What do you know? Not guess, or suppose, deduce, or assume. Not what you mighta heard. What do you know? And be careful, Amos. I'm the senior judge here, no matter what some others might believe. If I think you're making something up, I'll toss you in the pokey so fast your head'll spin off and take flight."

Amos blanched, looked for help at the table, and when none was forthcoming searched the crowd. "Mabel?"

"Your wife can speak on her own if she's got something to say. What do you know about the accused?"

Amos gulped again, looked at the Bible now sitting on the edge of the long table, and dropped his head. Since the seraphs came, people who lied on the witness stand had been known to drop dead. Not often, but once was too many times. "Nothing."

"Would the witness please speak up?" Audric asked.

Amos shrunk lower in his chair. "Nothing."

"Fine." Shamus banged his gavel. "The witness is dismissed. Mabel, you got anything to say? If so, get on up here, swear the words, and say it."

"Just that she's a whore. All mages are whores. We all know that." Every head swiveled to locate Mabel. The TV cameraman maneuvered and focused tight on her face.

"Yeah!" another voice yelled. "Hang the mage!"

"Let me have her first for a while," a third voice shouted. "I'll show her how we treat mage whores in Mineral City."

"They have sex in the streets," Mabel called out, "tempting man and seraph both, leading immoral, licentious lives. Orgies and—"

Shamus banged his gavel so hard I feared it would come apart, but Mabel just raised her voice.

"—wild parties, and drunken revels. Dancing with her clothes off." Someone whistled a cat-call. General laughter filled the hall. "Sinning and carousing and—"

"Guards, escort both the Ramps out, and take Mabel down to the jail. Gag her if necessary," Shamus shouted over the sound of Mabel's rhetoric, the clamor of the crowd, and his own rapping gavel. The two robed guards wearing Tasers and billy clubs waded into the crowd. One with a gun at his waist lifted Amos beneath one arm and assisted him off the stand and toward the cold. The number of opposing weapons in the room was cut in half.

"And if anyone else thinks they can flaut this court by speaking outta turn, or speaking opinion or gossip, think again. I'll have you in the jail in two seconds flat. You can spend the night in a cell next to Mabel there." The crowd roared with laughter as Mabel's tirade was cut off in mid-accusation, a gag stuck between her lips and a length of duct tape slapped on. She windmilled her arms, landing a solid thunk on Tobitt's head before she was cuffed.

Watching the men on the bench with him rather than the action on the floor, Shamus said, "I take my responsibility to the edicts of the High Council of the Seraphim very serious and everyone gathered here better take it serious too.

"Guards, when you get back from locking Mabel up, I want one of you at the front of the meeting hall and one at the back doors. If anyone opens his or her mouth out of turn, arrest 'em." The gavel banged again. "Anyone got anything specific to say about the accused?" When a hand was raised in the back of the hall, Shamus said, "The court recognizes Ken Schmidt. Come on up and get sweared in, Ken."

Schmidt was a miner who occasionally sold some fine quartz crystal to Thorn's Gems, specimens he had strip-mined from his claim near the old feldspar mine. A big man, he was bearded, with cold-reddened hands and a lumbering gait. We had dated once not long after my divorce. The blind date had been arranged by Rupert and Jacey, and had been a dismal failure. I had no idea if he would speak for me or against me, and from the look on Culpepper's face, half wild hope, half angry despair, neither did he.

Wearing rough clothes that looked as if he'd come straight from his claim, Ken sat, making the chair squeak, and was sworn in by the remaining guard. Waldroup said, "Say your name and address, and speak your piece."

"Kenneth Schmidt. I'm a miner. Got no mailing address, but I got a claim, duly registered with the claims office. I pay my taxes. I go to kirk every single meeting when I'm in town or when the weather allows me to trek in. I dated Thorn St. Croix once." A buzz started in the room. Ken looked at me from under bushy brows. "I been looking for a wife, long time now. I got a good claim, I make good money, and I can provide for a woman and kids." His heart was in his eyes, his whole soul there for me and the crowd to see. Ken Schmidt was in love with me, or thought he was. And he intended to save me.

"We went to dinner at the Blue Snail. She had a salad and I had the spaghetti. And then I took her home."

"Did the accused at any time try to seduce you? Or indulge in inappropriate behavior, actions not suitable to a chaste and virtuous woman?" Shamus asked.

"No, sir. She was perfectly, wellt, perfect. Just the kind of

woman a man would want to take as wife. Honest. Kind, too.
When I asked to see her again, she said it wouldn't work out
between us. She let me down all gentle like. And that's all I
got to say."

The next witness wasn't so kind. I recognized him as a
fiddler, one of the town's musicians who played at early
thaw feast days and holidays. One of the musicians who
had played for the dancing Audric and I had won. And he
had lost.

When he had been through all the preliminaries, Eugene
looked at me, met my eyes, and lied. "She and me been
having an affair. She won't let me alone. Calls me, comes to
my door and window at night, climbs in bed with me and
has her way. I'm ashamed and need to confess, need to
clear the air and find a way to get free of her immoral hold
on me. I want her locked up. That's all I got to say," he
echoed Ken's closing words.

"When did the accused last come to you?" Audric asked.

"This morning just after dawn."

Audric looked at the bench. "May I address the senior
judge as a witness?" Shamus' brows rose toward his bald
pate, but he gestured permission. "As a baker, you must
rise every day at dawn. Do you look outside?"

Shamus nodded. "Check the weather, just like every
businessman who depends on people being out and about.
Bad weather, we get less customers, so we make less bread.
Why you asking?"

"Your bakery is across the street from Thorn's Gems.
This morning when you looked out, were lights on above
the shop?"

Shamus scratched his bony chin. "Reckon they were."

"And could you see in the windows?"

"No, can't see in from the street, what with the porch
over the walkway. But come to think of it, there might
coulda been some shadows moving. Why?"

"The witness lies. Thorn St. Croix and I were practicing
savage-chi and savage-blade from before dawn until eight
o'clock. You saw the evidence of that movement in her
windows yourself proving she was at home, not in the witness' bed."

Shamus stared from Audric to me to the man on the witness seat. When he spoke, his voice was too low to carry off the dais. "Eugene. You want to reconsider your accusation?"

Red-faced and uncertain, Eugene pulled on his collar as if it was too tight. "Well, maybe it wasn't this morning."

"Some sweet young thing crawls in your bed and you don't remember when? I don't think so. Recant, or I'll think you need some time to reflect. Maybe a long time to reflect."

Eugene's breathing had sped up and a slight sheen of sweat beaded his face. When he looked at me, something malevolent swam in the depths of his eyes. "She's a mage. Mages are all whores." Voice filled with revulsion, he said, "She's evil. She's a temptress."

"But she didn't come to your bed?" Shamus, the chairman and chief judge, clarified.

"No. I guess she didn't. But she tempts a man. Just having her in this town is a cause for immoral thoughts for every man and boy. She's a wh—"

The gavel banged as Shamus cut him off, his face darkening, his dark-skinned knuckles pale on the wooden hammer. "That's enough. Guards, escort him to the jail." Two bailiffs lifted the witness by his arms and shuffled him off the stage. "Maybe a few days in a cell will convince you of the error of bearing false witness to this court, Eugene. And you're lucky the seraphs didn't strike you dead for lying."

"Well, I got something to say," a voice called from the back of the room.

"The court recognizes Derek Culpepper," Shamus said. "Come on up, son. And to prevent any conflict of interest or unethical proceedings, I'm sure the elder Culpepper will agree to remain impartial, and not vote his opinion on any evidence brought before this bench by his son. Elder?"

The elder didn't look as if he thought that was a good idea at all, but a quick glance at the camera convinced him of the futility of argument. Culpepper jerked his head with ill grace as his son bounded up the stairs to the witness stand. Derek was a flamboyant businessman, partial to vivid-colored clothing, a man with more money than taste. Today he was dressed in a gray wool suit with a tiny yellow pin-stripe, a cranberry-toned overcoat, and a purple shirt. His tie was a bright spring green. And his shoes were orange leather. It nearly hurt to look at him.

Holding to both chair arms, I opened a skim and my sight together. The world reeled and tottered like a top around me. Gorge rose in the back of my throat. The *otherness* of the blended scan stole my breath, but I saw what I needed to see. I released both senses.

As Derek took the witness seat and was sworn in, I lifted a finger, attracting Audric's attention. When the big man bent almost in two, I said into his ear, "Get him to say if he hates mages. And if he does, make him empty his pockets."

Audric turned a curious eye to me, but I offered no explanation.

Derek accused me of inviting him to my loft, drugging, and then seducing him. I didn't bother to hide my grin at his words. Even if I'd been in heat, a condition that had been known to cause mages to mate with a reckless lack of inhibition, even across species, I'd have had better taste than to choose Derek. A couple of women in the crowd must have agreed, because a titter rippled through them at my smile.

I didn't bother to listen to the dates and times Derek offered, occasions when I had my lascivious way with him. I just stared at his left overcoat pocket, waiting. When he finally fell silent, Audric said, "Are mages and their conjures a danger to the human population?"

"Yes. They should be wiped from the face of the earth. The Mage War was proof of that. The US military tried to destroy them, over eighty years ago, and would have if they hadn't been attacked by magic and annihilated." The crowd murmured uneasily and I could feel the weight of human eyes. "The nuclear weapon that was aimed at the mages would have left the Earth a clean and chaste place, worthy of the Most High. Now, because they're still here, still polluting the face of the world that the Lord hath made, God the Victorious won't come and finish the cleansing that was the apocalypse."

That was a new one. I'd heard all sorts of reasons for

killing mages, but never a claim that mages were keeping the Most High from coming to earth.

It was an accusation I couldn't answer, an allegation that was pure prejudice. The end of the world hadn't been exactly what the ancient prophets had been expecting. There had been seraphs, winged beings with swords who appeared in every major city in the world. There had been plagues and wars and rumors of wars. Most of the population had died.

But to the consternation of Christians and Jews, there hadn't yet been a rapture or a messianic appearance. The Muslims had been devastated to discover that other religious believers had survived too. Only nine hundred people in Utah had lived through the plagues. The Hindu messiah, the Kalki Avatar, hadn't come. Most telling, the Most High had not yet appeared, though smart people never said so aloud. People with big mouths had been known to drop dead when making that observation. Derek Culpepper, gloating and satisfied, left the dais.

An accused had the right to speak, and because Derek hadn't asked a question, I didn't have to answer one. I could, however, speak to the prejudice, and to the fatal altercation between a handful of mages and an entire army. The Mage War was taught to every mage child from the cradle up. It wasn't taught quite the same way in human schools. *Truth,* the tourmaline ring whispered. *Use only truth.*

Chapter 7

*T*ruth? How much truth? I stood, smoothing my skirt, drawing attention to the strange clothing, so different from the severe dress of the orthodox; to my skin and scars, both radiant; to my jewelry, which was ostentatious, and not a style humans would wear. It wouldn't hurt to remind them I was a mage, with weapons hanging around my neck. And that I had never used them against the town. I allowed myself to be sworn in.

In the singsong voice used by mage storytellers, I started speaking. "In the Beginning of the End of the World, came seraphs bearing the judgment of the Almighty, and the plagues they brought that punished the humans. War followed the plagues. Few survived.

"Darkness came, the Darkness that was of the spirit and the flesh. The handful of living descended into anarchy and violence or chose sides, joining the seraphs fighting the Dark, or joined the Darkness and the lures they offered. Evil walked the earth, stalking humans, killing, eating them. Darkness that raped and pillaged and kidnapped and bred with human captives to create new demons to cavort with the old. In all, nearly six billion died."

I heard the crowd muttering, and I knew what they were saying—that mages were the result of Darkness raping human women and getting them with child, false accusation based on prejudice. I drew on the tourmaline to amplify my voice, and slowly walked toward the edge of the dais so all of them could see me. With each firm step I let my boots ring like a drum on the wood floor of the platform, and made my skirt bells chime, the speaker becoming part of the storytelling art. In Enclave, mages lived for the story, and I wanted the humans to hear the neomage version of the end of the world. Wanted them to hear the truth. "And during the End of the World, neomages were born." I told them of the human babies born during the time of the plagues, infected or dead at birth. Malformed, genetically damaged.

"Nine months after the first plague, at the end of the final plague, a few hundred thousand human women survivors, those who had been in the first trimester of pregnancy at the Beginning of the End, gave birth all around the world. These children were viable offspring, beautiful children. Children of human fathers and mothers. But they were not human themselves. Conceived just before the first plague, carried successfully through all three plagues, the pestilence and disease had twisted their DNA into something different. Something new. Something never prophesied in all the years of human existence." I reached the edge of the dais. The TV camera was positioned at an angle to catch the crosshatch of scars on my cheek and the solid glow of scars on my left hand. I put it from my mind.

"The Last War was decades long and hard. The ice age began. When the first neomages came into puberty, in the fourteenth and fifteenth years of the war, their talents and gifts erupted. These children of man had no power of their own, but could use the power in the world around them, the leftover energies of creation. They could see these energies in the rain and storms, in the heavens, in the wind and the sea, in growing things and in the earth, in rocks and minerals. And they began to experiment with the power that was theirs to use.

"It wasn't illusion or trickery, it wasn't magic, not in the way of fairy tales or dark fantasy. It wasn't religion or sorcery. It was the unused energy of the Most High, the residue of creation. But the mages had no training. No one to guide them. By accident, some released wild energies—what, for lack of a better word, they called wild-magic. Mages died. Humans died. Humans they loved. Pain and anguish rang through the world."

I arched my neck and looked high at a round, stained-glass window. I raised my arms as I had seen the priestess do in telling the story of the Beginning of the End. "And humans feared." My voice rang off the walls of the old church. "They killed us by the tens, by the hundreds. Perhaps by the thousands. Small bands of neomages gathered in every part of the globe, despairing, frightened, untrained. In Louisiana, in the French Quarter of New Orleans, a small group of teenage mages gathered, sharing their newfound power. Attacked, hunted, trapped, they stood before an army of humans."

I looked down, dropping one arm in a sweeping wave, not saying "humans like you," but the gesture implying it. My glowing neomage eyes picked out the faces in the crowd. European, Cherokee, African, and Asian genetic backgrounds were all visible, all human, all facing a boogeyman, a nightmare, just as in the Mage War. The crowd had fallen silent, staring at the apparition who stood above them, a pagan wild child, a wisp of a woman, so much smaller than they, so much weaker. Wielding power they had never known.

And I spoke the story that humans denied, repudiated, claiming a revisionist history that protected them from the truth of what their forebears did, or tried to do. "Some of the humans were parents, fighting their own progeny. They bombarded the small band of teens with rockets and mortars. The children of man devised shields and weapons," I chanted. "But the neomages knew not how to manipulate the energies they could see and taste and feel in the world around them. With a single gesture, the human general ordered the ultimate weapon dropped, the nuclear bomb intended to destroy the neomages. And the mages called on the seraphs."

The crowd gave a collective gasp. From the back of the church, a voice thundered, "Seraphs and God the Victorious don't hear soulless mages. They're not human!

They're animals!" I found him at the doors. It was Tobitt, the young acolyte guard who had sworn in the witnesses. He was holding a gun in both hands, out from his body, pointed at me.

Without thinking, I called on the white onyx fish that held my sphere of shielding. I didn't snap it into place, as it would be like building a wall between the assembly and me. But I got it ready. And I watched Tobitt's eyes as I spoke.

"They don't hear Godless, heathen whores!" someone else called.

"The Most High don't see no mages," another said. "That's why they're in prisons!"

Watching Tobitt, I whispered, "Neomage children, the teenage children of humans, called on the High Host of the Seraphim, and upon the Most High. 'Mage in battle, mage in dire, seraphs, come with holy fire.' It was a child's nursery rhyme, chanted by innocents filled with fear. And the seraphs came." I raised my voice. "A dozen of the Holy Ones appeared in the air above the battle-field. One reached out his wings and caught the bomb as it plummeted. Another took the bomb and departed with it. It did not detonate. But the neomages had built up power while defending themselves. Much power. My an-cestors were foolish, afraid and untaught, facing an army of well-armed, angry, frightened humans. They didn't know what to do with so much gathered might, or how to control it.

"In their inexperience, they released the power. And the human army fell. Thousands died. By *accident,* not by in-tent. And the children of man screamed and mourned even as they tried to draw back the might that escaped from them. But there was no tool on earth or with the seraphim, to pull back so much power once released. And the ener-gies rained down on the human army, on their own fathers and mothers." I shared a small, sad smile. "A great anguish went up to the Most High with the souls of the human dead."

The mage account listed all the names of loved ones they had killed that day. I mentioned only the best-known one. "General Bascomb, the human who ordered the nuclear bomb dropped, was the biological father of one of the mages he battled. Bascomb died that day. His son was orphaned. His son grieved."

The church full of people had fallen silent again. Tobitt's gun wavered from me, dropping to dangle, pointing at the floor. *Truth,* the sigil had suggested. Well, here it was. Truth that the human and neomage communities had never shared.

"In punishment, the seraphs gathered the mages they had saved, forcing them into the first Enclave, the shielded haven now universally called the New Orleans Enclave. All around the globe, seraphs collected embattled neomages and established Enclaves, where the few still alive could work and study their gifts in safety. Where they were imprisoned. Nearly one hundred years have passed, and still we are captives. We may not depart without seraphic approval, visas, and scrutiny by the Administration of the ArchSeraph."

I looked around the hall. There was a lot I hadn't said. I hadn't mentioned that proximity to each other set neomages and seraphs into heat. Only recently had the Most High and the High Council of the Seraphim produced the sigils that controlled mage-heat for a few hours at a time. All that I kept to myself. "Even today, we mourn those we killed. Even now, we do penance for the death of humans, the death of our parents, in the Mage War." This was truth untaught in human schools. Truth that might disarm the angry and contain the vitriol.

"To atone, we help where we can, where asked. We accept payment, yes, as each of you accept payment for services and goods. Yes, we have power, but it's sealed inside the Enclaves with us, so it won't harm humans by intent or accident ever again."

I looked at Tobitt. Orthodox, weaned on mage hate, taught by elders focused on cementing their own political power. "You're right. We have no souls. When our spark of life is extinguished, we die forever. There's no afterlife for us. Don't fear us; pity us. We're empty vessels. We are the unforeseen."

"So how did the seraphs hear the mages?" Tobitt asked, curious at last.

I shrugged. Bells rang softly, a funeral cadence. "We think it was innocence that called to them. Since that time, seraphs always hear the call of mages in dire. It's their pact with us, though to call the capricious and volatile seraphs is always a danger to nearby humans."

Audric touched my shoulder and gestured to the chair set aside for the accused. I walked back across the small stage, my boots and bells loud in the quiet church. When I was seated, my champard asked, "Are there more accusations?"

Derek Culpepper raced up the stairs to the dais and shouted to the crowd. I had forgotten him and was almost surprised when he spoke, his face filled with rage, a finger pointed accusingly at me. "Don't listen to her wiles. Can't you see she's trying to seduce you with words? She's spelling you all right now!" When no one agreed, he said, "They take our money and make us dependent on their trinkets. We're *humans,* the highest creation of the Most High, beneath the seraphs. We don't need mages or their conjures or amulets. They're immoral and depraved."

"Is there no good to be had from mages?" Audric asked. "No good at all from the conjures and amulets that humans buy and use?"

"No!" Derek shouted.

"Then the accused requests that you empty your pockets," Audric said.

Derek paled and clenched his hands. Shocked, he looked to his father, and I followed the glance. The elder raised his eyebrows. Derek turned to me, taking in my small smile. I didn't know what kind of amulet he habitually carried, but I'd seen him worrying it during a previous town meeting, his fingers caressing it like a lifeline. He opened his mouth and snapped it shut, a crafty glint in his eyes.

"She spelled me with it," he said.

I didn't know exactly what kind of amulet he carried, but to my mage-sight it glowed a yellow-green of earth-magery, the gift of life and all things growing. It had been quite powerful the first time I noted it on him. I breathed deeply and caught the scent of the conjure. It smelled warm and verdant, like sunlight on spring leaves.

"Show us," Audric commanded.

Derek's triumph grew. He reached into his pocket and pulled out the amulet. He held it between thumb and forefinger so the crowd could see. The audience sucked in a collective breath, swept back from the truth of the Mage War story into habitual, ingrained fear. Ignoring them, I studied the amulet from my seat, smelling oak and age and the working of a powerful mage. The amulet was made from the root of a live oak, a thin disc about two and a half inches around and a quarter inch thick, like a large coin, carved through with symbols. To my mage-sight, its energies weren't beautiful, but it was powerful. The fact that it glowed with power was significant. It had been recently charged.

"What say you?" Shamus asked me.

"I can't use that amulet," I said.

"Say what?" Shamus asked, surprised.

"There are different kinds of mages and energies. I'm a stone mage. That's an earth mage amulet. I can see the working of the conjure but I can't use it, make it, or alter it." I lifted a carved quartz rose on the necklace I wore. "This is an amulet for peaceful thoughts. This I can use because it's made of stone and mineral, but not that. The amulet carried by Derek Culpepper is a kamea, an oak-carved, Oriental-style amulet, likely inscribed with the name of the seraph Garshanal. It brings success in financial negotiations to the one who carries it. He bought it from a licensed mage and had it recharged on a recent trip. Didn't you?" I asked.

Before Derek could answer, Shamus said, "You're still under oath, Derek. We've had one witness lie on the stand today. I ain't gonna abide a second one. If you lie and survive it, and if I can find the mage you purchased that thing from, I'll have you tarred and feathered. And you know I mean it."

Derek looked at me, loathing leaking like sweat from his

pores. He ground out, "I bought it. From a licensed witchy-woman. A mage whore in Atlanta."

In the silence that followed, Shamus Waldroup bent to the men at the judgment table, murmuring. My hearing is good, but I caught only a word or two before the chairman banged his gavel twice.

"By a majority of judges and elders, Elder Culpepper abstaining, we find that Thorn St. Croix is a legally licensed mage, and all accusations made today are proved false. Unless someone has specific charges against her, charges with hard evidence to back 'em up, I intend to declare this case closed." When no one offered damning evidence, Shamus banged the gavel once and said, "The accused is found not guilty. In fact, the accused is not and never was the accused. You're free to go, Thorn, and this bench offers its heartfelt apologies for this fiasco. Prejudice is something we ain't usually got to contend with in this town. I'm ashamed of my fellow citizens and of my fellow judges." He banged the gavel again and stood as he spoke. "Recess. I need to get the taste of lies and collusion outta my mouth."

Intense relief hit me and I shuddered, cold rippling across my skin with a soft jingle of bells. I would have slumped back in the chair, but my shirt's steel supports held me upright. Audric leaned down and gathered the collar of my cloak, securing it. "Damp your neomage attributes," he murmured. My hand stole to the amulets, first releasing the shield I had ready, then damping the glow of skin and scars. My flesh dimmed to human, untouched by magery.

"Need I carry you, little mage?" he asked.

I clamped my lips on a witless titter. "No. I'm fine. I think."

He grinned at me, sculpted, full lips parting, eyes sparkling in his dark-skinned face. "You were magnificent. But if you fall on your ass crossing the stage, you'll spoil the effect."

I laughed, a breathy sound. "And the sight of you carrying me off won't ruin it?" I stood, knees wobbly, drained and invigorated, all at once. Along with all the other mage children, I had studied the art of storytelling, but had never practiced, not before an audience.

"She's got a touch of the ham in her, doesn't she?" Rupert said, tucking my right hand into the crook of his left arm.

"She's been around you too long," Audric said. "It's rubbed off."

"Just remember, dearie. There's room for only one queen in Thorn's Gems, and I am she. What's this?" he asked, lifting an amulet hanging on my necklace.

I looked down. In work-hardened fingers, he held a poor-quality sapphire, crudely carved into a fat owl, an amulet I had purchased at a swap meet without knowing what it did. It came from the time of the wild-mages, from before the Mage War. And it was glowing. "I don't know," I said. "I really don't."

He could hear the soft pad of human-style boots on the stone of the passageway. They were early. His wings weren't healed over. It hadn't been twenty-four hours yet. Despair swamped him. How long? How long would penance last?

He pictured Daria in his mind: her dark hair and fine brown skin, long lean legs wrapped around him, her amulets flashing with wild-magic. Her flashing eyes so full of mischief. He could almost feel her fingertips as they caressed his face. However long it lasted, she would have been worth it. How does one ask forgiveness for a sin one doesn't regret?

The cell door opened and a voice said, "Barak. Rise and shine. We got a randy one for you. She can smell you already." They laughed. There were only three of them this time. And it hadn't been long enough. Something was different. Something had changed. Shackles clinked. He kept his head buried in the crook of his arm, breathing deeply.

"Yeah. It's your lucky day. And ours, if you continue being stupid about 'em."

"A bonus, you wingless wonder." A boot landed in the small of his back. A hand clicked a thick cuff around one wrist, while another captor wrenched back his other arm.

"We made Forcas happy and so we get the next one, and only three of us to share. And when she—"

Barak, the fallen seraph once called Baraqyal, lashed out with both legs and the partially healed stub of a wing. All three tormentors crashed to the floor.

Chapter 8

I had thought my troubles were over when the gavel banged down the last time. I was wrong. When my two champards and I stepped through the oversized front doors onto the covered porch of the old church, the steps and the walk leading to Upper Street were lined with black-clad humans. Rupert and Audric tossed back their cloaks and drew weapons. The sound of steel on leather echoed down the silent street.

In two rows, facing one another, the town orthodox had re-created the gauntlet, a silent condemning jury, hating me, letting me know that though a judge had set me free, they had judged me guilty. Several elders and the most zealous of their followers, perhaps three hundred, lined my passageway. I counted three brown robes before I looked away.

"Theatrics would come in handy now," Rupert said with tense humor. "We could cancan down the street."

I grinned at that, and my rising fear dissipated. "Thanks," I said, catching his eye.

"If you can walk on your own, a little extra weaponry and some hocus-pocus might be useful too," Audric said.

"I'm not attacking humans," I said softly. "Where's a TV camera when you need one to hide behind?"

"No one has a gun out," Rupert said. "No blades, no dynamite. Let's brazen our way through it. Show 'em your clothes again, Thorn. Make eye contact. Let them know you know who they are."

I looked at the first dozen people. I didn't know a single one. Somehow, that lightened my heart. I folded my cloak back, exposing my neomage finery and freeing my arms but keeping my head covered. Like a queen walking to her beheading, I started down the steps, Rupert and Audric following. We reached the street before I recognized anyone, and it was the owner of the laundry I used. Arms crossed over her chest, she held my gaze, glaring. I'd be looking for a new place to wash my clothes. Sleet started again, a thin rain of ice that bounced off my cloak.

Behind me I heard the scrape of boot on stone. Faster than humans can see, I whirled and drew my sword. It was Elder Jasper and his wife, Polly. And their new child, who hadn't been with them earlier. Polly sucked in a breath to scream. I lowered my sword.

His voice ringing into the street, the elder said, "Polly and I wondered if you had a healing amulet. She cut her finger opening a can last night. It's paining her mightily."

I looked back and forth between them, sword poised. A long moment passed. Polly, trembling, handed her baby to the elder and walked down the stairs. She held out her hand to me. A makeshift bandage was taped to her thumb. I stared at her extended hand; her human aura was blazing with fear and determination, a bright golden glow. She stared at my skin, and I realized I had released my attributes as my defenses went up. Slowly, so I wouldn't startle her again, I sheathed my blade and took the bandaged hand in mine. To her credit, she didn't flinch, though her trembling worsened. Her blue eyes fastened on me.

"I have a curative amulet at the shop," I said. "It'll speed healing and lessen the pain."

"That would be a blessing," Polly said. She gripped my hand, a simple human gesture that meant more to me than anything else she could do. I turned with her toward Thorn's Gems. Together, hands clasped, we passed my champards and took the lead down to the ice-covered road.

"Are you scared?" she asked, voice pitched low.

"Out of my mind," I said, seeing hate in the eyes of the farrier who shod my horse.

"Me too. But God the Victorious will protect us."

Having never learned what reply was appropriate when confronted with a faith I was genetically unable to share, I remained silent as we moved through the throng of black-clad, self-appointed judges and left them behind. At the end of the line stood Jacey and her brood, Eli and his mother, and a dozen or so others, including Ken Schmidt. They fell into the void behind us, a human shield. I wondered if they thought of themselves in that way. When we reached the curve in Upper Street and left the old church behind, I leaned to Polly. "Is your thumb really cut?"

"I will confess the sin of lying at kirk this evening," she said serenely.

"Thank you, Polly." I didn't know why she had helped me. We weren't friends in any sense of the word, barely nodding acquaintances, but I wasn't questioning her help.

Once at the shop, we entered while Rupert and Audric stood outside beneath lowering clouds, guarding for possible attack. I gave her a charm, one that might calm a restive baby. For her help, I'd have given her a charm for wealth and long life if there were such a thing. Waving away my thanks, she kissed my cheek, took her baby from the elder, and moved outside, down the street, leaving me alone.

From the back of the shop, a man emerged. I appraised him in the instant I pulled my sword and plucked a throwing blade. Hands up, palms out in the universal gesture of peace, he hesitated. Both cheeks wore brands, the left cross old and pale, the right still healing, perhaps only a few weeks old. He was dressed for the cold in layered, shabby coats and mismatched boots. Alone in the shop, I drew back the throwing blade.

"I'm unarmed," he said quickly.

"Give me one reason why I shouldn't gut you for breaking and entering."

"I'm with the EIH," he said. "And we want you to join with us against the seraphs."

I had no idea at all what to say to that one, but I didn't release the throwing blade, flipping and tucking it away instead. Silent, my sword in a low defensive position, I stud-

ied him, watching his hands. He could have been anywhere
between thirty and forty, his face weathered brown,
creased deeply at the eyes and around his mouth. His
Cherokee heritage showed plainly in the beak of his nose
and black eyes, even without the braids lying on either
shoulder, framing his long face. "You have one minute," I
said.

"Do you want to know the real reason why seraphs put
your people in Enclaves? It wasn't that silly fairy tale you
recounted back there." That ticked me off, but I raised my
brows in a parody of polite manners. He lowered his palms
a fraction and said, "It was because neomages can't breed
fertile offspring on humans, but you can with seraphs."

"Forty seconds." Everyone knew that human and seraph
offspring, the second-unforeseen—half-breeds, *mules*—
were indeed sterile, often with incompletely developed
genitals, while the offspring of mages and seraphs, the
kylen, were capable of reproduction, able to breed with
humans or mages equally. He was saying nothing new.

His eyes shifted to the door as it opened, letting in a gust
of air. Speaking fast, he said, "It's because you're genetically closer to seraphs than to humans."

Audric and Rupert stepped into the shop. I could almost
feel them maneuvering to my left and right, out of the way
of my blades. "What's this scum doing here?" Rupert asked.

"Chatting. Leaving," the man said, hands still out, placat-
ing. "Name's Joseph Barefoot. You want to talk, leave a
white rag hanging at your back window. I'll be notified.
Think about what I said." He eased away, backed down the
small hallway, and disappeared from view. I heard him exit
the shop by the back door.

Not looking at my friends, I sheathed my sword. Battle
rage drained out in a rush. My legs and arms were heavy,
tired, and I hadn't even drawn blood. I rested a hand on a
display, head hanging down. "What now?" I asked.

"Now we lock up the shop and mount a watch in case
one of the more fervent zealots decides to break windows,
toss firebombs, or paint slogans on the walls. Jacey's sending Zeddy over to spend the night here, and her next two
largest will keep watch in the barn."

Humans. Putting themselves and their families at risk. For me. I wanted to be sick. "Fine." I managed a smile at the picture they made, tall and muscular, swords at their hips. Audric's cloak was the basic black leather worn by the second-unforeseen when they went to war, though no one at my trial had commented on it. Unless the reporter had noted the dobok and delved into his past, his secrets were still safe. Rupert's new blue velvet had a trendy swath of lace at the throat. "You made great champards," I said. "Very flashy. But—"

"If you think you're taking off to keep us safe, don't bother," Rupert said, untying the cape and brandishing his new sword in its scabbard. "All for one and one for all, dearie."

I had been about to say just that. Unexpected tears sprang into my eyes and I hiccupped, half sob, half laughter.

"Go lie down," Audric said. "You're dead on your feet. Oh—and the tense was incorrect." When I looked my question at him he said, "We *make* great champards."

A tear rolled down; I caught it on my wrist. As I turned back, I saw Eli Walker across the street. He was leaning against the wall outside Shamus Waldroup's bakery, one knee bent, foot flat against the building, rifle cradled in his arms. He tipped his hat when he caught my eye. Eli worked as a tracker, sometimes for the kirk, sometimes for the Administration of the ArchSeraph. Neither liked me much. I wondered who he was working for today.

Thadd walked by Eli, talking to Jacey, the cop animated, his body language angry, Jacey calm, her red clothes a beacon in the gray light. Eli's gaze followed them, speculative. I remembered that neither Thaddeus Bartholomew nor the assey Durbarge had been in the meeting house. I'd have smelled Thadd. Durbarge, as an Administration of the ArchSeraph Investigator, would have been forced to stand beside me on the dais, his eye patch drawing frightened looks. I was a legally licensed mage, accused in a court of law. Part of an assey's job description was protecting mages in the human population, and he hadn't been there. Because he had been kept away as part of the ploy by

Culpepper's brigade and the orthodox? Or because he was colluding with them?

Farther down the street, the reporter who had been at the trial was doing interviews, currently talking to a member of the orthodox, an elderly man with a full beard and a deer-hide hat that came down over his ears. She was getting an earful, and I imagined most of it was mage hate. The reporter had perfect tanned skin, chin-length blond hair that curled at the tips, and clothes that came out of designer shops in Atlanta. As if she felt me watching her, she looked up and met my eyes. Immediately, she ditched the man and raced toward the shop.

Not wanting to listen to her pitch, I turned and climbed the steps, my booted feet heavy and cold. Behind me, I heard the bells over the door jingle and Rupert intercept her. Romona's tone wasn't happy, and I caught the words, "the Trine," and "ice cap," and "Darkness." It wasn't good, if the press had put that much together, but I still didn't go back down.

At the top of the stairs I stopped. The EIH provocateur had entered the shop, and was watching my home and me. *It's because you're genetically closer to seraphs than to humans.* It was an obvious deduction, yet one I had never made. So far as I knew, no one had made it. And I had no idea what it might mean. Speculating, I went in.

My loft was one huge open area, once the hayloft of the two-hundred-plus-year-old former livery that housed Thorn's Gems. The walls were three feet thick, four in some places, made of old brick, some of which I had plastered and painted rich greens and blues. Complementary window hangings were teal and sea green tapestries, to match colors from my childhood and the stained-glass window at the back of the loft where hay bales once were inserted. Wood floors were covered with rugs except in the kitchen and bath areas, where I had laid teal tiles. The furniture was dun and tan and soft, soothing colors, clustered around the freestanding natural gas fireplaces. There were no closets, and the armoires still hung open, clothes hanging out. The place looked like it was owned by a slob.

I tossed my cloak over the coatrack near the door and untied my boots, leaving them piled near the door so the ice that had crusted on the soles could melt and drain. I put away the cuffs, earrings, and rings. Hanging up the mage-skirt, I thumped a bell for a last little jingle. The shirt was harder to get off than it had been to put on, but I finally got it unlaced and hung on a hanger. For some reason I didn't want to look at too closely, I didn't put them back out of sight, hooking the hangers over an armoire door instead. The clothes looked exotic and foreign in the human apartment. Cold, I pulled on leggings, slippers, and a fuzzy turtlenecked sweater, and turned up the fire to warm the apartment, my necklace around my neck.

In a sudden need to restore order to my life, I made the bed with ruby red silk sheets, fluffed the teal comforter smooth, and arranged lavender, ruby, and turquoise pillows. The emerald bed skirt and an inch of ruby sheets were contrasting jewel tones. When the bed was made, I dusted, swept, vacuumed, and cleaned the bath, working up a sweat. As I worked, lazily turning fans overhead pushed heated air back to the floor from the rafters.

I checked my blades to see if they needed attention. Constant wet was a prelude to rust, but I had been careful to keep them oiled and so far I'd been lucky. In mountainous areas, sword blades needed oil once every three months, and I was weeks away from that timeline, but two blades looked dull, so I wiped away the old oil with a soft rag and sprinkled the blades with talcum powder to remove the excess oil. Lastly, I wiped each clean and applied a coating of light oil before laying them aside.

I was standing in the kitchen staring into the refrigerator at my sparse lunch offerings when I heard footsteps and smelled the food. Though it had been months, I recognized both the stride and the menu. Roast duck for him. Roast vegetables for me: potatoes, zucchini, and mushrooms sliced and marinated in herbed oil. Fresh onion bread, still hot out of Shamus Waldroup's oven. A salad with more of the herbed dressing would be in a sealed container to complete the meal. I couldn't smell it—but he wouldn't have forgotten the salad.

They were my favorite foods, and had once been part of a well-planned seduction that ended with my being stretched out on my mattress, losing my virginity with eager abandon and getting engaged to the man of my dreams. Who then cheated on me and broke my heart. Right. Remember that, I told myself, even as I closed the fridge door and went to greet him.

"Peace offering," he said when I opened the door, craning his head around a bag of food. I just looked at him, so he added, "I have wine and beer."

"I have food," I lied. "And wine and beer," I said, more truthfully.

"I have a foot rub." His blue eyes gleamed with mischief. I felt my toes curl up.

He shifted the bag. "And a shoulder rub, if you want. I remember how your shoulders ache when you drill stones all day." When I still said nothing, his brows went up and his voice dropped into a low register that sounded like pure sex. "And three kinds of hot peppers and cheesecake and red grapes and divinity candy imported from Louisiana."

My belly did a funny little dip and curl, leaving me breathless. I couldn't help it. I said, "You are an evil, wicked man, here to tempt me with fat, protein, and alcohol."

"Don't forget the hot peppers, fresh fruit, and candy," he said. Something in his voice reminded me of a vision I'd had of him not long ago, emaciated, in a dungeon, his neck scarred by fangs. I crossed my arms over my chest but my foot pushed the door wide. It was an ambiguous invitation at best, but he didn't wait for better. Lucas Stanhope walked back into my loft and my life with an unrepentant grin and the scent of really great food.

He went straight to the kitchen, where he began to unload the bags of edible treasures and set the table. I hadn't rearranged the dishes after he'd moved out. His hands went straight to the plates, the wineglasses, the salad bowls. Taking the bottle of wine and a six-pack of Dancing Bear Brew, he walked through the apartment as if he belonged there, and out onto the back deck, where I watched him brushing snow off my beer cache. He deposited the new six-pack and the wine in the snow, bringing four cold bottles back inside. He twisted one open and held it out as he passed. I had no intention of taking it but my arms unfolded and my hand reached out on its own. My fingers wrapped around the bottle. As he passed by, I found I was watching his butt. Drat. This was not good. A woman in town claimed they were married. Jane Hilton, a breathtakingly beautiful blond with vivid eyes and a sculpted face. Lucas was married. *Married.* Maybe.

I needed to tell him to leave. Now. Instead, I said, "Thanks," and took a swig.

I told myself it was the smell of roast veggies and the way the little potatoes glistened in oil and the sight of the salad greens all crisp and curled that shut me up. But it was the dried cranberries that did it. That and the almonds. They were a sure sign that this wasn't a spontaneous gesture on Lucas' part.

The other food could be obtained in Mineral City from greenhouse farmers or a trader who made regular runs on the mule train. But not almonds and dried cranberries; they had to be imported all the way from Atlanta. At fabulous expense. I was the only person I knew who craved slivered almonds and cranberries. None of the locals even knew what they were.

My mouth watered when Lucas set a small china plate mounded with pieces of fluffy white divinity candy studded with pecans in the center of the table. He dribbled raspberry sauce over the cheesecake. The china was the set we had used when married, the pattern an ancient Pre-Ap one, the plates and dishes from Audric's claim at Sugar Grove. They had been one of many engagement gifts from my fiancé.

Lucas lit candles and set out cloth napkins I hadn't used since he left. He looked up at me. His blue eyes were the exact shade of the Gulf of Mexico at sunset, the far-off water touching the darkening horizon. He was wearing a black button-down corduroy shirt over a cotton T, black jeans, and pointed-toe boots made of tooled leather. I had given him the boots.

"Get out," I said. Only it came out as, "I don't have any coffee." To go with the cheesecake. He smiled that smile that had blown me away when I first met him and pulled out my chair. The chair I'd sat in when we were married. I didn't tell him I'd taken to using his chair when he left. I just walked over and sat. And I bowed my head when he prayed a blessing. He'd never prayed a blessing when we were married. Never.

He raised his head. As if reading my surprise, he leaned over and kissed my cheek before placing my napkin over my lap. "Eat."

The bastard. If he'd tried to kiss my mouth I'd have cold-cocked him. Instead, I met his eyes. And was lost. I picked up my fork and took a bite of salad.

Chapter 9

While we ate, we talked of innocuous subjects like the weather, the kirk and the political situation in Mineral City, food, beer, and the ice cap that had mysteriously disappeared from the top of the Trine, followed by a six-foot snowfall to the east. I had caused the snowmelt, but almost no one knew that and I wasn't telling. Mysterious woman of secrets, that was me. Over dessert—which was coffee Lucas brought, tea for me, divinity, and cheesecake—we talked about the latest seraph updates. The presence of an SNN news crew in town. Ciana. Nothing more personal. Until he said, "I almost died down there."

I put down the teacup with a rattle. His lips were tight, the expression bleak, ashamed. In my vision I'd seen the underground cell where he'd been kept in the pit on the Trine. Seen the strange, radiant food they had fed him. I'd seen what a Darkness did to him while Lucas was drugged—a daywalker with his fangs in Lucas' throat, sucking his blood, stroking Lucas possessively. A daywalker whose eyes changed from a lucid blue-green by day to a glowing red by night, a walker who called himself Malashe-el, who gave me his true name and therefore gave me power over him. A daywalker who attacked me, tried to kill me, and apologized for it. Strange and stranger. I still didn't know what it all meant.

"I stayed alive for three things," Lucas said, drawing me back to the present. He took my fingertips, holding them lightly. "One was Ciana. She needs me. Marla isn't evil, but she can't give a child what she needs to feel secure and loved." I nodded, watching our hands, my tongue thick in my mouth. "Two was to tell someone what they're doing down there."

I sat up, mage-sight opening. The room brightened as the energies became visible and I could see Lucas' life force, his aura. It was a wondrous, shimmering blue-and-gold halo that followed the contours of his head and shoulders, and spilled across the table as if reaching for me. In two places a shadow swirled, small spots near his jaw.

He smiled wryly. "It's your lucky day, Thorn St. Croix Stanhope." Before I could correct him on the name, he said, "You're the one I'm supposed to tell." Fear flushed through me. With my free hand, I clutched for the walking stick hilt, but I'd left the sword by the door. "The Darkness' name is Forcas. It was once a Minor Darkness, but when its boss was captured with a chain and Mole Man's bloody sacrifice, it got promoted. Now, it's conjuring with Stanhope blood. Mole Man's blood. My blood."

I put it together with the history of Mineral City. Mole Man was the Cherokee name given to local war hero Benaiah Stanhope, Lucas and Rupert's several-greats grandfather, after a not-so-small mopping-up operation at the end of the Last War. He went with a group of winged-warriors into the hills, underground, tracking a Major Power, its human helpers, and half-human offspring. The battle lasted three days, during which the mountain, now called the Trine, cracked open. Light and Darkness spilled out over the land in battle dire—the spiritual warfare between Light and Dark. The townspeople prayed. Benaiah gave his life to save a high-ranking seraph, using his blood sacrifice to coat the chains that bound the Major Darkness. The seraphs came back out. Benaiah died underground; his body was never recovered. Hence the name Mole Man.

"I think it's making a chain—an antichain, maybe," Lucas clarified, "to free the Dragon that the seraphs captured and bound using Mole Man's blood."

An antichain. Like an antidote. Now that would suck

Habbiel's pearly, scabrous toes. When I found my voice, I asked, "Why are you telling *me* this?"

Lucas stroked my hand. "You're a licensed mage. Your visa links you to a Realm of Light. You can call on seraphs. And this town is about to need some. Pretty badly."

I almost told him I didn't know how to use it, but I kept my mouth shut. There was a lot I didn't know about the visa and GPS band, just as there was a lot I didn't know about being a mage. I'd left Enclave in my fourteenth year, when my mage-gift came upon me all at once. At puberty mages were supposed to find their gifts, their source and method of using the energies of creation. They weren't supposed to have their minds ripped open and the thoughts, hopes, and emotions of all twelve hundred mages in Enclave dumped in. Mages weren't supposed to go insane. I was different and that difference nearly killed me.

It resulted in my being drugged, carted out of Enclave, and shipped here. I was only half trained. I had no idea how to use the visa I'd been granted. And I had never shared my story with him. I almost told him all this. Almost.

Before I could speak, he stood and began clearing off the table. I sat and wrestled with his words and what he might want from me. Sipping my tea and watching him move. Lucas wasn't liquid grace. He wasn't sex in motion like Eli Walker on a dance floor. He didn't smell like a brothel/candy store like Thadd, or set my body to quivering, throbbing, mating heat. But when he moved, my eyes were inexorably drawn to his butt, flexing in tight jeans. Lucas had a wonderful butt. I remembered the feel of it flexing under my palms—

"You didn't ask my final reason for staying alive," he said.

My eyes whipped to his and my face flamed. *Seraph stones.* I looked around. The table was clear, dishes washed and put away. A lot of time had passed while I remembered all the good things—the very, very good things—about being married to Lucas Stanhope. "What?" I asked. Not in answer to his question, but to find my place in the entire conversation. "What did you say?"

"The third reason I came back was to say I'm sorry. I'm sorry, Thorn. I hate that I hurt you. I hate that I cheated on you. Marrying you was the best, smartest thing I ever did. Breaking up was the worst and dumbest." Lucas held up his hand. He was wearing the wedding ring I'd made for him, beaten gold and a series of ruby chips, similar to mine. How had I missed seeing it on his hand? I stared at it, appalled.

Though Rupert had shown me how to work the gold and answered questions while I fashioned it from a nugget found in a creek three mountains over, I'd made the wedding ring totally without help, for the man I thought I'd spend my life with. My best friend had watched as I heated and hammered and shaped, watched as I set the stones, not once telling me the marriage was a mistake, though his disapproval had been clear even then. Rupert had known his brother was a cheat.

"I love you," Lucas said. "I want you back." When I didn't answer, he walked to the door, carrying the now-empty food bag, the top folded over and rolled down.

I followed him, feeling as if I was saying something with the action, but not knowing what and not knowing how to stop saying it.

"I intend to court you," he said, his voice a low burr. He looked over his shoulder at me. "I intend to win you back. Marry you again." His eyes were resolute, unwavering, fixed on me like blue lasers. My belly did a little somersault, thinking he might kiss me. Might. My heart thudded.

"You're married," I whispered, remembering the utterly beautiful face in the moment I discovered he had remarried. I hated him for that, for marrying a beautiful woman. "You married Jane Hilton. She said so on live television."

"She lied. I never married Jane. And in my heart, I never left you. Never," he said, one hand holding the door open. When I didn't reply, he released the door, turned away, and walked down the steps. Cold air blew in from the stairway.

I wasn't sure what he had thought I might say, and I had a feeling he was disappointed by my reaction, but I didn't know what to do about it. I followed him down, shutting the loft door behind me, hearing our feet echo on the steps.

At the shop entrance, Lucas waited as I found the key and opened the door. Night had fallen while we talked. It was after six and the town was shut up, the citizens safely inside their homes. Only fools and evil walked alone in the dark. The sleet was long gone and the temperatures had dropped, the cold so intense it was blistering. Overhead, the clouds were breaking up. A black velvet sky peered down at the town, the moon bright, throwing shadows on white snow. Lucas stepped outside.

I lifted a hand to tell him to wait. I would get my sword. I would walk him safely home. Instead, he mistook the gesture for something else and pulled me to him, arm hard around my waist. His mouth came down on mine.

Warmth and need rose so fast they shocked me. His lips were demanding, beguiling, and punishing all at once. I heard a moan and knew it was me. One arm slid low on my hips to support me. The other hand slid around my neck to cradle my head. My mouth opened. His kiss deepened, hardened. Distantly, I heard the bag drop. My arms went around him.

He smelled of soap and beer and roast duck. He tasted of something else entirely. Something new and unpolluted, an unknown seasoning that flooded my mouth, faintly reminiscent of anise and nutmeg, sweet as honey. I knew it hadn't been part of our meal. Want rose in me like a primeval spring, splashing joyously, to puddle low in my belly. My fingers slid through his dark hair, against his scalp.

His palm was hot against my face. His tongue touched mine. I reeled deeper into the kiss, nearer to the taste of him. That strange taste. I could hear myself moaning, knees weak, the world spinning around me. My head lolling back, I remembered to breathe, and he kissed my throat, his lips hot on my flesh. Where he touched, cold followed, the air chilling. Lucas pulled me tighter, backing me against the doorjamb to keep me from falling. I clung to him as his mouth sucked the soft skin above my collarbone.

I ran my tongue over my bruised lips, tasting him. It was like the *otherness*, some part of me noted. The sensation I wasn't able to name when I blended two mage-senses into a single scan. An *otherness* I had been afraid to practice, afraid to use because it left me dizzy and befuddled. Now Lucas produced the same effect in me.

Lightheaded, faint, I pushed at his shoulders. Lucas pulled back, his blue eyes black in the dim light of the moon. "Whas at—" I stopped and licked my lips; they felt tender, swollen. "What's that taste?" I managed, only a little slurred. "On your mouth? Like anise?"

Lucas stepped away fast, horror on his face. I caught myself on the doorjamb with both hands. "You can taste it?" he whispered. When I nodded, he said, "I think . . . it's manna. I think it's manna." With that he turned and walked away, his boots crunching on the hard-frozen snow. He didn't look back.

Searing-cold mind-clearing air brushed me. Feeling abandoned, I eased inside and closed the door. *Manna?* I touched my mouth, which tingled slightly. Lucas had kissed me. I'd wanted him to. And he'd eaten the food of angels.

When the sense of inebriation passed, I found myself sitting in the dark on the stairs to my loft, chilled to the bone, shivering, Lucas' bag in my frozen fingers. I didn't know what to think, not about Lucas, his declarations of love, or his intent to marry me. Marry me? Once bitten, twice shy. An old aphorism that didn't take a kiss like Lucas' into consideration. What was I going to do? I traced the contours of my mouth. It was sensitive from his lips.

I remembered the name he'd spoken, the name of the Darkness trying to do an unspeakable evil. It wasn't the beast's true name, but it was a beginning, and research might provide me more. I pulled my fingers from my mouth and my mind from the kiss. *What a kiss.* I shivered in the cold. *Forcas. Yeah.* "I can't do anything about you, Lucas Stanhope. But I can do something about that," I said, my voice a whispered echo in the stairwell.

Well, maybe. Maybe not. But I stood and went to the computer to look up the evil called Forcas. For once, the computer in the little nook under the stairs worked at the same time as the Internet, though I had to leave my amulets hanging on the knob outside. Mage energies disagreed with sensitive electronics.

Online, I discovered that Forcas was not a nice little beastie. The occult lore didn't indicate what rank Forcas once held in the angelic hierarchy, or to what order he belonged, but he was generally considered one of the minor seraphs before the fall. Since, however, he had become something far more powerful. When he lived on earth, he had been a teacher of rhetoric, logic, and mathematics. His gifts included being able to render people invisible and restoring lost property.

And according to Lucas, who had been a prisoner in the pit on the Trine, Forcas was the resident Darkness, a talented Fallen, and he had grown in power. He was practicing the Dark arts with Stanhope blood.

I closed down the computer. I was chilled through, and not just because it was cold outside. Because Stanhope blood wasn't the only thing the master of the Trine was working with. If my guess was right, Forcas also had a few ounces of my blood, taken when I went underground to keep Ciana safe. I shuddered at the memory of the pit, the smell of sulfur and brimstone harsh in my mind. Never again, I promised myself. Never.

Before heading back upstairs, I walked into the stockroom and placed my palm on one of the metal boxes that contained the amethyst, the lavender stone I had thought was dead, yet which had generated the cobra. The first time I ever touched one of the metal boxes, I had been met with a frisson of heat, a whisper of power, and the touch of mage-perception. I had known that there was stone inside, stone imbued with power. That first time, sweat broke out on my arms and tingled down my spine. Not now. Straining, I lifted the metal box to the floor.

I touched the second box, which also contained stone. And behind it was another box, similar to the first two. I studied the boxes in the dim hallway light. They were an ugly green, painted with pale white pigments, words hidden under the crisscrossed security strips. A number six was clearly visible on one, the number two in a different place on another. They were Pre-Ap, US military ammunition boxes.

I sent a mind-skim into the box under my fingertips. The first time I had done this, the stone inside had swirled around me in an eddy, testing, toying. *Something* had touched my mind, recoiled a bare instant before it wrapped around me, seized me, and pulled me in. Something with unheard-of might. *Such power.* It beat into me, demanding.

Now there was nothing, not a whisper of power. I opened the box, its hinges twanging softly, and unexpected gloom settled across my shoulders at the sight of the once wondrous amethyst. Now it was pale, almost clear, like good-quality quartz, spotted with slightly darker inclusions in half curves and spots like eyelids and pupils. After the cobra, I had hoped it might be restored.

I lifted a fist-sized specimen and sent a tendril of thought into it. There was nothing there, no tremor of energy. I replaced the amethyst and closed the lid, feeling the chill of the unheated room through the soles of my feet. Fighting dejection, I turned off the light, went back upstairs, and found my bed. I was asleep almost instantly.

The lynx sat on my back porch railing, purring, body erect, stubby tail curled around its back feet. I placed my hand on the ice-rimmed window and leaned closer to the huge black cat. It was between sixty and eighty pounds, its waterproof outer coat of hair harsh and glossy over an inner coat that fluffed for warmth. Moonlight brightened white facial hair and its pale-haired belly, and white tufts sprouted from erect ears. It was prim and proper, until it opened its mouth and growled at me. Two-inch fangs caught the moonlight. My breath fogged the glass—and I woke, the echo of the growl reverberating in the apartment around me.

I came awake fast. The loft was cold, silent, and very dark.

I had left the fireplaces on medium to combat the winter chill, and their flames should have cast wavering light on the walls. They didn't. The fans should have stirred the air with warming currents. They didn't. The air should have smelled of fish and potatoes and beer and candles. It didn't. I caught a whiff of fresh roses and moldering leaves. Beneath it was the dank stench of standing water, mold, and mildew.

I opened my mage-sight and scanned the room; the furnishings, walls, ceiling and floor were lit with soft blue, green, and pinkish tints. There was no hint of Darkness, but the scent continued to grow, as if it—they—sat on the foot of my bed. *There were two of them.*

I slid my hand across the sheets to my amulets but encountered only cotton. They weren't there. I remembered taking them off at the computer nook. *Stupid. Stupid. Stupid.* Head full of kisses and beer, I hadn't put them under the pillow before sleep. I didn't remember where they were, and broke into a sweat of fear. My hand met a solid object. The kris—no, not the kris, I remembered as I forced myself more fully awake. It was gone, broken off in the belly of a Minor Darkness. What I touched was the hilt of a throwing blade.

I slid my hand around it. The knife was beautifully balanced, but wasn't shaped right for close fighting. It needed a longer blade with a honed edge, not just a sharp point. The hilt was bone, tapered and smooth, to slide from a hand without a hitch, which was great for a throw; not great for cutting. No help against a being of spirit. But it was what I had.

I slid from the sheets, a soundless action, and placed my feet on the icy floor. As I stood, the flames came on with a quick puff of natural gas. A click and hum overhead indicated the fans were back on. The other scents faded as if they had never been. I looked around, the blade catching the light.

Had the smells been real or a dream? Had the heat gone off? Had there been an interruption in both electricity and the supply of gas, leaving only enough to keep the pilot lights lit? Then when power and gas were restored they both came on at once? Was such a thing possible? Were the two forms of power linked somehow? Or was I going nuts? I looked at the black-pig clock in the kitchen. It was three a.m. I was wide-awake.

Unsettled, I crawled back into the warm bed. Unable to sleep, I stared at the ceiling, waiting on something. Anything. Time passed. The loft warmed. What seemed like hours later, I heard an almost silent click, a distant sound, muffled and muted. A quick glance told me it was now four, and I slid from the bed again. I gathered the practice swords Audric had given me, thin and pliable bamboo staves. Careful to keep from stirring the air currents, I crept to the door and crouched beneath the bar that separated the kitchen from the entry.

Stealthy as the lynx that invaded my dreams, Audric opened my door and entered my apartment. Until now, I hadn't figured out how he got in, but my eyes were adapted to the dark and my position was perfect. I saw him pocket a key as he stepped over the threshold.

Without warning, I attacked. I got in three deadly strikes, stabs in each kidney and one cut across his spine at shoulder level before the half-breed managed to master his surprise, turn, and raise his weapons. "Dead," I said softly, feeling triumphant. I should have known better than to gloat.

Audric countered and slapped me four times with his staves, any one of which would have killed me. Even prepared, I didn't get a single block in. After that it was downhill all the way. I lost count of the ways I died. Audric killed me with the walking horse, the dolphin, and three versions of the crab, an ugly move that I should have been able to block with my eyes closed, half asleep. He killed me with the scissors, the lion rampant, the lion sitting, and the lion resting. He killed me with a half-dozen moves whose formal names I didn't know and had never seen. I had bruises on top of bruises.

When my Thursday-morning lesson in humility was over and Audric let me rest, I fell across the couch, gasping and groaning. My teacher turned on a lamp and studied me. He wasn't even breathing hard, standing over me in his white dobok, arms crossed, staves beneath one arm. The light gleamed across his freshly shaven skull. "I smelled the evil when I entered," he said. "But not as strong as before."

"Let me guess," I gasped. "It distracted you and that was

why I killed you three times before you responded." When he inclined his head, I whispered, *"Bloody seraphs."* And then, boneless across the couch, desperately needing to rest, I told him about the lynx whose cry waked me some mornings, the dreams of Raziel, and the incubus who had tried, but been unable to gain a foothold this morning. Audric listened as if he had been solely my champard, and not the bound servant of the seraph, the winged-warrior Raziel himself.

Chapter 10

I laid my amulets aside, wearing only a healing conjure to lessen my practice session aches, and ate breakfast—oatmeal, because two teeth were loose from the fighting. A knock sounded on my door and, distracted by the sting of yogurt on a busted lip, I answered it in my bathrobe, the ruby velvet soft against the abrasions on my shoulders. Any knock while the shop was closed had to mean Rupert or Audric. Both had seen me in much less.

As I unlatched the door, the smell hit me and my entire body clenched. *Kylen.*

Caramel, brown sugar, and vanilla with a gingerlike hint of heat. My body reacted instantly. I threw the door wide, mage-sight flashing on before it banged open. Thaddeus Bartholomew was a huge form composed of reddish-gold with hints of green light. I reached for him, heat rising in me like lava from the earth's crust, like a megatsunami. My lips found his mouth. He tasted like a bakery. He smelled wonderful.

Distantly, I heard a voice say, "Get her amulets. Quick."

I could hear panting. Need thrummed through me. His hands pushed aside my robe. I tore at his clothes, found his throat with my teeth, and bit down. Hard. His arms came around me, lifting my bare bottom with heated palms. His seraph ring flared, scorching my buttock. My legs wrapped around him, pulling him closer.

Something slipped over my head. The world tilted.

Agony and blistering cold twisted through me. I gasped
and drew back, hissing with pain. My spine arched back
and wrenched forward in an electric spasm. Mage-sight
snapped off, leaving a whiteout of frozen emptiness. Heat
paled and cooled so fast it crackled through me like breaking ice. Like a glacier calving and falling. I dropped to the
hallway floor, fingernails carving into the old wood.

"*Blood of Michael,* what was that?" someone asked.

I threw back my head, tossing my hair, which had come
undone. I smelled kylen. I *wanted*. But some minute, newly
rational part of my brain catalogued the symptoms and
knew what had happened. I pulled that stable fragment of
myself around me even as I tugged the torn lapels of my
robe over my naked flesh. I was panting, and I could smell
my heat, a raw, wild smell of roses and almonds and a hint
of blood. From my place on the floor, I looked up.

Rupert and Audric were restraining Thadd, who was
growling like an untamed animal, his face twisted in need
and fury. He battled the two big men as Rupert found
Thadd's police sigil with one hand and opened it. The sigils carried by the state police had built-in conjures, including an antimage conjure. Rupert pressed it against
the cop's bare chest. Thadd screamed.

That cool, composed part of me registered that he was
emitting kylen pheromones at an unprecedented rate. His
genetic makeup had been hidden from him his whole life,
arrested at conception by a powerful seraph conjure held
in a turquoise ring, its band shaped like angel wings. My
buttock stung where the ring had been pressed against
my bare skin as it battled against mage-heat. The ring and
his heritage had been a forbidden secret kept by his
mother.

Until I made him take off the ring. The transformation
that should have taken place in the womb had been held
at bay by unknown incantations and unimaginable power.
When the ring came off, it had begun in the body of an
adult. His bones, organs, and cells had begun trying to
transform him into a kylen from the genes up, in a single
instant. With the ring back in place, the process was interrupted, but he was still kylen, still part seraph. Still

smelled of caramel and ginger and hot, fierce, furious sex. *I wanted him.*

As the police sigil pressed into his bare chest, his scent faded. Intelligence returned to his eyes and they met mine. In their depths, I saw his anguish. The transformation and the constant low-level mage-heat were making him crazy. Only the partial protection of the ring and the sigil were keeping him sane. That and the fact that I wore my amulets almost constantly, which gave us both protection from my effect on him.

I gathered my robe closer. One-handed, I levered myself up from the floor. Reaching my feet, I caught the wall unsteadily and looked at our rescuers. Rupert and Audric were flushed and sweating. Blood streaked their faces and hands. I smelled it: human, half-breed, mage, and kylen. I'd torn at Thadd's throat with my teeth, wanting the taste of his blood, and reopened the tear in my lip. I'd ripped at Rupert and Audric as they tried to separate us. The image of two rutting wolves hit me and I laughed. A shaky sound, but lucid. My friends were staring at me, guarded and cautious.

"I'm okay," I said, almost like myself.

"That would sound more convincing if your mouth weren't bloody," Rupert said wryly.

I licked my lips, tasting kylen and mage. Heat threatened to rise again, but the amulets sent a burst of something into me, like a shot of a powerful drug. I hadn't drawn on them, even instinctively, but I recognized the pulse of power from the pink tourmaline ring. Clearly part of its purpose was to help control mage-heat.

Leaving the door wide, I walked into my loft, touching the amulet in the doorknob to damp my neomage attributes. Behind me, I could hear the three males entering as I grabbed clothes from the armoire storing casual wear and pulled a screen around the bath area to shield it from the rest of the apartment. With icy water and a coarse rag, I scrubbed the smell of kylen from me, abrading my flesh to help with the last vestiges of heat. I stuffed the robe into a bag of salt for cleaning later. When I could find a new laundress and someone to stitch up the ragged tear.

Naked, I looked at myself. Beneath the amulet necklace, my body was mottled with fresh bruises from this morning's training, and on top of the bruises were the imprints of Thadd's hands. I inspected the visa, feeling the power of the four-inch stone doughnut and thinking. A mage in the human world would sometimes encounter a seraph or kylen. They would need something to keep heat at bay. The visa had a lot of powers I needed to know about. It would all be funny if I thought the amulets could control mage-heat for any length of time. They couldn't. I could feel it starting to rise and clamped down on it hard. I dressed in layers for warmth and separation from the kylen. From the look of my robe and his shirt, it might not be enough.

When I emerged, they were drinking coffee made from the bag Lucas had left last night. Water for my tea simmered on the gas stove. Warily, Rupert and Audric watched me. "I'm okay," I said, risking a look at Thadd even as an embarrassed flush rose in my cheeks. Tooth marks ringed his throat. Great. "How about you?"

He took a slow breath. "I'm okay. I guess. That was ..."

"Mage-heat."

"Yeah. Explains why I've been feeling—" He stopped again and flushed.

"Right," I said. "So why are you here?" I didn't mean it to sound so abrupt, but didn't apologize or take it back, either.

"Two things. You made SNN's breaking news last night, and it's still on this morning." When I grimaced, he said, "And you're under surveillance by the AAS."

"Why?" Audric asked, responding to the surveillance part.

"Because she's the only sanctioned mage living among humans who doesn't have a specific job to do."

My mind gave a drawn-out, unconscious, *Ohhh, of course,* at his words. When no one responded, he continued. "All other mages are diplomats, working to stimulate and facilitate trade between our respective governments. Thorn—" He paused and started over. "You—"

"Are loose and running around, having fun. A bad precedent for the immoral to be allowed among the *holy*

humans," I finished sarcastically. As I spoke, I found the remote and clicked the television on. I didn't even have to
wait. On the bottom left of the screen was footage of me
holding a sword to the elder's throat. I winced and turned
it back off.

"And your Lolo keeps calling me." He fished out his
satellite phone and looked at it. "I've tried blocking her.
I've had headquarters try to block her. She keeps getting
through. She's driving me nuts."

"What does the priestess of the New Orleans Enclave
desire of you?" Audric asked in that disconcertingly formal
way half-breeds sometimes employed in the presence of
kylen, seraphs, and mages.

Thadd shrugged, that odd, seraph-like gesture he used, a
lifting of shoulder blades, and shifted his gaze to the wall
behind me. "She implies that she wants us to mate."

"She would not. Such matings are forbidden," Audric
said before I could reply.

"Like hiding my birth was forbidden?" Thadd asked,
looking at me. "Somehow, your Lolo knows what I am, and
she wants something. I don't think it's a plan she just came
up with. I think it's been in the works for a long time. Like
since before I was born."

The same thought had occurred to me, and to avoid the
penetrating looks of the males, I went to the kettle, which
had started to sizzle, and busied myself with the ritual of
tea. I chose almond cookie tea, a comfort flavor, and measured a heaping tablespoon into the kettle to swirl in the
hot water. I found a mug I liked, one Audric had dead-
mined from his town. On it were the words BEST FRIENDS
ARE CHEAPER THAN SHRINKS. I liked the concept. As I
worked, I thought about Lolo.

Rumor claimed the priestess was old, maybe over a hundred years. If that was true, it would make Lolo one of the
Mage War survivors, alive when seraph and mage were
free to mate, when kylen had been born in high numbers.
Some mages wanted a return to the freedom of mating
when they wanted, and with whom. Some mages wanted
Enclaves abolished. Some hoped there was a way to coerce
the Most High into giving us souls so we might join the

elect and go to heaven when we die. Rumor said Lolo was among those, but rumor was often false.

Except: I had lived among humans freely. Free mages were thought to be a rumor too, but they weren't. Lolo had placed me in Mineral City, hidden me here, ten years ago. Was the old woman involved in some plan that required me to be in this town? Required the birth of Thadd, part seraph, part mage, to one of Mole Man's descendants? Required him to be here, at the base of the Trine, where the original sacrifice took place? And Audric, too? I had wondered all this before, but I couldn't see it—yet I had long ago learned to disbelieve in coincidences. I sat at the table and added crystallized honey to the tea, sipping slowly to keep from burning my split lip. I remembered Thadd's teeth against it. My flush deepened.

"Durbarge is taking a special interest in you, Thorn," Thadd said. "Be careful."

"Did he see you enter the shop?" Audric asked.

"Probably. But if we get back downstairs and I buy something, and if I report back to him on our conversation, I should be safe." When Audric lifted his brows in inquiry, Thadd said, "We talked about the weather; about the ice cap on the Trine melting. About the device that rose from the mountain peak. Thorn shrugged and said she thought it was all weird. I couldn't get anything from any of you, even in friendly conversation."

"I'm cagey that way," I agreed solemnly.

"Be careful. And keep those amulets on," he said, sounding rueful. "Please."

I smiled at him, seeing him for a moment in memory, a radiant reddish-gold aura sparkling with green light. Feeling his hands on my bare butt, kneading. I took a deep breath to steady myself. "I'll try to contact Lolo," I said. "Maybe she'll let something slip. Or maybe she'll answer a direct question. But before you go, I have a bit of information that might shed some light on all this." Or might not. I still wasn't a hundred percent certain that I had really seen what I thought I'd seen. It could all have been illusion created by the Darkness, and if so, would only cloudy the muddy waters even more.

Quickly I told them the vision I had seen beneath the Trine, of the seraph with clipped wings, the cherub, and Zadkiel. I finished with the caveat that it might not have been real, but even so Thadd looked at me like I was nuts. "Seraphs in a hellhole?" he said. "I don't think so."

Because I doubted what I had seen myself, I didn't get riled at his reaction—but it was a near thing. Rupert patted my shoulder, checked his watch, and stood. "Whatever," he said. "We can talk about angels and demons later. Let's get Thadd something from the shop. Something to convince his boss this visit was business."

As I followed them to the door, I took a small amulet from my necklace and handed it to Thadd, careful not to touch him. "Here. Put this over the tooth marks on your neck. It'll fade the bruises in about an hour. Keep your scarf on until then."

"You bit me?" he asked, hunger freshly alight in his eyes. His fingers found the raspberry red places on his neck. His mouth parted and he surged toward me.

"Down, boy," Rupert said, grabbing the cop and pulling him to the stairs.

"Yeah." I ducked my head under the amused expressions of my friends. "I bit you. Sorry." They closed the door in my face. I was alone in the loft, which smelled strongly of caramel, less strongly of ginger. Seraph and kylen pheromones changed with emotion, just as humans' and mages' did. When Thadd fought, he smelled of ginger. When he was aroused, the other scents were more powerful. Like now.

Forcing the rising heat back down again, I pushed the kitchen table away and got a bag of earth salt. Though used, it was potent enough to scry for Lolo. The old bat and I had a lot to talk about, not that I'd ever call her that to her face.

I poured water into my sterling silver conjuring bowl and lit a candle before sitting within the circle, at the open space in the salt ring. Spine erect, I crossed my legs yogifashion and closed my eyes, blew out a tension-filled breath and drew in a calming one. Again. And again. Serenity fluttered close, just out of reach, held at bay by mage-heat that still quivered through my nerves. I had a feeling I wasn't going to get any closer to calm today, and dropped the final handful of salt, closing the conjuring circle.

Power seized me. The fire of creation burned along my nerves and bones, pulling at me, tempting me, but as usual in the last few weeks, I batted away the temptation to take creation power for myself, to use as I willed, and stabilized the energies needed to scry for Lolo. Once, rejecting the temptation would have been difficult, nearly impossible, and many mages never gained any kind of restraint. I should have been worried about having such control, as it had been the gift of an outside force, but I wasn't. Never had been.

My heart beat slowly, my blood pumped, breath moved through my lungs, and all glamour fell away. Scars bright, my body pulsed with a pink coral radiance, and a lavender underglow, as if I sat on a pillow of lavender light. But there was no big purple cobra this time, so maybe I was getting lucky. Luck, fickle and random, was something else I didn't like to depend on. Only fools depended on the providence of good fortune.

My loft shone with power. Every window and doorway, and even the floor surfaces were charged with pale energy, glowing with subtle shades, their purposes working together to form the harmony that was my home.

Calm, relaxed, I called on Lolo. After several minutes, the water in the bottom of the bowl began to shimmer, brightening with an image. In it, a female form sat on a pile of pillows in a dark room. A flute played in the background. Drums beat a slow, steady rhythm. Candle flames bent in an unseen breeze. The priestess was in her chambers, attended by her musicians and acolytes. Finally, she had deigned to answer my call.

I repeated the incantation for scrying one last time as the vision came clear and tightened on the face of the seated woman. Lolo's black-on-black eyes looked out at me from the water, her lips turned up serenely. Her voice filled my head. *What you want, girl?* she asked, her Cajun accent present even in her mental voice.

"Four things," I said aloud. "I want to know how to call for seraphic help without calling mage in dire."

Yes, Lolo said. *I can teach you dis ting. It part of you visa.*

"I want to know what the visa can do and how to use it to its full potential."

Dat too, she said.

Good. Small steps. Now the bigger things, I thought. "I want to know if you were involved in the breeding of Thaddeus Bartholomew."

Lolo's eyes flickered once, and her tranquil smile faltered. I'd not have noticed had I not been watching her so closely. "Last, I want to know about the seraphs in the pit of Darkness."

Her hand lifted and the vision wavered as if I had lost focus for a moment. And then she was gone. The water went dim and I could see the silver bottom of the bowl.

I had lost her. Though I tried twice more to call the priestess of New Orleans Enclave, I failed. The water in the bowl remained only water, reflecting back the candle flame. I swore silently, thinking I should have put stones on the bottom for added power. When I knew my attempts would continue to be futile, I recharged the defensive amulets placed around the loft; not that they seemed able to keep the incubus out, but they were all I had. Marginally satisfied, I reached over and opened the circle, the energies flowing back into me.

As I cleaned up the salt, I thought about Lolo's face when I asked my last questions. Her shock. Her dismay. There had been no disbelief, no denial, only surprise that I had asked the questions. Only distress that I knew to ask. And something akin to alarm. Perhaps I hadn't failed after all.

At the end of the workday, I was feeling antsy. To banish the remnants of mage-heat, I dressed in work clothes and went out back to the old post-and-beam stable, one of several in a row. Zeddy, Jacey's teenage stepson, was there before me, mucking out the stalls by lantern light as the geldings—Audric's palomino Clydesdale and my huge black Friesian—and Rupert's mule munched feed and hay.

I grabbed a shovel and started on the far side of the barn, feeling the pull of muscles in my shoulders and back. The air inside was brisk but not miserably cold, heated by the bodies of the horses and the activities of two workers. Building up a sweat, Zeddy and I worked in silence, Jacey's stepson nearly a match in size for the workhorses. We had cleaned the stalls and most of the common area when the horses threw up their heads, inhaled and blew, snorting. Clyde stamped in agitation. The mule trumpeted a hee-haw of fear.

"Miss Thorn?" Zeddy said. "Something feels wrong."

The stink of brimstone and sulfur blew through the cracks in the barn. *Seraph stones.* I gripped the shovel and moved to the doors facing the back of Thorn's Gems. Holding the shovel like a bowstaff, a martial art weapon, I eased open the door to the night, the lamplight a wedge revealing snow trampled with three-toed footprints. "Spawn!" I shouted, as something crashed against the door and I jumped back. Mage-sight kindled instantly, turning the world shades of pink, indigo, purple, and pale yellow.

The big barn door slammed just as a three-fingered, clawed hand tried to thrust its way in. Without thinking, I rammed the blade of the shovel, severing the fingers. A howl sounded through the closed door.

"Spawn never come this far down the Trine," Zeddy said, his voice shaking.

I knew differently. Spawn went anywhere they wanted. I scanned the barn. I had no weapons but the shovels, a crow-bar, and a toolbox that housed a claw hammer, nails, and a couple of screwdrivers. I could throw a shield over the barn, but that would just send the spawn next door to eat my neighbors' horses. Or my neighbors. A thud landed on the roof, followed by several others. Something scrabbled again at the barn door. "How loud can you scream?" I asked. "If we make enough noise, Audric will hear us. He'll come." With battle-lust in his eyes and enough weapons to start a small war, I could have added, but didn't.

"Yellin' I can do," he said.

We let out bloodcurdling screams, and I drew on the visa, adding decibels to mine, until the horses reared and I had to stop or have the animals tear down the barn. Zeddy took his shovel to the post-and-beam walls, beating them, and when that proved unsatisfying, he dropped it and beat the walls with his bare hands. The horses pranced in alarm, terrified of the noise and our scent of fear, and of the reek of danger that gusted in through the chinks in the walls and beneath the door. If they started bucking, we were toast.

More spawn landed on the roof. I smelled smoke. *Seraph balls.* The spawn had brought fire. The hair on the back of my neck rose, even as defensive incantations and tactics presented themselves in the corners of my mind and were discarded. I hadn't recharged all my amulets. Most were half empty, yet even if they had been fully charged, they would not have been enough. Smoke wafted in through the chinks. I rammed the shovel at the wood walls, my voice shrill, fighting panic, trying to think.

If I turned my back on the town and shielded the barn from flame, I might live but my neighbors would die. If my shield missed even a corner of the barn, that part of the building would be vulnerable to fire. Smoke would penetrate the shield, suffocating us. Worse, the section of the barn enclosed by the conjure would be filled with hungry spawn.

I hadn't expected an attack. Spawn liked mule trains and the rare, lone, unwary traveler. They didn't attack cities. Spawn didn't plan an attack at all, as they were beasts of opportunity.

I started coughing. Homer snorted and pranced, ears back, eyes rolling. The mule, overlooked in my worry, hee-hawed and kicked in a circle.

Claws scraped the frozen ground and a body scrabbled under the door. I beheaded it with the shovel, ichor flying and burning holes in my shirt. It took three strikes to cut through the spine. Spawn were faster than humans and half-breeds, some said faster than mages, and they healed from almost anything except a beheading. It sounded as if there were dozens more. We were in trouble.

In the lantern light, I fingered my amulets. One that I would never utilize in warfare presented itself to me.

Coughing, I said, "Zeddy, get over here. Keep the horses calm." When the big teen slid between the workhorses, I said, "Cover their eyes if you have to, but stay put. I'll try to put out the fire." He dropped his shovel and clutched the animals' halters. I flicked my thumb over an amulet and opened a small shield over them. The horses, Zeddy, and the mule were protected from projectiles and attackers, but not from airflow. It was a pretty nifty defensive weapon and I had never figured out how the first neomages came up with it. Nifty, that is, unless smoke was about to smother you.

Outside the shield I primed two amulets, drawing on the cat amulet's stored power. I cracked open a door, aimed a charm to heat bathwater at Rupert's loft, and threw it, transferring power into it from the cat. A lot of power. It ripped through me with a searing electric charge.

The energies stored in the tossed amulet released when it landed on the stairs. Instantly the snow on the roof, porch, and steps melted, falling to the ground with a crash, like a wave on the beach, hopefully alerting Audric and Rupert while putting out the fire. I jerked back as talons reached for me, slammed the door, smoke billowing up beneath it.

Chapter 11

Outside, Audric shouted, "Thorn!" It was a battle cry. Relief whipped through me. Before I could reply, the barn door clattered. Three-fingered hands pried around it on three sides, claws gripping the wood. I slashed and hacked, severing fingers that flipped into the air, splattering black blood. Spawn shrieked in pain. With a squeal of tearing metal hinges and splintering wood, the spawn ripped the door off the barn. I almost swore as they raced inside. Long-legged, mole-bodied, and red-furred, patterned in indistinct stripes and spots, spawn had bat ears and big teeth shaped for tearing meat. And poisonous saliva and acidic blood.

I whirled the shovel. Slammed it into the face of the closest spawn, cut and slashed the next two. Audric bellowed again, this time from ground level. The battle cry was one I had never heard before. "Raziel! By blood and fire!"

My blood heating, I shouted back, "Jehovah sabaoth!"

The spawn entering the barn slowed at the words, and I knocked three to the ground before they found whatever wits they had. The shovel wasn't sharp enough to behead them, but I did serious damage to their throats. Battle-lust and mage-speed heated my blood, burning out fear.

It was full night, the ground an unfamiliar, muddy dark from the melted snow. Audric raced to the barn entrance, moving like an African-Asian prince, his katana and wakizashi flashing in the dim light of the upstairs windows.

Without losing the pace of his cutting and slashing, he
threw two long-bladed knives, impaling spawn at my feet.
I tossed the shovel and grabbed the hilts. Beheading the injured was the work of two swings, one left-handed, one
right. The tantos blades were pointed to allow for throwing, but double-edged for cutting, and wicked sharp, the
blade length more suitable for shortswords for my shorter,
more slender arms. I spun them once. I liked them. A lot.
They were perfect.

Blood splattered hotly across my back. Acidic spawn
blood, not Audric's. I felt the burn through my clothes.
"Need light?" I asked.

"Yes," he said shortly, breath fast but steady, his concen-
tration focused on sounds and currents of air that signaled
spawn movements.

Mages have better night vision than most half-breeds,
and a lot better than humans. I swung at three spawn, taking both arms off one and sending the others back. One-
handed, I tossed two illumination amulets onto the
ground, where they splattered into the water. Audric
swiveled so we stood back-to-back. "Horses and Zeddy are
shielded in the barn," I said.

Audric beheaded two spawn with a single swipe, his kill
totals rising now that he could see. "Snow?"

"Fire." I took one and damaged another.

"Smart. How many?" he asked, cutting the legs from beneath a beast.

I counted. "Seventeen dead or injured. Maybe six left on
the ground, four on the roof. Odd thing, though," I said,
darting close to a spawn, pricking it through the lungs, and
darting back. "They aren't eating their dead. And they're
better organized than most spawn."

"Make it four alive on the ground. Leader?"

"Could be. I haven't seen one. Three," I said, dispatching
another. Just then two spawn leaped out of the dark, from
overhead. One landed on Audric's back, knocking him to
his knees. It bit down. Audric bellowed and I switched my
grip, wedging the point under the spawn's nose and ripping
toward me, taking off the top of its head. It fell, and Audric
knocked the lower jaw and body loose, kicking it away. He

moved with a grunt of pain. He was hurt. Maybe hurt bad. I handed him a healing amulet, hoping it would be enough.

"Two o'clock," he said. "Red eyes."

To my right I saw an indistinct form at the back doorway of the linen shop, its shoulder pressing against the brick. Though I only caught a glimpse, I knew it was Malashe-el, the daywalker who had fed off Lucas. Enraged, for reasons I didn't examine, I shouted my battle cry again, lunged, and cut, taking two spawn heads at once. Malashe-el moved into the dark, beginning to fade from my thoughts. It carried a rune of forgetting, a dangerous and powerful tool. I struggled to keep it in my mind, following it with magesight.

The world suddenly quieted and, weapons held in defensive postures, I looked around. The spawn were all down. Audric moved among the bodies, beheading the ones still twitching. He moved with a limp. I tossed him a second healing amulet, and he caught it in the dark. We were both glowing; we had released control of our neomage attributes. He lifted a hand and touched his throat, activating his lightning-bolt amulet. His skin faded to human dullness and he picked up the illumination amulets, pocketing one and handing me the other. No townsfolk had come to help us, though we had made an awful racket. *Cowards,* I thought viciously.

When I looked back, Malashe-el stood an arm's length before me, holding an amulet. Audric and I had forgotten all about it. Its eyes blazed red, fangs ratcheted wide.

Lightning-fast, I slashed. The walker moved faster, stabbing toward my left side with the amulet. As it moved toward me, demon-fast, I saw the talisman. A talon. No. A spur. A dragonet spur. Under my guard, faster than I could block, the spur pierced my side. Pain exploded. I stumbled. My heart stuttered as if poison pumped through it rather than blood.

From behind, I heard Audric bellow and the sound of blades slashing, grunts and the impact of weapons on flesh. I doubled over, gagging. Malashe-el caught me, seized the tantos, and threw them. He hammered the amulet into me. The world tilted. Agony like a spear of hellfire burst through me, tearing. Dazed, falling, I reached for my prime amulet. I had a moment to wonder about Audric. Burning blood sprayed over me. Pain razored deep. My fingers scrabbled to find the four-inch stone, my prime ring.

Malashe-el lifted me and spun to race away. My face was pressed into its shirt. I smelled flowers and mold. My fingers encircled the ring. Brain fuzzy, having no incantation prepared, I summoned power gathered in the melded stones of the prime. Desperate, wordless, I called to it. I felt energies gather in the prime and in my torso, centering beneath my sternum. My vision was going dark. My hand was so heavy I could barely lift the ring. I pressed the prime amulet to its chest.

The daywalker stumbled and fell to one knee. I heard the swing of a sword, and the thunk of bone as a blade impacted the walker's calf. He dropped me, and as we separated, my heart thundered in my ears. The fall to the ground took two heartbeats, heartbeats coiled with pain from the stab wound. I hit and rolled, the breath knocked from me. My prime blazed.

I lay staring at the black sky, trying to remember how to breathe. My skin flared with pain as melted snow drenched through my clothes. Snowmelt stung like liquid fire, draining my energies pulling power from the primes to protect me. Water saturated the acidic spawn blood absorbed in my clothes, washing it against my flesh. If I'd been able, I would have screamed.

The torment flared, doubling, as I took a breath. The prime amulet in my hand was hot to the touch, flooding my body with stone power. I released it. One-handed, I felt my side. And found nothing, no torn flesh, no spur amulet, though my hand came away bloody.

I heard feet racing near me, one set, uneven. Two blades hit the ground near my outstretched legs. The tantos, by the sound of them. They'd need serious attention from the ill usage of this night.

Two breaths later, I rolled to my knees and followed the footsteps, plucking the weapons Audric had tossed out of the ground. Audric was chasing the walker in the general direction of my spring. I almost laughed.

I drew on the amulets, all of them, to stabilize my heart-beat and breathing, and to fight the poison of the psychic injury. I veered around Audric and the wounded walker. Shaken, slowed, I was still fast. The walker's blood sprayed in arterial spurts across the wet ground, brighter in the snow as they headed uphill. Audric grunted with each breath, limping.

I herded them both toward the ring of stones and my spring. It was protected with a conjure to keep it hidden from the attention of any nonhuman, and to capture any supernat that touched its ringing stones. Circling around, I came hard from the south.

Just as Malashe-el limped past the spring, I threw one of the tantos. It thumped into the walker, the blade penetrating under its right arm. It fell, one hand out to catch itself, and touched a rounded boulder that ringed the spring.

The first part of the double-whammy conjure snapped into place with a sizzle of sound, the trap-shield rising and covering the spring and the boulders that contained the power for the conjure. This part was little more than an inverted shield, meant to keep prey in, not predators out. As Malashe-el fell and rolled, the spring erupted with part two of the incantation, drenching the walker with water, the conjure draining much of its Dark power. Malashe-el screamed, the keen long and furious, then pained, as if it were two instead of one.

Audric skidded to a halt, staring at the spring. It was the most complicated conjure I had ever attempted. I was apt to use raw power to bully my way through most problems. This was a thing of beauty. As an unanticipated side effect of trapping it, the pain in my side lessened. I bent over and rested my hands on my knees. Breathing was suddenly easier.

Gasping, Audric sat on the frozen ground, landing hard, his longsword across his thighs, the shortsword on the ground. Both dripped blood onto the snow. I sat beside him on a rock peeking from the ground, the remaining tanto reversed, pointing behind me. "Very nice," he said, catching his breath.

"Thanks." Sitting in the dark, watching the walker howl

and roll in pain, I handed Audric a final healing amulet. "Put it over the fang punctures. It'll neutralize the toxins." A human might have died from the venom in the saliva, but Audric wouldn't. He'd be sicker than plague-stricken monkeys, however, unless we counteracted the poison. I had made some amulets following my last encounter with spawn. I couldn't count on the presence of a friendly, helpful seraph every time I got into trouble. Seraphs hadn't given the human world much attention in the last few decades, and the neomage world even less.

In its cage, luminous blue and green energies and gold sparkles arcing over the spring, Malashe-el writhed and cursed and beat against the walls. Its red eyes spit hatred each time they landed on me. It pulled the tanto from its side with a gush of blood and threw the blade at the shield. It bounced off, clanging on the stones.

"Will it live?" Audric asked, breathing hard.

"Probably. If it gets control of itself in time to reserve some blood. If it gets to eat."

"What are you going to do with it?" Audric asked after a few minutes. His voice sounded more normal.

"I don't know. But see its eyes? They used to be blue-green, like labradorite stone. Almost incandescent."

"Meaning?"

"I don't think it was originally pure Darkness. I think it was created out of the genetic patterns of a Major Darkness and something else." When Audric didn't laugh or shoot down my theory, I said, "Either it chose Darkness, or it's possessed. If it chose the Dark, we'll kill it. If it's possessed against its will, the control will lessen with daylight." Thinking about the questions Lolo hadn't answered, I said, "Maybe we could get some information out of it."

Seconds passed. Audric watched Malashe-el thrash. The daywalker pulled the spur amulet from its pocket and attacked the shield, stabbing at the energies with ferocity and speed that was hard to follow. The shield was unchanged, though it sizzled with the blows. When Audric spoke, his tone was deceptively casual. "You know how to exorcise a demon?"

"Not yet. But I might by morning."

"And the weakness in your side, left from your vision underground? I saw what the touch of that amulet did to you." I had nothing to say to that. We both knew I had a problem.

"Hey! You want to let me out of here?" a voice shouted. "Thorn?"

"Oops. Forgot about Zeddy," I said.

"I'll keep watch over your daywalker," Audric said. "You release the boy and tell Rupert what happened. Ask him to bring me a sandwich and some water. Maybe a blanket."

"You don't have to stay here. The trap won't fail. The walker was drenched with water from the spring. It's stuck until I release it." Zeddy shouted again, wondering if I was alive. I shouted back to hold his horses, hoping the humor would give him some patience.

As if he hadn't heard me, Audric said, "I'll wait here until you try an exorcism. Or until it dies. But you get to clean up the spawn. They'll stink by morning, even in the cold."

He was right. Spawn smelled like rotting meat, their decay process fast. As helpful townspeople had yet to appear, I'd pay Zeddy to pile and burn them, but I didn't think it would be cheap. And I wondered what the town would say about the unwanted mage attracting a horde of spawn. Whatever they came up with, it wouldn't be nice. They would have let me die out here, and probably been tickled pink about it. Tired, aching, feeling the pain in my side like a boil, I rose and went to the loft.

I showered fast and hung a healing amulet inside my T-shirt when I dressed, one that would help the acid burns, the cuts, and the pain in my side. As I dressed, I realized that Joseph Barefoot hadn't appeared to help with the spawn either. Maybe if I'd had time to hang a cloth in my window, I thought wryly.

After the bath, wrapped in an afghan, I ate cottage cheese, frozen blueberries, a bowl of canned beans, and a fresh pear, which had been trucked in on a mule train. The pear had cost me dearly, but was worth every dollar. Fresh

fruit in winter was for rich people. Or someone willing to
do without necessities. I fit into the latter category, and had
gone without much protein for the past month. In an ice
age, one had to choose between survival supplies and
pleasure. Paying for the pear had been one such choice. I
ate every part of the fruit except the seeds, which I kept for
Rupert and Jacey. I couldn't grow weeds in summer, but
my best friends had greener thumbs. Maybe they could
grow a pear tree.

With my aches and pains relieved, and appetite ap-
peased, I curled in bed and studied the *Book of Workings*,
trying not to think about Audric out in the night, watching
over my detainee. The *Book of Workings* wasn't a magical
book. It had no special powers or energies, and few ready-
made incantations. It was more a roadmap, a schoolbook,
a compilation of the learnings of the first neomages. Having no teachers, they had been trying to find out what they
were, and what they could do. The book was divided into
three parts, the back of the book devoted to warfare. It was
to that section that I turned, covers up under my chin, two
blades in the bed, and my amulets around my neck.

Toward midnight the smell of burning and rotting spawn
filtered in, the scent harsh as burned feathers in the back
of my throat. I was breathing the foul flavor when I found
the pages on exorcism. Unlike seraphs, mages are mortal
and, unlike humans, we have no souls. Mortal and soulless,
mages can't call on the One True God, God the Victorious,
for help. Prayer doesn't work for us. He doesn't hear us.
Seraphs will hear us if we, or innocents, are near death, but
many theologians insist that God won't. Other theologians
contend that if he doesn't hear an intelligent creature, it
proves he isn't real and never was, but that was a theolog-
ical argument for passionate believers and heretics, and all
I wanted to do was cast out an evil demon, if it could be
done without calling on the name of the Most High.

To my knowledge, Hindus, Muslims, and Jews did not
traditionally cast out demons when their people were
possessed. Some Hindus tried to placate Darkness, leaving offerings so demons would depart. Only Christians historically cast out minions of the Darkness. Christians, who,

by faith, called on the blood and name of Christ to over-power a possessing demon. Blood given in willing sacrifice had great power over evil. I had been raised Christian by my parents and the Enclave priestess, who hoped to per-suade the Most High to give us souls. It hadn't happened. And since I had become an outcast, I hadn't really wor-shipped, the faith of my childhood waning. Ergo, I wasn't equipped to deal with a case of possession.

In the pages on exorcism, I discovered two things that might help me. A conjure to track a Darkness through mage blood, and a seraph who offered its power to first bind and then exorcise demons. The winged-warrior Mu-tuol promised his name and power to help mages defeat evil in one-on-one spiritual combat. I studied the imple-ments and methods offered in the resource book for mages.

Once bound, the incantation on exorcism might work. A daywalker was not technically a demon—an immortal being who was spirit but could manifest in one or two physical forms. A daywalker was mortal, a Minor Dark-ness, restricted to one physical shape. It was soulless—much like neomages, though few mages would have accepted the similarity. My Bible beside me, my blades on the tables and floor around me, I studied the incantation suggestions, sought scriptures to bring Light and power to them, and made copious notes.

This wasn't some conjure to heat bathwater. This was warfare. I had to do it right or I might die in the process. Many early neomages had.

Chapter 12

They threw him into the cell, weak with blood loss. He fell hard on his severed wings, the bones bending with his weight, buried his head in his arms, and wept. He didn't hide his sobs, his voice broken, like cracked bells and splintered flutes. The pain was beyond anything he had experienced since they'd first clipped his wings, rendering him unable to fly from the deeps of the pit, unable to defeat time, unable to contact another of his kind. Since that time, the Darkness had merely shaved the stubs of his wings every twenty-four hours, the trimming keeping him bound. Until today, they had merely allowed the heat-driven mage to try to force him to mate. Merely.

Today, to punish him, they had cut him deeper, much deeper. Using human steel, daywalkers had removed his wings to the shoulders. They had broken him utterly. It was the smell that ruined him. The growing aroma of sex and death, like nothing he had ever smelled before. He had failed the Most High. Because of the scent, the strange odor, he hadn't been able to prevent them from taking his essence.

Fists clenched, he beat his bed until his hands bled, screaming, his broken voice echoing down the hallways. His blood trickled across his naked back and onto his feathers, blood that smelled of life and Light, of blooming flowers, scents that taunted, recalling the earth that he had once loved enough to abandon heaven. The scent nearly overpowered the smell of the walkers he had killed, their rancid blood sprayed against the walls and spilled over the floor. His blood, a thing of life and healing, a construct of heaven, had been turned against him. He screamed, his agony long and loud. Somewhere near, he knew the Darkness was laughing.

"Watcher?"

His cries stopped, breath ragged.

"Watcher?" It was the bell-like voice he had heard before while in pain.

He laughed, the sound ugly, defeated; raw with the torture he had endured. "What? What do you want now? I did what you suggested. I fought. I killed them with my fists." He remembered the sound of bones breaking; the heated spatter of blood. "But they had locked the cell door behind them. I was still trapped. And more came." He dashed tears from his face. Across his back, dried blood cracked with the motion. "They clipped my wings to the shoulder. I am ruined."

"You are not ruined. A mage is near. You can call her. She will come."

"I don't need another *mage*," he said, his tone heavy with loathing. "They took my essence today. And they gave it to a mage. She will deliver a litter of first-generation kylen to the Dark. The Most High will condemn and drain me utterly. I will have no more chance of penance until the end of time and the human judgment."

"There is hope," one voice trilled in his head. *"Help is at hand."*

"A mage has freed my wheels," another voice belled, higher-pitched, softer. *"She will rescue us."*

"The Most High will not drain you unto death, Watcher. When we are freed, we will carry your claim to Him. We will trust you, and you will trust us."

Slowly he sat up, severed nerves flooding exquisite agony through him. His unhealed flesh split, blood running in rivulets. "You say *we*. Yet I have heard only the name of Zadkiel."

"I stand above my mate's prison, a place the Dark One created to trap her."

"Your mate? A *cherub*?" he whispered, startled. Except for the Watchers who had allied with the High Host, no Darkness had ever successfully trapped a winged-warrior. And he had never even considered that one of the cherubim could be imprisoned.

"Yes. She feared for me," he crooned. *"She left the Most High in the Last Battle Glorious, the battle where I was nearly destroyed. Her prison and the snare that holds me are new constructs. New things such as I have never seen."*

"There are no new things," Barak said, his mind racing with possibility.

"So we had thought. 'No seraph, Holy or Fallen, has imagined or created any new thing,' " he quoted from the *Book of the Light*, *" 'except for sin. Except for sin. Selah. Only the Most High can create a new thing, only God the Victorious and his humans, who breathe with his breath, may dream, devising that which they have not seen, humans with their stories, songs, and poems, humans with their machines which they imagine and build. So it has always been,' "* he finished the quote, his tone dropping low with disquiet. *"Until now."*

He wrapped his knees with his arms to stop their trembling. "And now?"

"Beasts, dragonets, have entwined themselves upon me. They smell of Mole Man, and the scent slows my defense. Though I still have my wings, I am unable to fly, unable to transmogrify, trapped in a substance that secures me. My mate is chained and imprisoned within my sight. All this is new. Selah," he whispered, seraphic for, "Think of that."

"Humans built it? Humans working with Darkness?"

"Humans and mages. But a mage has seen us, possibly one of the foretold *ones."* His tone rang with awe. *"The essence of this mage, this daughter of man, was similarly trapped, yet she escaped. She is still near. She can save us. You can summon her."*

"How? I have no token of hers."

"You have access to the daywalker, the boy. She claims him. She takes his blood," Zadkiel said.

"The boy is mine," Amethyst belled softly. *"Mine."*

Barak wasn't sure what they meant, but if they offered freedom, he would agree to anything. "If your words are faithful and your bargain fair, call me by my true name." It was a test and a barter. No seraph called a Fallen One by his true name, that given by the Most High at creation, the name forfeited at his abandonment of the Light. Watchers were Fallen, even those like him, who hoped for redemption, who allied with and fought beside the High Host in the ongoing war. No Watcher was *sanctified*. No Watcher was holy.

"Baraqyal," the two voices belled together. *"Baraqyal."* And the seraph said, *"Gird thyself, and bind on thy sandals."* It was a warning to prepare for battle.

Audric didn't wake me Friday morning by sneaking in for my daily beating; my eyes opened on their own. My head was resting on my arms, neck cricked into the pillow. The black-pig wall clock chimed. I'd slept two hours. Roosters sounded, their calls demanding. The charcoal sky held a silver wedge of clouds in the east. Beneath my cheek was a page of notes and a finished incantation. Groggy, I sat up and reread the paraphrased text taken from the Old Testament. It would have helped if I knew Forcas' true name because then I could have used it in the binding, but even so, it wasn't bad. Not bad at all.

Stretching to ease my petrified muscles, I went to the back door and out onto the deck. The scent of coffee reached me. Audric toasted me with a cup in the dim light. He was wrapped in blankets, sitting before a secluded fire. Rupert was a bump beside him, unmoving. I held both fists out to Audric and flashed my fingers open three times. He toasted me again and nudged Rupert, who rolled over.

I ate and pulled through the primary moves of savage-chi, stretching protesting muscles. Dressed in two sets of underleggings and tees, extra socks, and my dobok, I made sure the seams were straight, the blades easy to pull, and that the amulet necklace was secure around my waist. Then I phoned Jacey, told her what I needed, gathered up supplies and my pages, the result of my wakeful night, and went into the cold, my breath misting in small puffs.

The sky was patchy blue through the clouds with a red frosting of sunrise on the eastern mountain tops, the tem-

perature a cold twenty-one degrees. At the edge of the
shield, I set down my supplies, all but one of the pages I
had worked on in the night, and studied the being in the
trap. The legendary daywalker. It looked human, sitting on
a rounded boulder shaped like an egg with the pointed end
buried in the dirt. One knee was bent, its arms around it.
Like so many of the locals, like Rupert and Lucas, like the
Cherokee, its skin had a pale olive cast in certain light, and
it wore its black hair in braids. The walker wasn't dressed
for the cold, but wasn't shivering, and it stared at me, its
eyes still red, but now flecked with blue.

I gripped the handle of the walking stick, the bloodstone
hilt warming my hand. If I'd carried it last night, I would
have remembered more about the walker. The prime
amulet had many uses, including being a repository for
memory. My memories of the daywalker were contained in
it, along with the incantation of the rune of forgetting it
carried.

Holding it, I studied the walker, comparing it against the
first time I saw it. Then, it had worn cornflower blue pants
and shirt, its eyes like fine labradorite, a pellucid blue and
green. Today it wore brown pants and a dull green shirt,
both crusted with splatters of dried blood. Its eyes glowed
the red of the pit, but blue flecks grew wider as the sun
rose.

Suddenly it appeared right in front of me. I stepped back
fast. Fangs unhinged, it laughed, tossing the tanto in a glittering arc, catching the hilt one-handed. I steadied myself.
The beast was contained in the shield incantation. It
couldn't get away until I released it. It spat at me, and this
time I didn't move, the spittle splatting and sizzling on the
shield.

Satisfied, I turned to Audric. "How was it?"

"Lovely. Nice breeze, two owls keeping me company,
Rupert snoring. Good fire. Coffee. Could have used a
book, but the walker kept me occupied with constant
chatter." He had let the air out of the mattress and rolled
it up, and put out the fire. He looked invigorated and
steady, not like he had spent the night exposed to the ice-
age weather.

I looked far less refreshed. I had seen my dull, unglamoured skin and the circles beneath my eyes in the mirror when I brushed my teeth. "You learn anything from it?"

"It seemed surprised that I knew its master had your blood. It has an entire litany of things it wants to do to you and with you. Nothing new or inventive, but all entertaining. It offered to share you with me."

I grinned. "Stupid of it."

"Very. What's your plan?"

I indicated Zeddy and Jacey, who rounded the building, coming from the alley. They each carried shovels and Bibles. "It's complicated."

"Humor me," he said dryly.

I told him. When he stared at me, I shrugged, found a stick, and traced a dotted outline of a ring around the outside of the shield holding the daywalker. Using a shovel borrowed from Jacey, I set the blade against the frozen ground and started digging. It wasn't easy. I looked up to see Zeddy digging too, starting across from me. Luckily—or maybe he knew more about incantations than I gave him credit for—he was digging clockwise. Audric and Jacey were speaking in low tones, their backs to us. Just as well. Audric hadn't had to share his opinion of my plan. His expression said it sucked Habbiel's pearly toes.

When a four-inch-deep, four-inch-wide, miniditch ringed the spring and stones, I stopped digging, breathless, body wet with sweat. I had left a foot-wide space, not yet dug. Zeddy, who had finished his arc before I did and looked much more refreshed than I, even after a night of burning spawn, would have dug it as well, but I waved him away. "The rest I have to do," I said. "You should get ready to help me. Like I said when I called."

"Sure, Miss Thorn," he said. Shouldering the shovel, he walked to a tree, sat down on the roots, and picked up his Bible. "Which book?"

"Genesis 14:20. 'And blessed be the Most High God, which hath delivered thine enemies into thy hand.' But keep a finger in Psalms. If I have problems with him, recite those verses on the list there"—I pointed to the page I had put by my supplies—"in the order given." The page was covered with verses in Psalms that referred to defeating enemies.

I positioned my candles and the stones I had brought from the loft, looked again at the incantation, and shoved the paper into my dobok. I had never created such a complicated conjuring circle. I had no idea if it would work or if I could control the energies I was calling up. A walking circle was a dangerous construct, the conjure not as stable as one where the energies were called and then cut off when they reached the critical zenith. The energies in a conjuring circle were stabilized with salt. This circle was stabilized through the body of the mage herself. If not utilized, the energies would just keep rising.

Walking beside the path of the circle, I lit candles, placing each in the lee of a rock, protected from the wind. Satisfied, I positioned a bag of goodies I might need and drew my walking stick blade. I was prepared to fight, should the new circle break down the inner shield I was trying to encompass, and free the walker. I put both feet into the trough we had dug, one in front of the other. "Okay," I said. "Start the chant."

"And blessed be the Most High God," three voices said in unison, Jacey, Rupert, and Zeddy. They had positioned themselves equidistant around the circle, each just beyond a candle. I hadn't told them where to stand, and wondered if Audric had positioned them or if they had known it themselves. Or maybe it was just luck.

Balancing with one foot in front of the other in the shallow trench, I set the shovel into the earth and completed the furrow, closing the ring. With a crackle I felt in my bones, power rose, ascending slowly through the soil beneath my feet. A pale blue light, darkening to indigo at the ground, it gathered within the ring and lifted, like a wide river at high tide. My breathing sped up and my heart rate increased in reaction. I started walking the ring.

Inexorably, the building energies climbed slowly over my feet, calves, and thighs. It was uncomfortable, at the edge of pain, like salt in a wound or a buildup of static electricity, like the energies the cobra had forced onto me and which I still didn't understand. I wanted to jump from the trough but knew I couldn't. My friends continued their chant, voices measured and clear in the chill morning air.

According to the *Book of Workings*, because I was walking along the path of the conjure and was already wearing the amulet necklace, the energies should rise, power the circle, and fall off to a trickle I could use for other things. Theoretically, I should be able to see and monitor the levels of power within the circle, using them or siphoning them off before the whole thing exploded. Theoretically, as long as I walked, it should maintain and remain stable. The energies rose over my chest, a horrid pressure that made breathing difficult. The urge to jump away was almost too strong to disregard. I gasped. The walker growled; it sounded like hunger. Not a good thing.

The power reached my shoulders, which meant I could start using it now. The inner shield had held, so I sheathed the walking stick and passed it through a loop in my belt. From the bag of stones I took an egg-sized sphere of pink marble. Letting all glamour fall from me, I set the stone into the trough. As it touched the ground, I said, "Mutuol, O winged one. Mutuol the bright star, I call on your power."

Inside the shield, the walker laughed, a low rumble. I remembered the voice of the daywalker, and this wasn't it. This laughter was the Darkness. Three feet further on, I placed another stone, repeating the phrases calling on Mutuol. When I reached my starting point and passed the first stone, I set the empty bag beside the trough and continued walking the ring, calling on the winged-warrior. The walker fell silent. The sky brightened with day. The energies rose to twenty feet in height and tightened at the top, pulling in like a drawstring bag. I could see the sky through the opening, and the shield below it. The walker watched it as well, its face twisted in revulsion.

Still nothing happened until the top of the conjure was nearly closed, the mouth dinner plate–sized. The walker's eyes were on me, and they were blue with only a fleck of red. *I call myself Malashe-el*, it had said, once. Its eyes had been blue then, too. Whip-fast, its body twisted in a serpentine spiral, the darkness remaining in it struggling against the power all around. It snarled, jaw unhinging, moving like a snake.

A faint throb of power trembled through the tide of energies. From Mutuol? I looked up into the sky, but saw nothing, no flashing wings, no scent of all things living and edible. The energies throbbed again, a heartbeat, steady and true. The construct of the walking circle shimmered with faint blue light, touched with rose, yet the seraph himself didn't appear.

I considered the oddity of using seraph power without the presence of the seraph. It was possible that Mutuol had stored energy in a reservoir mages could draw upon, much like energy was stored below each Enclave. But this power was dedicated to one purpose. With each throb of light came information, syncopated surges of data about the walker, more than I could process, more than I could understand.

The rhythm of the surges matched my heartbeat, which was odd. I looked at the daywalker in surprise, remembering the smell that had come from him once, the sweet scent of seraph. The walker saw the beginning of knowledge in my eyes. With a final snap of its body, demon-fast, it raced to the confining shield and crashed against it, eyes flashing with red fire. Fangs extended, it struck. I flinched, nearly stepping off the path before righting myself.

Suddenly the flames in its eyes went out, leaving it looking startled, like an abused child rescued by gentle arms. With a strange, dispirited cry, it crumpled to the ground.

The desire to comfort it throbbed through the seraph light. The yearning and the information I was receiving weren't coming from Mutuol. Couldn't be. And it wasn't coming from the Darkness. Compassion wasn't an emotion Dark ones felt. Perhaps the Mistress? Though I was uncertain where the knowledge originated, I could use it.

Carefully, I placed a hand on the wall of the shield. It sizzled where I brushed along it, burning my palm. From the incantation I had written and memorized, I said, "I will bind you fast, but surely will not kill you. By the power of Mutuol, I seek that which was lost, and will bring back that which was driven away. Will bind up that which is Fallen, and will strengthen that which was sick." Looking into its eyes, I spoke its true name. "Malashe-el! Malashe-el, by the power of your true name and by the power of Mutuol, I command you! Join me! Join the battle on the side of the Light!"

It took a breath. And, as if it had been waiting for me to say the words, it smiled. As if it wanted me to say them. Eyes gray and blue-green, it retracted its fangs, stood straight, and shook itself, the motion catlike. "I thank you," it said. With a quick toss, it sent the tanto whirling. I almost jumped from the ring, breaking the conjure, halting myself just as the blade slid along my palm and thumped into the ground at my feet. It hadn't cut me; I knew that. But I wanted to inspect my palm just the same.

"My Master is gone," it said, and touched its chest, looking down as if it could see inside. "Not even a whisper of his thoughts are with me." It breathed deeply, as if the air tasted better, cleaner.

I watched it, waiting, walking, sliding my palm along the shield with its sizzling energy. This had been easy. A lot easier than I had expected. Too easy? The chanting continued. I could sense Audric nearby, guarding, his apprehension like a sour smell on the morning wind. He moved into my field of vision, both blades drawn. "Who is your master?" I asked, my palm smoldering on the shield, the pain growing. "Give me its name."

"Forcas." It looked up and heaved another deep breath. "The Master of the Trine. By night I am in thrall to him. By day I am sometimes free, as my Mistress desires, though that becomes more difficult as his power grows."

Easy. Way too easy. "Who has my blood?" I asked. "Is it Forcas?"

"Yes. My Master took your blood as an offering from one of his servants. You had wounded it unto death. For the gift, the Master awarded it true life and a place at his side."

True life? I wanted to ask, but didn't know how much time I had. I focused on the information I had to have. "What is Forcas' true name?"

"I do not know, but my Mistress does. Call on the seraphs and save her. She can free you from Forcas' summoning."

Everyone wanted me to call the seraphs. Why hadn't someone taught me how? And then surprise flooded through me. It *wanted* me to call in seraphs?

"If you don't free her and destroy him," Malashe-el said, "Forcas will claim you as his own, you and the blood he seeks." His mouth turned up at the corners and I saw a hint of fang. "The blood is strong. When combined with the blood of Mole Man and the blood of the Fallen, it creates much living power for his use. Enough to change the world as he desires."

I studied the walker, not letting it see my confusion. Forcas wanted my blood to combine with Mole Man's? But it had mages in its power already; I had seen them. I deviated from my plan and said, "Tell me about the blood Forcas wants."

Swiftly, it lifted the blade and exposed its forearm, the flesh pale, human-looking, the blade glinting in the rising sun. With no sign of pain, it drew the point of the blade along its skin. Blood welled in the cut. Red blood, when some walkers had blood blacker than the night sky. Its scent reached me through the shield, human, and familiar. Because the beast had drunk from him, I expected to scent Lucas, and indeed there was the scent of Stanhope. But above the Stanhope blood rode something more. Something fresh and unexpected. Something I hadn't noted in the heat of battle.

I sniffed again as I walked, my feet dragging slowly through the heavy weight of the conjure's power, drawing it deep, breathing it in, and as I did, Malashe-el grinned. Its fangs unhinged fully, hanging on its lower lip. "Vampire," Audric murmured. But it wasn't. Vampires of legend walked only at night. Malashe-el lifted its arm in the light of the partially risen sun and licked at its blood, its eyes on me.

Suddenly I placed the scent, recognized the owner of the blood. The same scent was in my closet, on my dolls, dolls given me by my foster father. Wild energies prickled my skin. Above me, the hole was gone, sealing me in the walking circle with the beast. The beast who smelled like family. I had stopped walking the path, and took a step, my foot encumbered in the thickness of the energies.

The walker mocked, "You don't know. The priestess didn't tell you." It licked its wound, eyes filled with red flecks of gleeful scorn. "You are ignorant and untutored. But Forcas knows. And I know." It cocked its head. "I'll tell you if you beg."

The walker's possession ran deep. Even surrounded by daylight and Mutuol's power, it was malevolent. When I said nothing, the red in its eyes faded, leaving it with a frustrated pout, bad-tempered, like a teenager denied a parent's reaction. My feet pushed through a dozen steps and the energies softened, making progress easier. My brain cleared.

"It's a puzzle, a riddle devised by my master. The mother of Mole Man's progeny was daughter to Adain Hastings." It smiled again, fangs hinting, as if the information was important. When I didn't react, the smile faded. Irritated, it turned its back to me, spotting Audric. In a flash, it crossed the spring and slammed against the shield wall. Audric didn't flinch. Enraged, the walker howled and threw itself against the wall, bouncing away only to rush in again. Its eyes flashed red fire.

While it beat against the cage, I parsed its words. The mother of Mole Man's progeny was the Stanhope matriarch, Gramma Stanhope. Hastings was the last name of my foster father, Lemuel, who died just after my eighteenth birthday. I still missed him. And often, like now, I wondered what he would have done and felt had he ever learned I was a neomage.

Adain Hastings was Uncle Lem's father's name. Which made Lem Gramma's brother.

A cold shiver quaked through me. I was glad Audric held the walker's attention. The beast would have gotten a kick from my reaction, and maybe a foothold in our conversational disputation. Again, my feet had slowed, and energies had built up as I pondered. I increased my pace, pulling the excess power into me, into my amulets, filling them to the brim and taking the excess energy into myself,

beginning to feel drunk on the rising power. While I
thought, I recited the incantation freeing Malashe-el, calling on Mutuol.

Lolo had sent me to Mineral City after my mind unexpectedly opened to the inhabitants of Enclave. The move
was supposed to save my life and sanity. But what if the
move had been planned long before? The question rippled
through me. What if Lolo had wanted me here for some
devious, nefarious reasoning of her own? What if the old
bat had planned my move, planned the secret breeding of
Thadd's mother—Rupert's aunt—to a kylen, planned the
marriage between the matriarch and patriarch Stanhope?
There were love conjures in the *Book of Workings*. What if
she had masterminded it all? What if she had a plan that
had been in the works for . . . what? Decades?

*Blood of the saints! What was the priestess of Enclave up
to?* I pulled a blade, the silver ceremonial blade I used
when I needed my own blood in a conjure. With the point,
I reached down and traced a loop in the soil, inside the
walking circle, making a protected place. The *Book of
Workings* said this would work for a short time. If not, it
would kill me. Decisively, I stepped from the trough to the
loop. There were no explosions, no wildfires, no bloody bits
scattered across the hillside. The voices of the chanters
sounded tense, as if they knew what I had just done was
dangerous. The next move was even more so. It would give
the walker access to me.

I flipped the knife. Stabbed into the shield.

Heat erupted out at me, a blast furnace. My body rocked
back, nearly making me lose my footing in the loop.

Eyes flaming fully red, the walker launched itself at me.

Chapter 13

It was holding the tanto, and I the silver knife. The walker slashed, faster than I could follow, demon-fast, moves I had never seen. The first drew blood as I blocked with the ceremonial knife and pulled a throwing blade. The silver knife was too soft for fighting, and I slipped into the egret, blocking the successive cuts with swooping, winglike moves. Suddenly Malashe-el was six feet away, laughing, eyes sly. It was a victorious sound, arrogant. As calmly as if it hadn't moved at all, the beast licked my blood from the tanto's blade. Its other hand twirled the spur with nimble fingers and closed its eyes in pleasure.

With a quick flick of my wrist, I loosed the ceremonial blade, saying, "Mutuol."

The knife thunked deep into the walker's chest. It staggered, eyes wide, and dropped its head to see. Blood welled around the silver blade. The daywalker screamed and dropped both the tanto and the spur conjure.

"Now, Zeddy!" I shouted.

The chanted words changed, almost as if they had rehearsed it. The incantation from Psalms was softly chanted from three sides of the walking circle. "I will call upon the LORD, who is worthy to be praised: so shall I be saved from mine enemies." Humans could call on the Most High. I was hoping it would be enough.

Backed by the scripture, I stepped over the loop cut into the ground and carefully placed a foot inside the walking circle. I didn't have long, as the energies would continue to build, but now I could fight. "Mutuol, the bright star. By his power I bind you."

Fangs wide, the walker pulled the silver knife from its flesh, the motion quick. It dropped the knife and sucked its blistered fingers where the silver had burned it. Bright blood spurted in steady arcs from the hole in its chest. I kicked the tanto and the spur away, and they clattered against rock that ringed the spring. I thought it might attack again, but the daywalker fell back and sat on a stone, its breathing ragged. "So, worthless mage. You have me trapped. What now?"

Ignoring the insult, I judged by the color of its eyes that it was free of its master. "Answer my questions. Provide me with information."

"Yes. And then?" it asked, voice rough with pain.

"Information first. Tell me all you know about the"—I paused, remembering the phrase it had used—"the mother of Mole Man's progeny, who was daughter to Adain Hastings."

"The riddle. My Master will be disappointed." It pressed its hand over its wound. The bleeding slowed and darkened, but didn't stop, and its lips were blue from blood loss. "Forcas thought you would ask something important, but so be it. She is a murderer, who killed her own grandson, siphoning him dry. She is full of greed, keeping much of the blood she stole. She is wise, bargaining with the rest for great gain. But my Master has murdered millions, killed his own children, is greedier by far than she, and wiser than his Dark Lord."

"That's it? Tell me everything."

Malashe-el laughed, a breathless sound. "She is a queen, soon to be the mother of thousands. That which was lost shall be restored."

Darkness was a hierarchical organization, so the Dark Lord concept was logical, and, if Gramma had allied with a Major Darkness to become a dark human, other parts of the riddle made some sense too. Jason, her grandson, had been dead some time, and though I hadn't known she killed him, the revelation wasn't surprising. Gramma hadn't come to Jason's funeral, odd behavior for a human. They often revered the dead more than the living.

I had met the old woman, a keeper of secrets, tight lipped and watchful. The daywalker's blood smelled of her, which meant it had recently drunk her blood. One of Forcas' powers was to restore lost property. Gramma was once rich, but her husband had left *her* fortune to his grandkids. Had she thought herself wise enough to bargain with the devil? Had she bartered all she had and was to get back what she lost? Had her blood sealed the bargain? Had greed and vengeance been keys to her soul? Whatever she had bargained for, Forcas had tricked her, taken her, changed her, and now she was something else.

I searched through the knowledge the walking circle and the strange rose glow of energy had bequeathed me. Yes. A possessed daywalker could make bargains for its master. It would drink blood to seal the deal. "What kind of queen?" I asked.

It took a moment for it to answer, its throat working as if dry. Its fangs unhinged and extended before it could speak. "The mother of thousands. The breeder."

No help at all. This was getting me nowhere. I pulled the walking stick blade and bent for the ceremonial knife, covered in the walker's blood. Backing away from the walker, I found the supply bag I had set within the circle. In it was a small stone jar and a swatch of cloth.

One eye on Malashe-el, I scoured the silver knife on the cloth, polishing the gleaming metal. The blade was nicked from Malashe-el's sword, which annoyed me. When it was clean, I opened the stone jar, exposing the earth salt within. I thrust the silver blade inside, deactivating any microscopic traces of blood. The scent of brimstone billowed out.

A silent click, a sound I heard in my mind and not in my ears, alerted me that the visa had activated itself. I didn't know why the official amulet was working, and I had no way to figure it out.

I inserted the cleansed blade into a sheath sewn in the dobok. The bloody cloth I tucked into the stone jar. The daywalker's mouth tightened and I grinned at it, showing my teeth. I might not have fangs, but my meaning was clear. I had its blood. For the moment, I owned it. Face pale, it took a wheezing breath, as if air entered its lungs through the chest cavity. If it had been human, it would be dead.

"Tell me of the seraphs beneath the Trine," I said

Its eyes, growing bluer as it weakened, darted between the silver hilt and the stone jar in my left hand before it answered, panting. "Privacy is a gift."

Understanding, I found an amulet by feel. With a thought and a delicate squeeze, I activated the incantation stored in it, letting the building energies of the walking circle power a privacy circle. Strangely, a discomfort I hadn't noticed eased with the privacy circle. The energies were still building. I didn't have long. "You have your gift," I said.

"Barak. Succubus. Queen. Larvae. Baraqyal." It put out a hand, steadying itself on a nearby boulder. Its blood smeared the stone. "I am dying," it said, sounding astonished.

"So?"

"Alive, I am of use to you," it bargained. "Alive, my Mistress has a conduit. Ask me of her."

"Who is your Mistress?"

"Holy Amethyst, mate to Zadkiel, the winged-warrior."

"Where is Zadkiel?"

"Trapped above her prison. Hurry. I am dying." Malasheel slipped from the stone to the ground. Blood coated its ugly shirt. It was shivering.

It hadn't been a dream. I had seen Zadkiel, the winged-warrior, in a vision, and had thought it a nightmare, some representational image I would someday understand. But it had been truth.

"Reset the trap," he—it—said. "Set me free and I might yet live."

"At the behest of Forcas or of the Mistress?"

"Your choice. You have the power. She knew you had the power. She watches you."

Its face was whiter than the snow beneath it. Its blood, a scarlet stain on the white, had slowed to a trickle. The walker was no threat. I sheathed my sword and pulled the silver knife. With a single slash, I opened the privacy circle and buried the silver point against the earth at the broken loop that had modified the walking circle.

Thunder sounded in the distance. "Get down," I shouted. Rupert fell, followed by Jacey and Zeddy. I had a single instant to shield my eyes. A flash hit the ground. The earth erupted. Rocks and soil flew. When I opened my eyes, Malashe-el was gone. I was lying faceup on the ground, my legs spread in snowmelt and mud. Tree branches above me smoked. The air smelled of sulfur.

Zeddy held a shovel at the ready. Rupert and Jacey bent over me, staring, faces concerned. Audric was standing over me, both swords drawn. "The swan," I said, identifying the position of his swords. "Very flashy." I started coughing.

Audric grinned and sheathed both swords. "Yes, I am." He held an arm to pull me to my feet, steadying me as the coughing fit passed. "Almost as flashy as you releasing both a privacy circle and a walking circle with a sword and sending the daywalker back where it came from."

I caught my breath, looking around. The spur that had conjured the injured place in my side was gone. "I didn't. Exactly." At his look, which was mostly unreadable, but certainly not happy, I said, "Well, I did open the privacy circle with it. But not the walking circle. I was just going to cut into the earth underneath the trough and release the energies back into the ground. The explosion wasn't me."

His face shut down. "Your eyebrows are burned off," he said before he turned and walked away.

Following another shower and two cups of strong black tea to fortify myself, I sat down at the computer and signed on to the Internet. I wasn't sure what I had accomplished in the walking circle, with the talk of riddles. All I really had were the five words Malashe-el said when in the privacy circle. "Barak. Succubus. Queen. Larvae. Baraqyal." Barak and Baraqyal I thought I recognized from old neomage legends, but nothing came readily to mind.

It was not yet nine in the morning and I had another

hour before the shop opened when I secreted myself beneath the stairs to my loft, my amulet necklace on the
doorknob. For the second time in a row, the Internet was
agreeable, which was sort of scary in a Murphy's Law
kinda way, and I quickly found a ring of sites run by a
mage-chaser, one of the humans who follow and document
every bit of neomage news, history, gossip, and lies, detail-
ing every fact and fancy about each documented mage, and
lots of foolishness about undocumented ones too. Until I
acquired my visa, I hadn't appeared on the site, so either
the mage-watcher had limited resources or I was very well
hidden. But I was there now.

Unable to resist, I pulled up my own page. "Saint's
blood," I whispered. There was a full page of text next to a
photo of me in mage-garb at the trial. One arm was extended at the elder's face, the point of the sword touching
his throat. I faced the crowd, glowing like a light bulb. I
looked . . . well, Lolo wouldn't be happy. I didn't have the
heart to read the text. I hit the BACK button and found
Barak under the pages classified as "Verified Anecdotes."
I expected to find that one part in four had a basis in fact,
but was surprised when most of the story was true to my
memory, though told from a human perspective.

*The fallen seraph called Barak, an Allied One, for-
merly named Baraqyal, was badly burned in a battle
over the Gulf of Mexico twelve to fourteen years Post-
Ap. The soldier-seraph landed and was found on a
white sand beach by a nomadic human clan. He was
burned almost to nothingness, nearly dead. Nursed
back to health by the small clan, he stayed with them
for some time as his skin and wings regenerated and
new feathers grew.*

*Though damaged, he offered them protection at a
time when little was available. In return they gave him
sanctuary and a family such as he never knew. Barak
was nearly healed when Daria, the adolescent pictured
here, entered pubescence and was revealed as a neomage. The seraph recognized the presence of a new
creature when her gifts blossomed and went wild. Un-*

able to resist her, he mated with the first-generation witchy-woman, stealing her virginity and altering the fledging world of the neomages forever.

The union produced a first litter of three boy children, half seraph, half mage, all with full-sized wings but incapable of flight or transmogrification—the kylen. The second litter produced four viable, winged offspring as scientists called them. Daria and Barak had six litters before the seraph disappeared in the major battle that destroyed Mexico City. **See section: Mage War.

The twenty kylen were incorporated into the New Orleans Enclave and grew to be powerful and prolific neomages. When they reached adolescence, they created an unexpected heat in the neomages. A mating frenzy resulted. Rumors of that event are responsible for what the orthodox consider the licentious sexual practices of mages. **See section: Mage Breeding Habits.

In the second generation, the crossbreeding of seraphs and kylen with neomages was banned following an accidental discharge of wild-magic that killed many. The neomage population stopped expanding with the edict. Without seraphs to stimulate mage females into heat, neomages don't breed easily or quickly. **See section: Mage Breeding Habits.

By seraphic decree, kylen now mate only with humans, and all offspring are taken at birth to a Realm of Light. Mage-powers demonstrated by the first generation have been diluted with the human gene pool, and the wings have vanished entirely from recent generations. Yet kylen, who have vastly longer life spans than humans or mages, are known throughout the protected domains as wizards who answer the call and will of the High Host.

Though I had some answers, I was left with more questions than when I started. What were Allied Ones? What was a nomadic human clan? I didn't remember that from schoolroom studies. What did it mean to be burned almost

to nothingness? And what was this about the New Orleans
Enclave being the site of the first mage-heat, and the birth-
place of most of the kylen? I had lived there for fourteen
years and never heard that. Was Daria still living? The
photo was grainy and blurred, the face unfamiliar.

Next I searched for *succubus*. That was enlightening. A
succubus was a noncorporeal demon who could temporarily coalesce to take on the physical form of a human female, or who could possess a human female to lure human
men into sexual sin. Occasionally a succubus would then
bring the man to its master or kill him, sort of a demonic
black widow. I couldn't see Gramma—who had to be
eighty—being successful at the possessed part at all. A succubus had to be sexually alluring and Gramma . . . wasn't.
Not by a long shot.

Next I looked up queen, and found thousands of sites,
books, and papers relating to human queens, queen bees,
Pre-Ap queens who were beheaded, queens who used to
be human males, which had to be painful, and hundreds of
other types of queens. I didn't find one single reference
that might fit the daywalker's obscure words.

On a whim, I tried succubus queen and hit pay dirt. A
succubus queen was purported to be half human, half
demon, a rare supernat capable of casting a glamour that
could fool even seraphs. When bred with a Major Darkness it could produce thousands of eggs. The hatchling larvae would all be female succubi—true female beings,
capable of giving birth when mated to anything male. If
Gramma had been replaced with a succubus queen, or
been possessed by a succubus, capable of a glamour to hide
her physical appearance, that might fit. Though why a sex
demon would want to possess Gramma was a mystery.

Still not satisfied, I looked up more sites mentioning
Baraqyal. The name turned up on an incomprehensible
site dedicated to seraph watching. Seraphs had groupies,
much like mages did, and not all were totally rational. The
keeper of this site surely wasn't, with whole sections rant-
ing about seraphs, mages, evil, sex, and demons, none of it
comprehensible except the dictionary of seraphic names,
which was organized and coherent enough to have been

imported from another site or created before she lost her mind.

There was also a Web page listing the traits of seraphs, including their limitations, which was a surprise. Most humans seemed to think they were omniscient, omnipresent, all-powerful beings. They weren't. According to both current and ancient theology, their power and knowledge were finite, often held in check by the Most High.

In another section, I found pictures of seraphs, which made my blood pound and my breathing speed. I shifted from page to page and found a picture of my own special seraph, Raziel. He looked back at me in full color, with blazing ruby irises, scarlet feathers, crimson hair upswept in a breeze, and muscles that looked as if they had been chiseled from marble.

My knees went weak. Heat, never far away, threatened. *My seraph.* It was how I thought of him, in lots of carnal circumstances and positions. Dangerous thoughts in light of the death penalty imposed upon mages who mated seraphs. Reluctantly, I went back to my search. But I bookmarked the page and the picture.

Baraqyal was listed as one of two hundred Watchers, fallen but repentant seraphs, as referenced in Enoch I. I hadn't heard of Enoch I. But the description matched the seraph I'd seen in the pit on the Trine, the silver-haired one with clipped wings. Barak was in a list of nearly a hundred missing Allied Ones, most not seen in decades. A quick search proved that Enoch I was not available on the web. Neither was a picture of Barak, and that bothered me.

I hadn't known there were repentant seraphs among the Fallen, and that most had joined the Allied Ones. There was an awful lot I didn't know, not with my neomage schooling and training cut short, terminated by the priestess of the New Orleans Enclave, and most of the Internet information was confusing. But one thing was clear in all the accounts of Baraqyal, Barak, and kylen. They had been in the same Enclave where the first litters of kylen were born. Where the first mage-heats took place.

Apparently, Barak had allied with the winged-warriors, the seraphim, in the Last War. He was also a Watcher, a fallen but repentant seraph. Was Barak really Baraqyal? If so, then another part of the puzzle that started and ended with Lolo, the priestess of the Enclave of my birth, was making sense.

Little facts and bits of memory were beginning to fall into place in the depths of my mind. Thoughtfully, I signed off the Internet. I had to have a long chat with Lolo.

Chapter 14

♦

Friday was my day to work in back, while Jacey and Rupert handled shop business. With the clearing weather, there should have been a lot of walk-in traffic, but things seemed awfully quiet when I came down the stairs dressed in jeans and layered T-shirts. Jacey was sitting at a display, with an adding machine, pencil, and notepad, doing the books and Rupert was resetting a cabochon in an old setting. Repair work. No customers.

"You guys look relaxed," I said.

Neither looked up. Rupert said, "Taking it easy after a wild morning trapping demons, chanting, and getting blown up."

Ouch. "Sorry about that," I said.

"You got a customer in back, though," Jacey said. She hit a button and a paper strip unrolled from the machine. "I turned on the heat." I didn't like the way she said "customer."

When I stepped into the work space, I found a woman I had passed on the street and at kirk. She was midfifties, face wreathed in wrinkles that had been created by laughter. Dressed in layers, like me, but in proper skirts and blouse, she had thrown her overcoat to the side and stood with hands clasped behind her back, inspecting globs of glass on Jacey's workbench. She wore pink, which meant she was a reformed or a progressive. I couldn't remember what her name was. I cleared my throat.

She flushed and looked up with a hesitant—guilty?—smile. Had she been stealing? Thinking about pilfering? Her first words cleared up that question. Hand outstretched, she crossed to me, saying, "I've never been to a mage for help before. I hope you'll forgive me. I don't know the proper protocol." At a loss for words, I accepted her hand. She shook mine once, firmly, and let go. "I'm Sarah Schubert. My husband and I own Blue Tick Hound Guns. We want to purchase mage-steel."

I tried to keep my brows from touching my hairline. "Oh," I said. Mage-steel was used in blades and other devices that required a strong temper, yet an elastic flexibility. "I can't help you." At her blank look, I added, "There are different kinds of mages. You need a metal mage. Specifically a steel mage specialist. I work only in stone."

"Oh. Well, of course," she said. "But you have diplomatic contacts at Enclaves." From her sleeve she pulled a sheaf of papers, tightly rolled. "You can contact a steel mage, send him these drawings, and he can quote us a price. Our go-between. Yes?"

I had no idea. But I was a licensed neomage, with the visa and the GPS bracelet and whatever authority came with them. Traditionally, licensed mages made contracts with the outside world for trade. I realized the silence had stretched too long. "Um. Sure. I can make the contacts." I hoped. Maybe. Unless I screwed up. I didn't even know any steel mages. They were a minuscule minority in the small number of metal mages. The skin along my spine started to itch. *Seraph stones.*

"Look, Sarah, I'm new to this," I said. "Really new. You would be my first trade negotiation. I might not do it right. I might take longer than someone who's been doing them for a while. Maybe you better go to someone else."

"I appreciate your candor. But you're here. Atlanta is the next closest option." She rattled the papers in her hand. "Someone else might be faster, but you're Mineral City's neomage. You'll try harder to get us good value for our money."

Heaven help me. She meant it. She was claiming me for

the town. I had been revealed as a mage for a long time, but this was the first time anyone had openly accepted me for what I really was. I couldn't keep a small flame of delight from igniting in my chest. I took the drawings. "Sure." The word felt huge, as if it wanted to lodge in my chest. "These aren't your only copies, are they?"

We agreed that I would handle the trade negotiation via phone, Internet, postal service, and "mage ways," as she called scrying. And that I'd take expenses and a percentage for my time. Sarah seemed pleased with the four percent I asked, assuring me I could have gotten more. But I had no idea what I was doing. I just hoped Blue Tick was happy to pay me anything once it was all over. When the particulars were settled, we shook on it and Sarah left. Out the back door of the shop, which surprised me.

While I was still getting over the shock of her circuitous egress, a second person knocked on the back door. It was the mortified, blushing, middle-aged wife of a kirk elder, wanting a charm for improving her sex life. Being exposed as a licensed mage, not having gone to jail for it, and having an elder purchase a charm for his wife seemed to have freed the citizens to use my services. But not yet freed them to be up front about it.

After the fourth indirect visitor, I was pretty well ticked off. I wasn't a whore or a guilty pleasure, so I hung a sign on the back door. "Mage appointments and services will be provided on Monday, noon to three. Enter at front." After that, I had no more interruptions. I might have no appointments Monday, but at least if I did, I wouldn't feel shameful.

Near eleven, I finally pulled my one-piece work uniform on over my clothes and settled to work on a double fist of dark green aventurine. Overhead, a new CDS disc played, an ancient, Pre-Ap rock-and-roll singer named Rod Stewart. He had a smoky, rough voice, but with a pathos I liked. The crystal digital storage disc had been released in a batch of Pre-Apocalyptic music, and my partners and I had been listening to new, but long-dead, artists every chance we got.

For decades rock and roll had been prohibited, though no one knew what the Administration of ArchSeraphs had against the music. Rod's rough voice seemed made for cutting stone. Jacey had come to appreciate a guy named Sting, and Rupert was currently listening to the Eagles, a band called Traffic, and Casting Crowns.

I secured the large hunk of rough into a vise and turned on the wet saw, showering water and wet stone dust all over me with the first cut, and excising shapes that I would later carve and link into a necklace of overlapping leaves. The diamond-tipped blade roaring in the saw, I slowly removed roughly triangular shapes from the motherstone. The matrix was stable and tightly grained, a pleasure to work with.

I had learned to inspect the crystalline matrix of the rock with my mage-senses as I worked, sending a skim into the heart of the stone. The aventurine responded, a green-glowing resonance, an echo of power, though I hadn't charged it with anything yet.

Maybe I could use a bit of the stone for the kirk elder's wife's sex charm. Something carved into an orchid, a bloom that looked like a male sex organ. I grinned as I worked, imagining her expression when she saw it. She'd never wear it in plain view.

As the hours passed, I relaxed into working stone, my affront fading as I cut and shaped leaves, and then worked some rose quartz for another necklace of overlapping roses, a commissioned piece for an out-of-town customer. It was cool, and I was glad of my extra layers, wishing Rupert and Jacey were working with me, their flames and braziers helping warm the room. My hands were icy when I finally stopped for lunch. There were customers in the front and so I ate alone, juice and yogurt, while sitting at my workbench. When I went back to cutting stone, I was marginally aware that Jacey, and then Rupert, stopped for lunch too, though we didn't speak.

Near five thirty the light dimmed. My shoulders were aching, muscles bunched and tight from the hours of work. I had excised enough stones for a half-dozen necklaces, and several large pieces that would work up into nice focal stones. Others would consider my day boring, but I thought it was wonderful.

I went to bed early, the previous sleepless night catching up with me. In Pre-Ap times, town activities might have kept a sleepy person awake, but, like all small towns, Mineral City now pretty much died at nightfall. Big cities could afford streetlights and mage-shields, and the citizens found protection in sheer numbers—places like Atlanta, Mobile, Daytona, and Boca Raton. But in the rest of the world, not much happens after dark, not since the coming of Darkness. So the town went silent as night fell, and I went to sleep.

I knew I was dreaming when I found myself in Enclave and sane, alone inside my own mind. I was sitting with Lolo, who rocked back and forth in candlelight, positioned on a pile of pillows in the big front room in her house. I thought I might be able to wake myself, but I didn't want to. I wanted to see what would happen next. And I liked the free-floating sensation of this dream. It was soothing and tranquil.

The priestess' home was near the corner of Bourbon and St. Louis Streets, a two-story house with a black, wrought-iron balcony and tall windows with working shutters. The night was mild, a breeze billowing the gauze curtains, flickering the candle flames. The room was large, with scattered tables and chairs, fans turning lazily twelve feet overhead, casting shadows on the pressed tin ceiling. My dreams painted the room a deep rose with pale pink trim, and made the pillows a hundred shades from dusky rose to dark wine.

Nearby, a flute played in a minor key, and drums beat a soft, steady cadence. They followed the tune of a distant trumpet that came through the windows, playing a mournful melody. On her pillows, Lolo swayed to the beat, eyes closed, her ancient skin hanging in folds, her skull nearly bald, brown skin shining through sparse, corked strands. She was alone but for the flutist and drummer, her wrinkled face smooth and relaxed.

The room spun slowly, and I was the one sitting on the pillows. I opened my eyes, seeing the walls and fluttering curtains in a wash of power. Bowls and vases of flowers scented the air. Night-blooming jasmine and lilacs flamed with bright pink and blue energies, their very scents power I could bend and use. I held up my hands, seeing smooth, young, dark-skinned flesh and slender fingers. Not my hands. Not Thorn's. Someone else's hands.

Bells draped around my neck tinkled with my movement. In the mirror across from me, I was beautiful, dusky-skinned, and power surged around me like the waves of an incoming tide swirling around coral reefs. I was Lolo. Lolo when I—she—was young.

The seraph stepped toward me, wings folded back, his hair too long, worn loose on the breeze, silvered by moonlight. He was naked, aroused. I trailed my gaze up his body, my lips full and bruised, much kissed. I lifted a hand, holding a stem of lilac in my fingers. I waved it toward him, seeing the strength of an incantation swirl into the air like yellow butterflies.

The sense of his gaze was no dream, but solid and real, a memory or a vision. I couldn't remember if I had ever been old. Surrounded by my conjure, Raziel—no. Not Raziel. Another. One with iridescent green feathers and desire on his face. He moved across the room and knelt on the cushions, one hand on my shoulder.

His wings lifted and brushed along my body, raising my flesh into prickles of tight peaks. His head lowered and I reached for him. Something clanked, capturing my hands. I caught it and pulled it over my head. Heat blossomed up like a garden blooming all at once, perfuming the air with desire. His nevus gleamed silver like moonlight, like his hair. A silver glow that pulsed with life.

No. That wasn't right. Not growing things. But like a wave of magma, rising, burning its way toward the surface. I cupped his face with one hand, and lower I found his need, guiding him to me. His body glowed, fulgent in the moonlight. The seraph fell on me, his mouth on my breasts. I arched up to meet him, screaming, "Now. Now!"

I woke, still screaming. Mage-heat locked itself in my

body, demanding, the wave of lava still rising. I rolled over, reaching for the seraph. He was nowhere to be found. I was alone in my bed, in the bitter, frozen Appalachian Mountains. My hand encountered something hard, and a morsel of my mind returned to me, fighting through the waves of need. The scent of flowers altered, sour, like funeral lilies, dying.

I gasped a breath of frigid air and looked down at myself. I was myself, not the woman in the dream that hadn't been a dream. My amulet necklace lay tangled in the sheets.

A cry beckoned through the windows—the lynx, its voice coarse and low. From farther off, a wolf called plaintively. I pulled the necklace over my head. With it in place, I was able to separate the foul scent from the smell of flowers. Mold and dead leaves.

I gripped the hilt of the walking stick and rolled from the bed. Except for the smell, I was alone. The lynx called again, the sound seeming to come from the front of the loft rather than the back, where it usually appeared. Barefoot, naked, not knowing or caring where my nightclothes had disappeared to, I crossed the room to the front windows. They were arched, like the windows in my dream. Like the windows that memory told me were in Lolo's house in New Orleans. How had I lived here for so long without noticing the similarity? Had I unconsciously chosen this place for that reason? Tall ceilings and arched windows—

Banishing the thought, I lifted a tanto from the kitchen table where I had left it for a thorough cleaning. One blade before me, one held backhanded, pointing to the rear, I reached the front windows and stared at the silent street. A gibbous moon hung in a black sky, silvering puffs of low clouds, rimming the buildings with pale light. Windows were dark. Churned, crusted snow and mud were rutted in the street. The smell of mold grew.

A form moved from the shadows of the bakery across the street. Bareheaded in the night, his long coat unbuttoned, Thadd stared up at me, the angle allowing him to see me from the waist up. Though it was dark, I knew he saw me standing there, blade raised, naked but for my amulets. I could sense his heat, his need, desire stronger even than the seraph's in my dream. My body responded to the fire in his eyes, nipples tightening.

He was refusing the kylen transformation, fighting it. So what was Thadd becoming? What would happen if I, if we, gave in to the attraction between us and fell on the bed, as the seraph and I had fallen together in my dream?

Thadd's hand lifted. Asking what? To come inside?

The scent thickened. It wasn't the aroma of Thaddeus Bartholomew, kylen and cop, nor was it the smell of seraph. I broke our gaze and turned to my loft. Opening mage-sight, I swept the open space, seeking. I had done just that only a day past and had seen nothing out of the ordinary. Now, near the back door that led out onto the small back porch, I saw a spark of reddish brown swirling with black. My nostrils flared, and beneath the smell of flowers and mold and rotting vegetation, I caught the stink of brimstone.

I moved through the dark apartment with ease, the overhead fans blowing icy air over my bare skin. At the back door, behind a privacy screen, was a woven reed basket of folded sheets. The glow came from within it.

I lifted the sheets. On the bottom of the basket was an egg-sized piece of wood, river-carved and smoothed. An earth amulet. Its foul stink roiled out.

In mage-sight, the Dark conjure caught in the cells of the wood appeared as an intricate web of shadow and orange light. I didn't touch it, but I recognized an incantation spelled to stimulate heat. Someone had put it in my loft. Someone had climbed the loft stairs from the shop or crept along the back of the building and up the stairs to the porch. I checked the door. It was locked. How did he, or she, get in?

I turned on a light and placed the blades on the foot of the bed. I had several stone jars filled with used salt, and I took one. Opening the top of the jar with a glove, I shoved the driftwood amulet inside, deep into the salt, and closed the lid.

Only then did I put on a robe and return to the front windows. Thadd was gone but the stink remained. Had Thadd put the amulet here? One of the townsfolk? I knew the scent of the conjure that had trapped me in the dream memory. It reeked of incubus.

Chapter 15

B efore I climbed back into the now-cold bed, I had to
  ward my home or I wouldn't be able to sleep. Pulling
on a robe, I carted my silver bowl from window to window,
gathering the stones that protected me. Stones that had not
been enough security against whatever or whoever had entered my loft. When the bowl was uncomfortably heavy, I
carried it to the kitchen and shoved the table to the side
with my hip. I placed the stone spheres and eggs—agates,
quartz, marble in shades of pink, white, brown, and
green—on the floor and sat beside them, clicking a circle
around me. I was so exhausted that, if I tried to pour a salt
ring and conjure a proper circle, I might incinerate myself,
but even using a stored circle, I could do a quick-and-dirty
protection that would get me through the night. I hoped.

Filling stones with power was the work of hours, unless
I used a shortcut. It might not be a terribly safe shortcut—
throwing around creation energies when tired, cold, and
horny as a burning bunny was never wise—but it was what
I had.

Mages in Enclave didn't have to worry about their protection, and if they needed a lot of power, they could call
on one another for assistance, or they could draw quickly
from the power sink stored deep in the earth below them.
I had discovered that distance made it harder for me to utilize that source. Living on my own, I had learned to bend
the rules.

But this is different, a warning voice whispered inside my head.

I closed my eyes, blew out a tension-filled breath, and drew in a calming one. Serenity fluttered just out of reach, distanced by exhaustion, and by a niggling doubt as to the wisdom of this. I had been thinking about this kind of conjure, but I hadn't tried it before. And using a portable circle meant that I located and used power in different, less controlled ways. But I was so tired. And I knew I could do this. I knew I could. I breathed out my tension.

Crossing my legs, I let my back slump. The floor was icy beneath my bottom, chilling my thighs. I hadn't bothered with candles. This would be nothing but power and stone.

Again I breathed. Calm slid closer. The silence of the loft settled about me, only the black-pig clock ticking over my shoulder, soothing, a part of the stillness. Calm finally rested on me, heavy, enticing me toward sleep. My breath smoothed. Peace entered me with each inhalation and wrapped itself around me, warm, thawing the cold tiles beneath me.

My heart beat a slow, methodical rhythm. Behind my closed lids, I saw the gentle radiance of my own flesh, the brighter glow of my childhood scars like a horrible map of old pain down my legs and arms. I opened my eyes, seeing with mage-sight.

The loft pulsed with power: bath, bed, fireplaces, every window, the floor; all glowed, charged with pale energy. To enter here would cause Darkness terrible pain. Except for near the back door. There I saw a dull black stain, where something had conjured an opening. It hadn't come fully inside, but had knelt and touched the laundry basket. It had made contact with the door in three places. Scuffed traces of its fingers were on the basket. The mark of Darkness was already fading, but my breathing sped at the sight.

My skin burned brighter than the apartment, a pearl sheen with the hotter radiance of scars. The amulet necklace I wore was a bright constellation of power, resting on my chest.

Sight open, I focused on the structure of Thorn's Gems,

and my home above it. The building was over two hundred years old, constructed and rebuilt over time with whatever was handy. The outer walls were several feet thick, built with a mishmash of materials: brick, mortar, and stone gathered or quarried nearby. Because brick and mortar were composed of minerals, I could use them in the conjure too, but it was the rocks, some weighing hundreds of pounds, on which I concentrated. In the radiance of the other materials, they smoldered with raw power. I fixed each in my mind and reached down, toward the center of the earth.

Power seized me. Power from the beginning of time, heard as much as felt, it swept up through the earth and caught me, a humming, singing echo of the first Word of Creation. I could *see* the thrum of strength, the force, the raw, raging power deep in the earth. It burned, a molten mantle seeking outlet. Finding me, rising within me.

But the amulet necklace already around my neck tempered my reaction. The might of the earth writhed inside me, melding me to it. Instantly I was refreshed, my aches and pains, the dregs of the cold that settled into my bones, eased, along with the ache of the spur amulet that had pierced my side. Strength flowed into me.

Seeing the outlines of the hidden construction of my home, I directed the energies into the walls. They rose like a wave of lava, replacing the air pockets in the mortar, filling the cracks and sealing the building. Like magma, it pooled in the foundation and walls, swirling into and through them. The walls blazed.

I filled the bowlful of stones, and all my amulets, and directed energies around the lintels and jambs of the doors and windows. Nothing of the Dark could enter now. And still the power rose, a solid force of might that stopped where the walls stopped. I had no power over the wood roof supports or the metal roof, but the walls and foundation sizzled with energy. As an afterthought, I included Rupert's loft, Audric's storefront, and the foundation of the stable in the conjure. The fortification glowed, a sharp, multitoned energy that glistened with massed power, making my home into a weapon. I paused. Calling the power of

leftover creation had never been so easy. I hadn't known I
could store power like this, in a building. I studied the protection I had made. I wasn't certain that anything or anyone could pass through it anywhere at the moment, not
even me, except maybe through the roof. I'd need to turn
it off by day and on by night. And I didn't know if I could.

Well, that's just ducky, I thought. I had created a prison
for myself.

With a touch, I ended the conjure, feeling the backlash
of energies as the circle opened. I stood and walked
around my loft. This was not good. At the back, I looked
out into the night, seeing the spring, its ring of rocks, and
the trap I had reset. Some of the boulders were much
larger than they appeared, their bases spreading below the
ground beneath, sitting on bedrock.

If I channeled some of the power over a bridge into the
rocks at the spring . . . No, that wouldn't work. Stone-power
would dissipate into the air. But a tunnel of energy *below*
the ground, like an underground stream of lava flowing beneath its cooled crust, that would work. Returning to my
place on the kitchen floor, I opened a new circle and envisioned an underground lava flow. With a mental push, I
opened a conduit.

The energies gyrated, spinning down the walls, coalesc-
ing into a thick cable belowground. As if passing through a
cylinder, they shifted under the barn, undulating along the
vaguely streamlike contour. They hit the stones at the
spring, rolling like a molten wave over and through them,
filling each, but not dissipating. I had created a power sink.

"Now that is just too cool," I said softly. I lifted a sphere
of green marble from the bowl of stones and set a trigger
into it. A simple on-off switch. On, the power flowed from
the spring and into the walls, forming a stronger protected
fortress than any devised by castle builders. My loft, the
shop downstairs, and Rupert's loft next door were all
warded. Off meant the power flowed away underground,
into the spring and the rocks banding it.

I drew the ward back into the building and clicked the
circle open. I was exhilarated from handling so much
power. I was also slightly drunk from it.

Carefully, I set the marble globe beside the bed and crawled back under the covers, my head denting the down pillow with a soft whoosh. I curled in the fetal position and pulled the covers over me, creating a warm nest. An hour had passed, though it seemed a lot longer. Time was uncertain during a conjure. Curled tight, I evaluated the walls around me, feeling a deep satisfaction in the sight. "Not bad for a half-trained mage," I said.

I snuggled down to sleep. Under the pillow was my walking stick, the blade unsheathed. Beside me were two tantos and a half-dozen stone spheres, good for throwing or braining an assailant as much as for the power they carried. I might have a way to fast-charge future conjures. But, even with my new handy-dandy ward in place I would go heavily armed from now on. I was taking no chances.

Saturday morning dawned clear but icy, the temps conveying the promise of the blizzardlike change forecast by SNN. Audric didn't wake me, giving me a rare and unanticipated respite. I lazed around until nearly eight, and would have stayed in bed even longer than that had the door not slammed open, crashing back on its hinges.

I remembered the conjure. Battle-lust surged through me. Mage-sight flashed open. I levered myself up on one palm, reaching for my weapons, gripping the hilt of a tanto. I glimpsed a flying figure with long dark plaits barreling across the loft at a dead run. I slid the tanto from the covers. Battle-lust surged.

At the last instant, I saw a down-filled coat, knitted scarf, and hat. Ciana. Or a Dark being glamoured to look like her. Yet the conjure was still in place in the walls. *Not possible.*

Knees landed on me. My breath was expelled with a whoof. "Morning, sleepyhead," she shouted.

Adrenaline pumping, I rolled with her momentum, pinning Ciana beneath me. She was giggling as I trapped her wrists beneath my knees. "How did you get in here?" I demanded, shouting, the tanto raised over her. "How?"

Her face fell, chin quivering. Tears pooled as her eyes sought first the blade, then my face. My heart clenched.

Seraph stones. It was really her. "I'm sorry," I said, releasing her, shifting my weight away. "I'm not mad. I'm not," I insisted as tears ran from her eyes across her cheeks. I dropped the blade and sprang up, pulling her with me as she started to sob. "I thought you were a Darkness. I'm sorry. I'm sorry. I'm sorry," I said, wrapping my arms around her and hugging tight. "But you scared me. I set a conjure. And you walked right through it."

"Really?" Her tears stopped as if I'd turned off a faucet. She struggled against me, pushing me away, and unbuttoned her coat.

Fear at my own reactions and shame at causing her fear brawled within me. I pushed the blade out of sight. I might have skewered her.

"Maybe it's my seraph pin," she said. The pin, which was shaped like a seraph wing, was given to her by the seraph Raziel. My seraph. It was shining like a beacon. "Cool," she said, touching it with a finger.

No, it wasn't. This was not cool. I reached for the marble sphere and touched off the ward, sending the energies into the trap at the spring to wait for my need. If the pin was a way for her to call Raziel, and she had activated it, and he got here and nothing had happened that required his presence, well, seraphs were notoriously volatile. And a ticked-off seraph was not good to have around.

Ciana was caressing the pin like she'd stroke a cat, the movement of her finger slow and gentle. She cocked her head and closed her eyes, a half smile on her face. I didn't like the look there. It was too mature, too ripe . . . too something. I touched the pin. It went dark. I jerked back my hand.

Ciana laughed and opened her eyes, meeting mine. "I think you just told him everything is okay. Can you take me to the library? Mama has her new *boyfriend* over," she said, adding a slur of emphasis to the word, "and I got a school project due Monday."

Relief, barren and stark, flashed through me. "Sure." To hide my face, I hugged her again, seeing in my memory her eyes swimming with tears, and in them, the reflection of the tanto raised over her head. Seeing the expression in them when she opened her eyes just now. A *knowing*. But what did she know? Was the pin more than an offer of seraphic protection for a child of Mole Man's blood? And how did I find out? What had I really seen in her eyes in that fraction of time? "But I have to work today," I said, taking refuge in the innocuous. "What time does the library open?"

"Nine. If we hurry, we can spend an hour. Uncle Rupert won't mind getting the stock out of the safe and setting things up."

"I'm sure he won't," I lied, still trying to calm my racing heart.

We ate breakfast, which Marla hadn't bothered to feed her child before sending her out into the snow for the day, and I dressed in copper-toned leggings and tunic while Ciana played with my dolls. When her attention was focused on changing a doll's dress, and she was chattering about school, I slipped behind a screen and strapped sheaths to my limbs, inserting blades: one of Audric's tantos on my right arm, throwing blades on the left and both shins. To hold them steady, I added large silver cuffs on my wrists and wore high boots. It wasn't as good as a dobok, but I couldn't dress for battle every day. Satisfied that I had done the best I could, I glamoured my skin and picked up my cloak and walking stick.

Together we knocked on Rupert's door and told my sleepy neighbor I was otherwise engaged this morning and couldn't help open the shop. Rupert, who wasn't his queenly best, needing a shave and coffee, grunted, "Big surprise there," and shut the door in our faces.

"Grumpy, huh?" Ciana said, pulling me down the steps and into the cold, dim day.

"Yeah." I smiled, swinging her hand as we walked into the icy morning. "Very." Lowering clouds promised an early dusk and poor light, and probably snow. Again.

The library was on Upper Street, down from the shop a half block, and filled with stacks of books. A lot more than when I went there as a schoolkid to study and do research. The publishing industry had been mostly inactive for

nearly seventy years after the Last War, and had only recently reemerged as a power. Heavily controlled by the
Administration of the ArchSeraph, a dozen companies
nevertheless produced some twenty thousand books a
year.

The latest fiction publications, romances, mysteries, and
adventure were on the front shelves of the poorly lit room.
Reference books were midway back, and Ciana joined a
gaggle of kids already there, poring over the big tomes. The
older books, Pre-Ap books, were elsewhere. On a Saturday
morning, I was the only adult patron.

Fortunately, Sennabel Schwartz was disposed to help
me. The plump blond woman behind the counter had run
the library for years, since she was a teenager herself, and
had helped me look for reference books when I was in
school. She had seemed all grown-up then, but with the
perspective of time, she couldn't be more than five or six
years older than I was. And although she had been afraid
of me when I was first revealed as a mage, she had been
civil since.

A public servant, she wore an orthodox gray dress, but
with a rebellious, frilly yellow apron over it. Lined across
the counter in front of her were framed photographs of her
kids, the youngest in a high chair, laughing and looking
cute, if messy, eating something red and sticky.

"What can I help you with, dear?" she asked.

"I, uh." I unclasped my battle-cloak and tossed it over a
chair, adding gloves and my scarf. "I need to see a copy of
Enoch I."

Sennabel looked around to see that we were alone. Satisfied, her face lit with anticipation. "Is this mage stuff?"
she asked, her voice lower than her usual librarian hush.
"Study for fighting the Dark?"

I repressed a grin. "Yeah. Mage stuff."

"I have an old copy. I can't let you take it with you, but
you can use it here. And I can provide you with a notebook
if you need to take notes."

"That would be very nice," I said, at my most polite.

Sennabel bustled into the next room and returned carrying a thin book and a pair of white cotton gloves. "This

volume is well preserved. It was translated with annotations back in the early nineteen hundreds. That's Pre-Apocalyptic times," she lectured me. "It contains Enoch I and the other books of Enoch, along with Greek fragments, but according to scholars, only Enoch I is worth much for seraphic studies." She led me to a table, where she placed the book, gloves, a pen, and a pad. "The other books may be of Byzantine origin.

"Wear these gloves to protect the pages from the oils on your fingers. Make whatever notes you like on the pad, tear off the pages you use, and leave the rest. And I hope you find what you're looking for. If I can help in any way—any way at all—just let me know."

I was surprised at her chattiness almost as much as by her willingness to help. "Thanks."

"And if you get a moment someday," she said, her eyes glistening, one hand at her throat, "we could, maybe, have tea? Or coffee?"

I finally realized that Sennabel had become a certified mage-chaser in the weeks since I was outed. Mage-chasers made good friends, and I was in pretty short supply of friends in Mineral City. "I'd like that," I said.

"Oh. Well," she said, pleased, her hands fluttering. "I'll get back to the children."

"You're good at that," I said, the words coming from nowhere. Sennabel flushed to the roots of her hair, said, "Oh," a few more times, and all but raced away. Smiling, I laid my walking stick across the table near to hand, sat down, and put on the gloves, which were far too large. I understood what an honor Sennabel had bestowed on me. She had left me alone with an ancient Pre-Ap book; not a recent copy, but a book well over a hundred years old. Carefully, I opened it, hearing the crinkle of old paper. I paged through the introduction, and started reading.

Enoch I was apocalyptic in nature, dealing with the end of the world and the judgment of the unrighteous. Typical of scripture, it was flowery and hard to follow in places, but I understood that Enoch was purported to be a man who was righteous and holy before God, living before the time of Noah. Quickly, I found the first mention of Watchers, who were angels who went "to and fro on the face of the earth," watching humans.

In chapter six, I got to the good stuff. "And it came to pass when the children of men had multiplied, that in those days were born unto them beautiful and comely daughters. And the angels, the children of heaven, saw and lusted after them, and said to one another, 'Come, let us choose us wives from among the children of men and beget us children. . . .' And they were in all two hundred, who descended."

There followed the names of Watchers who had come to earth for the purpose of mating with humans. I recognized one of the names associated with Satan, a name heard in newscast video from the Last War. *Azazel*. A cold chill found its way under my clothes. Had the Fallen seraphs chosen their names from this manuscript after they came to earth at the apocalypse, as the EIH insisted? Or were they the true High Host, fulfilling prophecy? Blocking out the children's voices in the front of the library, I read on.

"And they . . . took unto themselves wives, and each chose one for himself. They . . . defiled themselves with them, and taught them charms and enchantments . . . and made them acquainted with plants. And they became pregnant and bore great giants . . . who turned against them and devoured mankind. . . . And began to sin . . . and to devour one another's flesh and drink blood."

It sounded a lot like the minions of Darkness, especially walkers and spawn who drank human blood and ate human flesh, and didn't much care if the victim was dead first. I heard Ciana's voice and a burst of childish laughter as I read on.

"And Azazel taught men to make swords, and knives, and shields, and breastplates, and made known to them the metals and the working of them . . . and the use of antimony . . . and all kinds of costly stones. . . . And there arose much godlessness." Unsettled, I skimmed the next few chapters, seeing other skills the Fallen taught humans, and perceiving parallels that baffled me. Parallels that had as much to do with the history of neomages as with humans.

I found myself sitting back in my uncomfortable wooden

chair, staring up at the ceiling, gloved fingers laced. Ciana, as if to reassure herself that I was still here, peeked around a tall library stack and waved at me. I smiled and waved back. She held up a book and stage-whispered, "Can I check some books out?"

I nodded and her head disappeared. I hadn't made a single note, but now I wrote, "Stone mage, metal mage, earth mage, sun mage, moon mage, sea mage, weather mage, water mage, are all the things the Fallen Watchers taught mankind. Gifts that are now practiced by mages, using creation energies." Was that significant?

My eye was caught by a name in a list of Watchers and the hidden knowledge they taught humans, and the hairs lifted across the back of my neck. "Baraqijal taught astrology." Was he the same Fallen as Baraqyal, the seraph that sired the first kylen after mating with a neomage? Had he been a Watcher? Had he been Fallen?

I read on, discovering that angels in heaven heard the cries of humans who were being tortured, humans begging for help from the cruelties and horrors of living beneath the rule of the Watchers and their immortal descendants. "And Michael, Uriel, Raphael, and Gabriel looked down from heaven," and saw the evil on the earth, the evil perpetrated on humans by the descendants of Watchers and women. The four high-order seraphs, each a prince, took the prayers of humans to the Most High and asked him to judge the Watchers. The Most High was angered at the Watchers and their offspring who were abusing humans. He warned that a flood was coming to wipe evil off the face of the earth. The same flood that Noah survived.

"And again the Lord said to Raphael, 'Bind Azazel hand and foot, and cast him into the darkness: make an opening in the desert . . . and cast him therein. And place upon him rough and jagged rocks, and cover him with darkness, and let him abide there forever. And on the Day of Judgment he shall be cast into the fire. . . . To him ascribe all sin.'"

The Most High continued, as he damned the immortal children the Watchers bred on human women. They had become giants, warriors, and so were condemned to fight among themselves and kill themselves off. They were condemned to live in physical bodies no more than five hundred years, and after physical death they became demons, until the end of time, when the Most High would judge and destroy them.

The Watchers themselves were stripped of many powers and bound to the earth, unable to ascend to the heavens again. In desperation, the Watchers asked a human man, Enoch, to intercede before the Most High. The Lord said no to that plea. And the Most High added that humans would judge the Watchers at the end of time.

The chill that had invaded me deepened by the time I got to the end of the book. I wrapped my battle-cloak across my shoulders and curled my toes in my boots. The story of the Watchers explained a lot about the End of the World: the plagues that had come with the appearance of the seraphs of death, the wars and pestilence, the deaths of over six billion humans. While it didn't explain the appearance of the neomages, it did hint obliquely at us. If I was reading the meaning correctly, the book of Enoch I was the first ancient scripture implying the advent of mortals who could work with forbidden knowledge. Had the Watchers stolen the next creation from the hand of the Most High? Had the mages been expected at some point? My thoughts were blasphemy. Sacrilege.

And Forcas? Was he one of the Fallen Watchers? One of the Watchers who had not repented? Or a demon child of a Watcher?

Forcas had both my blood and Stanhope blood, and blood from Gramma's line. He had a seraph or two and a cherub imprisoned in his lair. And he was making plans to free his boss. *Crack the Stone of Ages.*

I had to learn how to use my visa so I could call for seraphic help before innocent blood was spilled. And I had to learn fast.

Chapter 16

🗡

As I was closing the book, a loose, folded page fell to the floor. It was as brittle as the *Book of Enoch*, though it was thicker, heavier paper, and larger than the book's pages. I opened it, revealing a handsome script penned in ink. I read the words. "Now, the End of Time has come. Watchers fight on both sides of the Holy War, some allied with the Dark, some with the Light. Those allied with the Light search and hope for grace, for forgiveness. Humans are caught between, neither of the Dark, nor of the Light. They alone are able to choose."

It wasn't dated or signed. But when I looked at the note with mage-sight, it glowed softly. Though a mage may not have written the words, sometime, somewhere, a mage had held the note. Had imbued it with power. The *Book of Enoch* showed no such energies. It didn't shine with power at all.

I turned the sheet of paper over and over. Lolo? Had she put the page where I might find it? Was this one more in the long list of her intrigues?

"You ready to go?" a voice whispered. "I have all my research done." I looked up at Ciana, her head again peeking around the stack of books.

"And how many books are you checking out?" I whispered back.

"Seven. Miss Sennabel says they're reprints from Pre-Ap times. And they're really cool. Is that okay?"

"If Sennabel says they're appropriate for your age, sure." I stood, tucking the mage-marked note back in the *Book of Enoch*. Maybe some other mage would need it someday. If the library and the books survived whatever was coming to Mineral City.

On the way out, I tucked the thin volume into the crook of Sennabel's arm, along with the gloves. "Thank you," I said. "If you would like to come by Thorn's Gems at closing, we could have tea or coffee. That is, if you live close enough for me to walk you home after."

"I'll be there," the plump woman said, her face lighting with pleasure. "Tea would be lovely. I'll bring shortbread cookies and some strawberry preserves I put up last summer."

"Great," I said, meaning it, as I followed Ciana out and into the street. Together we walked to Thorn's Gems, where my stepdaughter curled up in a corner to work on her report, and I went to work filling Internet orders. From the nook beneath the stairs, I heard the far-off cry of the lynx. Hunting? A warning for me? What else could go wrong in my life?

False dusk deepened throughout the day as blizzard-strength winds blew in and back out. Disputatious, the storm deviated from the forecast, heading farther south than expected. As blizzards went, this one was a bust for Mineral City, but heavy clouds remained, hiding the surrounding peaks, settling onto housetops, turning the town dim and murky.

As the shop was closing and false night was falling, Sennabel opened the door with a jaunty clanging of the bells overhead and peeked inside. She was dressed in a bright blue cape, a red tunic, and leggings. Her hair had been freshly washed and plaited, coiled into a crown. Hanging prominently around her neck was a necklace of glass beads with a focal stone of pale green agate carved into a turtle. It wasn't expensive, but it had been crafted and sold in the shop. Over her arm she carried a covered basket that smelled of cinnamon, yeast, and honey. Sennabel had clearly left the library hours earlier and gone home to get ready.

Taken together, it was a public affirmation of me. A lump rose in my throat at the extra time and care that had gone into planning for what had been, to me, a nearly insignificant visit. I felt dowdy and callous and ill-prepared. All I had done was make tea on the shop's gas-log heater, though I had gotten out the good china and the silver spoons Audric had dead-mined from his claim, and some starched and ironed linen napkins.

Behind Sennabel came Polly, the elder's wife, equally stylish and well dressed, wearing full skirts and a Thorn's Gems necklace. My mouth fell open. Sennabel seemed delighted at my surprise. "I hope you don't mind," she said. "I brought another—"

The display window beside her shattered. Instinctively, I covered my face, ducking as glass shot in. An explosion sounded outside. Screams echoed, full of terror. Through the open door and empty window the warning sounded. "Spawn! Devil-spawn! To arms!"

With an expression of disbelief, Sennabel touched her face. Blood trickled on one cheek, and she stared at her hand in confusion. Polly fell, bumping the librarian to the side. A spawn gripped her waist, its teeth buried beneath her breast. Mage-fast, I grabbed Sennabel and spun her inside, out of the way. As she was falling to the floor of the shop, cape swirling wide, I pulled the tanto from my right sleeve and raised it over Polly. With three fast cuts, I severed the spawn's head from its body. For an instant, its eyes rolled up and looked at me. In a death spasm, its teeth clamped down tight. Belatedly, Polly screamed. I pushed her inside and grabbed the walking stick from the umbrella stand at the door.

The stench of sulfur filled the shop. A massive dose of battle-lust thumped through my blood. Mage-sight flicked on, and my flesh burned bright. I reached for my amulets but saw spawn attack a man in the street, his body a silhouette on the snow. First, I had to get outside.

"Audric!" I shouted, whipping the blade from the walking stick sheath. I slammed and locked the door to the shop and whirled to the broken window. Four spawn, their naked molelike bodies mottled shades of red and

gray from dove to charcoal, were crawling inside, three-
fingered hands ripping out broken glass to make the hole
bigger. Spawn blood coated the sharp edges, black in the
evening light. Rows of razor teeth snapped, their reddish
bodies writhing. I dropped the sheath and beheaded two,
slicing the arms from another. A dozen more shoved the
dead from the window and wriggled in.

At the top of the stairs I heard Audric's battle cry, "Raziel! By blood and fire!"

The window of the door cracked and shattered. Spawn
crawled through the new opening. Claws scrabbled on the
porch above the door, on my porch. Behind me, Polly's
screams had subsided to a panicked litany, "Get it off get it
off get it off get it off!"

A fleeting look showed her peeling at the spawn's head,
their blood mingling in a gory rush. Jacey and Sennabel
were bent over her. Ciana peeked around the opening beneath the stairs. She had been researching online. I sliced
and cut, taking down half as many as I needed to protect
them. "Ciana. Bring me the marble sphere from beside my
bed!" In a flash she raced around the corner and up the
stairs. Her seraph amulet was blazing at the presence of
the spawn. Dodging her, Audric and Rupert ran from the
stairwell, swords drawn, and scythed into the pack rushing
in.

A horde converged on the broken windows. Time dilated and stretched, my blades spinning in apparent slow-
motion. A smell like rotting roses and stagnant water blew
in, for a single breath overriding the spawn stench of sulfur
and brimstone. Outside, a man fell to one knee in the
street, stabbing a spawn with a long-bladed knife. Another
spawn rushed from behind, sinking its teeth in his neck.
From the side, a second blade dropped, cleaving through
the top of the beast's head to its spine. It fell, shuddering
like an insect. A second twisting sword thrust decapitated
it. Eli stood over the injured man, pouring fluid over him
from a clear bottle. I had a second to wonder what he was
doing. And then spawn were inside.

Audric and Rupert took up positions to my left and
right, Rupert at the door with its broken window, Audric

eight feet from me, standing in front of Jacey and my visitors.

I spun into the swan, the move flashy, used to cut multiple opponents at once. Five spawn fell to the floor. My feet slid in bloody muck, my shoes smoking. I kicked spawn bodies to the side. I wasn't wearing battle boots. The leather of my shoes smoldered, sliding on blood or sticking to the wood floor with each step. The black blood ate through my copper-colored tunic, burning my flesh. I ignored the sting of the acid blood. If I lived, I'd heal.

In the street, something long and multijointed raced past, too fast for sight, leaving the impression of many legs and an armored exoskeleton. Bodies were lying on the snow in the gathering night, dead humans and spawn tossed together.

Ciana shouted, "Thorn. Here." Underhanded, she tossed the sphere. It lifted from her palm, twirling and spinning beneath the lights overhead. I stabbed the tanto into the body of a squirming spawn and reached up, over my head, to catch the sphere.

"Outside," I said to Audric. He leaped over the opening in the window. Rupert sprinted through the broken glass of the door. "Behead the spawn. Then stay put," I shouted to the women, pulling the tanto from a lifeless body. "You too," I said to Ciana.

Two strides took me through the window, landing beside and behind Audric. The snow cooled my heated shoe soles, icy wind cut through my clothes, and my skin rose in chill bumps even as my night vision sharpened. I opened the ward stored in the sphere. Instantly, the entire building came alight. Spawn screamed and plummeted from the wood porch and metal roof, surprising me. I hadn't expected residual power to cross them. "Nice," Audric said as he and Rupert whacked at spawn. "Too bad you can't do the whole town."

"Yeah," I agreed, sucking in deep breaths and stretching, preparing while I could.

South of us, across the street, spawn crawled through broken windows into shops. People screamed. Gunshots exploded with flashes of light. Though spawn are hard to kill with bullets, humans often resort to them, and cordite scented the air. West, to our right and downwind, Thadd and the assey Durbarge stood together in the night, hacking a six-foot-long beast, something that looked part centipede, part wolf. Three women stood to the side, watching, seemingly calm.

Odors of sulfur and brimstone were interspersed with the more repulsive smells of rot and dying flowers, scents reminiscent of incubus, but less harsh, more sour and cloying. Looking fast, I scanned the street upwind and saw a woman knocking on a door. In every particular she was human, but for the smells that gusted on the frozen wind and the fact that she was naked beneath a sheer gown. In mage-sight she looked like a mannequin, her flesh dull. She was glamoured. A man opened the door of the house, light falling on her face.

I knew her. Jane Hilton. The woman who claimed to be Lucas' wife. Opening her clothes, she reached in for the man. He touched her breasts. Fell on her. *Feathers and fire. A succubus.* At another house, a second succubus knocked on the door. It too opened, and inside a man and woman fought; the woman to keep him inside, the man to reach the beast who called to him. She too looked like Jane.

I scanned the three women watching Thadd and Durbarge. They were succubi as well, but were visually different from the Janes. I started in shock as a light fell across them.

They looked like me. *Crack the Stone of Ages,* they looked just like me. Except they were voluptuous, like sex toys made for a man's erotic dreams, and they had no scars.

As I watched, Thadd dispatched the thing he fought, cutting it in half. Spinning, his seraph ring spitting sparks, he attacked the nearest succubus, slicing her across her huge breasts. She squealed and raised her arms in defense, the sound of an animal in pain. Thadd wouldn't confuse us. Not a kylen. But the smell of her blood was a mingling of the familiar. I stood still, the longsword hanging in my hand, trying to parse the scents. A spawn attached itself to my ankle and I flipped the blade, decapitating it. The smells blew away. My mouth felt strange for a moment, a bitter taste coating my tongue.

A shadow from above warned me and I lifted the tanto, the blade meeting a body, catching on bone with a jar I felt to my teeth. Spawn legs went one way, the torso the other. It would have landed on Rupert's shoulders and bitten into his neck before he could respond. None of us were dressed for battle and, like mine, his neck was exposed.

To our right, Eli Walker fought three mole-bodied beasts with a sword and a strange-looking gun. All I could see of the weapon was a two-foot-long, inch-wide barrel with a bag strapped beneath his arm. He beheaded a spawn with the blade, turned, and fired. When he pulled the trigger mechanism and squeezed the bag, a cloud shot out the barrel, ignited by a spark. It was a one-handed flamethrower, but the flames it shot weren't ordinary fire. Spawn liked fire, dancing in rings of it at Dark Feasts. But with this fire they screamed and burst into flame. Above the stench of roasting spawn, I smelled eucalyptus and rosemary, kirk oils used for anointing.

Just beyond Eli, Zeddy fought in front of Jacey's door, bleeding from multiple bites, lit by the ambient light from the window. A horde of spawn tore at him. My weight on one heel, I twisted toward him, an instability in my stance.

Three spawn sprinted demon-fast at me. Lifting the sword to block, I reached for a throwing blade, my fingers tingling. The hilt caught on the sheath strap, altering the downward momentum of my hand. I lost my grip and dropped the throwing knife and the tanto into the snow. Almost in slow motion, they disappeared into a drift.

Panic caught at me. I looked up, repositioning my feet. I still had the sword and slashed at the attacking spawn, taking off a hand and part of a head in a fountain of blood. My face and neck burned where it splattered. My hands, coated with spawn blood, were blistered, but I felt nothing. They were numb. The spawn fell back. I saw Zeddy fall. Spawn swarmed over him. "Zeddy!" My voice sounded thready, my breath uneven.

Trying to pull a second throwing knife, I stumbled, my

feet clumsy. White-hot pain ripped across my thigh. I looked down as a spawn claw, three-fingered and venom-tipped, dug in. Heated blood pulsed through my leggings and sopped the torn fabric. Acid pain burned inward from the wound. The claw jerked back, taking a chunk of my flesh with it.

"Need help?" Eli took the third spawn down with a gout of flame. In two swings he beheaded the ones I had injured, fighting the way he danced, with fluid grace. I pointed at Zeddy, and Eli called to anther man, dim in the night, who sprinted over to Jacey's stepson.

I pulled my last two knives, holding them by the hilts in one hand, the blades opposite one another, one pointing forward, one back. I had dropped the walking stick sheath in the shop, abandoning it for the tanto. Now I swung the makeshift weapon, knowing it was good only for stabbing, as the knives weren't made for cutting. A tip caught on the fabric of my tunic. I sobbed once in frustration.

"Watch my back," Eli said to Rupert. He slid his gun barrel into a loop at his waist and stepped to me. Brusquely, he jerked my blades free of my clothes. With his knife he sliced off the hem of my tunic and bound it around my thigh, pulling on the knot until I gasped with pain.

"I've seen you fight," Eli said, standing watch as I put weight on the leg and repositioned the blades. "What's wrong?"

My leg felt numb. Had I been wearing my dobok, that claw would have been less than a scratch. "*Death and plagues.* I don't know," I said, my mouth tingling. "My hands feel strange."

I looked from my leg into Eli's face and the surprise etched there. I had cursed in the presence of Darkness, a foolish, deadly thing to do. *Too late now,* my brain said, and I looked past him into the shop, my eyes arrested by the sight of the women.

Polly, the elder's wife, and Sennabel, the local librarian, had come to visit me, just like they might any other woman in town—any human woman. They had come for tea. And I hadn't been able to protect them. Tears gathered in my eyes. My hands felt heavy, the blade tips drooping to the ground. One had bitten Polly, and spawn venom was often deadly to humans. I was useless. I hadn't been able to kill the spawn. I hadn't been able to call for seraphic help, because I didn't know how to use the visa. I was *useless*, just like always.

"Thorn. Toss some light amulets around so we can see," Eli said.

I pulled several clear quartz nuggets from loops on my necklace and threw them into the street. My hand seemed to rise and fall in slow motion, as if pulled by a heavier gravity. The amulets cast pools of illumination that brightened splatters of blood, dead spawn, and clusters of fighters. I saw Audric and Rupert back-to-back, fighting spawn, swords slashing. Across the street, Zeddy went down again, landing on the motionless body of the man who had gone to his rescue. I started toward him but stumbled.

A succubus stepped in front of me. She wore my face, her—my—hair plaited in a war-braid. Unlike the other succubi who looked like me, this one was small-breasted and lithe. But for her red-irised eyes, she was an exact duplicate, down to the scars on her cheek. And she was dressed in a dobok.

She raised a sword toward me in the sitting lion and cut across my body. My block was ugly, but it stopped her blade. The jar vibrated up my arm into my spine. I slipped on the crusted ice, landing on one knee. The succubus bent over me, pressing the point of her blade against my neck, her eyes holding mine. A triumphant grin lit her face as she reached for my waist. I felt the heat of her fingers against my side. She was going after the amulets.

Her head wrenched back and she fell across me, drenching me with blood, Audric's sword buried in her chest. A small shock speared me. It was like seeing myself die, a prophecy of my own demise. She landed across me, and I was showered with the sweet scent of mage blood, my blood, tainted with brimstone. A Dark mage glamoured to look like me? Or one created with my blood to look, feel, smell, and react like me? A Dark clone? Dark mist flowed out of her flesh as she slumped to the street.

"What was she supposed to do?" Eli asked. "Take Thorn's place?"

"Not with those eyes," Audric said, twisting his sword back and out of her flesh.

Across the street, I spotted Ciana and screamed. My throat tore on her name. She was stepping over ruts and across dead spawn, walking with a measured, steady gait. She passed a group tearing into a man's body, eating. They didn't look up. Drawing on the bloodstone hilt, I lunged toward her, stopped by a four-foot-long serpentlike thing with hundreds of jointed legs. It hissed and snapped. Before I could react, Eli hit it with flames. I cut its legs off in a two-foot-long swath, my sword dragging through the snow beneath it. The thing tumbled to one side, burning, the stench like rotten meat and butyric acid. I gagged, stumbling away, screaming for Ciana through the gathering smoke.

She was barely perceptible, sitting beside Zeddy. A conjured shield was wrapped over her and the downed man, rendering them nearly invisible. If I hadn't known where to look, and if her pin hadn't blazed like a campfire in mage-sight, I would never have seen them. How had she opened a shield? Humans couldn't manipulate creation energies.

I wiped my mouth, which was bleeding from some injury I hadn't noticed. I looked from my blood to the shop, which still glowed in mage-sight like a beacon. This was twice Ciana had gotten past my ward without burning herself to a crisp. How? Questions for later. I repositioned the knives, feeling clumsy and jittery. Uncoordinated.

"What's wrong with you?" Eli demanded, stomping on a jerking leg and breaking it into small pieces. When I didn't reply, he pulled me around and slapped my face. My head whipped back, the pain a keystone my mind could grasp. My cheek stinging, I met his eyes. His fingers dug into my shoulders and his mouth landed on mine, the kiss hard and searing and tasting of beer. He pulled back, his amber eyes blazing. "Snap out of it, girl."

I nodded and took a breath, searching for my center, placing my feet with care as he released me and triggered the flamethrower, burning a cluster of spawn to crisps. Only minutes since the start of the attack, yet spawn were everywhere, scuttling up and down the street in a well-coordinated attack. Spawn couldn't coordinate their own bodily functions, let alone a battle. I searched for a Darkness directing the fighting. The war-torn street was full of men throwing up barricades in front of homes and elders chanting prayers and hurling plastic bags of water. Thadd and Durbarge fought back-to-back in the night.

From the north, the direction of the Trine, forms darted into the street, human-shaped but demon-quick, carrying blades and guns. "Daywalkers," Eli whispered. "I count nine." Six moved toward Thadd and the succubus he still fought. Durbarge fell to the ground, barely moving. The remaining three walkers came for us, moving slowly, spreading out in a three-pronged attack pattern. "Hold this," Eli said, thrusting a cross into my hand. "And hit 'em with these." He gave me two bulbous plastic bags sloshing with fluid.

"Bags of water?" I asked.

"Wastewater. From the kirk." He laughed, as if that weren't bizarre. "Used baptismal water and purification water is cheaper and more plentiful than water from the Dead Sea. It slows them down, makes them easier to kill." His tone said I should have known that. "Especially vampires," he added.

"Daywalkers aren't vampires," I said, my lips swollen and numb. "Day. Walkers. It . . ." I licked my lips, losing track of my thoughts for a moment. "It sorta defeats that whole 'beings of the night' thing." I must have sounded witty, because Eli laughed.

The three walkers surrounded us, moving like hungry lions, half-crouched. I shook my head and set the bags of water on the snow at my feet, assuming the walking horse stance, the cross held with the weapons in my left hand. My arms were heavy, my grip weak; I was afraid I'd drop them.

The two nearest Eli attacked; he drew knives from his belt and threw. "They're sexless, half-demon things that drink blood," Eli said, drawing breath between strikes. "I'll give you the sunlight part, but try the cross. Holy icons work."

Holy icons? A human was giving me advice about holy icons and fighting Darkness. A *human*. Tears rose at my uselessness and I looked down at the cross, two hunks of wood wrapped with lengths of metal. It had no power, no stones for me to draw on. And I had no soul and no faith to give it power. Watching the walkers tease Eli, I sheathed the two throwing knives and gripped the cross in my scarred fingers, movements clumsy. My hands felt strange, stiff and buzzing. The walker nearest me grinned, showing fangs like slender needles.

Beside me, Eli fired his flamethrower. The daywalker blazed into a fiery dervish even as he turned to the next. It crouched, grin wiped away, fangs flashing, shock on its human-looking face. Eli held up his cross and picked up my two bags of baptismal water; the beast reared back as Eli aimed and tossed. The bags burst on contact and the walker screamed, batting at its body. I was still standing, feet planted in the ice.

"Thorn! Move!" Eli shouted. The world smelled of eucalyptus and rosemary, roasted meat and rotten things. The third walker laughed and darted forward. I stared at my death. Time slowed, dragging at my mind.

My bare hand held the cross, fingers frozen around the base. *Useless.* The word was a gong of power in my head. The cross was a primitive thing, wood and metal. Shouldn't an icon, a thing of power, look sculpted? Be beautiful? *Useless.* It was useless. I was useless.

My hand, and its scars, was a dull, blotchy white on the bare wood. Ugly. Ugly scars.

The walker was roaring, a long raucous note, its mouth ratcheting wide in slow clicks of motion. Beyond it, in a circle of light, a small band of teenagers attacked two spawn. A girl fell, bleeding. Aware I was moving with mage-speed as time dragged around me, I shifted to watch, turning from the walker. In an instant, two others fell, a boy and a girl, trying to pull the first to safety. The others circled around, hacking the spawn with kitchen knives.

Distantly, I was aware of blood, of someone nearby shouting my name. *Useless,* the word gonged again, and something quivered across my skin. *Useless.* I looked at my other hand and it quaked weakly. *Useless,* it whispered to me. *Useless.* Children were dying.

"Thorn?" Eli called, his voice far away. In my peripheral vision, the walker reached for me.

I stared at my hands. *I've been spelled.* My brain struggled with the concept. My hands were coated with some *thing.* I knew how to fix that. Didn't I? Screaming, Eli crashed into the walker, striking with a blade and firing a handgun. The explosion was deafening. I smelled cordite and a wisp of hyssop, rosemary, and salt. Holy water.

Half a block away, four screaming women beat at a spawn that was munching on something small lying in the snow. Almost lazily, it reached up and grabbed a woman's wrist, pulling her down to its open mouth. It bit down on her throat. Two other women raced up, carrying automatic weapons, firing into the spawn's body.

Still holding the cross, I reached beneath my ruined tunic and gripped my prime amulet, the stone ring that incorporated my blood, that had been tied to my genetic structure by master mages at my birth. I drew on it, calling on both primes, the bloodstone hilt of the sword and the prime ring.

Heat from the amulets shot through my frozen hands and up my arms. Electricity zinged through me, arching my back, clearing a small lucid place in my mind. I dragged my gaze from the fighters. I could see the spell on my hands. It was conjured of thin bands, and dull orange energy traced around them like veins, forming gloves made of infirmity.

My brain was too drugged to form an incantation to free them; instead, I drew on the power stored in my amulets and simply directed it against the curse. Nothing fancy. Just raw power. Blue light sizzled across my flesh and deeper, into my bones. As my mind cleared, I noted the intricacy of the incantation that had formed it, a subtle and complex conjure.

Eli shook me, his singed, blood-splattered face inches from mine. "Wake up, woman," he shouted. He'd been burned, and blood trickled down his face from a cut bisecting his left eyebrow. I raised my hand, the cross in my palm resting in his hair, and touched a fingertip to the wound.

Blue energies made a soft hiss against his skin. His face
hard, he pulled me close and kissed me again, his lips sizzling with the same energies. "Son of a seraph," he whispered softly, the curse dangerous. But my mind was
elsewhere.

I remembered the *Book of Enoch* and the gloves I had
worn. Sennabel? No, not Sennabel. And not the gloves. It
would have been too risky; they could have been misplaced, discarded, used by another. Yet, someone had
known I would want that book.

The strange piece of paper inside. Ah. The note. A trap
laid for me, one weakened or delayed by my wearing protective gloves. Maybe triggered by falling night. Had my
touching the *Book of Enoch* this morning initiated this attack on the town?

Mind clearing for the first time in long minutes, I pushed
away from Eli, handing him his cross, his emblem of faith,
useless to the soulless, whom God never hears. Zeddy was
down. Had gone down fighting to protect his family, including his half sister, Cissy, a child of nine. An innocent. I
could have called mage in dire. The criteria had been met
long ago. And if the seraph who answered also decided to
punish guilty humans? That was the catch-22 of mage in
dire. But I didn't have a choice, hadn't had one since the
spawn attacked. Feeling the last of the nebulous spell dissipate, I stepped over dead bodies of daywalkers, gripped
the visa, and called. "Mage in battle, mage in dire, seraphs,
come with holy fire!"

Eli stepped back and looked up.

Overhead, something screamed.

Chapter 17

"Too late, little mage." The words echoed across the buildings. "Too late to change the course of this night."

Eli swore, or perhaps prayed. He lifted his flamethrower and hefted a plastic bag of baptismal water.

I followed his aim up, into the black sky. Above the town hovered a leathern, seared shape, crackling with dark energies, wings outspread, clawed hands reaching wide. Its naked body was muscular and strong, but disfigured, flesh puckered and scarred, wings featherless, the skin between the bones thin and ridged with scar tissue. It was a huge being, power rippling across ruined flesh like black lightning. Yet its face was wholly, flawlessly exquisite, as if carved from a slab of perfect white marble. The face of a seraph, created by the Most High to be entrancing, captivating. Not a Fallen Watcher. Something much worse.

I almost cursed, but swallowed down the words before it could hear and think it was summoned. It was a Major Power, and I knew—I *knew*—it was Forcas. One of the true Fallen. A seraph who had gone his—its—own way. It looked at me, meeting my eyes.

Eli wound up like a pitcher and threw the water. The bag hit Forcas on the arch of its foot, rupturing and splattering. The water sizzled and smoked into vapor. Forcas laughed. Eli fired his flamethrower. A gout of fire rose into the air. Forcas inhaled, drawing the blaze up its body to its face and into its lungs, still laughing. Eli stepped back, rigid with shock.

It swept its wings open. The cloud-smeared sky and distant moon shone through the scorched skin stretching between the wing bones. With a tremendous rush of frozen air, the wings closed and opened. Eli raised a gun, firing a barrage of shots, the bullets filled with holy water. With a negligent wing, Forcas knocked him aside and landed. An amulet hung on a thong around its neck. The spur. Sweat trickled down my spine, prickling like broken feathers.

I raised my sword, a puny weapon in the face of such might. It pointed one long, slender finger at me, holding my eyes. Its irises, in that white, perfect face, were violet, like the velvet of flower petals, but brutal, cold, pitiless. Its voice boomed, "I have you again, body, blood, and spirit."

My damaged side spasmed. The pain spiraled out, smoldering, entwining my torso, piercing through the invisible wound where a talon had speared me twice. But there had been no physical wounds. Psychic injuries only. A taloned hand reached for me.

My legs gave way and I fell, twisting my knee and thigh muscle where the spawn had clawed it. A dead walker broke my fall and I gasped, whispering mage in dire again.

Ciana looked at me from across the street, her eyes looking older through the shield, wiser, and full of grief. Her mouth formed my name. I rolled from the walker to the blood-soaked snow. My side contracted again in unbearable agony. Forcas laughed. "Mine," it said.

The pain exploded. Violent violet pain, the color of Forcas' irises, a ruthless anguish, ripped through me. Lying on the snow, my head lolled down, my face in the frozen mass. Dying. I was dying.

From somewhere, some distant place, lavender eyes watched me, eyes so similar to Forcas', yet darker in hue and full of mercy. *Eyes . . .* I had seen these eyes before, in the face of a cobra, in my dreams, and, once, on the Trine. The eyes of Holy Amethyst's wheels. *Eyes.* Wheels within wheels, covered with eyes. Like the Mistress herself. Eyes. The eyes of El Roi, *the god that sees me.* I knew it, but I didn't understand, didn't know where the knowledge of the name came from.

I heard the wheels softly singing, like bells and wind instruments, and the bellowed breath of a distant galaxy. "We cannot come. We cannot. We are not yet healed. Are caught in *time*. Sooo sooorry . . ."

Taloned hands wrapped around my waist and lifted me. The agony, which couldn't grow more, penetrated deeper, a torture so great my breath froze solid in my lungs. Forcas pulled me close to his face, his strong white teeth bared in a grin.

A fireball landed on the snow with a spit of sound. Eli's flamethrower? Shooting at us? Two other blazes, brilliant white, round balls of lightning moving in unison, touched down on Forcas' hands. The Darkness roared and wrenched away. My body flipped in the air, my hair a spiral around me. I landed again on the snow, face to the sky, and air *whoosh*ed out of me in a pained grunt. Fire was dancing all around me, coiling, curling balls of energy, gusting blue smoke, seven globes the size of conch shells, moving and whirling in concert.

One landed on my face and I flinched, but there was no pain. Closing my eyes against the brightness, I managed a breath, cold air blistering my lungs, the movement of air fluttering the flame. It landed on my scarred hand, settling like a bird at its nest. I opened my eyes and watched as six others chased Forcas into the sky. Ridiculous sight. Tiny, spherical flames chasing the oversized Darkness.

Forcas cursed the Most High, a curse so foul it shivered the air. The spheres divided into groups of three to Forcas' left and right, arranged themselves into arrow formations, and attacked. Darting beneath its wings, they pierced Forcas' sides. I blinked my eyes against the flare of colliding energies, brilliant plasma streaking the night. Minions of the Light.

Relief swept through me, so intense I sobbed. The Flame on my hand wavered with the sound and darted up to perch on my mouth. Suddenly I could breathe, could think. The fireball, a searing orb of light, seemed to wink at me, and danced away, taking my pain with it, leaving something else in its place, some other emotion. One so improper for a battle that it took a moment for me to identify it as it bubbled up in me. A blossoming euphoria. The blaze jetted away, joining its brothers as they harried Forcas, who hovered in the air above me, wings beating.

I was sure they were Flames. More correctly, Minor Flames. Though I had never seen them, I had heard of the self-sustaining, intelligent creatures. Spirit and energy, they were thought to be composed of plasma and were members of the High Host, part of the Seraphic Council. They were warriors, holy beings not capable of transmogrification, beings who always looked like fire. Historically, they followed seraphs at the call of battle dire.

High above the town, Forcas pulled its sword, demon-iron sweeping up, a shivering cold like black light dancing off the blade. The Flames whipped in and out, slicing and burning where they touched, then darting away before the Power could react. Forcas bellowed and I covered my ears at the sound, a low-pitched roar of fury and pain. Harried by Flames, Forcas ducked and wove, swatting with its blade. Its blood, blacker than the night sky, splattered to the snow with spits of steam.

At Forcas' head, light appeared, blinding, wrenching, taking away the night. In its midst was a seraph. He had heard my call. I sobbed, sucking in air, lying on the snow in the blood of daywalkers at the feet of a Major Darkness, staring at the battle in the heavens.

The teal-feathered seraph in scintillating battle armor threw power from one bare hand. Bolts of white light stabbed at Forcas. Only inches from its body, they spread into crackling pools that skimmed away, moving in smooth arcs, bouncing off its shield. From Forcas' sword, blackish-purple light burst outward. The seraph vanished and reemerged, as if flashing out of and into reality. The black-light power slid past him. The seraph drew his shield, a glistening disc that bent light like abalone shell. Their wings beat the air.

I rose up on my elbows as energies shivered above me. The hair on my arms and head lifted, electrified. The seraph, dusky-skinned, with curling, smoke-colored hair and a widow's peak, drew his sword in a steel-on-steel swish, a harsh sound like pulsing blood and slicing pain and death. The blue steel, silvered and gilded with light, raised up, trapping Forcas between the Minor Flames, the earth, and escape.

The seraph screamed his name, the word echoing off the distant hills like thunder, like massive brass bells. "Cheriour! Cheriour! To me!" At the words, the Flames darted in, formed three groups, and attacked Forcas' eyes. The Power screamed, a desperate sound, and whirled in place, scattering the Flames. Two were slammed to the earth and lay on the snow, pulsing slowly. Wounded.

Cheriour's wings rose, tips touching, far over his head. His scent flowed into the street, lemon mint and sage, spicy and cool. My body clenched in reaction, my eyes fastened to him. The down beneath his wings was pale, shading to black at the tips. His armour shimmered, an aurora borealis of might. Bombarded by the remaining Flames, Forcas curled its body in an impossible coil and shot up, high into the sky.

The seraph raked his teal-irised eyes over me where I lay. A golden disc rested on the center of his chest, a sigil, a seal of office in glowing amber. In a burst of thundering light, Cheriour followed Forcas into the sky.

I blinked at the explosion and curled into a tight ball. I knew this seraph. In the lexicon of seraphs he was known as a "terrible angel," a seraph charged with the pursuit and retribution of criminals, his sigil protecting him from mage-heat. He was the Angel of Punishment who had judged me, and allowed me to stay in Mineral City. Though I hadn't known his name, I remembered his power flowing over me like a cloud, intimate as a lover. I had survived his touch, but when such a seraph draws his sword, humans die. Always.

Up and down the street, the sounds of battle penetrated: shouts, screaming, the crack of gunfire. I unwound from the snow and struggled to my feet. Scant moments had passed in the battle between the Light and the Dark. Around me, the more mundane battle between humans and Minor Darkness continued, humans and spawn and daywalkers in clusters, fighting in the light of my tossed amulets, or lying on the snow, still with death.

No humans had fallen at the appearance of Cheriour. Not yet. But from where I stood, I could see a man and a succubus coupling on the snow. Cries of pleasure and passion mingled with cries of pain. Similar sounds came from open doors up and down the street. If the seraph returned, if his sword was still drawn, there would be a slaughter. I looked for Eli and spotted him with a group of elders fighting two walkers, standing over the bodies of another elder and a succubus, dead. Had they killed both, executing kirk judgment?

I had to destroy the succubi before Cheriour returned. Disregarding the hurt in my side and chest wall with each breath, I chose a group of fighters who needed help. Bending, I picked up my sword and two throwing knives, and cleaned them on the snow before positioning them in their sheaths. The cross, half buried in a rut, went into my waistband on my left, near the wound that wasn't, the wood icy and soothing against my skin.

When I tried to stand upright, pain erupted from my side. I caught myself with an arm around my waist and fought for breath that wedged in my lungs, an inferno of torture. I held myself, pressing the cross against me, and finally found air, a sweet agony of frigid oxygen. *Sword of Michael,* I thought, more prayer than curse.

As I inhaled, I smelled vanilla spiced heavily with ginger, and knew Thadd was near. A Minor Flame swooped close and halted as if inspecting me. I was pretty sure it was the one from before, though I couldn't have said why. It landed on my hand again. Seemingly satisfied, it soared away, leaving me blinking, my night vision lost, my pain undiminished.

"Are you hurt?" Thadd asked from behind me.

"I don't know," I managed, looking around. The battles had moved on for the moment, most taking place in the wash of illumination from my amulets. I tried a breath and agony shot through me like a red-hot spear. I gasped. "Maybe. But I don't think it's a physical injury. It's something that happened first in a vision and then when I was

fighting a daywalker. And again just now." Three times injured in the same place. Was that significant, even if Forcas
hadn't touched me with the spur this time?

"You want to explain?"

Bent over, I tottered to a set of narrow steps leading
from the street to a store and sat, leaning back against the
small porch, stretching my spine as much as I could. My
feet burned with cold through the thin indoor soles and I
flexed my toes to restore circulation.

The cop followed and settled beside me, a gun dangling
from each hand, exhausted, watching for attackers. As my
breathing returned to normal, I told him about being
trapped below the Trine, and of the spur that pierced my
side. I told him about the daywalker. And because the
fighting had passed us by for the moment, I told him
about the poisoning and my hands. He listened without
comment.

"Dragonet," he said when I finished. At my expression,
he explained, "That's my guess. Dragonets have been reported in the nearby mountains." He jutted his chin at a
bloody pile of chitinous body parts. "Like that one. It's why
I'm still in Mineral City. Dragonets have spurs." He
glanced at me once and then away. His scent was changing,
the smell of honey growing, the smell of ginger fading. His
heat was overtaking the fight-or-flight of battle. "Seraph
blood can heal psychic wounds," he said diffidently.

"Yeah, well, when he comes back, after he finishes killing
off half the town, maybe he'll fix me up good as new."

Thadd laughed softly at the bitterness in my tone. "Good
point."

Something crashed in the center of the street. Faster
than the detritus that blasted out from the impact site,
Thadd rolled over me and pulled me beneath the porch.
We huddled in the narrow crawlway, his body over mine,
his arms supporting his weight to keep from crushing my
thinner, more brittle bones. A spray of acid followed the
explosion, the heated mist boiling the snow, polluting the
air with brimstone and sulfur. Things, sizzling and hot, fell
from the sky, hitting the buildings like thunder. Fighters
screamed, both human and Dark.

Thadd grunted and lifted a hand. Blood smeared his palm. Shrapnel had cut him. His scent grew in the small space, and my amulets glowed, fighting the heat his blood and body were stimulating. My arm snaked around his waist, my eyes on his hand. I wanted to lick the blood. Another explosion sounded in the street, the vibration of the blow shuddering through the earth. I slid a hand inside his coat and found the warmth of his chest through his shirt.

Thadd laughed softly and lifted my torn tunic. He pushed the cross to the side and placed his wounded hand on the bare flesh of my side. Instantly, as with the touch of the Flame on my mouth, my pain subsided, but this was a deeper ease, a profound relief. He stroked along my side, his blood smearing my skin. His lips found mine, filling me with the taste of vanilla and honey and brown sugar. I cupped his head and pulled him closer, sighing into his mouth. His hand pressed hard over my side, kneading the muscles, his seraph ring heating on my skin.

I pushed aside his coat and shirts, stroking along the valley of his lower spine. Heat gathered between us, a throbbing of blood that settled deep in the pit of my abdomen and high in my breasts.

Thadd's body slipped between my thighs and settled at the center of me, thrusting with a gentle pressure. I sighed into his mouth and his tongue swirled against mine. I pulled him closer, wanting the weight of his body, moving my hands up his back. I touched softness. Feathers. Thaddeus had feathers where before were simply raised ridges. Wings had sprouted on either side of his spine.

My fingers moved into them, stroking. His scent grew. He moaned against my lips and moved a hand up, cupping my breast. I traced his wings, the humeri longer than my hands, the bones lighter than air. The primary feathers were nearly fourteen inches long. They quivered beneath my palms. A thought insinuated itself into my mind. He would soon be unable to hide the fact of his part-seraphic heritage. I bit down on his lip, sucking it inside my mouth. He groaned and I thrust up at him, grinding, wanting him closer.

"What manner of Darkness are you?" The words belled through the night. Thaddeus pulled away, gasping. I groaned in want, my fingers sliding from his feathers. The sound of combat intruded, the clash of sword and the crash of energies. I smelled ozone and sulfur and blood. My heat began to ebb. Sense returned. Crawling on our elbows, we scuttled to the edge of the porch.

Hovering above the street, his wings beating powerfully, Cheriour fought swarming fiends, beasts leaping up to the seraph from the street, ten feet into the air. Dragonets.

Each was unique. One was shaped like a centipede with a wolf's head, a pair of human hands, and barbed hooks at every joint. One was a striped serpent, its mouth open like a striking rattler, but it was furred in shades of orange and black. Its tail was hooked, a poisonous barb like a scorpion. Another was scarlet, with tendrils like kelp dragging along the earth. They had dozens of sets of leathery bat wings, each spanning a foot, and with them spread, they could jump from the earth as if they had springs. I was pretty sure I had seen them before, in the vision while I was trapped underground, when I was first speared in the side.

They moved with the quickness of demons, so fast that I wasn't certain of their number. Maybe ten. Yet they smelled unlike any demon in the texts or histories. There was little sulfur, ichor, or acid; rather, they smelled like Lucas. They smelled like Stanhopes. The seraph hesitated, his defense slowed by the vow to protect the blood of Mole Man.

As we watched, the scents of heat and blood and seraphs and Stanhopes mingling in my nostrils, the furred scorpion's stinger whipped up and under Cheriour's shield. The seraph bellowed with pain and fury, bringing his sword down on the beast, the blade flashing with reflected light. The furred serpent was cleaved in two, the halves rolling into ruts in the street, thrashing as if in pain. But still alive, even after the touch of seraph-steel. The wounds sealed over with gelatinous caps the shade and texture of clotted blood.

"That's not good," Thadd said, pulling a semiautomatic from a thigh holster.

The two halves pulsed, palpitations that ebbed and flowed beneath fur. Faster than I thought possible, a rounded bone protruded from the neck opening: the top of a skull. As one half grew a head, the other grew hind legs. Wings sprouted on both. The new beasts were smaller than the original, but the transformations were fast, energy for the metamorphoses sucked from the air and snow, leaving hot air currents blowing into the street and the snow evaporating. There had been dragonets in the Last War, but none since; none in so long that they had fallen into the category of legend. And none quite like these.

Resting on his elbows, his head bumping against the porch overhead, Thadd pulled back a sliding mechanism on the top of his gun and checked the chamber. A brass cartridge gleamed inside. A sterling silver tip protruded from it, shining in my returning night vision.

"Holy water?" I asked. Holy water was imported from the Dead Sea at dreadful cost, but it was known to be deadly against Darkness. If one had enough of it—and there was never enough.

"Yeah. A drop in the tip. It's designed to shatter just after impact, depositing water-coated shrapnel." The chamber closed with a metallic click as I gathered my bloody sword to me and pulled a throwing knife, missing the tanto. "How's your side?" Thadd asked.

I paused, surprised. I was out of pain, my mind clear. I wasn't cold, though I was dangerously underdressed for the temperatures. I met his eyes and said, "What did you do?"

"Seraph blood can heal psychic wounds as well as physical ones," he said, shrugging. "I smeared some of my blood on you. I figured kylen blood might work too. You ready?"

Out in the street, Cheriour screamed a battle cry, the note painful to my ears. I smelled seraph blood, a lot of it, and knew he had been wounded badly. "Yeah. Go."

As if we had rehearsed the move, we rolled from the protection of the porch and to our feet. We were running before anything saw us, attacking the two winged halves. Thadd shot one. I sliced into the other with a double Zorro move, cutting off its legs, wings, and tail. As I cut, it spit at me, the saliva spurting into the snow, melting it with a hot hiss. As battle-lust claimed me, I called out, "Jehovah sabaoth!" Blood erupted as I removed its new head and hacked its torso in two. I jumped back and its pieces coiled into tight balls, pumping blood. Finally, its death throes stopped and it lay still.

Thadd shot again, his beast still moving. "These things don't kill easy."

I spun a throwing knife at him. It landed beside his foot, sliding along his boot sole, and Thadd's eyes went large. "Use that," I said. "Mine's dead. Cut them enough and they bleed out."

From 2 Samuel, I quoted a stone mage's battle mantra as I picked another dragonet and cut into its tail, my arm moving with the tempo of my voice, "God, my rock"—cut and cut—"in Him will I take refuge." Cut and cut and cut. The beast was a scaled, catlike thing with four-inch fangs. It whirled, its back feet and most of the tissue from one hip gone in a bloody heap. It snarled, spitting venom, and sprang at me, raking the air with razor claws. "My shield, and the horn of my salvation." Three cuts.

Choosing a move based on its form, I ducked beneath its lunge and stabbed up in the sleeping cat move, into its tender underbelly. Its momentum carried the killing stroke deeper, eviscerating it. The jar of its landing traveled up my shoulder into my spine. Its entrails splatted on the ground and uncoiled in a messy heap. I beheaded the beast with a single strike. Settling into the rhythm of fighting, I hacked it into pieces. "My high tower, and my refuge; My savior, thou savest me from violence." At my feet a second dragonet bled out, mewling like a kitten as it died. It was in dozens of pieces. "Four down, five more to go." The assault of Darkness was in a group of nine. Most of them were concentrating on the seraph overhead. Easy pickings for us.

From across the street, Eli and a ragtag cluster of humans raced from a pile of dead spawn and daywalkers toward the seraph. I picked out another dragonet. Thadd shouted advice to the approaching humans on how to kill the beasts. The group spread out and circled an eight-foot-long wasplike thing with demi-wings and knifelike claws. I shouted scripture and attacked another beast. A trio of Flames darted in and pierced its flesh to either side of my sword. They disappeared inside. The beast howled with pain.

Above me, Cheriour tilted his body at an impossible angle, his feet to the sky, head toward the earth, arms reaching down. Like me, he was chanting scripture, a single line over and over. "And behold, a pale horse." It was a quote from Revelation, and as war cries went, it seemed pretty pallid, but I wasn't complaining. His sword no longer simply cut the dragonets in two. Now he was slicing and dicing, leaving them in numerous pieces, none large enough to regenerate. And then I remembered the full scriptural quote. "And behold, a pale horse, and he that sat upon him, his name was Death." Cheriour was calling upon one of the four horses of the apocalypse. I shivered. It was warfare most extreme.

I dispatched my target and whirled, seeking another, searching up and down the street. Groups of humans were killing succubi, stabbing the woman shapes while they screamed, entreating mercy, or bared their breasts, offering sex. Beside me, humans finished off their dragonet prey. Thadd, reeking of ginger, stood over the unmoving bodies of two others.

I sucked in a breath that sounded like a bellows and lowered my blades. The muscles in my arms were stiff, my fingers frozen in place on the hilts. I hurt in a dozen new places. I was burned, bitten, and had sustained a glancing blow from a fast-moving stinger. But I was alive. Euphoria shot through me and I raised my head, howling in exultation. All the Darkness were dead. The town was saved.

Cheriour landed beside me in the street, his primary flight feathers brushing the snow as he closed them with a whoosh like storm wind. I turned to him, grinning with victory. And saw his sword. It was still drawn, raised over his head. Beside me, a man fell to his knees, then face-first onto the frozen, crusted snow.

Chapter 18

D own the street, a fighter fell. In the shadows, the man who had been consorting with a succubus lay still, blood flowing from his mouth and nose.

"Stop," I said, horrified. "Stop." I stepped to the seraph, instinctively raising my sword.

I heard a woman scream from an open doorway, a wail of grief. A child called for its father. They were dying. The Sword of Punishment had been raised against the town.

Cheriour looked down at me, and at my raised sword. His victorious face transformed, the light of battle in his eyes dying. When he spoke, his voice was touched with sorrow. "You would wage war against the High Host, little mage?"

My joy and battle-lust leached away, leaving horror in their place, knowing it was hopeless. Even if I attacked him, he would win. And even more would die for my insolence. Slowly, my sword arm fell. "No." Fighting was worthless now. No one, no mage working alone, could defeat a seraph. Perhaps with an army . . . but I didn't have an army. Rebellion and fear warred inside me, my fists gripping so hard on my weapons that they ached.

I didn't want to do this. I didn't want to beg.

Forcing my hands to unclench, I dropped the sword and knife to the snow at my feet. Hearing the cries of the dying, feeling the weight of them in my deepest heart, I crumpled to my knees. From the Psalms, the book humans and mages called upon during war, plague, and punishment, I pleaded, "O Jehovah, have mercy upon me. Heal my soul; For I have sinned against thee."

Cheriour answered, voice like a gong, and I recognized Deuteronomy. "When the LORD thy God shall deliver them up before thee, and thou shalt smite them; then thou shalt utterly destroy them," he belled. "Thou shalt make no covenant with them, nor show mercy unto them."

Thadd knelt beside me and quoted, the lines also from Psalms, "Have mercy upon me, O Jehovah, for I am in distress. Have mercy upon me; For I am desolate and afflicted."

Cheriour looked at him as if seeing the cop for the first time. His teal eyes widened, and his nostrils flared. After a moment, he said, "I will be gracious to whom I will be gracious, and will show mercy on whom I will show mercy."

More scripture. Was that a good thing? I bowed my head.

A kirk elder, the hem of his brown robes splashed with gore, stepped close. Others clad in black moved and fell to their knees near him. When he spoke, I recognized Culpepper's voice, quoting, bouncing around in Psalms, "Hear, O Jehovah, and have mercy upon me. Mercy and truth are met together."

The others near him began to pray. I heard the words in an overlay of litany. "O turn unto me, and have mercy upon me." "Give thy strength unto thy servant." "Save the son of thy handmaid." Culpepper knelt in the snow beside me, unexpectedly close. In my peripheral vision, I saw more townspeople falling to their knees. Beyond them, bodies dropped in the street, lifeless.

"Please. You can't kill them." Ciana's voice jolted through me. I raised my head. Cheriour whipped his sword down. It sought her chin, the point touching the tender flesh of her throat. I froze, one hand lifted.

"You reek of Mole Man's blood," Cheriour murmured, his tone a minor chord of uncertainty. "As did the beasts."

"They stole the blood of Mole Man's progeny," Lucas' voice called from the shadows, growing clearer as he neared. "They held me prisoner. Raziel, second to Michael the Archangel, the revealer of the rock, he rescued me. But

not before they took my blood. Not before they used it to
make new dragonets that smell like Mole Man's blood,
and that heal from mortal wounds."

"Is this possible? That the Darkness has made a new
thing?" Cheriour whispered, his words the rustling of hollow reeds in a summer wind. "Darkness has made no new
thing since it created sin."

"The evil smells like both Mole Man's blood and Darkness. The creatures you fought in the sky are old things
conjured with my blood and with the blood of Darkness
and with the blood of seraphs. Ciana, come here."

Ciana stepped back from the seraph's sword, blue eyes
staring in her pale face. Raziel's pin blazed like a torch on
her chest, casting light to the snow.

"The human speaks truth," Audric said. "I am bound to
Raziel—"

"Audric, don't!" Rupert shouted from the darkness.

"I have to. For the town. I am his for beck and call," Audric said, voice so low it scarcely breathed into the air, "my
blood and bone and sinew." The ancient words of binding
a half-breed to a seraph. Cheriour hesitated, the point of
his sword arcing down to point at the ground.

Culpepper stared at Audric, his eyes cunning. My heart
clenched tightly. Audric had given himself away.

"For Mole Man," Ciana said, staring up into the seraph's
face.

Lucas said, "Show mercy to the town he died for."

The seraph looked out over the growing crowd, their
shuffling feet and labored breath loud in the night. "You
wish this, little human child, progeny of Mole Man?"

"Yes. Please." She folded her hands together, her dark
hair loose and curling around her waist. If her dress hadn't
been saturated with Zeddy's blood, and if blood hadn't
dried in the ridges of her hands, the pose would have made
a lovely picture. But her eyes and face no longer held the
innocence of a child. They carried the weight and knowledge of war and death in them. She had seen too much in
the past hour.

Cheriour looked from Ciana to me to Audric. Lastly, his
gaze fell on Elder Culpepper. The older man raised his

hands and clasped them together in a sign of piety and entreaty. A cold wind blew along the street, whistling through the buildings, a high-pitched paean over the whispered scripture. I shivered hard, clamping my teeth together to stop their chattering. Cheriour breathed the wind deeply into his lungs. The snow beneath his feet melted in a sudden rush, leaving him standing on ancient, cracked asphalt in a shin-deep puddle. A teal-colored mist seeped from the surface of his skin, glowing with a faint light. He inhaled again. The water at his feet steamed.

As if he had forgotten us, the seraph stepped up onto the snow and walked down the street, snow melting with each footfall. His sword dropped, as if forgotten. Thadd looked at me, a question in his eyes. "I don't know," I said.

Cheriour stopped at the body of a man and a succubus, their blood mingled in a frozen crimson pool. With the point of his sword, he nudged the Darkness. Her full breasts were bared, and moved with languid enticement. Standing alone, he bent over them, breathing deeply. He was sniffing the succubus. Snow melted beneath him.

His wings shifted, the feathers rustling. Slowly, they rose, long flight feathers brushing the street. The pale down beneath was caught in the glow of an amulet, one of the ones I had thrown early in the battle. The nevus, the major vessels feeding the wing structure, were glowing. As I watched, they brightened, the blood superheated as if for flight, his pulse rapid and uneven.

At his groin, the flesh brightened between the seams of his battle armor, pulsing in time with his heart. His scent filled the street, carried on the cold air. The first time we met, when he judged me. Battle-lust and his sigil had protected us from mage-heat. Even now, he hadn't gone into heat at the presence of a mage, the golden disc of his sigil protecting him from me.

But he was going into heat at the presence of a succubus.

The light on his face, his neck, beneath his wings, glowing from the joints in his armor, blasted out. I turned away. But not before I saw the expression on his face. Lust. Hot and demanding. Cruel.

At the sight, my own lust rose, a throb of need low in my

belly and high in my breasts. I covered my face, hunger beating in time with my blood. Cheriour turned to me.

"The next great war begins. A mage is in place," he said, his voice like low brass bells and wind instruments, again playing in minor chords, mournful and stricken. "A harbinger she is, and a guardian." He strode to me, the packed ice melting in his path and running across the snow, water mixed with blood. His wings closed and opened, his scent caught in the wind they made—the smell of sex. My knees went weak.

"The beast came for Thorn," Lucas said from beside me, his voice rigid with anger and fear. "It said, 'I have you again, body, blood, and spirit.' Did Forcas have her once?"

I took Lucas' arm to keep me upright, desire purling through me. His question rode above the need, and I said, "I was taken by a Darkness when I was a child—"

The seraph raised his sword, point down, and slid it into the sheath. Seraph-steel rasped like the dying breath of an army as it slid home, echoing up and down the street, cutting off my words.

His wings lifted and swept down, and he leaped, his body shooting for the sky. The downdraft threw me to the ground, wrenching my grip from Lucas. And he was gone, questions unanswered. The mage-heat that had been building fell away like a wave splashing on the beach, sliding back out to sea, leaving only a trace of want in its wake.

Snowflakes drifted down, a silent dance of lacy ice. They settled on my exposed skin and melted, pinpricks of pain. A hush settled on the town. No one moved for a long moment, every face turned to the clouds. Ciana slipped her small hand into mine and I gripped it hard, feeling awe and wonder at the presence of a seraph.

"That's really cool," Ciana said, and I agreed.

"Take her," Culpepper said, his tone commanding.

Before I could react, a crowd of men surged in. With a soft click, a shield opened over us, Ciana and me in the center. I hadn't opened it. I hadn't even reacted. I looked down at my stepdaughter. "How—?" Her hand was on the seraph pin gifted to her by Raziel. Obviously, a seraphic shield of protection was contained in the pin. Somehow,

Ciana knew how to open the conjure, when even mages couldn't use seraph energies.

Beyond the shield, a group of elders stood. Ringing them were blood-soaked townspeople, all dressed in black; the orthodox, watching us. My shields were created to hide me from sight. Not so with this one. The dense crowd surged together, several deep, only yards away. Weapons that had recently been buried in the dying bodies of spawn were lifted in tight fists. The power of the shield burned into the snow, showing a clear line where its protection began. The throng circled around us.

"You cannot hide, mage," Culpepper called. "You brought the Darkness here." The crowd murmured agreement, faces hostile and bitter, fists clenched. "You called the Darkness to you with your wanton ways," Culpepper said. "The evil of sexual sin came at your behest and now good men are dead because of your siren's call."

Between the shield wall and the black-clad townspeople, raced a narrow ring of my supporters, weapons drawn. Thadd, Lucas, Eli, and Audric. Rupert and Jacey, her young daughter Cissy, three of her sons, and Big Zed, Jacey's husband. Sliding around the shield wall from behind came old Miz Essie, Sennabel, and Polly. The elder's wife walked with a limp, her dress stained with blood. Her face was flushed and sweaty from the spawn poison coursing through her body. I gripped Ciana's hand and blinked back tears at the unanticipated presence of friends.

"Get away," Culpepper demanded, his fists clenched. "You cannot defend a whore."

"The seraph didn't call her a whore. He called her a harbinger and a guardian. A guardian of this town," Miz Essie said, her old voice crackling.

"I reckon that's so. Heard it with my own ears," Shamus Waldroup said, edging along the front of the shield, followed by his wife Do'rise. Polly's husband, Elder Jasper, stepped through the crowd, pushing aside the orthodox, and took his wife's hand, feet planted in a runnel of bloody water.

"Look at her, stealing a child away from its mother, kidnapping her beneath the vile shelter of mage-power," a woman shouted.

I didn't answer. Marla didn't come forward to add her complaints to the elder's. I had no idea where Ciana's mother was, but it was likely under the sheets with her latest fancy. And the fact that the town thought the shield was one I had made was protection Ciana might need. So far, no one had ever noticed the pin Raziel had given her, and that was a very good thing.

"Whore," another woman shouted from the edge of the mob. She lobbed a stone; it hit the shield and bounced away with a spark of light the humans could see.

"Why do you defend a mage-slut? Would you fools die for the likes of her?" a man near the front called out.

"Would you murder your friends to get her?" Elder Jasper asked. The man he rebuked frowned and looked at the bloody weapon in his hand. He hefted it and dropped it into his palm as if considering his answer.

Three men in rags, their feet swaddled in strips of leather and old tires, brands on their cheeks, moved next to the elder. Members of the EIH. They carried bloody weapons, clearly part of the town's defense. *Tears of the seraph,* what were they doing? Another elder, his face set in hard lines, slid in, trailed by two black-clad women, Mrs. Abernathy and Florence Watkins. They had been among those who judged me before my trial and found me wanting. They stood with me now, facing their neighbors, the other orthodox. My tears fell in earnest, trickling slowly through the dried blood and gore on my cheeks, burning the injured skin.

A phalanx of miners carrying bloodied picks and shovels, guns at their waists a clear threat, entered from the west. I recognized several of them as men we had bought from over the years. Another group of miners looped around from the east. All were dressed in jeans, plaid shirts, jackets in browns and yellows, colors often worn by members of the reformed movement. At their head was Ken Schmidt, the miner who had a crush on me.

A Jewish family joined my supporters, grown sons carrying bulky automatic weapons in both hands, heads topped by black yarmulkes. The women wore olive green, and handled similar weapons with a surprising confidence.

Pushing their way through the crowd, ten men in braids
and jeans, carrying both traditional stone axes and hunting
rifles, joined the supporters. They moved close to the shield
wall, standing equidistant from one another, facing out.
Cherokee.

The numbers standing for me were growing, but so was
the opposition. Rumbling and name-calling began, calls of
slut-lover and mage-lover used interchangeably. Someone
in the back cried out that I should be burned at the stake.
Some of my supporters racked their weapons at that one.
Another quoted scripture, calling for my death.

We were facing civil war, the orthodox against the rest of
the town's religious groups. Fighting among humans in the
name of the Most High was a sure means to draw an angry
seraph back, especially an Angel of Punishment. I didn't
know what to do. At my side, I could hear Ciana whispering. It sounded like prayer, and her pin burned brighter.

A small man shoved his way between the two groups,
limping. He was bathed in blood, and his skin, showing
through cracked and drying ooze, was blistered and
burned. One foot was mutilated, boot half torn off, exposing mangled toes. Beside him was a television camera,
perched on the shoulder of a woman. Durbarge, his face
below the eye patch pale and drawn in pain, glanced at
me, his eye full of angry promise, meeting mine between
the shoulders of my supporters. He turned to the crowd
before I could interpret his expression, his arms raised.
The camera scanned the mob, panning until it focused on
Durbarge.

"Townspeople of Mineral City," Durbarge shouted.
"You know me. I'm an investigator with the Administration of the ArchSeraph, entrusted to protect sentient beings and to prevent religious violence. This mage is legally
licensed, free to live among humans with the permission of
the AAS and the High Host of the Seraphim. Any violence
against her will be construed as violence against the seraphs of the Most High. There will be no more blood
spilled. Go home. Prepare to bury your dead."

At that, the camera swiveled smoothly until it captured
my face. I must have reacted, because Ciana squeezed my

hand reassuringly. It was the reporter who had tried to get an interview with me, her coat splashed with blood, her shoes sticky with it.

"Thorn St. Croix brought succubi into this town," Culpepper shouted, his face red, a vein throbbing in his temple. "She brought those . . . things." He pointed at the dead and mangled body of a dragonet. The reporter moved for a better shot of the townspeople and the angry elder. "Before she came, Mineral City was a peaceful town. She brought us discord. She brought us lust. She brought us evil and death!" he screeched.

Suddenly, fireballs danced above Ciana's shield, leaving trails of phosphorescent blue and green, their brilliance blinding. They swooped at the crowd, flying into the mass of orthodox, scattering them, then back, to hover directly over me. The support of the Minor Flames was clear. I counted five, and remembered the two who slammed to the earth early in the battle. I hadn't seen them since they fell.

The reporter's face was smoothed in professional lines, her mouth unemotional, but her eyes were full of fear. If civil war broke loose and the seraph returned, she would die, along with the combatants. "This is SNN reporter Romona Benson," she said into the sudden quiet. "We are here in Mineral City, covering the events surrounding the appearance of winged beasts called dragonets, and the seraph who answered a call of mage in dire."

In front of the shield, Durbarge put a hand out, grasping at air. Slowly, he toppled, hitting the snow, his face whiter than the crust he landed on. Thadd, lurching to catch him, followed him down and placed two fingers on the assey's throat. Mouth tight, he rolled Durbarge to his back, white face to the sky, and hit the assey hard, one fist slamming to his chest. He checked the pulse again and slid one hand beneath his head, the position opening Durbarge's mouth. He breathed in and the assey's chest expanded. I had never seen CPR done in person, but I had seen the method demonstrated on SNN. Durbarge was dead.

Chapter 19

✦

"**D**rop the shield," I said to Ciana. Without demur, she touched the pin on her chest. The energies fell to the snow with an unfamiliar crackle of power, a backlash of electricity that stung the skin on my legs. Pushing the reporter aside, ignoring her incessant questions, I knelt at Durbarge's side as Thadd again breathed into his mouth.

A small voice in the back of my head whispered that my life would be a lot easier if the assey were dead. He had never done a thing to help me. Even his current defense could be construed as self-serving. I lifted a healing amulet from my necklace and snapped it loose, placing the stone, a mottled black and clear agate carved like a frog, on his stomach. Thadd placed his hands on Durbarge's chest and started pumping.

The Flames, all five of them, whirled around my head, darting in front of me, stealing my vision and leaving plasma burns on my retinas. One landed on Thadd's hand, and he yelped, knocking the Flame tumbling. It regained its shape and shot toward me, hovering at chin level, blinding, emitting an awful, high-pitched buzz. I closed my eyes against its glare and swatted at it. "If you can't heal him, get out of the way," I said.

Instantly, the Flame darted at Durbarge's torso and disappeared inside. Thadd jumped back, yelping again as if stung. Durbarge's body lurched on the snow. Lurched again. A second Flame darted to Durbarge's side, penetrated a three-fingered claw wound, and vanished inside. The other Flames whirled over him, making that shrill vibration that hurt my ears. Thadd didn't seem affected, but I wanted to slap something. Durbarge jerked a third time. And took a breath.

"Tears of Taharial," the reporter whispered into her mike, her mouth at my shoulder, the mild blasphemy going out over the SNN airwaves. Thadd risked a shock and touched Durbarge's carotid.

The two Flames reappeared, plunged once around Thadd's head, and joined the mad dance over the assey's body, singing a bright song that was giving me a headache. With a final swoop, the Flames separated and flew in five different directions, each landing on a wounded human or darting inside a body.

"As you've just seen, the mage commanded the Minor Flames to heal," the reporter said to the anchor only she could hear, "and they did. Healing is a talent never demonstrated by these minor seraphic warriors. How did you do that?" She thrust a mike under my jaw, eyes imploring, knowing the danger had been lessened but was still present.

All I could think of was, *seraph stones,* much more vulgar language than she had used. Someone called my name and I turned away from the reporter. Miz Essie was bending over a teenage boy and I moved to help, pulling another healing amulet and activating it with my thumb.

The boy watched wide-eyed when I placed the amulet on his bleeding wound. The mob, which had had fallen silent, began to stir.

Thadd pointed to a knot of miners. "You men. Get some stretchers. You"—he pointed to a man in the front of the mob—"find some medics and get triage started. You. Get a fire brigade and start a bonfire to burn the spawn and succubi." Thadd pointed at Culpepper and ordered, "You. Get the meeting hall open for the wounded." Culpepper opened his mouth to argue, but stopped when the camera focused on him for a close-up. Casting one last furious look at me, he turned to obey. The mob began to break up.

At my side, Ciana sighed with relief. I touched her chin

and turned her face to me. "Thank you. But if you ever again step in front of a seraph to save me, I'll beat you black and blue." She grinned at me, a gamine expression, unrepentant. "How's Zeddy?" I asked.

The small girl shrugged. "Okay. I guess. I left one of those things over him."

Following her finger, I saw Zeddy propped against the wall of his house, Jacey bending over him but not touching him. Arching over his supine form was a pink shield, prickling with ruby lights, a shield I could see with human vision. I had never seen anything like it and moved to get a better view. "What is it?"

"I don't know. The pin told me to open it."

As we approached the edge of the shield, I inspected it with mage-sight. The conjure was a healing incantation in the shape of a bell, the force of it pulsing with power that rolled across the sides like sound waves and into Zeddy's body. I had no idea how it was made.

Jacey, seeing Ciana at my side, grabbed up my step-daughter and hugged her hard, weeping, trying to get words past the joy clogging her throat. "Thank you. Thank you so much." Ciana grinned at me over Jacey's shoulder, her legs and feet swinging.

Zeddy opened his eyes and whispered, "You'll crush her, Mama." Jacey laughed, a broken sound, and set Ciana on her feet, stroking her face and hair. The huge boy's cheeks, neck, and shoulders were puckered with wounds in half-circular spawn bites, indentations where flesh had been torn away and eaten, dried blood where the teeth had pierced. There were dozens of bites along his legs and torso. Hundreds.

No human could survive that much poison; Zeddy should be dead already. Even a mage would have a problem surviving that many bites. The scars tracing my arms and legs zinged with remembered pain. Beneath the shield, Zeddy was alive, his bleeding had stopped, and the wounds were scaling over. It would take a while to clean all the spawn poison out of his system, but I was pretty sure he would live.

I looked at Ciana. "Can you make more than one of these shields at a time?"

She shrugged again, and I could see exhaustion in the set of her shoulders. "Maybe. Why?" It wasn't fair to ask what I wanted, but if she could make other healing shields, she could save some of the more grievously wounded. I explained what I wanted, and she looked down at the pin on her chest. It was glowing softly. "I can try. But then they'll know about me. And the pin." She didn't add that they would fear her, as they feared me.

"If you want, you can pretend the shields are mine."

She slid her hand in mine again and said, "That elder would try to take away my pin if he knew it was me."

Ouch. But I agreed with her assessment, as well as the plan to fool the town. "Okay."

Satisfied, Ciana and I walked together toward the old Central Baptist Church. The fighting was over, but we had a second battle before us, as dangerous and difficult as the one with the Darkness. Many had been bitten by spawn and were poisoned. Except for the Flames, if they stuck around, and healing amulets, there wasn't much that would clear spawn venom from a human bloodstream.

For me, the rest of Saturday night and all of Sunday passed in caring for the injured while the town fathers burned Darkness and cleaned up the town. Abbreviated services—praise for the survival of the town, mourning for the dead—were held in the town hall when the kirk was found to be fire-damaged. I didn't attend.

It was three a.m. Monday when I locked my loft door and reset the ward over the building. Ciana was asleep in her nook of a bedroom at Rupert's, my worn-out friends sleeping the sleep of warriors. It would be dawn before I could rest. I had too much to do.

Before I cleaned myself, I rinsed my weapons in the kitchen sink, then thrust each into a bag of cleansing salt to remove microscopic traces of Dark blood. I oiled each blade, inspecting the cutting edges for nicks and slivers, and piled the weapons and my amulets on the kitchen table as I peeled off my ruined clothes, tossing them onto the gas-fire logs. The bloody cloth blazed up in a cloud of sulfur and acid. Darkness could use the smell to find me if they wanted. Once that would have frightened me, but now I was pretty sure the Power on the Trine knew where I was. When it was ready, Forcas would come for me again. For me, and for Mineral City.

Standing under a hot spray of cleansing water, I inspected my hands and feet, arms and legs as caked black and crimson-rust blood dissolved and washed down the drain. I was a lot better off than I had expected. Close proximity to Ciana's healing shields had provided a residual effect, leaving me with fresh, shiny, red skin in place of blood-crusted wounds. The new skin was thin, filled with fluid, and very tender, but it was way better than open wounds. Even my feet, which should have been burned and frostbitten, looked better than I expected.

I had suffered three spawn bites and one really nasty claw wound—enough to kill a human—and they were partially healed as well, the surrounding flesh creased and tight, the wounds themselves knitting together. I wasn't sick from the poison. I had learned the hard way that my childhood exposure had given me an immunity to spawn poison. As silver linings went, that one was pretty good. Too bad I didn't have an immunity to ugly scars. The new batch were pretty gruesome, and I smeared ointment over them after the shower.

I wasn't thinking about the fight. Wasn't thinking about the attack of the townspeople in the street. I was trying to keep it all, all the blood and stench and death and betrayal stuffed into a little pocket in a corner of my brain. So far I was succeeding, but as I cleaned up my body and my weapons, little bursts of memory occurred, vivid blasts of individual images. The sight of a man's face, bled out in the snow, lips blue, skin crusted with blood and ice. A severed dragonet leg, twitching, the joint opening and bending shut. The remembered smell of rotting meat brought me to my knees, gagging. The sound of a child's scream as it found its father dead. The crying of another child, dying of spawn bites.

Ciana's pin had helped to heal me, but it hadn't restored me, hadn't taken away the shock of real war. The only time I had fought before, except for the mock battles with Audric, was underground, alone. It had been followed by an attack on the Trine; a handful of humans, Thadd, and me against a small horde of spawn and daywalkers. Neither had prepared me for all-out war, with women, children, and men dead in the street, dinner for spawn.

I knew I'd never sleep. And though I was exhausted, I still had work to do. I had to have a little talk with Lolo. Blinking away the images, I dressed in soft, warm clothes and turned up the heat in the loft.

Sore in every muscle, I pushed aside the kitchen table. The five Flames had disappeared. The two I had seen wounded I had picked up and carried back to my loft in a pocket. They were now among the pile of weapons. The burned-out Flames looked like smoky quartz with black coal-like inclusions. I held one to the light and wished I could fix them both, just like their buddies had healed so many of the townspeople.

The makeshift hospital was filled to capacity with bell-shaped healing shields and recuperating townspeople, many of whom had been healed by the Flames. Thadd had taken over the defense and military organization of the town. The reporter, whose name I had forgotten, had probably won a Pulitzer or a wartime certification for her footage on the attack and the town's defense. And the healing of the fighters afterwards.

I figured I was famous. Which would have really ticked me off, had I any energy or emotion left for trivialities.

I set the Flame down and cast a charmed circle, using clean earth salt. Around the outer perimeter I placed seven aromatic candles, because their spruce scent would clear my head and remove the smell of dead and burning spawn that filtered through my windows. In the center of the circle I placed my silver bowl filled with springwater, its bottom lined with a layer of moss agate nuggets for life and growth. My ceremonial knife and amulets went beside it. I didn't need the stones or blood to scry for Lolo—all I supposedly needed were salt, water, and a calm, meditative mind—but after my last failure and the attack by Darkness, I wanted to be ready for anything.

I closed the circle the old-fashioned way, with a call on

creation energies in the center of the earth. When I had enough for the working, I placed my necklace over my head, and the power draw stopped. I called on Lolo, speaking aloud. "Lolo. Hear me. Awaken, priestess," I added, remembering it was the middle of the night. "Lolo." I called for several minutes but nothing happened. It was like talking to myself. I wasn't getting through. It was as if Lolo had blocked me. Or as if I was doing it all wrong, or as if the overused and drained amulet necklace was sending feedback, any and all of which were possible.

I wasn't very good at scrying. It was a use of power that required that a mage's gift be alive and open to study and attempt. I had left Enclave before I could learn, and I had never practiced. Who would I have talked to? No one knew I was alive except Lolo, and she wasn't the chatty type. Pulling the bowl to me, I took my prime amulet in my left hand, settled myself, and leaned over the bowl. I set the amulet into the water and chanted softly, "Lolo, hear me. Open to me. Knowledge I seek. Truth I seek."

On the third repetition, the water in the bowl began to change, gradually darkening, growing murky. But it wasn't the Enclave priestess I saw in the bowl. It was a small clapboard house, painted white, with a low-pitched roof and aqua shutters. It was our vacation house on the Gulf when I was a child. The only vacation we had ever taken. The only time my parents had been certified to leave Enclave and, even then, it was only a few miles east, almost within sight of the extravagant, ornamental prison.

Palm trees waved in a brisk wind, fronds bending, all to one side. Dark clouds raced across the sky as my position changed, and waves crashed on a nearby shore. Lightning cracked across the sky and sheets of rain pounded the ocean, moving closer. But the vision was murky, cloudy, shadowed by the passage of time. I heard neither wind nor ocean nor approaching storm. Only silence. And the sound of my heartbeat as it began to race. I leaned in closer, hoping to make the vision in the bowl come clear, fearful, yet unable to look away.

A woman walked from the front door, a mage visa around her neck glinting in the sun. One hand shaded her eyes as she looked out to sea. Her mouth opened, calling. Calling. I knew her. I knew what she was saying. I remembered this day. It was my mother, and she was calling my twin and me, wanting to get us inside before the storm hit. "Thorn-y-Rosie." All one word, the way she always called us. "Thorn-y-Rosie!"

I knew what I was seeing. I knew what was about to happen. Once again I had bungled my attempt at scrying. I had performed a truth vision instead. I shivered, my throat closing up, my eyes on my mother's face as my tears blurred the scene. Out on the water, the Gulf of Mexico, a cloud twisted into a long roll along the length of the sky, a cylindrical shape, spinning, as warm and cold air masses collided; a tornado trying to take shape.

I watched as if hanging in the air. That day, Rose and I had been playing our version of hide-and-seek, and I was searching for her, hoping to catch her in the backyard. If I answered Mama, my twin would run, reaching home before I could tag her. So I didn't answer. And neither did Rose.

A tornado formed over the bay, arching first one way, then the other, vaguely S-shaped, dropping slowly. When it hit the storm-tossed sea, it whitened as a waterspout developed. It headed straight at the small house.

Mama shouted, her face frantic, mouth open wide in distress. Daddy ran from the shed in back also shouting. The wind picked up. It had been howling. So loud. Now was only silence. Daddy looked angry, and I remembered being afraid, not knowing what I had done to make him mad. Because I knew where to look, I could see myself, kneeling in the dirt beneath the lilac bush. I remembered the smell of it, lush and heady. And the roaring of wind and water, like nothing I had ever heard.

Tears trickled down my cheeks, my eyes aching, my chest so tight it might explode.

Over the storm's roar, Mama screamed. The waterspout came right at her. Fast. Unearthly fast. Daddy—a stone mage like me—was in the midst of casting a shield when it hit the beach. The spout picked up Mama and spun her like a wheel, sucking her into the white roar, the serpent of

swirling water. She was gone in an instant. The roof went
next. The palm tree. And then Daddy. He was just gone.
Gone.

My tears fell into the water, making small rings that circled out, distorting the surface. Mama and Daddy were
gone. Even after all these years, I was empty, still shocked
at the sight. I couldn't react to their loss. Didn't know how.

The waterspout fell apart, drenching the house and
grounds with a solid deluge of seawater and rain. The lilac
bush crashed around me and I fell forward in the water, instantly soaked. I pushed back to my knees, my bare skin in
a puddle of water. The sun came out. Tiny fish darted
through the puddle where I knelt, bright forms flashing. Silence settled on the entire world, broken only by the dripping and trickling of water as it ran off and away.

Mama and Daddy tumbled onto the ground, landing
with horrid thumps and splashes I felt through my knees. I
could see them lying on the wet grass. I knew they were
dead. They lay so still, twisted and broken, blue and naked,
even their visas gone. I stared, unable to move, frozen to
the ground as the sun came back out and threw its warmth
over my shoulders. A *thing* dropped from the sky and
stood over them, looking at them.

It was like a man, but taller, with a blackened and
twisted body, and a white head. It had wings made like
Lolo's drums. It kicked Daddy. Hard. And it laughed.

Rage woke in me, a blaze of white-hot fury. I stood and
raced at the thing, hit it at the knee and beat it with my
fists. It laughed again and picked me up, holding me, dangling down, above its beautiful face. I socked it with my
fists, which made it laugh harder. "I have you," it said,
"body, blood, and spirit. You are mine."

It spread those terrible wings; they beat at the earth.
Suddenly we were aloft, racing for the clouds. I looked
down through the missing roof of our vacation house.
Looked into Rose's eyes. She was saying, "No," reaching
for me, a hand extended. The image froze on a picture of
her face, palm outstretched, perhaps the last thing my
young mind could handle. I broke away from the vision
and pulled back hard, the water in the scrying bowl murky.

I didn't follow the vision into the next moments, into the dark, and the cold, and the pain of spawn claws. I shuddered so hard my teeth clacked as I stared at my last memory of that day. My sister's face, viewed through the water, its surface uneven from my involuntary movements.

I hadn't remembered the attack in any kind of detail. Neither had Rose; not even with the best psychiatrists and healers the Enclave had to offer. Now, I stared at my parents' bodies tumbled in a pile on the shore. I was a lost little girl, helpless and broken. From somewhere, I heard a hopeless, helpless sound, a mewl of pain and terror.

I was choking, staring at the broken bodies, gray-blue in death. Staring at my sister. My hands were going numb, my muscles jerking with reaction as I sobbed, making waves in the water of the scrying bowl. Remembering. Remembering it all. A snap of pain slapped me, an electric jolt that burned across my skin. With a crack, the vision vanished into blackness and I fell forward, toward the bowl, toward the telescoping night of unconsciousness.

"Thorn?" My name brought me back, shouted, angry-sounding. My body shook like an earthquake, my head rolling. I opened my eyes to see Lucas, his beautiful face only inches from mine. "Thorn?" He sucked in the word on a frightened breath. I managed to raise a hand and placed it on his cheek. He needed a shave, black hairs prickling.

Ciana appeared over his shoulder. As if mimicking me, she touched my cheek and her fingers came away wet. "You screamed," she said. "You were crying."

"It's okay, sweetheart. The circle's broken. I have her now." Lucas' voice was unsteady, filled with some emotion I didn't recognize. Without taking his eyes from mine, he nuzzled his daughter's shoulder with the side of his head. "Thank you for the use of your pin," he said to her. He raised his voice, speaking to someone nearby. "Can you make Ciana some calming tea?"

"Sure. I'll make enough for us all." I recognized Rupert, and the tears started to fall again, burning my face. Forcas wanted him. Wanted Ciana and Lucas and Rupert for their blood. Wanted me. And I didn't understand why. I heard footsteps and the door closing. Lucas slid an arm under

me, lifting me, and carried me to the couch. It made a soft
sigh beneath us and Lucas settled me on his lap, wrapping
me in an afghan knitted of soft mist-green yarn.

I laid my head on his shoulder. "Forcas killed my mama
and daddy," I said, my voice shattered and crushed, like the
little girl I had been. "It killed them with a waterspout and
it took me." Lucas said nothing, just tucked my head beneath his chin, tightened his arms around me, and rocked
me while I cried.

As grief flooded through me, it occurred to me that Forcas might also have been the Darkness that attacked and
killed my twin, Rose, leaving me the only member of my
family alive. And Lolo sent me here. To its lair.

Chapter 20

I must have slept, because when I woke I was in bed, my head resting on Lucas' shoulder. My mage attributes were blazing, mage-sight fully on in the soft light. I didn't know if it was dawn or dusk or cloudy midday, but I was warm and cozy, limbs heavy with sleep. And I was safe.

Lucas glowed, a beautiful, soft blue touched with gold. His aura used to be yellow, I remembered, yellow banded with green and blue. It had changed after he came back from the Trine. And had changed again in just the last few days, deepening into a richer hue, like Gulf water on the horizon at sunset, just where it meets the sky to the east.

"Morning," he said, his voice that soft scrape of sound that came after a long, silent night.

Warmth traveled through me, sleepy and contented. I reached up and touched his face, his beard softer than I remembered it from our marriage, but no longer than the night before. There was so much I should have said, wanted to say, but what came out of my mouth, in solemn curiosity was, "Your beard doesn't grow much anymore, does it?"

His mouth quirked up on one side, but he answered the question as if it were of great import. "No. Not much." His voice slid into a whisper. "Since I was a prisoner on the Trine, since I ate manna, it doesn't grow."

"Your aura has changed. It's blue now."

"I'm . . . different," he agreed. He shrugged his shoulder,

my head moving with the motion. "I don't need much sleep. Don't need much food." He smiled and said, perhaps only half facetiously, "Even my clothes don't seem to wear out." His fingers followed the length of my jaw, feather-light, letting the silence speak.

Far off, a rooster crowed. Farther, the lynx called, a roaring cry. Not a warning, but a lonely sound. The warmth beneath the covers was soothing, part memory, part security, part solace. Part something more that I didn't want to analyze.

With a forefinger he traced the hatch-mark scars on my cheek. "You've changed too," he said. "You have old scars that you used to hide. You have new ones." The smile died. "Lots of new ones. You glow. You can do magic."

"Mages don't do magic. We work with leftover creation energy."

He shrugged again, the light returning to his eyes. "Whatever. You're different now. You're not human."

Our forearms entwined, I stroked his jaw, finding his beard softer than down, the bones beneath sharp and distinct. "I was never human," I said. "You just didn't know it." I was almost afraid to ask. "Are you? Human?"

A long moment passed. The pig clock ticked into the stillness. "I don't know." He skimmed a hand along my body, caressing, as if he stroked the length of an animal. I was still dressed in the soft, loose leggings and sweatshirt I had worn to scry for Lolo, the clothes bunched and out of shape, my body warm and languid beneath the covers. "I don't really know."

By increments his head dropped, as if giving me time to think about it, to stop him. He kissed my nose, my closed mouth, the scars on my cheek. Lips trailing to my hairline, he breathed in my scent, mouth pressed to my temple. When he pulled back, my fingers found his mouth, traced the curve of his lips, so well remembered. So greatly missed.

His eyes on me, he slid questing fingers beneath my shirt, to rest on my rib cage, tentative, waiting. When I didn't pull away, when I just watched him, the expression in his eyes, the ripples in his aura, he deposited fluttery kisses, like butterflies, down my jaw. He touched his lips to my neck at my pulse.

"Oh," I whispered. "Oh. . . ." And I felt his mouth smile against the tender skin there. His lips trailed slowly, so slowly, the length of my throat to my collarbone, which he kissed, mouth open, breath blowing. Even slower, he kissed back up to my left earlobe and paused. Mouth poised, one hand still on my ribs, he cradled my head in his other palm, his thumb tracing my windpipe, back up into the sensitive hollow where throat met ear and skull. His lips opened. He sucked my lobe into his mouth.

I arched up. His palm slid up my body, under my shirt. Covered my bare breast.

And I was lost.

His mouth followed the shirt as he pulled it over my head. Settled on my breast, teeth grazing the tight point. He gripped my waist, hands just above my hip bones, and slid down my leggings, tugging them from my toes with his own. The sheets were warm and silken below me, my skin roseate against the ruby silk.

As if we had all the time in the world, as if the world itself had never ended, I peeled off his jeans and shirt, tossing and pushing the clothes aside, movements indolent. I traced his naked back, skin like heated silk, muscles long and rigid.

Lucas breathed on my breasts, his breath warm until he licked first one, then the other, his tongue hot and rough on the sensitive points, the chill air making them even tighter in his wake. He pulled one whole nipple into his mouth, sucking it down, elongating it, creating an unbearable pressure on the deeper flesh that tautened low in my belly.

I trailed my hands up his body, over his shoulders, finding the indentations of bone and tendon. Wrapped my hands around his head, holding him close, hearing the whimper of my breath, my fingers tracking ridged fang scars beneath his jaw.

Shifting his torso between my legs, he balanced on elbows and knees to take away his weight. Kisses rained across my ribs, following a faint scar down my stomach, across my abdomen to the point of the hip on the other side. Cooler air followed the warmth of his mouth, the comforter sliding away to reveal me, covers caught on his body. His lips moved on my flesh at the jointure of hip and thigh, tongue trailing in circles. I heard my groans and his laughter, heated and satisfied. An almost dangerous sound.

He moved his mouth slightly slower, the circles continuing, his tongue pressing, the tissue beneath sensitive. My legs opened, and he paused, drawing down the covers so he could see me, all of me. I remembered that, that he liked to watch my body when it stole from my control, when it became some other thing, untamed and feral, needy and demanding.

Mage-heat, kept close to the surface by the presence of a kylen, blossomed and spread through me, beating in time with my heart, pulsing through me on a wash of need and want, scenting the air with cookies and almonds. Taking his shoulders, I pulled him close, but he held away, his eyes locked on mine as his mouth moved down my thigh to my knee. He lifted my leg and sucked the soft tissue behind it into his mouth, teeth grazing the tendons. I reached between us and clutched him, moaning, the timbre changing from want to demand, my fingers urging him up to me.

"Not yet," he said, a hint of laughter in his tone, which was rough with his own need. He turned me, putting my cheek to the pillow. I struggled, trying to rise, but he held me in place with his stronger human muscles, pressing my body into the mattress. He stroked along my sides, the backs of his hands trailing from beneath my arms to my thighs, so very slowly. I shivered in want. He smelled like anise, nutmeg, and male, familiar and yet all new, different. I breathed him into me, tasting his scent. Wanting more, but unable to force my will on him.

I gave up resistance. His tongue touched just above the top of my buttocks. Swirled at the edge of the fissure and up, along my spine. Again and again, tasting me. My muscles were loose as warm oil when his hand slid between my legs. I wanted this. Oh, *fire and feathers*, how I had wanted this.

He lifted my hips and entered me, slowly, one hand hold-

ing my hips high, the other sliding to the front, teasing me.
I shoved back against him, hard, pushing with my hands,
raising my body off the mattress. Guttural breaths came
from my throat as he rocked me, my hands gripping fistfuls
of sheets. Mage-heat pulsed through me. I wanted. *Wanted.*
And still he held back, moving his body so slowly, too
slowly, his rhythm a bass drum beaten with a single club, vibrations pulsing out, his fingers moving only slightly faster.
Heat built as waves surged and flooded through me. I
could see his hand below me, his blue aura meeting and ex-
ploding against my own in tiny gold discharges, pinpoints
of light.

When I thrashed, he withdrew, fast, leaving me empty. I
ground my teeth, holding in a scream, reaching back to
scratch him in anger. Mindless. He turned me again, all in
one motion, dropping me on the mattress. I landed with a
small expulsion of breath, one knee on a pillow, my head
back, half off the bed. He plunged hard, slamming into me
with his whole length, filling me up. I screamed then,
throaty and breathless, head back, my mouth open.

Lucas rose above me, braced on his hands, elbows
locked, eyes on my face. His strokes filled me and retreated, rapid, rhythmic, hitting the deepest part of me in
internal blows of desire. I clawed at his shoulders, wanting
him close, closer.

He settled to his elbows against me, stomach to stomach,
grinding into me with a deeper, corresponding rhythm. I
bit his flesh on the pad of muscle below his collarbone,
sucking hard and tasting the anise and nutmeg in his
blood. He pushed my head aside, and his mouth found a
breast. Teeth grazed along the nipple, pulling, stretching. I
arched up, following him, my heart beating like thunder.
My legs wrapped around him, gripping his hips hard and,
arching my body, I took his buttocks in my hands, fingers
digging in.

Passion spiraled up from my depths, a swirling whirlpool
of sensation. His eyes were open and watching, staring into
mine. Waiting. Stroking. Knowing. Lightning shot from the
center of my body, along my nerves. It coiled in my breasts
in a sizzling surge of pleasure. My extremities curled up

hard, clutching and wrenching, and I screamed. Something tore in my throat with a hoarse note of pain and pleasure. "Yes," I breathed, the sound harsh. "Now."

He thrust into me, brutally beating into my body. Electricity followed the swell of passion, crackling and burning, rolling through me, up through my bones, along my skin. Thrashing waves of passion gathered and folded over, tightening with surface tension. And fell. Exploded in an eruption of power from the center of my body. Through my skin, along each pore and out my fingertips. His hoarse cry echoed mine.

We lay there afterward, our bodies sweaty, heated, our breathing loud in our tortured lungs. Oxygen-starved, I sucked in air, wondering if what I had seen with mage-sight had been real, the light that burst out between us in that final moment, rose and blue, creating a lavender and purple haze that undulated out from our center. Wondering, but not really caring.

When he could move again, Lucas pulled the down comforter over us and settled more deeply against me, his weight a little to the side so I could breathe. We lay there, head to head in the dark. Warmth gathered under the covers, a languorous, lethargic ease.

My stomach growled and Lucas laughed.

He fell to the floor of his cell, tripping on the shackles, overshooting the supple resilience of his wings and rolling into the far wall. He crashed into the stone, back-first, as they intended, his severed wing humeri hitting with painful thunks. Since he had killed three of them, they had been more cruel, less willing to place themselves in danger. He eased away from the wall, leaving his blood in a long tracery.

The key to the shackles landed on the stone floor and bounced with a snap and tinkle. "Open the cuffs. Toss 'em over here along with the key."

"Scared to get too close, Ephrahu?" he taunted, breathless with pain.

"Too smart, Watcher," the human said, moving a bit of straw from one side of his mouth to the other. He propped a

shoulder against the wall outside the cell and relaxed, crossing his arms. "Move. Or I'll put a mage in heat across the hall
from you again. See how you like it two days in a row."

He didn't think he could withstand another day of that
particular torment, but he didn't want them to know how
close he had come to succumbing once again. So he chuckled and bent for the key. The demon-iron spat when he
touched it, searing his fingers. But the key was the only
way to take off the shackles, and leaving the shackles on
only meant more pain.

He inserted the key in each cuff, at the wrists first and then
the ankles, and let them fall to the floor. He kicked them all
to the cell door, close enough so the human could reach
them. He tossed the key beside them. He'd learned the futility of rebellion. Whatever he did, they always had something
worse they would do to him. And now, for the first time in
too many decades to count, he had a reason to live.

When the human was gone, he settled slowly to his severed feathers and lay face-first in the down. The smell of
them was sweet, the remembered scent of freedom, of
flight, of holiness. A state of grace he had thrown away,
thinking it slavery, and now longed for as the perfect liberty.
Because intense pain opened something in his mind, and
was the only time he could reach them, he marshaled his
thoughts and called to the seraphs. "Zadkiel. Amethyst," he
whispered.

"We are here," they belled, their words and tones a sweet
harmony.

"Little time *has passed,"* Zadkiel said, his emphasis on
the second word. *"How are you able to call again so soon?"*

"It's been over twenty-four hours," he said, raising his
head in alarm.

"Not here. Less than an hour," Zadkiel said.

"How? Unless Forcas has found a way to dip into the
river of *time.*"

"Danger," Amethyst said, a paean of distress. *"His plan
is close to fruition."*

"Seal the covenant, then," Barak said.

"You ask much," Zadkiel said. *"In return for our freedom we can promise to free you. That is acceptable."*

"Not enough," Barak said, taking the chance he had been hoping for, waiting for. "I ask your oath, by feathers and fire, in the river of time and beyond. Your oath to intercede, to speak for me before the Most High, to seek a return of my seraphic gifts, transmogrification, a return of true seraphic power, a regifting of my place in the High Host of the Seraphim."

"The time limit you propose is foul," Amethyst moaned. *"You ask perpetual intercession. Everlasting. Such has never been granted to the Fallen. And the Most High has never granted redemption to your kind for your sin."*

"This for your freedom," Barak bargained. When they didn't reply, he ground out, "Agreed then. For your freedom, I ask only your oath for intercession between the Most High and this Fallen one, such negotiation to last one decade in the river of *time*."

"If the Most High does not consent, the Host may imprison you," Zadkiel warned, "until the end of days."

"I understand," Barak said. "And I accept."

Zadkiel breathed out in resignation. *"Mate?"*

"I agree to all he asks. I long for paradise."

"Don't we all," Barak snarled. "You have been apart from the Most High, lost in the river of *time* on this accursed world, for a century, cherub. I have been lost for all of human history."

Knowing their time was short, neither answered that it was his fault, his choice, his failure, and for that he was both resentful and grateful. Instead they belled together, *"A covenant is sealed between me and thee."*

"A covenant is sealed between me and thee," he said in return. A covenant between seraphs of the Light and one of the Allied, once an impossibility. "Who is this mage?"

"We have memories of her. We can share our knowledge. And perhaps we can show her to you," she said.

"We shall try," Zadkiel murmured.

A vision opened in his mind, of the surface of the world. The sun's rays blazed across the sky in a golden wash. Snow, crusted and coarse, glistened with the light. A soft mist traveled across the ground, pale and white, touched with the brightness of the sun. It was winter. But his mind didn't linger there, in the cold air and the sunlight, but swept with the swiftness of flight, down to a town, and inside a building made of stone.

Instantly the sweetness of winter was replaced with the heat of sex and mage. He focused on the woman, the mage-warrior, her body radiant, scars shimmering brighter still. She stood before a sink, her hair loose and curled in a scarlet tangle, a worn wool robe belted over her. She wasn't lovely. Wasn't beautiful and perfect of form. But there was terrible strength to her, and a fragility as well. The dichotomy was arresting. Intriguing.

Water poured over her hands. Suddenly her head came up, nostrils flaring. In a burst of mage-speed, she raced to a window. His perspective moved with her and followed her gaze out into a street. Below her, standing on the snow, was a man, his face tortured with desire and need and the agony of . . . transmogrification. A *kylen*.

Barak remembered his sons, the children he had sired on the neomage he cherished. *This being belongs to me.* Speaking quietly, so softly that his breath barely brushed the feathers near his face, he said, "Zadkiel. Amethyst. A new bargain. I can bring unto us the mage. And gift to you a kylen as well. What would you give me for this?"

"A kylen?" the cherub belled. *"One lives among men?"*

"For you to keep such a one free breaks a covenant only now sealed. Are you not allied with the Light?" Zadkiel asked. *"What game do you play here?"*

"What *game*? Long, long ago, I was a member of the High Host. Then, a Watcher of men," he said. "Tempted, I was lost from the Most High. Yet, in the War of Heaven, I fought with the troops of Michael. In the Last War for Earth, I was allied with the High Host fighting with the winged-warriors. Though I gave my body to be burned, I remain unredeemed, unforgiven. It is the way of my kind to *renegotiate*." Barak smiled into the crook of his arm. In the hallway, the smell that caused his most recent sin grew. A mage had been placed nearby. Humans laughed.

Small red lights appeared in his irises. And began to grow.

Chapter 21

⚭

I rolled over, reaching for him, to find the sheets warm but empty. His smell was heated, comforting, and my body tired and at peace. Lucas wanted me back. How could he want me back? And how could I possibly be so stupid as to want him? *So stupid as to spend the night with a cheat and a scoundrel?* a wiser part of me asked. That was a question I couldn't answer. *He claims to be a changed man.* I banished the tempting thought.

Once again, Audric didn't come after me for savage-blade practice. Maybe bruises from real battles were as good as bruises from play battles. Stiff and sore, I rolled out of bed and got ready for the day.

Downstairs, Jacey and Rupert were standing at the remaining front window, staring out into the street, the aromas of coffee and tea strong on the air. Though it wasn't yet ten, they were dressed for work in the back, as was common on Mondays, when the shop was closed. Spawn blood and broken glass had been cleaned up. From somewhere they had found plywood and covered the missing windows, which made the shop darker than usual. In the confusion that had followed the battle, I had forgotten the mess in the shop. They had done a mountain of work while I was elsewhere, working on the injured.

I stopped in the doorway to the stairwell and stared at them. They had to have heard me come down, yet neither turned. Something was up. "Morning," I said.

"You missed Ciana. I walked her to school with Cissy," Jacey said without looking my way.

"Oh. Sorry," I said, trying to interpret her strange tone. Her body was tense, stiff. Something about the two made me wary. "I'll catch her later."

"We'll continue to clean up in here. You can work in back today," Rupert said, his back still turned.

I folded my arms, sensing a scheme to keep me out of sight. "Why?"

"Did you reset that thing you did last night, to protect the shop? During the battle?" she asked. "That shield that glowed?"

The ward. Oops. No, I was too busy having really good makeup sex with my ex-husband. But I didn't say it. And I remembered that I still had to find out how Ciana got through the ward without an explosion, and where the energies went when Jacey and Polly walked out. "No. Why?"

"After you risked your life fighting for the town, and healed the survivors, someone paid us a visit," Rupert said, his shoulders hunched, voice bitter. "They left a little warning."

I walked across the shop and peered between them. Swathes of red paint marked the unbroken glass. Grabbing Rupert's new blue cloak from the coatrack, I went into the cold. During the night someone had painted slogans on the walls. DIE MAGE WHORE. DIE MANLOVERS. DIE UNBELIEVERS. It wasn't very original, but it got the point across. Rupert's cloak dragging in the slick slush, I turned in a slow circle and surveyed the street.

The road had been plowed, something the town fathers did only rarely, as snow-el-mobiles and horses could navigate over most anything, and cleaning out the accumulated snow several times a week wasn't practical. The asphalt was scorched in places: large circular spots, where humans had battled behind barricades; smaller areas where flamethrowers had melted the snow and singed the road; where the seraph had stood or walked. Smoke blew down Upper Street in gusts, reeking of charred spawn. Windows up and down the street were boarded over. Only ours had been decorated with slogans.

I bunched the cloak in front of me and walked down the middle of the street, passing numerous townspeople: some I recognized from business, some from school years ago, some from kirk, some from my trial. Fewer from the fighting. None met my eyes. Not one.

He may not have actually said so, but Rupert was right. It wasn't fair. There was an old saying among mages. Give humans your best and they'll kick you in the teeth.

Fury and hurt welled up, a noxious brew in the back of my throat. I pulled the cloak tighter, feeling cold.

"Miz St. Croix?"

I turned to find Do'rise, Shamus Waldroup's wife, behind me. The old woman wore the shapeless black dress of the orthodox, but with a white apron over it. The apron was embroidered with bright red strawberries, a pie with slits in the top through which steam escaped, and a bluebird on a stem, an odd combination, but pretty. Her gray hair was in a bun and she was stooped, a widow's hump rounding her back. She held out a long loaf of bread wrapped in paper. I caught the smell of yeast, hot and fresh over the scent of rancid smoke.

"You and your partners probably haven't had time to eat this morning," she said loudly. "It's just out of the oven." Softer, she said, "Shamus chased the kids away. The ones who did that." She indicated the graffiti with a jerk of her head. "He'll be speaking to their parents today. My husband would consider it a personal favor if you would accept their apologies when they make them. And attend the funeral." At my blank look she said, "There'll be a mass funeral for our dead tomorrow. You should be there."

Funeral. Right. The town had lost citizens, elders, men, women, children. I blinked against a momentary image of a teenage girl being eaten in the street. I couldn't seem to stop the words but I felt selfish and arrogant when I said, "Apologies don't fix the hurt."

"No," she said gently. "But they are a step on the road to forgiveness."

After a moment I heaved a breath in agreement, and Do'rise extended the loaf. Reluctantly, I accepted it. "Thank you for the healing," she said, again speaking so her voice would carry. "Some fools haven't realized that you saved the town when you called the seraph. And the ones who died in judgment did so because of their own sins and choices."

Her piece said, the wife of the most powerful elder and most powerful town father turned and walked back into her shop and out of the icy morning. Only then did I notice that she hadn't been wearing a coat. Flaunting the bright colors on her apron.

Smoke blew across my path, and I turned upwind, seeking its source. Keeping my mage-attributes hidden, I opened mage-sight, the extra cells in my retinas that humans lacked, allowing me to see creation energies. The town was a bright place, constructed mostly of brick, stone, and mortar, but the smoke that drifted through was tainted with Darkness. I followed the wind, and knew they still burned spawn near the Toe River that bisected the city.

Below my feet something caught my eye. Buried in the street, a part of the rocks, tar, and the frozen slush that was freezing into black ice, there was a dim shimmer forming a perfect circle. The contour incorporated Thorn's Gems, the bakery, and large parts of Upper Street. *Seraph stones.* It was a seraph's sigil, embedded in the earth.

The cloak tight against me, I rotated in a tight circle, trying to see what it said, or what it did. It was too weak for me to be certain, but it looked familiar, flames jutting toward the center. And then I knew. Cheriour had twice stood in the same place in the street, the first time after he judged me, when I was revealed as a mage before the town, and last night when he fought. I had never heard of a seraph leaving a copy of his sigil anywhere, but the Angel of Punishment had left his twice, once in the shop, on the display cabinet, and now in the street. I didn't know what it meant, but I guessed it was a sign of a verdict, a legal ruling. It might not mean the town was doomed, but it gave me the willies.

I shook my head and spotted Romona Benson, the reporter for SNN, standing in front of the shop. In the last weeks, she had come by Thorn's Gems several times, but Rupert had always managed to divert her before she could bother me. Now, unless I was willing to pull the cloak over my head and run like a scalded dog, I was going to have to speak to her.

Romona stood in the cold, arms crossed, one foot angled out. She looked haggard, hair mussed, no makeup, her clothes wrinkled as if she had slept in them, or hadn't slept at all. Strangely telling, her cameraman was nowhere to be seen. Her back to the street, she was studying the slogans painted on the remaining shop-window glass. I stopped beside her, our reflections wavering in the glass.

"Imaginative little cusses, weren't they?" she said. I said nothing, and after an uncomfortable pause, she went on. "I had a several times great-grandfather who was killed at Auschwitz. That was a place the Nazis killed Jews in one of the World Wars." Having studied world history in school, I was familiar with the war and the atrocities and genocide that took place. "It started like this," she said. "With hate."

Romona turned and studied me. "Some of the elders think you saved the town," she said conversationally. "The rest think you brought down judgment on it. Which was it?"

I still didn't reply, and she added, "There are also rumors that you melted the ice cap on the Trine, then vaporized the snowmelt to prevent a flood." I shook my head, not denying it, but not responding either. "If so, that makes you a hero. You saved the town and didn't charge the town fathers a hefty mage-price." When I pressed my lips tight, she turned back to the window and sighed, trying to smooth the blond chaos of her hair.

"I'd like to tell your story," she said more softly, finger-combing a snarl. "Add it to the footage I have of you fighting and healing. You and your champards were pretty amazing. I'll sweep this year's awards without it, but an interview would complete the story of what happened here. I admit it's a self-centered motive, but that and curiosity are all I got."

"Where's your cameraman?" I asked, almost idly.

She opened her mouth, hesitated, and I could see her riffling through possible answers. She dropped her hands from her hair and settled on a reply, but when she spoke, the word was strained, as if pulled out of her by force. "Dead."

I held her gaze in the reflective surface, waiting.

"He went with one of those *things*," she said, her tone for the first time revealing emotion. "Had loud, crazy sex with it in the hallway, on the floor outside my door at the hotel, while I filmed the fighting from the balcony. When he got quiet, I turned off the camera and peeked into the hall." She looked a little sick and I guessed what she had seen. Succubi were reputed to eat their conquests. "I ran down the stairs into the night and started filming again. But I still can't get the picture of him out of my head." She made a fist, knuckles white in the morning light. "And I still—" Her voice broke. "I still don't know why."

"That's why I won't talk to you," I said. "Because I don't have any answers. I don't know what's going on in this city. I don't know what's going on up the Trine. I don't know any more than you about why I'm here."

She searched my face again in the glass. "May I quote you on that much?"

"Sure. Why not."

"Thanks." She started to walk away, but stopped and pressed a business card between the folds of cloak bunched at my waist and the loaf of bread. "If you ever decide to talk, remember me, okay?" I stared at her. "You can call the number on the card and my service will get back to me. Your story is important." This time, she didn't look back.

I was left standing alone in the cold, gazing into the glass at words that called me a whore, that condemned Rupert and me both. In the reflection, I saw a man walk down the street and enter the bakery. Lucas, dressed for the weather in a bulky vest and layers. My heart went from cold to warm in an instant and a smile pulled at my mouth. Through the layers of glass I watched him as he leaned over the counter and pointed inside, and I wondered if he was buying lunch for us. Maybe a picnic on the floor in front of the fire. On a down coverlet. With wine and grapes and more fresh bread. My skin warmed at the thought and I knew that there were some things that were still good in my life.

The girl on the other side of the counter laughed at something he said. She had dimples and a sunny smile. And bouncy breasts straining at her dress. Lucas shook his head, pointed at something else in the case, and leaned across the counter, weight on one elbow. She cocked her head, pushing back her hair. The girl bent into the display and then held her hand over the counter to Lucas, offering him a taste. I turned to watch, faint disquiet stirring.

He took her hand in his, directing it to his mouth. He bit into the sample, holding her hand, smiling into her face. And then he kissed her fingers. I watched as she blushed, her perfect, unscarred, unblemished skin glowing with simple human health, blushing with frank sexual attraction. She giggled. Pushed back her hair, fingers lingering in the tresses.

Around me, the smoke of burning spawn blew in, adding a putrid fog to the murky day. It reeked of rot. Silent, I turned and entered the shop.

I changed clothes and went to the workroom, turning on the gas logs. Though the expenditure of energy was unforgivable, the stock was frozen and my equipment was stiff. My breath blew clouds and the cold was searing on my exposed fingers. I was afraid the saw and drill would heat the crystalline matrix unevenly and cause any stone I worked to shatter.

I poured a bowl of cool water over the dark green aventurine I had previously excised and set it aside. The due date for the necklace of stone leaves was close. I could warm the pieces slowly, starting with cool water and adding warmer water to it several times, and it would be fine until the room warmed above freezing.

Until then, I was at loose ends and feeling edgy. I didn't want to put stock away or rearrange the bins that needed attention. I didn't want to sweep or clean. My movements were erratic, and my mouth was a tight line of hurt and anger. I ought to stop and look at what I was really feeling before I hurt myself or broke something.

But I refused to think about the night before. Refused to think about his mouth on that girl's fingers. And more importantly, I would not cry over him. Never. Never again.

I took a shuddering breath and forced the hurt into a deep, dark place inside me. It was getting full, that region of my heart where I shoved all the stuff I didn't want to look at. I breathed deeply, trying to find a peaceful place within myself. I wasn't sure one existed anymore. My hands quivered with inaction, my heart with a painful rhythm, and my eyes burned like brands. But as I forced long, steady breaths, my muscles relaxed, my breathing evened out, and the threatening tears dried into a hot, scalding mass in my chest.

Firmly, I buried my ex-husband and my love for him. I truly had cried my last tear over Lucas. I would not grieve for him, or for my dead marriage, again. I would not look at that part of my life. Instead, I pulled the three wild-mage stones from the time of the first neomages off my amulet necklace and inspected them.

At my trial, one of the mage-stones had glowed—yet I had never filled it with power. It should have been as dead as weather-beaten rock, holding potential, but nothing more. I held it up to the light; a sapphire with lots of dark inclusions, a poor-quality stone carved in the shape of a fat owl. It didn't look any different from my other amulets, but it had to be. I thought the owl might have worked on, and with, my mind to allow improved psychic reactions. During the trial, when I tried blending the mind-skim and the sight into one, I hadn't been as nauseated as before. In hindsight, I was pretty sure the amulet had started glowing about then, and had somehow facilitated blending the two gifts. Maybe it had something to do with the *otherness* as well, that odd sensation that flooded me with the blending.

Centering myself, I opened both sight and a skim. The world whirled drunkenly around me, and I gripped the edge of the workbench to steady myself. The sapphire nugget was glowing, a sunlike glare I blinked away. Mentally, I reached out and touched the otherness. It felt bubblelike, solid and ephemeral, like a cell wall of energy enclosing, yet not binding, me. Testing, I hooked a thought in it and tugged.

Suddenly I was on the other side of . . . something,

standing beside a river glowing like lava. In a quick glance I saw humps and lumps, like boulders in the lava flow, and sparkles and flares, like tiny explosions. I turned to step back, but there was no doorway, no opening, just the wide, endless plane. I heaved a fear-filled breath and felt myself shift, hard. I landed back in the workroom, my fingers cutting into the bench top, holding me in place.

"Tears of Taharial," I muttered coarsely. That had sucked Habbiel's pearly toes. I wouldn't be trying that again anytime soon.

When I caught my breath, I inspected the second wild mage-stone. It was a citrine nugget; the sparkling, translucent, soft yellow gem was shaped like a pear with a nub of a stem and a small leaf carved at the top. The final wild-mage stone was a green zoisite carved like a cherry. A tiny ruby inclusion looked like a gemstone worm in the matrix of the zoisite.

I placed the wild amulets on the workbench, adding the two extinguished Minor Flames. They were unlike anything I had seen before. Their color had changed overnight from smoky quartz to the color and opacity of peach moonstone. Today they were malleable, like putty, and warm, slightly warmer than my body temperature. In mage-sight, they had a dim glow, like a candle through a distant window in a night of dense fog. Experimentally, I touched a Flame to each of the wild-amulets. Nothing happened, not even in mage-sight.

From the frozen stockroom I carried one of the metal ammo boxes of amethyst. It still looked dead, unchanged from the time on the Trine when I had pulled its energies to me and drained it totally. *Except for the cobra*, some small part of me reminded. Unlike normal stone, it wouldn't take a recharge, meaning it didn't accept the restoration of creation energies like ordinary stone. I had tried to fill it once before, and the energies I could bring from the heart of the earth bounced right off. It really was dead stone. Yet, there was that danged cobra and the purple mist I had breathed.

I added water to the warming aventurine and returned

to the workbench. It was harder than normal to calm my heartbeat and breathing, a current of anger still spiking through me at the thought of Lucas. But I didn't want to go messing with unknown energies while ticked off, so I made a space and hopped onto the workbench. I sat, my legs curled, and opened a portable charmed circle. I probably should have gone out back, away from people, but I wasn't going to try anything tricky. I just wanted a quick look-see into the stones.

I never found a peaceful, slow heart rate, but I did relax. When I had calmed myself, and my own temperature had cooled from grief and anger to merely unhappy, I began inspecting all the stones in mage-sight. I placed the sapphire in close proximity to one of the Flames, and nothing happened. I tried the amethyst with the sapphire. I tried several combinations of Flame with the visa, with my prime ring, and with the sapphire. Nothing.

But when I tried the extinguished Flame with the amethyst, both sparked. It was just a flash of light, like a jolt of recognition, but it was there. Nothing happened when I added the sapphire or the zoisite. But when I brought the pear-shaped citrine nugget close to the amethyst and the Flame, there was instant heat, and the Flame began to glow. I separated the stones and sat there on the workbench, staring at them.

Carefully, I brought all three stones close again, holding a sliver of amethyst and the citrine wild-stone to a Flame. All three sparked again, and in the amethyst I saw eyes, eyes, eyes. I fell into the stone, deep into the matrix. Eyes watched me, blinking, entreating. It was as if I were part of the stone, part of the crystalline strength, as if it and I were made of lavender eyes. Through the eyes I saw the wheels. Amethyst's wheels. Interlocking rings of amethyst stone, glowing with life and power, similar to creation energy, yet subtly different. The size of the purple stone was lost with nothing to measure it by, but I remembered the size—long as a football field, nearly as wide, but with the gyroscope-like rings folded flat, it looked narrow, a faceted cabochon of eyes. Millions of them. The golden navcone—the navigation nosecone—was seated firmly and securely against the stone. And it was tethered with a glowing green rope that vanished out of sight. A living ship of the High Host.

In my vision, the wheels were singing to me, a wonderful, placid melody, a gentle lullaby. In the notes were words. *"We are nearly healed, little mage. Nearly healed. Soon to be released from time, time, time. Help us save our Mistress. Promise us this. To save our Amethyst. Promise us. Promise us. Soon, soon, soon,"* they—it—the ship caroled.

The vision faded though the soft singing continued. I returned to myself for an instant, seeing my hands holding three rocks, before plunging again into the stone, deeper inside where the light shimmered and glistened, rebounding through the crystal amethyst heart. It was dark and cold here, the song far away, a distant wind through standing stones.

I saw Amethyst and Zadkiel trapped underground. They looked at me, shocked. Zadkiel reached up to where I hovered, high over his head, yet deep in the Trine. His hand passed through me, a ghostly sensation. The seraph was badly burned. His bones showed through blackened flesh. Dragonets twined around him, fangs hooked into him, siphoning off his lifeblood. His sword dragged in the web, coated with their gore.

As I watched, he hacked, cleaving one in two. Yet it clotted over with a mucoid, gelatinous substance. Its chitinous surface regenerated instantly. He swung again. Nothing changed except that his burns grew deeper. The seraph was weakening.

Below him, still trapped in the crimson strands of her cell, wrapped in the chains that seared her, was the cherub, Amethyst. *She was real.* I hadn't been entirely certain. The cherub was a bizarre being, her entire body feathered in pale lavender, a mishmash of body parts, demi-wings, hands, feet, breasts, all secured by reddish-black chains that burned into her flesh. Every part of her body was covered with eyes, eyes shackled in demon-iron chains.

I remembered the scripture. "And every one had four faces: the first face was the face of a cherub, and the second face was the face of a human, and the third the face of a lion, and the fourth the face of an eagle . . . and their whole body, and their backs, and their hands, and their wings, and the wheels, were full of eyes round about. . . ."

She stared at me, her human face filled with hope. A light came from somewhere, bright as the heart of the sun. It burned my eyes and I closed them against the pain. Yet I could hear her crooning. *"Help me. Help us."*

Fear bloomed in the dark places of my mind. "I can't," I said aloud, opening my eyes again. "Forcas has my blood. I can't come back down there. I . . . can't."

"You are wounded. He has harmed you." Her voice was a delicate chime of compassion. *"Woooouuuunded."*

I knew she meant my side, the psychic injury I had first received while mired in the walls of her trap. She cocked her head, rotating in her prison, turning the eagle face to me. The beak parted. *"I hear my wheels,"* she said, her strange, pointed tongue speaking words.

Again she gyrated, her chains turning with her. The lion face spoke, a lyrical growl. *"You have bound them to you. Bound them. Save us. Come. Now!"*

Below the growl, I heard the wheels crooning to me. *"Soon. Your stolen blood will be restored. We will help you. And you will help her. You will rescue the Mistress. You will."*

I linked the trails of the warren beneath the Trine into a map and stored it in a sliver of amethyst, then slipped from the vision and the otherness like stepping from a pond, weird images sluicing away like water. When I came to myself, I was still sitting on the workbench, legs cramping. I clicked open the circle and slid to the ground. When my circulation had returned to my toes, and I could stand without pain, I picked up the stones.

The citrine was unchanged, but the amethyst, which had faded from a rich lavender the first time I had seen it to a clear crystal, seemed a deeper hue, as if contact with the other stones had restored some of its vibrancy. The Minor Flame, however, was glowing with a peachy, phosphorescent radiance.

"You look better," I said to the Flame.

It flashed a darker shade and then brighter. I could have sworn it winked.

Chapter 22

$\dagger$

Before dusk, I had shaped and carved all the green aventurine stones for the leaf necklace, and had taken them through the first polishing, most by hand. I didn't stop for lunch, or breaks, or time to think. I didn't stop for anything, and though it was Monday, and I assumed the sign was still on the back door, no one came to me for charms or favors.

By nightfall, my body had stiffened into the hunch-backed curve of an old crone. I had taken off my one-piece work jumpsuit and was stretching cramped muscles when Rupert, shooting me glances, came to the back. He put away stock, chattered about repairs on the town, about new items that had sold online, about orders from shops that carried our more pricey items. He shared an amusing tidbit about a dog that wandered in while the front glass was being replaced, and that a moose herd had been spotted to the south. He told me that Marla was back and Ciana had gone home with her, revealed the safeguards the town fathers had ordered for the night—el-cars loaded with well-armed guards, and elders praying in shifts.

My best friend was far too chatty, and after ten minutes of nattering on, during which he studied me with concerned eyes, I held up a hand to stem the flow. "What do you really want?" I asked, watching his face.

Rupert put a hand on his hip, all queenly indignation, something he did when he was uncomfortable. "You're too quiet. You haven't said a word all day. I want to know if you're all right. No, that's not quite it. I want to know what in Habbiel's pearly citadel is wrong with you," he said baldly.

I tested the words on my tongue, watching my hands as they hefted a fist of quartz. When I thought I could say them out loud, I set the quartz down and leaned against the workbench, bracing myself with my palms. "I made a mistake. I slept with Lucas last night."

"Oh," Rupert said, his face falling, his indignation collapsing. He slid his hand into his pocket, opened his mouth, and closed it with a click before speaking again. "Well. I see," he said. Without another word, he turned and left the room.

"That went just dandy," I said into the silence. I wasn't completely certain what Rupert's expressions had meant when I told him—all sorts of feelings had flitted across his face—but the final one had been dismay. Which pretty well summed up my own feelings.

Alone, I finished my stretching and cleaned up the stone-dust-and-water mess that accumulated when I worked stone. Feeling better having spent the day with my first love, I turned off the heat and went upstairs, my feet ringing on the old boards.

Oddly, Rupert had gone up without me. I had sort of hoped he would speak again, maybe invite me to have supper with Audric and him. I assumed they were arguing about Audric leaving town, but I was at loose ends. And out of food. I still hadn't made it to the grocery store. Too busy fighting Darkness, saving the town, and getting smeared by vandals. Unhappily, I remembered I had dirty sheets on the bed and on the porch. Those were probably frozen to the wood, stuck there until spring thaw. And no clean ones available.

I opened my door and stopped in the opening. A light was on, the heat was up, and candle flames flickered in the breeze of the overhead fans. The place smelled wonderfully of onions, garlic, potatoes frying, and seafood. Lucas was standing in the kitchen, flipping something in a skillet, a knack I had never learned.

After one flash of anger that left me empty, I wasn't sure what I felt as I studied him at the stove. Hungry for the meal he was preparing. Violated that he had invaded my home. Hurt that he thought he could make a place for himself in my life after cheating on me. Certain he had no idea that kissing a clerk's hand constituted cheating. Uncertainty as to whether or not it actually did. Absolute confidence that if I let him back in my life, I'd regret it. He would cheat again. Maybe not today. Maybe not with a clerk in a bakery. But with someone.

I was pretty sure Rupert had let him in and hadn't known what to do after our little talk, hence the peculiar look earlier. Why did things have to be so complicated? I closed the door. Lucas looked up at the sound, a welcoming look on his face. "I brought your pretty dagger back, love. An elder found it in the street." He held up the tanto.

Love. Right. I moved to the window across from the doorway and bent, blowing out the candle. Stalking clockwise through the loft, I blew out another candle. The smell of smoke and aromatic oils followed me.

"Thorn?" I heard the tanto clatter on the table.

Without speaking, I blew out another candle and another, until I reached the kitchen table and the tall tapers that were burning there. My beeswax candles, imported from Mississippi. He hadn't asked if he could use them. He had gone through my pantry cabinet to find them. I wondered what else he had gone through, the thought unfair, as Lucas wasn't snoopy. But he had walked in and taken over my home. *My* home. I should be furious. Instead, I was just drained and cold. On the way by, I blew the tall candles out too.

When they were all out, smoke swirled in the loft air and I walked back to the kitchen. Lucas had turned off the stove and stood against the counter, watching me, arms hanging limp, his expression guarded.

I crossed my arms over my middle, aware but uncaring that my body language looked protective, and leaned my butt against the kitchen table. Four feet separated us. It might have been a thousand miles.

"Last night was great," I said. His face lightened

slightly, his body unwinding fractionally. "But it shouldn't have happened." When he started to speak, I interrupted. "Flirting for you is as casual and unconscious as breathing. But it always hurt me. Always, every time. And you always knew it hurt, yet you still did it. And you cheated on me. And that hurt most of all.

"Stop," I said when he tried to speak. "I'm not finished. And I need to say this." I took a breath that pulled at my ribs, the air aching as it passed through my throat. "I know it didn't mean anything to you; that kind of flirting never did. But I saw you today, with the pretty girl in the bakery across the street."

"Are we going to go over this again?" he asked. "Every day for the rest of our lives? You know I love you. I've apologized for the one time—one time—I cheated on you. I told you I want you back. You, not some big-busted girl from a bakery."

I laughed softly through my nose, breathing the amusement and the hurt out together with wry acceptance. He clearly had no idea how transparent his statement was.

"I had plans. Supper made—pasta Alfredo, and salad, wine, dessert, great sex," he said, "and you have to go and—"

"Yes," I said into his tirade. "I know you love me."

"And I'll never cheat on you again."

"That I don't know," I said, tightening my arms around my waist. "I really don't. And I never will. Our ideas about what constitutes cheating are different. Our concepts about the sanctity of marriage are different. We're divorced, Lucas. And frankly, our marriage was probably over before it ever started."

Incredulity crossed his face. "Sanctity of marriage? *Sanctity?* Death and plagues, Thorn, you're a *mage*." He picked up a pot lid and slammed it down on the skillet. "Under the right conditions, you'll mate with anything that moves. In any combination. I've heard the stories."

Shock spiraled through me. Anger built in his eyes. "I know what I'm facing, married to you," he said, crossing the space between us, taking my shoulders in his hands, squeezing. I was bruised from the fighting and flinched, but he didn't ease his grip, forcing me to look at him. "You lied to me about what you were. Who you were. You placed me in deadly danger for sleeping with you if you were ever discovered. You're a *mage*. And I want you anyway."

Anyway. In spite of my genetic signature. I didn't know why that *anyway* hurt so much. I looked up at him, his blue eyes vivid, black hair falling over his brow, beard a black stubble on his lean cheeks. He was just as beautiful as the first time I saw him. Heartache tightened my chest. I had lied to him. In its own way that was an infidelity too.

"You will never be able to be faithful to me," he said, shaking me slightly. "And I still love you."

"You can't possibly be afraid of my cheating on you," I said. But he was. I saw it on his face and pushed my way out of his grasp. I placed the table between us, needing a clear head. This conversation was turning out entirely different from what I had expected.

"It's true," I said, "that when mage-heat hits us, we don't have a choice what we do or with whom. We go pretty much mindless. But in Enclave, a mage makes certain she's locked up with her intended partner on the proper date for the seraph flyover, the day our mage-heat is stimulated. Married partners make stringent plans to remain faithful, plans that involve locks and keys. If we had stayed married, I'd have made those plans." Lucas' eyes moved over my face, evaluating my words. "There'd have been no orgy in the streets."

I could have added that it was usually only the unmarried who joined in group mating, and those who wanted to avoid having a litter while single placed themselves with champards for servicing—sterile half-breeds, the second-unforeseen. But I didn't say it. When a woman chose a life partner, she no longer took part in the mass mating ceremonies. Usually.

And wasn't it different when a human cheated? Humans had a choice. Maybe that was splitting hairs, to parse it so closely, but we all made choices that reflected how we wanted to live our lives, humans and mages. And Lucas hadn't had to flirt with the big-busted girl. Yet he had.

Much like I hadn't had to kiss Thadd under a porch during a battle, hadn't had to because mage-heat hadn't fully awakened. I'd still had a brain, had known what was happening. Yet I had kissed him. More than kissed him. My face heated uncomfortably.

"What?" Lucas asked.

I scrubbed my face, feeling the grit of stone on my skin. I needed a shower, followed by a long, hot, soaking bath to loosen my muscles. I needed Lucas. And I needed him out of my home and out of my life. "I'm too tired to make a decision tonight," I said, dropping my hands. "Thanks for fixing dinner. We can eat. Then you go home."

"You're not kicking me out?" he asked, suspicion, and maybe a bit of hope, in his voice.

"I'm not sleeping with you, either." An incredulous smile lit his features. "I'm not," I said, making sure he heard me.

"Fine. It's a start."

I sighed, knowing I had made a mistake but not knowing exactly what it was. "I'll wash up. Then we'll eat. Then you will go home. Yes?" But Lucas didn't answer. He was already dishing up the food, which smelled like a little bit of heaven, making my mouth water. I washed my face and joined my ex-husband for pasta Alfredo. How stupid was that?

Lucas didn't want to leave, of course. He wanted to stay the night, hoping to convince me with his body that we were perfect for one another, and he was charming and totally absorbed in me throughout the meal, the conniving bastard. He was just as wonderful as he had been before we got married. Is that the way to a man's heart? Refuse to sleep with him? Kick him out early? Refuse to marry him? Again.

My emotions were still raw even after a great meal, and I knew better than to let him near me, even for the shoulder rub he offered as temptation, and which I really needed. But I was wavering. So as soon as we finished cleaning up the kitchen and putting away the dishes, I went to the door, opened it, and stood back.

He sat down in a kitchen chair, straddling it, his hands

on the tall back, his chin on his knuckles. He looked gorgeous, and he knew it. "You're really going to make me leave."

"Yes. Go."

"Right now."

I closed my eyes against the enticement he promised and rubbed my temples, my shoulders aching with the motion. If he touched me I was ruined. I'd capitulate. I knew it. "Please, Lucas."

"You're going to miss me," he said, rising, the chair legs scraping on the floor. "You're going to wish I had stayed," he said, closer. "You're going to think about me all night, wanting and longing."

I couldn't help the smile that pulled at my mouth. "I can live with that," I said, opening my eyes. He was standing right in front of me, the rugs having muffled his footsteps. His blue eyes were only inches away, staring into mine, and I felt an intense craving to just touch his mouth. Once. I curled my fingers into claws and tucked them behind my back.

As if he knew the reason for the action, he gave me that smile, that blasted smile. *Tears of Taharial.* "I'm not sure I can," he said. "But I guess I'll have to." He leaned in the six inches that separated us and kissed the corner of my mouth. One of those little feather-light kisses, like heated air brushing close. "I still have my key. I'll see myself out. I'll call you in the morning." And he was gone.

He was smug, complacent, and self-satisfied. And he still had a key to the shop. As if that were significant of something intimate. I hadn't bothered to get the key back, although I had changed the lock on the loft. Was it significant that he could get halfway to me? Had I deliberately left him with access to my life? Could I be that stupid?

Somehow I got the door closed and a bath going and my body stripped out of the dirty clothes. I set the ward, feeling and seeing the glow of the energies as they filled the walls and foundation. I added stones to the bathwater, for their restorative powers, then added a big helping of salt for the muscle aches and pains.

Just as I was about to step in, I heard something hit the

back stained-glass window in the original hayloft door. Or
rather, hit the ward over it. If the stone had hit the glass it
would have made a simple tap. Instead it was a sizzle followed by a sharp snap, as the stone shattered. A bright
light shocked through the windows. "Crap in a bucket!"
someone cursed.

I chuckled and wrapped the worn robe around me before pushing open the functioning window beside the
stained-glass one. I rested an elbow on the ledge and
looked down at Eli. He stood hipshot on the crusty snow,
feet spread, pointy-toed boots at angles, and a cowboy hat
on his head. I was a slut. I had to be. Because he looked
really good. But I had no desire to invite him up—well, not
much of one—so maybe I was only half a slut.

"Shop's closed."

"Is he gone for the night?" he asked.

"Yeah, he's gone."

"Want company?"

"I had company. I ran company off."

"Well that's good to know. Why would you want a slut-
puppy like him anyway? I mean, when you could have
me?" He spread his arms in display. "I'm clean, loyal, de-
pendable, charming, and sweet."

"You sound like a pet. Mages don't do well with pets."
Something about all the energies surrounding a mage
made them die young. Or go feral. Come to think of it, a
high percentage of humans did the latter.

"I'm also great in bed. Or so I've been told."

I laughed outright. Eli had offered to shake my world, in
a variety of innovative and athletic ways, and he was a
pretty thing. Amber-colored eyes had always been a favorite of mine. I cupped my chin and went with the flow of
the conversation. "Why would I want a man who's prettier
than I am?"

"Why would I want a woman faster and more powerful
than I? Speaking of which, did you ward the whole
building?"

"Looks like."

"Dang, woman. That's impressive."

Yes. It was. I liked him even better that he would know

that. And that he could tell me so. I studied him in the snow as the cold air cleared my head. He was indeed attractive. And charming. And I was lonely. If mage-heat were a factor, I'd invite him up in a heartbeat. But with me as just me, I wasn't ready, I decided. Not ready for any man.

Realizing that made me feel better. "Good night, Eli," I said, closing the window.

"Wait!" he called. When I paused, the sash in hand, he said, "The EIH wants to talk. They think they can help you."

"Do I need help?" I asked.

"You will. And when you do, remember the signal."

A white cloth in the window. Or was it red? "Good night, Eli," I said firmly, pulling on the glass.

"Good night, mage of my dreams."

The window closed. I pulled the tapestry over it, and slid the robe off my shoulders and my body into the hot water. Heaven. Pure heaven. And suddenly my life looked okay. Weird how a little honest attention from a pretty man could make the difference between a totally terrible life and a much better one.

Chapter 23

◊

I put three blades and the amulet necklace on the bed-side table near the ward's on-off marble sphere, and fell into the covers, pulling them up around my ears. I slept hard, dreaming of seraphs. One had teal eyes, a chiseled jaw, and pale down beneath teal wings, and one had ruby irises and scarlet plumage. The Angel of Punishment wooed me, standing in a jewelry store; the winged-warrior in red battle armor played at rescue duty.

I came awake to the sound of slow, steady dripping in the tub, sharp plinks. Outside, wind whistled as it whipped through the buildings. The old livery creaked, settling. There was nothing in the sounds to warrant the sudden chills that ran down my arms beneath the coverlet and across my scalp. Nothing at all, yet I was suddenly hyper-alert, skin tingling, breath fast, hands clenched as if to draw blades. Fear prickled along my flesh, lifting the tiny hairs on my body. Outside, just below the sound of the wind, I heard the distant cry of the lynx. That blasted portent. Drat.

Without giving away that I was awake, I slowly swiveled my head and took in the loft. A gray tinge rested in the eastern windows, the night stars dimmed by the promise of dawn. The apartment was still and silent. But the ward was gone, the walls unprotected. I hadn't done it. Ciana? Some-one using her seraph pin?

I breathed in slowly, and caught a scent, the smell that

had woken me, cloying and sweet, like flowers and rotting corpses. Incubus. *Tears of Taharial.*

Opening mage-sight, I scanned the room again; the furnishings, walls, ceiling and floor were lit with their usual soft blue, green, and pinkish tints. The stones at windows and doors were fully charged. There was no hint of Darkness, but the scent continued to grow, as if it sat on the foot of my bed. Beneath that scent I caught a whiff of something else, equally vile, yet subtly different. Fresh roses and dead leaves, standing water, mold, and mildew. *There are two of them. Incubus and succubus.*

Stealthily, panic crouched tight in my throat, I slid my hands out of the covers to grasp the walking stick and amulet necklace. The amulets clinked softly. In mage-sight, they glowed weakly, *wrongly*; even the bloodstone handle of the walking stick wasn't quite right, as if amulets could catch the plague or falter. Shock fluttered through me. Something had affected them. But they were all I had. I pulled the necklace over my head, then eased the blade from its sheath. Every noise I made seemed louder than the next, yet nothing happened, no hidden threat jumped onto the bed and gored me with its claws.

Somewhere on the Trine, the lynx growled. On the Trine, but close. *Fine, cat. I got it. Trouble. Danger. Now go away.*

In a single rush I threw back the covers, grabbed up an extra blade, and raced to the kitchen. Slammed my back against the wall. Three feet of stone and brick offered some protection, and the only window here was up high, long and narrow, the transom sealed shut with layers of paint.

Nothing moved; nothing attacked. My harsh breathing and the dripping tub were the only sounds. The scents began to dissipate, to slip away. The apartment grew brighter to my sight as the smells gathered into one spot and faded. I followed them with a mind-skim, my nose seeking their scents, to the front of the loft where they formed a cloud at the French door onto the porch. They weren't attacking me. *They were trying to get away.* Fury blazed through me, driving out the fear. I bellowed a battle cry. The mist of Darkness rushed beneath the cracks and out onto the porch where it re-formed into a loose column of black ink, almost indistinguishable from the night.

I drew on my prime amulets, the walking stick hilt and the ring, but they wavered weakly in response, and I surely drained them as strength trickled into me, an irregular stutter of energy. I sprinted to the door, slashing through the cloud. The smell broke over me, drenching my feet. I ripped open the door and cut through the dark mist as it tried to re-form. Below me, I heard a gurgle. Bare feet on the frozen boards, I sliced through the Darkness again and again as I dashed to the railing and looked down. Below me, standing in the street, were two dark beings. One was a succubus, Jane Hilton, her head thrown back, throat exposed. This one looked more real than the ones from the battle. Her breasts were normal-sized, not the overripe melons of the succubi. She fell to her knees on the cracked pavement as if I had cut her body along with the mist.

The thing beside her was Malashe-el, the daywalker, its eyes labradorite blue flecked with scarlet. From the bloodstone hilt, images flooded through my mind. Stored images of the beast overruled the rune of forgetting Malashe-el still carried.

The daywalker's rune sat high on its chest, a silver tracing of wire supporting a huge, white quartz crystal. I stared at it with mage-sight. A mage-rune, but different from one I might create. This one was shaped, not to destroy memory, but to blur memory away. The memories of this Darkness hadn't been stolen from me so much as clouded over, hazed into the mundane, their importance eradicated. I cut the mist again, but my pause had been too long. *Stupid!* It separated and slid off the porch, dropping to the street. I crossed the blades low over my body, breath heaving, heart racing, a cold sweat drenching me.

The succubus was fragrant with evil, but with an overlay of human scent. The thing had possessed Jane's body, an evil sprite hoping to capture men in a spell of lust. Lucas had slept with this thing. Jane clawed her throat. A single trace of black mist wriggled across the porch and I sliced it through, again and again. Jane gurgled in anguish, her body rippling. I was surprised at the alteration. For a moment, before she flowed back to her youthful appearance, she looked like Gramma Stanhope, bent and worn, full of old angers.

The daywalker stood beside her, watching as she writhed in agony. Finally, it looked up at me and spoke, directly into my mind. *"Come. My mistress calls you. There is not much time."*

Without thought, without plan, I reversed the small blade and threw it, overhand, the spinning toss aimed at its heart. Its pupils widened and it darted to the side, but the blade caught it beneath its arm, striking deep, close to the site where I had last struck it. I heard the thump of blade against bone, and smelled lilacs as the mage-steel cut through ribs and muscle and into its lung.

It crumpled to the street. The black mist coalesced around it. The woman who had claimed to love Lucas bent and withdrew the throwing blade. It gave a sucking sound and she threw it to the side, keening, holding her hand as if it burned.

Together, spilling blood in the moonlight, trailing a scent of death and destruction, they ran down the street and vanished into an alley. Not willing to risk a broken leg by a jump, I stood on the porch, staring down into Upper Street, my eyes seeing only ice, cracked pavement, and broken sidewalk. The fight, such as it was, had taken less than a minute.

My side, where the spur had touched me twice, gave a single mighty throb. It hadn't pained me since Thadd smeared it with his blood, but now it twisted brutally, like a muscle spasm, stealing my breath. I pressed my elbow against the hard knot, and it burned, feverish, like a boil. I glanced down, and was startled to see it pulse once in mage-vision, a wan yellow glow that faded and was gone.

Behind me, my door crashed open. I felt more than saw him whirl through my apartment. I could *feel* the spin of his blades and smell the faint whiff of sweat. I turned and stared through the window, though I could see only my reflection and the pale gray sky in the glass. After a moment, Audric stepped onto the porch. His blades were both at the ready, the tinge of oil tainting the air.

"They are gone?" he asked. To my mage-sight, Audric glowed a bright coral, blood coursing beneath his skin in tones of crimson.

"Yeah," I said numbly as I lifted the amulet necklace. Something was wrong with it.

"How did they get in? Did you set the ward?"

"Yes, I set it." *They did something to my amulets. Maybe during the battle?* "I need light." Audric followed me inside and turned on the light over the kitchen table. I removed the necklace and spread it over a clear space on the old wood. In mage-sight, everything looked wrong, dull and off-color; nothing stood out as the one cause, but when I shut off my sight and looked at the amulets with just human vision, I saw one that was nicked.

I would never attempt to use a broken amulet because damaged stone releases energies wrongly. Many can't be charged with creation energies at all, the power sliding across them and into the nearest whole stone. I lifted the quartz crystal and held it to the light. It was an amulet of illumination, like the ones I had thrown in the street during the battle.

The trinkets were cheap, energy-wise, and easy to make. I seldom searched for and retrieved one if I misplaced it after use. I had lost some on the Trine once. I had lost others in the street. I skimmed it, sniffing with mind and nose, catching my own scent, and the reek of old evil. "I made this. But something else changed it, then reattached it to my necklace."

"When?" Audric asked.

Lucas? I shook my head and placed the crystal on the table, nudging it with a finger. They had tried with the earth charm planted in my clean laundry. That hadn't worked, so they tried a more direct approach. Tag me, not the loft. And it had to have been done recently.

"None of us were prepared for the attack. I was in street clothes, the necklace tied to my waist, not in a protected fold in a dobok. There was this succubus dressed in battle garb." I looked up at him, the half-breed so much taller than I. "One of those who looked like me. She had her weapon at my throat, and she didn't use it." Audric didn't even blink, focusing intently on my words. "My tunic was cut half off. She touched my waist. I remember the heat of her fingers. Then you killed her." I blinked away the image. I hadn't realized how much it bothered me, but it had been like watching myself die, cleaved in twain by the sword of my champard. The image was a small shock that lingered still. "Her blood smelled like mine and Darkness fused."

"She had one assignment. To plant the amulet."

"It's empty now," I said. "Whatever it was supposed to do, is done."

"Perhaps simply to provide access to your home."

"Then why wait so long?"

"You were not alone last night," Audric said, his tone pointed.

I felt my lips twitch. It was the nearest thing to a smile I could manage. "No. I wasn't. I hit one of them with a throwing blade." I kept my eyes turned away from him. "It was the daywalker. The blade is in the street."

Audric looked steadily at me. "This is two times you have struck the beast. There is power in numbers. If you strike it yet a third time, you will gain power over it."

"How much? What kind of power?" I asked, thinking of the spur.

"I don't know. Power is dependent on many things."

I thought about my side. What would happen to me should the spur touch me a third time? Forcas had been calling me in dreams, had wounded me, had sent evil into my home.

"I'll get the blade," he said. When I put up a hand to stop him he said, "Raziel enjoined me to work with you." He canted his head in acknowledgment of a truth he was sharing. "Being your champard was a destiny I already desired. A fate painless to follow."

He disappeared into the stairway and reappeared below, surveying the block, weapons at the ready. At the far end, el-car headlights moved. When Audric stepped into the street and retrieved the throwing blade, placing his bare feet carefully, he was every inch the warrior.

As he lifted it, the moon caught on the blade edge and threw back a golden glow, beauty tainted by the Dark blood on the edge. My birth prophecy, mine and my twin's, had promised, *A Rose by any other Name will still draw Blood*. I had drawn the blood of Darkness. Lolo had always hoped I'd be a battle mage, my blood heating with fire at the thought of war. What else had she hoped? How had she planned to use me?

I lifted my mended amulet, studying the old break. Lolo had put me here for her own purposes, but I had caused my own trouble. I wasn't sure how, but it had all started when I broke my prime amulet, and healing it hadn't corrected things. Sadness welled up in me like a spring on the mountain, gushing and boiling with white-water force. Tears gathered in my eyes and I blinked them away. The orthodox were right. I had brought harm to the town.

I pushed away old wounds and new. I had no time for them. Darkness was here and it was my fault. Seraphs were here as well. Ditto in a convoluted kinda way. The conditions were ripe for a holy war, which would kill humans by the thousands. I had to fix this. Somehow. If I could figure out why breaking the prime amulet months ago had started the trouble.

Overhead, the moon broke through the clouds, a brutal radiance to stone mages. Yet I was unhurt, not drained by its power. I should have been exhausted by its light, energies drawn away like steel pulled by magnetism. But I wasn't. The amulets weren't working well, yet the humidity was causing me no pain. That too was indirectly because of the temper tantrum that led me to break the prime, because without its protection, I had been vulnerable to the wheels. The amethyst had changed me in some fundamental way. Lolo had been upset when she learned I broke the layered stone ring. Had she known of the amethyst on the Trine, that it might change me? Is that why I had two primes instead of the usual one?

I carried the charm that had been used against me to the bathroom and stuffed it into a bag of salt that held other contaminated things. I was running out of places to put objects of evil. I closed the bag as Audric climbed the stairs.

Lolo had to have known something, expected some-

thing. Constant contact with the amethyst had augmented
some natural mage-attributes and decreased others. Had
altered the way I could store and use the energy of creation in stone. Had damped my mage-heat to nothingness.

I didn't know if I was addicted to the stone, or if the
stone had become addicted to me. If the latter was true,
then the huge crystals boxed in the stockroom were some
new thing in the world of mages. A new construct. And
though they were nearly drained of their natural energies,
the amethyst had still gifted me with more power than I
had before.

"Thorn?"

"The daywalker was acting as an incubus," I said, thinking that didn't feel quite right.

"Or it had one at its command," Audric said.

"Yes," I breathed. That was it. Malashe-el had been directing the incubus, and Jane had been a conduit for the
thing that possessed her. The only reason to attack a mage
with a succubus and an incubus was to try to stimulate
mage-heat. That thought melted away the last of the
adrenaline. I turned, scenting the blood of the daywalker
in the dim light. "I need to clean the blade," I said. "And I
need Jane Hilton, the woman possessed by the succubus.
Can you track her? Bring her to me? Before full dawn and
without danger to yourself?"

"I can bring her. Mules are unaffected by such."

I nearly winced at the term. "I don't like that word," I
said.

"I am yoked to a seraph," he said, tone flat. "The second-
unforeseen are neither human nor mage. They are sterile
in every way—unable to manipulate creation energies, unable to procreate, unable to experience passion as humans
or mages can. We are from both races and are neither.
Mule. The term is appropriate," he spat.

I didn't agree, didn't argue. Audric had been free. He
had bargained that freedom away in exchange for his life
and was now enslaved to the High Host. In the bargain, the
life he once lived was gone. I understood. The reverse bargain was made for me once, and I had been severed from
the slavery of all mages, a slavery that linked us all in one

place, working together, living together, mind-to-mind and skin-to-skin. I had been forced into freedom. I too had grieved.

He spun my throwing blade and offered it to me hilt first. I took the small blade, tilting my head in acknowledgment of his pain. "When I bring her, you will have a ring of protection prepared?" he asked. "I do not relish having her infect every man in town."

"I'll be ready."

Without another word, he whirled and disappeared, moving as only a master of savage-chi can, totally silent. Way cool master of death with hands of destruction. Bound to a seraph. Lost to the world. And majorly pissed off about it all.

Chapter 24

I shoved the kitchen table across the room, out of the way, its leaves let down until it was a fifth its full size. The chairs I hung on wall hooks. The loft was straight and neat. I was dressed in my black dobok, my hair braided close to my head and out of the way, unable to be used as a weapon against me. Only fools and movie stars went to war with hair long and flowing, begging to be twisted around an opponent's fist and yanked.

All my blades were in place, secured up sleeves, down my collar, and strapped to my legs. The throwing blade had been cleansed by wiping it off on a strip of a rag followed by a quick thrust in a used bag of salt and a thorough rinsing in spring water. Once again it was freshly oiled and ready for battle.

Using a new bag of earth salt, I poured a salt ring on the kitchen floor, leaving a two-foot space open. I placed a chair in the center of the circle and gathered all the implements I might need: candles, a bell, matches, well water, my ceremonial blade, my three crucifixes on long chains, and duct tape. I didn't add the *Book of Workings*. I didn't have time to create and learn an incantation. This would be brute force.

From the depths of bags of salt, I removed stone jars filled with things that needed separating from the world, and placed them in the circle. I added a cloth and the bag of salt, just in case. Quickly, I closed the circle, feeling a momentary spike of fear. If I couldn't fix the amulets, bringing them to power, and fully charge the stones, I was lost. I would have to start over, carving new defensive amulets. I had been shoving that fear away, but looked at it closely now. Nothing should be able to affect a mage's amulets, draining them as had been done to mine. I had never heard of such a thing. And I didn't know what to do.

Was the spelled amulet a simple one-time switch, a sort of on-off switch that temporarily incapacitated my amulets? Or had it been much more, like a computer virus, permanently disabling them? That was a question I hadn't been able to look at or even acknowledge until now. The charm had been on the necklace, which I had placed near the sphere that activated the ward, and close to the walking stick hilt. Only those amulets had been affected, none of the others in the loft. This soooo sucked Habbiel's pearly, scabrous toes.

I calmed myself and directed my attention to the amulets. The stones in the necklace and on the walking stick looked dangerously weak, all of them almost totally drained. With a thought, I directed creation energies into them. The irregular pulsing of the amulets instantly smoothed. Within minutes, they began to look healthy again. I breathed a sigh of relief. They hadn't been poisoned. They had simply been drained.

Simply . . . Yeah, right. If that happened in battle I was toast. The amulets brightened, growing stronger.

Once, the act of recharging stones would have taken me hours and brought me dangerously close to the creation energies deep in the earth. Now, like the oldest, strongest mages, it took only moments for each stone to glow with strength. More than anything else, this speed of working with energy marked me as different from other neomages. For mages, different is dangerous. In Enclave, there were no unique mages. I was, once again, a singularity. A misfit, unconformed to either the world of humans or the world of mages.

The sky was brightening to a dull metallic sheen when I heard them on the stairs: the faint scuffling of boots, the muted sounds of muffled screams. I dropped the circle, smoothing a new aperture in the salt, opened the door, and stood aside. Audric entered, dressed in black battle dobok, a body tossed over his shoulder. It was wriggling, fighting, trussed, and gagged.

Audric carefully stepped between the edges of the salt opening and deposited Jane in the chair. She kicked him, catching him in the shin, hurting her toes. She screamed behind the gag in her mouth, rage and hate in the tones. Audric held her in the chair.

Stripping a length of duct tape, I secured her right leg to the right chair leg, wrapping the tape around and around. It would hurt like heck coming off, but that wasn't my problem. Jane had welcomed a succubus into her body, trading its power for the use of her bed. A woman who wanted a man who didn't want her might do such a thing. *Lucas*.

I taped her left leg to the left chair leg. Standing, I said, "Okay."

Audric freed her left hand from the bindings and I taped that wrist to the chair arm. Her right wrist followed suit. With the roll of tape, Audric wrapped her shoulders to the chair back and her hips to the seat in a single long winding. When he finished, he pulled away the cloth that had secured her.

Jane bucked hard, bringing the chair legs off the floor and landing with a solid *scuff-thump*. The chair was heavy. Unless she got a foot to the floor, she couldn't move it far enough to disrupt the salt ring. I gestured toward the opening in the ring and Audric stepped through. On the other side he pulled his blades and walked the perimeter of the apartment, checking through the windows, over the stable, into the street.

I sat on the floor and lit three candles, ignoring Jane's body-wrenching exertions. I had chosen new candles, never used, with clean white wicks. I placed them at the north, northeast and northwest sides of the ring, not aligning them to the compass, but balanced according to the Trine's peaks. Breathing, I quickly settled into a steady, calm state. Having just been in a mage-state, and having already determined what I would do, there was no time lag as my body adjusted to the needs of my craft. I was as ready as I would ever be. I closed my eyes. When I opened them, I opened my mage-sight.

With a handful of salt and a snap of power, I closed the ring and set my amulets over my head. Jane screamed, a long, agonized sound, half muffled by the gag, a sound that came from Jane's throat, but from the succubus' fear. It knew what I was about to do. Chatting with a Darkness was foolish. But I needed information, and hoped I had found a way to get it.

I had opened an inverted shield over us, not just a charmed circle. It was like the trap at my spring, an energy construct to keep us in, not to keep others out. Safely inside it, I thumbed a mouse carved from white howlite and opened a different circle, this one a simple privacy circle. Jane's screams sounded dead, dull tones instantly absorbed by the privacy circle. We would be as silent as if I still slept, alone and warm in my bed.

Not knowing which one would work best, I took up the three crucifixes, one in my left hand, two in my right. I had tried one method to dis-possess Malashe-el, and if the view of the walker and Jane together in the street was any indication, it hadn't been totally effective. Jane was human, and she had been raised Christian; I hoped this one might work on her.

I didn't pray often because, according to prevailing theology, the Most High didn't hear the prayers of soulless beings. But, just in case, I prayed aloud. "Hear me Lord of creation, the Most High One, King of Kings, God the Victorious. With your servant Mutuol, I do battle in your name." Beyond the circle, I noted that Audric had stopped pacing and was watching me, his back to the kitchen wall, blades crossed low and ready. "Mutuol, I claim your power to bind this evil." Jane's screams intensified and she bucked wildly, sending the chair legs banging into the floor like a drum. "To wrap it in chains. To remove it from the chalice that holds it. To free the body and soul of the woman who was so foolish as to call such a being. Forgive her, for she knew not what she did." I wasn't sure the last line was true, but I didn't know it wasn't, either.

Standing, I took up the ceremonial knife and cut away Jane's gag. Her screams were not much louder than when she had been gagged. She spat at me, spittle landing just short of my foot. "My master will come. You are dead, mageling. He will kill you with fire and iron. Or perhaps he will breed with you and produce a litter of sons and daughters before he tears your body to shreds. Children to serve him. My master—"

I backhanded her across the face with the ceremonial knife hilt. Blood flew from her split lip; I heard the sharp snap of a tooth cracking; the smell of sulfur wafted from the broken root, bitter and burning, sulfur mixed with Stanhope blood, Gramma's blood, the blood of others, my blood—familiar smells that shouldn't have been part of her. They had stolen my blood in battle and were actively using it against me. I had to get it back.

Jane spat and a tooth landed on the floor, broken and bloody. If she survived this, and if I was able to separate her from the Darkness, I could offer her an incantation to speed her healing. If not, well, there was no mercy shown to a human who cavorted with Darkness. A broken tooth was the least of her worries, dead or alive.

I held one of the crucifixes in my left hand, close to her head. She reared back, hissing. Teeth bared, her eyes widened, fixed on the silver cross with the body of the dead Christ stretched on it in gold. The metal warmed slightly in my hand. Okay, but not perfect.

I looped the chain on my neck to get it out of the way. Next I tried a crucifix made of wood. It once had a tigereye setting and a silver Christ. Now it was singed wood. Its temperature didn't change at all. I looped it, too, over my head.

The matrix of matter resonated in different ways with the matrixes of evil and good. Some elements of matter worked on some elements of energy, and some didn't. I would have been taught all about such sciences had I been able to stay in Enclave and learn. I would have known exactly what metals and stones to use on the woman and the thing inside her. Now it was hit or miss. But I did know, from the look in her eyes, that the icons were powerful things to her. Once, Jane had faith. That faith punished her, even now.

Holding the last crucifix in my right hand, I brought it close to her. The sound from her throat was the squeal of a piglet pierced through with mage-steel. She reared back as far as her head could stretch, muscles and tendons straining and exposed, her pulse pounding beneath her skin in a frantic rhythm. "Nononononononono . . ."

The gold and amber crucifix blazed. So did the blood-stone rings that layered my prime amulet, a green and roseate glow. That was strange. I had never seen sections of the prime work alone. No time to worry about that now. "Mutuol, cleanse her, by the power of the Most High. Transform her and bind the Darkness." The crucifix Jane had responded to was of the empty cross, hand-carved, amber-inlaid, in a gold setting, and hanging on a gold chain. Tiny little beads of red carnelian were inlaid at each end of the cross, at head, hands, and feet, the places where Jesus bled, if one didn't consider the thirty lashes with a cat-o'-nine-tails delivered by Roman guards that had flayed his back and chest.

"Cleanse her," I repeated. "Transform her and bind the Darkness." With the words, I reached out and let the crucifix rest against Jane's cheek. The cross blazed with light, so bright that I blinked my eyes. The smells of sulfur, dead leaves, and funeral flowers filled the conjuring circle with a black cloud. And the clean smell of heated amber—the scent of twenty-million-year-old fir trees.

"Cleanse her," I said a third time. "Transform her and bind the Darkness." With my left hand I pressed the cross into her flesh. The crucifix sizzled, popped and almost . . . *reached* . . . for her. Before my horrified eyes the amber melted and burned into her face. Shocked, I jerked my hand away, trying to pull the cross off her. The crucifix didn't waver, remaining firmly planted, deep as bone in her flesh. Black smoke rose from her skin and muscle and skull, a brand, like the brands planted by the kirk.

Jane howled, the sound of a full-grown boar being torn apart by wolves. Her skin rippled, the flesh mottled with Darkness, purpling and blackening like deep bruises. A pustule rose on her forehead and erupted, spilling yellow pus. Instantly, and way too late to do anything about it, I realized what I had in the circle with me, taped to the chair. Not a succubus inside a woman, but a succubus that had possessed, eaten, and replaced a woman. Jane's skin peeled back in little rips of flesh. Abscesses formed and burst on her chin, jaw, shoulders, and chest. Her clothes stretched as her musculature and skeleton rearranged.

My stomach turned over with a sickening lurch. "Yuck," I murmured. I backed away, leaving the gold chain dangling against the ruined skin.

The succubus' teeth elongated. Its breasts grew and formed points at the tips like little claws. *Wrath of Angels.* This wasn't just any old textbook succubus. This was a big-ass succubus. The mama of all succubi. *Seraph stones.* If it got loose from the duct tape, I was worse than toast. I was fried, fricasseed, and served up as an entrée. A laugh tittered in my throat. I was betting my life on duct tape.

"My master will come," it said, spitting acid. A droplet landed on the arm of my dobok and burned, the leather melting around it before hardening to protect my skin. It smiled at me through pointed teeth, incisors and canines like those of a small carnivore, which, of course, it was, if you consider that the flesh it ate was human male, starting with the private parts.

The succubus' head was still changing, forming a blunt snout. Its hands were clawed, talons tipped with bright red and orange striped nail polish that had been applied while in human form. The polish cracked and rippled as the beast changed. Red polish on the long, razor-sharp nails of her toes followed suit, drawing to the pointed tips. Tres chic, in a ruination of Darkness kind of way, I thought, still near hysteria. Its skin, where it showed through the torn clothing, was scaled and mottled. Jane was literally enough to scare a man to death, should it transform in the act of sex. "My master will come," it hissed again, writhing its head as if to get away from the cross that still burned into its flesh. "He will take me back."

That stopped me. *Take it back?* From what? From me? I stared at the cross charred into its cheek. Melted in.

Branded. I remembered the words I had used asking the Most High and his servant Mutuol to lend a hand. *Cleanse her. Transform her and bind the Darkness.* This thing couldn't be cleansed. It wasn't human, and only humans could be redeemed. But it could be cleansed of its human guise, transformed to its natural structure. And it could be bound. And I hadn't said what I wanted it bound to.

Feathers and fire. Had I bound the succubus to me? Oh, *seraph stones.* Somebody up there had a weird sense of humor.

That single thought brought me up short. Someone had heard my prayer. Mutuol? The Most High? And he—whoever he was—had done as I asked.

A shiver of fear slithered under my skin. The succubus laughed, thinking I was afraid of it. But I was a whole lot more afraid of holy things than of evil. To wipe the smirk off its face, I hit Jane with the hilt of the knife again. This time, black blood flew, sizzling when it splatted against the charmed circle. I had bound a succubus to me. *Crack the Stone of Ages.*

The succubus' eyes changed slowly as understanding came to it. "You aren't afraid of me," it said. When I didn't answer, it said, "You aren't afraid of my master." It cocked its head, looking particularly reptilian. "What do you want?"

The question thawed me from where I was standing, frozen at the sight of what I had done. What did I want, now that I couldn't have what I had intended? Ciana safe. The Stanhopes safe. The town safe. Me safe and able to stay in Mineral City. For starters. I had intended to dispossess Jane and then question her about what she knew of Forcas' plans. Could I still question this thing? Being bound, it had to speak the truth, or as much of the truth as it had. Some said pride was the first weakness of any Darkness. Pride had caused the fall of Lucifer and his followers. Pride could be used against them. What came out of my mouth had nothing to do with my thoughts. "I've never seen or heard of one like you."

The succubus' pupils were slit, goat-eye irises a coppery yellow, like stained sheets flecked with the brown of old blood. "I am the result of a triple mating between a Power, an unwilling mage, and a blood-demon drunk on Stanhope blood and your blood."

As a child, I had been underground, alone and afraid. Later, I had seen unwilling female mages, rescued from the Trine. If mages had been kept captive long enough to birth a litter, their minds might—would—be gone. And then I caught the timeline. Made of my blood? With that, I calculated its age at less than a month. How fast did these things mature? It acted like a spoiled, rotten child, bragging and testing me. Great. I was stuck in a conjuring circle with a teenaged, power-drunk Darkness. "What is your master?"

"I am a *new* being," it said, "created by a Power. A Principality. He desires you." It smiled. It was a really nasty smile. I couldn't help my reaction. Seeing me shudder, the beast slit its eyes, baring its teeth. "You fear. This is good that you fear me. I am unique, one not seen since the fall of man. I am a succubus queen."

I remembered my research into the obscure words uttered by Malashe-el when I had him trapped at my spring. And last night he reappeared with an incubus and this thing. And now I had it captured. No big guess that I was being led by the nose. "What else are you?"

"I am the mother of those you killed." When I didn't react, it lifted its chin. It licked its lips, tongue tar black and mucoid. "I am the mother of many larvae," it bragged. "Of thousands of eggs. My children will begin to hatch at dawn, and this batch will be even more powerful than I. My children will destroy your world and I will sit beside my master in a Realm of the Dark." Yep. Teenaged hubris. Just my luck.

But, even still, that sounded bad. Seraphs lived at Realms of Light. Sounded as if this Darkness' daddy had visions of grandeur. "What sins have you committed?"

"Sins are for humans and their children. We do what we will."

Okay. Big help there. How could I use this accidental bonding without being used by whatever sent it? More importantly, how could I survive an encounter with a beast that was a whole lot more powerful and a whole lot less mature than anticipated? Duct tape. Could I be any more stupid? I watched as it sat there, waiting. And then I realized that I hadn't asked a specific question. It couldn't lie to a direct question, but if it could find a way to misdirect, it would. So sue me. I had never cross-examined a big bad evil before. I was flying by the seat of my pants again. Which was not smart, no way. "What have you willed?"

It smiled at me, settling deeper into the chair. The motion was slow and languorous. Had it still been in human form, it would have been a sensual flex. "Much. I have seduced humans, including the female whose likeness I chose. And I ate them. They were tasty."

"I thought succubi were only interested in males." How could I use this? How? I had a strip of cloth marked with the blood of the daywalker. In the jar beside it was the blood of another being, a spelled human warrior for Darkness. Could I use them?

"The females were interesting. I liked the form of one of them. Men liked her form. It was pleasurable and necessary."

"Can you transmogrify?" I asked, surprised. Only seraphs should be able to do that, to actually alter shape and appearance at will. But this was a queen. She, not it.

"One form only," she said sullenly, her moods whip-fast. "The rest is illusion. But through my children we will regain our lost gifts."

That didn't sound good. "What have you willed in regards to me?"

Her eyes narrowed and I knew she didn't want to answer. The cross in her cheek quivered as she tried to contract the cheek muscle away from it. A long moment passed and I said nothing, waiting. If she were truly bound to me, she had to answer. But a better question might hurry things along. "What did your master tell you to do about me?"

Her lips peeled back, exposing teeth designed for tearing meat. "To search for you, as once we searched for the wheels. They were close. My master could smell them but not see them, sense them, but not touch them. Now they are gone, and you reek of their scent. When your scent came on the wind, he set traps for you."

When your scent came on the wind. When I broke the prime? Was that the first time the evil on the Trine had sensed me? "You have other mages. Why do you want me?"

She rolled her shoulders, pulling at the duct tape. The chair legs rattled on the floor. "You are different," she said, the words unwilling.

That didn't help. I didn't know what questions to ask, yet I had to find a way to encourage her to talk. Pride had worked once. "Better?" I asked, raising my head, exposing my throat and the amulets that hung there. "Do you mean that I am better than you?"

"No female is better than I," she said, a line of spittle sliding down her jaw.

Major yucks. This thing had been created to seduce, then eat its prey, but without its glamour or a body to inhabit, it would scare a man to death long before the first bite. "I'm better," I said. "Much better than you."

It spat at me, a sizzling spatter, saying, "My master will take you. You will call the wheels. He will mate with me, and then nothing in heaven or earth shall be denied us."

Ahhh. I socked the succubus with the ceremonial hilt. Really hard. Her head rocked back. So I hit her again. Several times. When she was lolling with pain, I rebound her mouth with the gag, taping it in place. With the tape, I wrapped the chair legs and pressed them to the floor, taping her toes to the tile too. By the time I was finished, I was breathing hard and had worked up a sweat. I was nauseated. The stink of sulfur, acid, and dead flowers was really vile. Sitting on the floor at Jane's feet, I pulled on the duct tape. It held. No wonder the Pre-Aps liked it so much. This stuff could do anything.

I had put both clean and used salt in the circle with me. With the clean salt, I made a third ring inside the first two, stepped outside the circle, and closed it. I thumbed the amulet that held a charmed circle and one flared into being, a smaller dome, created just for the succubus. She raised her head and tried to focus on me, snarling. I had hoped she would be out longer than that. If she figured out how to get the chair or her feet loose and break the circle, that would be dangerous. Deadly dangerous.

With a quick finger, I broke the privacy shield and the outer charmed circle with a soft pop. The candle flames flared and went out with the energy surge. Audric was on the couch, blades at his feet, watching me with pursed lips. "What is that thing?" he asked.

I told him what she had said and that I had accidentally bound her to me. Audric snorted as if that was funny. "Invasion of the body snatchers," he said. Which made no sense at all. He shook his head, looking down at his hands.

"Yeah. Okay. Whatever. Will you watch her? I don't have time to, now." The next words shocked me, coming from my mouth even as the thought formed. "I have to go to the Trine." *Feathers and fire. Saints' balls.* My breathing sped up. I was going to the Trine?

He stared at the succubus rather than at me. "The Trine. *Alone. Again.*"

Though I was sweating from the confrontation with the succubus, I shivered at his words. I had promised, never again. *Never underground. No. Never, never, never.* But did I have a choice? Fear and sorrow twisted together in my guts. I didn't want to do this.

"The town can gather troops. Or you and this unworthy champard can kill that thing and go together." His face was blank, and I knew I had hurt him. I was going to war. And I was leaving my champard behind. And he wasn't unworthy, which he knew when his feelings weren't all hurt.

Again, words fell fully formed from my mouth, as if I had thought it all out. As if I had an answer. As if I wasn't terrified. "They'll dither around for days before deciding to war, even after the attack on the town. A fast incursion by a small group, or one person working alone, has a better chance. But if we kill this thing, its master might know it and be waiting for us. I need my champard to guard Jane. Or are you going to talk me to death?"

"Guard," he said. "Got nothing better to do."

As if I stood outside myself, I watched as I tucked the stone jar and strip of cloth with the daywalker's blood into a canvas bag. Piled in a selection of stones, a tiny silver

serving tray, my ceremonial knife, a candle, and slung the
bag over my shoulder. "If Thadd comes by, you can tell him
what happened. And you can use this if that thing gets
loose." I poured clean salt into the silver bowl and placed
it by Audric, the water inside sloshing gently.

"Salt water? What good will that do?"

I dropped in a tiny shard of the amethyst. It was even
more drained than before, scarcely glowing as it *tinked* to
the bottom and rested on the layer of slowly dissolving
salt. "When she gets out, she'll want to restore the illusion
of her beauty, and for that she needs meat. A lot of meat.
Throw the salt water on her. Wet her down good. I think
it'll send her screaming away without eating you or the rest
of the town for lunch."

"That would be nice. I'd like to live long enough for the
holy war that's about to break out here," he said, softly
scornful, and clearly still mad at me. "That would give me
a chance to watch all the humans I love die while I'm tied
to the side of a winged-warrior."

The words dripped with sarcasm, self-pity, and quiet horror. The sarcasm brought me back to myself. I was going up
the Trine. I really was. "Yes," he finished, "that sounds like
a fine plan. Your champard is awed."

"Master of understatement," I said, my heart hurting for
him. But I wouldn't offer sympathy. I collected bottles of
springwater and raisins. Trail food. "I like that in a man."

"I'm not a man."

"Nope. Not a human. Not a mage. Have you decided
what you *will* be yet?"

Audric tilted his head, jaw tight. "I'm not interested in
being psychoanalyzed."

"Tough. I'm not interested in being a shrink to a pissed-
off, whiny mule, either."

His eyes blazed, fingers twitching as if reaching for his
weapons.

I laughed, knowing it was cruel, but needing to say this.
Maybe say it before I died. "Your life has changed. Okay.
Got that. Big deal. You wanted to bind yourself to a free
mage; instead you got bound to a battle-seraph, one of
the most powerful winged-warriors, a relationship that

most of your kind drool over. So you get to draw blood and kick Darkness' ass. Blood, guts and glory, huzzah. You get to stand at the side of the High Host. You didn't want it, but that's what you got. It's what your kind do. Deal with it." I thought he might jump up and pound me to a pulp. I was almost disappointed when he didn't. I picked up the walking stick and twirled it once, hearing the whistle of the motion.

"While I'm being catty I'll ask you a couple of questions. Maybe you're man enough to answer, maybe not." Audric gripped the hilt of his sword until the knuckles showed beneath his dark skin. I adjusted three throwing knives in the proper loops of my dobok while he struggled with my impertinence. When it looked like he had mastered his reaction and wouldn't cut me to ribbons, I said, "How long did it take you to find Sugar Grove?"

Whatever he had expected me to ask, it hadn't been that. "Four summers."

"What brought you the most glory, finding the town or dead-mining it?"

"Finding it," he said, half unwillingly.

"And how many towns are left to be discovered?"

He looked away when he answered. "According to my Pre-Ap maps, dozens were left empty by the plagues, and are now lost beneath the ice caps. A few others were destroyed by war and buried by landslides."

"And how many dead-miners have ever discovered more than one town?"

Audric's eyes pierced me, his mouth turned down. "None. It has never been done."

"You would be the first." Audric stared. I double-checked the placement of three vials of baptismal water, tugging to make sure they would stay in place, yet pop off easily as needed, not that I was convinced they would work against Darkness. I had yet to see proof. "A dead-miner with two towns to his credit. Glory, a name for yourself that would survive until the end finally comes. You can't, however, discover a second town if you're excavating a hole in the ice. But if you sold your claim you could research all winter and spend the summer months looking.

And you would only have to leave Mineral City for three months a year. You could have a home. A real one. It's just a thought."

I walked to the back window and hung a white cloth where it could be seen from outside. "Someone from the EIH will be coming. Maybe Eli. You can tell them where I'll be. Maybe they'll feel like helping."

My heart in my throat, I said, "If I survive, I'll be back before dark tomorrow." With those words, I grabbed up my insulated leather cloak, food, a small bag I had packed for emergencies, and swung out the door and down the stairs to the stockroom for the real supplies. Minutes later, I had Homer saddled and bridled and was leading him out of the stable and up the Trine, my cloak and the bags filled with necessities tied to the saddle skirt.

My breath came tight in my chest. My body was rigid with cold and fear, my hands too firm on Homer's reins. Picking up my agitation, he tossed his head and rolled an eye back at me. "Sorry," I said, patting his big shoulder and easing the pressure on the reins. I was going up the Trine again. I was going into the pit of Darkness. A hellhole. Tears blurred my vision. I didn't want to do this. I really, really, *really* didn't want to do this. *Stupid, stupid, stupid,* my brain shouted at me.

I looked up into the sky and sighed. I had lived in the mountains long enough to read weather signs, and what I saw was Murphy's Law in action. To the south, warm weather currents had gathered and slid north with the trade winds. From the north, a cold front had moved through the highest reaches of the stratosphere. A blizzard had begun to form. "Just ducky," I said.

Chapter 25

The day was well advanced when I reached the site where Amethyst's wheels had lain buried for a century or more. It was the first time I had come back since the amethyst ship had risen from the ground, reattached itself to the navcone—the ship's navigation nose cone—killed a whole army of Darkness, melted the ice cap avalanche that was roaring down the Trine, then vaporized the deluge. The ship had taken off into the heavens.

In the way of the battle-mages, it was my moment of glory. But no one saw it but the few humans who had been there and Amethyst, who had seen what was happening from her prison underground. I had sort of thought the cherub had been a figment of my imagination, and figments don't talk about moments of glory. And the men who had fought with me, well, they probably had big ideas about what had happened, but they didn't really know. As moments of glory went, it was pretty great. But pretty secret.

Signs of the battle were buried beneath several snowfalls, leaving the site looking pristine and white, not blood-splattered, heaped with the bodies of the dead, burned, charred, and gory. The clearing had once held a manmade cairn of boulders and stones, now crushed and scattered, covered by snow, and the huge oval mound hiding the wheels was now a deep depression. The snow made the hole look smooth, neatly scraped and shaped, as if God the Victorious had taken an ice-cream scoop to the mountain.

I'm really here. I'm really doing this. How stupid can I get? Fear whispered through my bloodstream.

Icy air moved through the bare branches of trees. Where once the mound had offered protection from the wind, now there was a barren desolation, and the sound was like the plaintive moans of bagpipes. I pulled the battle cloak over my knees and readjusted my feet in the stirrups. Battle boots weren't made for riding and my knees hurt, locked at an awkward angle.

I rode Homer to the edge of the cavity and looked down, the big horse snorting his dislike of the sharp precipice. It was a long way down. A very long way. The sight made me lonely in ways I didn't completely understand, but maybe it was just that no one wanted to die alone, and I had a good chance of doing that today. I had come close to dying the last time I went into the pit, and then I had some help from the wheels buried here. I had promised myself I'd never go underground, never again. I guess I lied.

A whistle sounded, echoing and reechoing up and down the mountain, a keening, mournful sound. I kneed Homer in a slow circle, searching for its origin, and finally spotted a row of horses below me, six of them, too far downhill to identify the riders, except for the bay in the lead. It was Thadd's mount. Joy spiked through me, followed by some emotion I couldn't name, bittersweet and painful, and I swallowed against a tight throat. Okay, so I wouldn't die alone. But if I died, I'd likely take them with me. Which was much worse.

"Hope you guys brought lunch and feed," I said to the cold wind, "because I can't take care of you all." Which was more true than it might seem.

I slid from the horse's back, led him away from the precipice to a flat area on the south side of a large rock, and loosed his girth. A bit of grass peeked through the snow, and Homer sighed happily before pawing at the ground to uncover more. I dumped two handfuls of feed at his feet for lunch and opened a jar of peanut butter and a package of crackers for me. I would need the protein. If I ate meat, now would be the time for a big juicy steak, some fried potatoes, and cake or pie for the sugar burst. I ate quickly and was standing on a boulder, my cloak tightly wrapped against the cold, watching, when the cavalcade came into view.

A heavily armed Thadd was in the lead, an automatic rifle with an unusual barrel design hung from his saddle. Joseph Barefoot rode behind him on a sure-footed mountain pony. Eli, wearing a fringed leather jacket, buckskin chaps, and cowboy hat, looked like a riding armament with knives in his hatband and belt, bandoliers crossed over his chest, and his flamethrower slung over his back. He rode a flashy Appaloosa, its coat apricot-colored with molasses-colored spots. At their six was Durbarge, the assey, his black eye patch and twisted features malevolent, his remaining, droopy-lidded eye hard. Thadd and Durbarge were wearing long leather dusters, fashioned to ride and to fight, the pockets bulging. Flames had healed Durbarge's foot, mangled in the street fight, and he rode without pain.

Between the assey and Eli, riding sturdy palomino mules, were two men I didn't know. Like Barefoot, each had a branded cheek; clearly EIH operatives. The Earth Invasion Heretics were poorly dressed in jeans and ratty leather jackets that stopped at their thighs, but they were well armed, and one had what looked like a shoulder-mounted rocket launcher strapped to his mount's withers. It was strange to see the EIH and an investigator with the Administration of the ArchSeraph working together. Durbarge's cheek, below his eye patch, was twitching, though whether because his eye pained him or because of the company I didn't know.

As they snaked toward the clearing, Eli took off his hat and waved it over his head, calling, "Hey, beautiful! Can you take on all six of us?" Thadd looked back at him, irritated at the innuendo.

I hid a smile, folded back my cloak, and lifted a hand, considering the six men. Together we made seven, an auspicious number, holy. Revelation 1:16 said of a seraph, "And he had in his right hand seven stars: and out of his mouth went a sharp twoedged sword ..."

I wasn't a star—nowhere near being a seraph—but I had a two-edged sword. And now there were seven of us. That thought cheered me as the men reached the clearing, dismounted, and began to open supplies. Eli, holding what looked like a ham sub, walked to the boulder and stood below me, munching. He talked between swallows, amber eyes squinting up at me. As he talked, the other men gathered around him. "You know everyone but Tomas and Rickie here." He indicated the two EIH men with his sandwich. "They saw you fight in the street battle the other day. Thought you looked interesting." I wasn't certain what *interesting* meant, but I didn't interrupt. "Got enough players to make a good-sized Pre-Ap boy band," he said. I rolled my eyes at his flippancy, and nodded to the strangers. "If this can wait, we can mobilize a good-sized force by morning," Eli said.

"I don't think it can wait."

"We got your message," Joseph Barefoot said, finishing off a beef jerky stick. "Brought enough weapons to wage a small war. Not what we'd have with some notice, but a bit. What's this your champard said about a succubus queen?"

I told the men about the queen who had given birth to the succubi, the voluptuous killers from the battle, and they listened with keen intent while eating and drinking water from plastic bottles. When I told them the new succubi were possibly fertile, capable of birth, and that thousands of succubus eggs might be ready to hatch, they moved uneasily.

"And how do you know this?" Durbarge asked, his droopy eye deceptively sleepy-looking in his scarred face.

This was the tricky part. Durbarge was contractually bound to assist me in my duties and in fighting Darkness, but he could also arrest me if I overstepped my bounds. As a licensed mage I could operate among humans, but having conversations with minions of Darkness wasn't exactly part of my rights. "The queen, uh, tried to attack me last night. And I, well, I kinda, accidentally, bound it to me." The men's expressions were comical.

"You bound a Darkness to you," Durbarge said tonelessly.

"Seems like it," I said, glad I was hiding behind my cloak so the assey couldn't see me fidget. "I thought it was human, possessed by a demon. I was going for exorcism, but it turned out to be a partially transmogrified Darkness. It's bound to me. I'm guessing its master will undo the binding when it gets free."

"Free? You left it alive?" Durbarge asked. Maybe I should have taken the fifth then, but I didn't, though it was a crime to leave a Darkness breathing.

"Yes," I said, and watched as he processed the information. He didn't go for his sigil to arrest me or his gun to shoot me. So far so good.

"So. You called a succubus—a succubus queen, as you call it—captured it, and bound it, all without the help of the AAS. Where is this *succubus queen*?"

I suppressed a flare of anger at his tone. He was right. It had been stupid, even if I hadn't planned it that way. "In my loft. Duct-taped to a chair in a conjuring circle. I was afraid that if I killed it, its master would know. If I can get to the nest before it gets loose, I can do a lot of damage. And if we get there before nightfall, we can surprise its master."

Durbarge sighed, rubbed his hand across his head, and slid the tip of a finger under the band that held his patch in place. Before he could decide what he was going to do about me, I added, "I learned the name of the Major Darkness on the Trine too."

"That thing that tried to take you in the street battle?" Thadd asked.

I remembered my horror and the pain of being held in its claws. "Yes. It's Forcas. Not its seraphic name, I know, but it gives us at least some power over it."

"And this can't wait until I can get reinforcements in?" Durbarge asked.

"Train is out until spring thaw."

"I can get troops in on military transports," he said. "Take two days, three at most."

"I don't know how much time we have," I said, shrugging, my cloak moving with the motion and catching the cold breeze. "She said the larvae would hatch at dawn. I'm guessing it's easier to kill eggs than larvae, and I know for a fact my circle can't hold the queen for long. She'll be free sooner rather than later." Their faces were indecisive, mutinous, or irritated, and I knew I couldn't wait on them.

Unable to conceal the anger in my tone, I said, "You guys decide what you want to do. There's water for the horses." I pointed to a runnel near Homer. "I'll be on the Trine." I jumped from the boulder, tightened Homer's saddle girth, and climbed a branch to remount. With a leap that threw my cloak flying, I was astride the Friesian and heading up the mountain. I tamped down my irritation as the men argued behind me. They would come or they wouldn't. Nothing I could do about it either way. *Men.*

As I rode, I studied the triple peaks. The entrance to the lair of Darkness was on the left peak, near the top. I wanted to reach the mouth of Forcas' domain way before nightfall, and with the ice pack gone and bare ground most of the way, that was possible. But I was, maybe, back to doing it alone. Just ducky.

Barak settled against his feathers, staring at the dark rock roof of his prison cell, his mouth turned up in satisfaction. It had been long and long since he had felt the presence of a kylen. But the near-breed was close and armed. He traveled with a mage, both of them prepared for war. It would not be long now. Zadkiel wanted him to bring the Light into the cavern, and chaos and war. Zadkiel wanted many things. Barak would settle for freedom.

In the corridor beyond the bars, he heard a soft soughing, smelled the mingled scents of Light and Darkness, of flowers and spring wind and freshening rain blended with the stenches of rotting meat and old blood, mold, stagnant water, and an overlay of brimstone. The smells had tantalized and beckoned to him, pulling him to the bars, once close enough to burn his face on the demon-iron. He had first noted the slight smells several hours ago, as time was counted here, and they had grown, the scents peaking some hours past. But they had weakened, and whatever had emitted the odors was gone.

*   *   *

Two hours before nightfall, I reached the hellhole, the smell of brimstone and dead things blowing across me, the entrance glowing a dull yellow and red in mage-sight. The men had finally made their decision and were only a few hundred yards behind, their mounts lathered, their faces inscrutable. No one looked happy to be there, not that I was dancing a jig myself. If someone—if Lolo—had sent me instructions on how to use the blasted visa I might not need to be here, at least not without seraphic support.

I dismounted and tethered Homer to the trunk of a long-dead tree, removed his saddle and the bit, and poured him more food. When he looked settled, I threw a shield of protection over him. He had drank deeply only minutes before, and water would be plentiful come morning as sunlight melted the snow. When he got thirsty he could pull the tether loose, pop through the shield of protection, and get to a runnel. Eventually, the Friesian could make his way down the mountain. That was assuming I didn't get out alive.

Before the men reached me, I drank a liter of water, found a secluded place to relieve myself, and scuffed a conjuring circle in the hard ground just below the lip of the hellhole. Sitting on a rock, I closed my eyes, and prepared for battle. I had been to war. I knew how it was done.

I was pretty sure I had sat on this exact rock to prepare myself the last time I came here, except it was in a different place and turned on its side. Melting snow had changed the face of the entrance, moving boulders downhill, cutting runnels in the dirt, carving out a ledge just below the opening to the lair.

Mage-sight open, I closed the circle, and the stench of evil intensified. The peak glowed the ailing greenish-yellow of snow, overlaid with the red and black of Darkness. Swallowing down the nausea of fear, I began to chant. "Stone and fire, water and air, blood and kin prevail. Wings and shield, dagger and sword, blood and kin prevail." Calm descended, as soft and gentle as seraph down. I chanted the litany created by the earliest neomages, a nursery rhyme chant that had followed us down through the decades. Breathing, feeling my heart beat, my blood pulse,

I centered myself, preparing for death, as all warrior mages must.

The stone beneath my thighs warmed, offering its strength to me. The stones I carried in pockets and my amulets soaked up the strength of the mountain as the sun fell toward the western hills and the stink of old death grew. Nothing came from the deeps to hunt. Nothing disturbed me, not even the men. When half an hour had passed, and I was calm and centered, I opened my eyes, stretched out a finger, and broke the circle.

The men stood or sat on stones in a loose circle around me, watching. I could guess that none of them had ever seen a mage prepare for battle. Humans prepare for war differently from mages. Humans expect to win. Humans plan to survive, with thoughts and plans for death limited to notes for loved ones, a lucky rabbit's foot tucked in a pocket, a quick prayer for holy assistance. Mages never plan for life. We prepare our bodies to be used up, destroyed. That way, nothing is held back in the conflict. We can truly give our all.

Last time I went into the pit, I had prepared like this, yet secretly, in the deeps of my heart, I had hoped to survive, hoped I could take a mortal wound, call mage in dire, and have help come before I died. Unlike last time, I wasn't the only candidate. This time I was taking humans in with me. Death would be so close that its wings would be folding around the victim before seraphs arrived. If they came at all. Either way, some of us would probably die. The weight of that settled heavily on my shoulders as I looked from face to face. The burden of death, theirs and mine, was a shroud. Feeling the mountain, sturdy beneath me, feeling my heart's slow beat, feeling the cold sweet air in my lungs, I said, "I've been down there. I've fought down there. Thousands of spawn live in a warren that goes down inside the mountain, probably two thousand feet."

"That's how much the Trine grew in Mole Man's battle," Thadd said.

"Last time, I thought I was prepared, and maybe I was as prepared as I could be, with what I knew, but I wasn't smart. I didn't think about being able to draw on the stone heart of the Trine for power. I didn't think about using a shield to hide my presence through the maze. I went in fighting, hoping to call mage in dire in time. I can hope to call mage in dire again, but it means a mortal wound before I can get us seraphic help—mortal for one of you, or for me. And if they come, they might execute judgment on you."

"All have sinned and fallen short of the glory of God," Durbarge quoted.

Thadd looked at his hands. Or maybe he looked at his ring, the ring that kept him mostly human. So far it had kept him from seraphic notice, but that might not continue.

Eli double-checked the positions of his weapons and of the strange flamethrower he carried, sliding the bulbous section under his arm. His lips were pursed as if he might whistle.

The three EIH men glanced from one to the other, and I didn't like the look of the exchange. They knew something. Or they were planning something. I raised my brows at Joseph Barefoot but he only lifted his brows back at me, assuming an innocent expression. It would have been more effective without the brands on his cheeks.

"There's that," I said, belatedly responding to Durbarge's scripture. "But this time I have a shield that's big enough to cover us and will move with us when we move. With the mountain to power it, the shield should be enough to protect us for a while. But I don't know its limitations. If we get separated, or if anyone steps too far out of position, it could snap off."

"How close?" Rickie asked. It was the first time he had spoken and his high tenor was a surprise. He had an almost girlish voice, at odds with the cross brand and his rough clothes.

"Twenty feet maximum," I guessed. "And it has limitations. If you fire a weapon from the inside, it shatters. It'll screen us from the sight of any Darkness we meet, but not from their noses, and once they smell us down there, they can track us. It won't stop the toxic fumes—we'll be breathing them the whole time. And the biggest problem is that I don't know where the nest is, but I'm betting it's as deep as the mountain."

I saw no point in telling this crew about Baraqyal, Zadkiel, and the cherub Amethyst. Thadd hadn't really believed me when I told him about them being trapped.
Durbarge had heard about Zadkiel once before and not
believed. We might come close enough to save the seraph
with shorn wings, as his cell was close to the surface, but
the cherub's prison was in the deepest part of the Trine. If
we made it that far, we'd never be able to fight our way
out. Of course, the nest might be that deep, in which case,
if we made it there, we might find the prison. Time enough
then to share that tidbit of info.

Enough chitchat. I threw back my cloak and pulled my
walking stick blade, the steel a harsh sound in bright daylight, the bloodstone hilt warming in my hand. I reached
under my dobok for the white onyx fish amulet that carried a shield of protection, the shield that moved with me.
Somewhere behind me, down the Trine, the lynx called, a
full-throated scream of sound. *Thanks for the warning,* I
thought, taking a step toward the center of the men.

A sharp pain took me through the throat. The explosive
sound of a gunshot instantly followed. I blinked in surprise. My knees buckled. Pain carried me toward the
ground.

I looked up as I fell, seeing Thadd's mouth open. Hearing the beginning of his ringing cry, the words lost beneath
the roar in my ears and the blast of the gun. The men scattered, moving behind rocks. Thadd fell over me. The shot
echoed. A barrage of others followed; cover fire, return
fire. Another round landed in the frozen dirt near me, a
puff of motion.

I couldn't breathe. The air in my lungs was hot, burning,
trapped. Blood fountained over me. I tried to force a
breath and sucked hot blood into my lungs. My throat
made a sucking sound as my windpipe spasmed shut.
Blood pumped onto the ground around me. *I'm dying.* The
thought was curious, a vague paradigm, surprisingly without fear. *I'm really dying.* Blood pumped again, into the air
this time, in a crimson spray.

My mind was suddenly lucid, my thoughts coherent and
orderly, an overlay of facts and possibilities, transparent,

cold, and deadly. I had taken a shot through the throat.
Left to right, clean in and out. Carotid clipped. Esophagus
gone.

My blood pumped, arching up, then down to splatter the
ground, steaming in the cold, a bright, glistening scarlet. I'd
be unconscious from blood loss in seconds.

They had known someone was coming. It had been an
ambush.

They had used guns, not creation energies. A trap for humans by humans.

I had taken a step forward, into the shot. Had they been
aiming at someone else?

I couldn't call mage in dire because I couldn't speak.

We would all die.

In the corner of my eye shadows moved, a glint of metal
in the sunlight. They were coming. *Ahh.* They wanted *me*—
alive. They had intended to kill my companions to get me.
They wanted my blood.

I thumbed the fish, and the shield snapped into place
with a shock wave of might. In mage-sight it was a purple
bubble of overlapped energy, like feathers layered over us.
Lightning sparkled through it. Thadd raised up, drenched
in blood, his face shocked white. He started to place his
hands over my throat and then pulled back. I could read
his panic. *How do I put pressure on a throat wound? I can't.
She's dead.*

The world darkened around me, my sight telescoping to
a tiny pinpoint of light, centered on Thadd. The muscles of
his shoulders moved. His mouth pulled down. I thought he
was speaking. Realized he was screaming. In pain. He fell
over me.

I opened my mind, reaching out to stone. Reaching.
Pulling it in. *Too late . . .*

The light shrank down. And died.

Chapter 26

I opened my eyes. I was cold. In pain. Confused. And out-side. Overhead, purple light shimmered and sparked, like holiday sparklers. It was shaped like a dome. *A shield.* I took a breath. And realized I was still alive. I touched my throat. It was tender and sore, the tissues weak and thin to my fingertips. The shield I had opened was taking hits; bullets bounced off of it. The battle was still taking place. Gunshots were deafening.

I smelled cordite and kylen blood. Heat stirred under my skin, coiling like a snake in the spring sun. I was weak, and the flesh of my arm looked desiccated, wrinkled, hanging from my bones as if I had lost pounds. Perhaps I had. My lifeblood had run across the frozen ground and pooled in the downhill edge of the shield.

The sun was still up. Half an hour had passed, surely no more. Thaddeus Bartholomew lay across my body, his weight pinning me to the ground. I wriggled an arm under him and pushed, rolling him over as I sat up. His arms flopped, one landing in my lap.

Through my clothes, my amulets blazed, as did the stones in my pockets. I pushed aside the saturated cloak and dobok tunic to see that the talismans were discharging energy at a constant rate, a steady blast of might. Uncon-sciously, I had drawn on them as I fell, dying. At this speed, the amulets should be totally drained, yet when I ran my hands over the necklace, stopping them cold, they looked pretty good. In mage-sight they were still full of power. They had to have drawn energy from somewhere . . . the mountain. I had opened a conduit as I . . . died. The amulets had been powered by the Trine, through the sleeping cat I had carved from the heart of a fist of bloodstone. I touched the cat and jerked my fingers back. It was blistering hot.

I shook my head and wiped blood from my face, my mind still sluggish. Someone screamed nearby. Rickie had been hit, or maybe it was the other one, Tomas. Human blood, sweat, and the stink of fear were carried on the breeze.

On my lap blood pumped from Thadd's wrist, kylen-sweet. There was a huge seraph ring beside me on the frozen ground, turquoise in a silver setting of angel wings. Off of his finger, it had reverted to its unconjured size, the biggest ring I had ever seen. "Oh, Thadd," I whispered, throat raw. I knew why I was still alive. Thaddeus had pulled off the ring for the second time in his life. Then he had cut an artery and let his precious kylen blood pour over me. To heal me. Around the edges of his duster, white feathers protruded, the softer-than-air feathers of a kylen youth. His transformation to adult kylen was now far along.

My mind cleared fast. I shoved the ring on his finger; it instantly shrank to fit. I ripped off a healing amulet and pressed it into the arterial cut. Like me, he had lost a lot of blood. It had taken a lot to heal me, with his wrist pressed into the wound on my throat.

Oh, saints' balls. I had kylen blood in my system.

I twisted the top off a bottle of water and dribbled some between Thadd's lips. He coughed and his eyes fluttered open. Chrysacolla green irises were clear and bright in his pale, white face. "More," he whispered. I lifted his head and held the bottle to his mouth so he could drink. He drained the water and lay there, gasping. I drank a whole bottle, hoping to restore my body.

"Call mage in dire," he said, his voice grating.

"If I do, they'll know what you are," I said. "And they might kill the others out of spite. And then they'll take you away." It hurt to speak and my voice sounded worse than his, a stranger's croak. I touched my throat again. A large patch of skin was numb and weak-feeling, as if it might burst open again. The wound had taken out a huge amount of tissue. My vocal cords must have been damaged by the gunshot, maybe destroyed and rebuilt from nothing. I wondered how much kylen blood had been deposited into my bloodstream. And what that might mean.

"It'll be dark soon," he said. "Then it'll be too late anyway. Dead if you call, dead if you don't. And I'd rather die any other way than to be eaten alive."

Spawn hunted at night. I looked around, considering. The horses were gone, except for Homer. The fighting was at a lull. Three forms hid behind boulders, one under the overhang of the hellhole. Durbarge looked around the rock where he had taken cover. He was prone, a long rifle cradled in his arms like a lover. "You two alive?" he called.

Thadd looked down. I felt shock surge through him, but he nodded and pulled his duster over his feathers. "We'll live."

I looked around, evaluating our options. There weren't many. The men were in close proximity to the assey, though, and maybe I could cover us. "Durbarge!" I shouted. "Turn off any assey gadgets you have." Asseys are equipped to trap and capture witchy-women—unlicensed mages. The devices might disrupt the shield. To Thadd I said, "We get to Durbarge. Then we put you and Rickie on Homer and send you down the mountain, out of seraph range. I can keep us alive an hour before calling mage in dire. Maybe."

"Durbarge already knows something's up. You can't protect me anymore," Thadd said bitterly.

I looked at the cop. "You don't have to worry about the assey."

"I'll have to worry about him as long as I live," Thadd said.

"Or as long as he lives."

Thadd's face grew even whiter as it drained of blood. "That's murder," he whispered.

"I'm not planning to kill him." I heard the fury beneath my words and felt a spurt of surprise at my own anger.

"But if it comes to it, well, I don't have a soul. Besides, they can only execute me once."

Thadd kindly didn't point out that I had been dead one time today already. Instead he said, "And if I do what you suggest—run, and let you commit murder for me—then what?"

"Beats me. Let's move." I rose to my knees, then my feet, feeling the world whirl sluggishly around me as my blood pressure stabilized. Thadd took my elbow, and I said, "Now!" We ran toward Durbarge, the shield moving with us, a mutable force, and fell behind the rock where he lay. Tomas and Eli fell over Rickie, stanching blood, checking his pulse. I couldn't tell if he was breathing. I tossed Joseph Barefoot two healing amulets. Long seconds passed before I saw Rickie's chest rise and fall.

"Call mage in dire," Durbarge demanded.

"She can't. Rickie's branded, not an innocent," Thadd said. "He didn't get wounded saving her, and she's not near death. When she couldn't speak, she used a healing amulet on both of us." Durbarge looked from me to Thadd, his face debating whether to call us on it. Not giving him a chance to dispute, Thadd outlined my plan, ending with, "Surprise is gone. Without horses, we'll never get down the mountain alive, even if Thorn could keep the shield open that long. I'll get Rickie to safety, and get Audric and Rupert and the town fathers. We'll start back up the mountain by dawn, if I have to shoot someone to get it done."

"We don't have much time," I said. "I smell the succubi."

"You can't. They aren't supposed to hatch until dawn," Thadd said.

"Time isn't always linear in a hellhole," Durbarge said. He seemed to reach a decision, and pointed to the left and right of the hellhole with his rifle. "Two snipers. I can take them out with these"—he pulled two egg-shaped objects from a band at his waist—"but they might damage the entrance. And any hope of stealth will be gone."

Eli chuckled. "I think it's pretty well gone now, bro. I don't think a couple hand grenades will make much of a difference. And Rickie's as stable as we can get him." He held one of the healing amulets to the light. "Pretty nifty little suckers. Hope you got a lot more."

My lips curled at the thought of needing a lot more.

Durbarge assessed his lethal weapons as if checking their weight in each palm. He explained how they worked, and said, "Let's do this, then. On three. One." Durbarge pulled a pin from the first grenade. "Two." I dropped the shield and Eli provided cover fire as the assey pulled the second pin. "Three." He stood, and threw one in a long arc. The second grenade followed it in a slightly different direction.

I snapped the shield back over us and dropped to the ground, not because I needed to, but because Durbarge did. The explosions overlapped, vibrating through the earth, hurling debris and shrapnel into the air. Shattered rock, dust, and traces of blood hit the shield and rained to the ground in a circle around us. The quiet afterward was absolute. Durbarge pointed two fingers to Eli, then to the right, to himself, and then left. I dropped the shield and they separated, rising from the ground and dashing up the scree on either side of the entrance of the pit at a dead run. I could have told them not to bother. I could smell dead humans.

Minutes later, Thadd was on Homer, Rickie sitting up strapped to his back, straddling the Friesian's rump, and heading downhill at a fast clip. I snapped the shield back over us and met Durbarge's one good eye. "Why didn't you call for help?" I asked. "You could have gotten troops here. Gotten seraphs here. That's what the AAS does, isn't it? Talk to the Seraphic High Council?"

"Troops are on the way, but a blizzard has formed up over the Mississippi River valley and is heading this way fast. There wasn't time for a mobilization before the storm hits. And seraphs don't listen to us much anymore," he said, as if it were a well-known fact, instead of mere supposition. "Haven't in two, three decades."

"Invaders don't have to listen to the conquered," Joseph said. Durbarge didn't reply to the heresy, and Joseph went on. "I told the men. Some operatives are gathering, but they come from the outlying hills and have to prepare for the storm first, so their families are safe. They'll be here at noon tomorrow."

"Too late," I said. "It has to be today. I can smell something from the entrance. Something that wasn't there the last time I went in. It smells like the queen smelled. It's a little late to be asking this, but does anyone have a better plan?"

"You mean better than following a sexy, redheaded, sword-wielding neomage into a pit, battling spawn, dragonets, a major Dark mojo, and trying to kill some kinda aphrodisiac larvae like in some bad, Pre-Ap, B-grade movie?" Eli asked with a roguish grin. "Can't think of one." He looked at his watch. "We got one hour till sunset. Let's boogie."

I chuckled, slung my bag of goodies over a shoulder, and drew two blades—the walking stick blade and the tanto—and tabbed open the moving shield. "Stay close."

With them trailing me, I levered myself up over the ledge to the mouth of the cave and stepped inside. Fear skittered up my spine.

Barak slammed his fist against the wall, drawing blood. The kylen was leaving. This was not acceptable. He raced to the bars and gripped them, oblivious to the pain of demon-iron as he shook them in the unyielding stone. His eyes, once a rich and vibrant shade of silver, had acquired dim red flecks. They grew with his anger. The bars held firm.

Across the passageway, a mage in heat moaned as the smell of his blood reached her. The sound brought up his head, and his nostrils quivered as he caught her scent. He swallowed, the muscles of his throat working harshly. "No," he whispered. "I will not." Slowly, the red lights in his irises began to fade and die. When they were gone, he stepped away from the doorway and fell to his feathers, dropping his head into his arms. "I will not."

It wasn't yet sunset, but I had learned to my chagrin that spawn, while nocturnal, were sometimes active in the protection of the pit when the sun was up. Once stirred to life, they were the same vicious little beasties they were at night. However, even with the gunfire and explosions, no one, and no thing, met us at the opening.

The passageway descended and the ambient light dropped off. I handed each man an illumination amulet and a healing amulet, and advanced into the dark at human speed. The air grew foul with the scent of death and sulfur, an acidic cloud. The men strapped on gas masks, looking like huge bipedal insects. No one had thought to bring a mask for me, but mage eyes and lungs are different from humans', and the gases didn't bother me as much.

Moving silently, following the map in my memory, we were down two levels by the time the sun set. A stagnant breeze blew up from the deeps. Chittering started ahead and to the sides as spawn began to wake.

At the sound, my amulets blazed into life, as did the stones in my pockets and in the bag I had slung across my back. The first spawn peered around the bend at our left. Before it could yowl a warning, I dropped the shield and beheaded it. "To the right," I said. "Fast." We made one more level before the alarm was sounded.

At a juncture of corridors hewn from the mountain of the Trine, new scents collided with the smell of waking spawn. Dragonets. Seraph. Mages. A ululating cry echoed through the tunnels. And the swarms attacked.

"Jehovah sabaoth!" I screamed. Moving with mage-speed, my skin blazing like a torch in the night, I advanced into the horde, blades flashing in the swan and the whirl-wind—moves created specifically for fighting spawn, taking off body parts. The spawn—always hungry, pulled their injured under them, feasting as others advanced to attack.

"Jesus," Durbarge prayed, easing to my right, slicing with his own blades, beheading and maiming. He began his war chant, which I thought was from 2 Samuel. "And dark-ness was under his feet. And darkness was under his feet."

Eli, to my left, shouted from Isaiah, "Thou shalt be vis-ited of the LORD . . . and the flame of devouring fire." As he yelled, he pumped the bag under his arm and shot gouts of fire from his flamethrower. Spawn screamed and burned and died.

The EIH fighters drew swords and shouted together, "I will draw my sword, my hand shall destroy them." The words brought me up short, and I misstepped. Teeth sank in my calf, above the battle boot. Pain shocked through me. With a single swipe, I beheaded the beast and kicked its teeth loose, the head flying away into the swarm. I settled myself with a simple crab move, wondering at the heretics' choice of scripture. They were speaking from Exodus, the words of the enemy of the people of the Most High.

"Jehovah sabaoth!" I shouted, the words that came to me the first time I went into battle, as all battle cries that fight Darkness are given.

"The seraph I told you about is close," I said to Durbarge and Eli. "I smell him." And a mage was close too, gibbering, insanity like a festering wound in her mind. *Take me, take me, take me, take me, take me,* she cried silently. I tripped and fell, landing flat. Eli stepped over me, shouting my name, firing his flames. But the mind of the mage pulled me down into the cramped and flashing corners of her tormented memories.

I see him. His wings are iridescent green, softening to a paler green, like new leaves, on the underside and down. Silver hair curls around his high brow, gray eyes flecked with silver, and a narrow jaw with pointed chin. Barak. Baraqyal. The seraph.

His nevus pulses with fear and desire. Demon-iron shackles him to the wall of a chamber set aside for torture. Laughing daywalkers cut into his wings, hacking with demon-iron blades and with human steel. Severing them.

Gagging with reaction, with horror, I jerked back out of her mind. But not before I saw through her eyes, across a shadowed corridor. The seraph she desired was there, in a cell, only feet from me. Holding my weapons blade-down, I curled under Eli's feet, between his legs, letting him fight over me. He held swords, and handled them the way he danced, with effortless ease. "Seraph? Barak?" I shouted.

"Here, mage!" he belled back, filled with joy. "Here I am! She sent you to me!"

She. The mage near him? No. Not her. *Seraph stones.* He meant Lolo. Suddenly, I was sure of it. I had the mage's vision of him just now. And in a dream, in the vision of Lolo's past, I had seen within the mind of the priestess a silver-haired seraph with green wings. Barak. *Baraqyal.* The name of the first seraph to take a mage as lover.

"Thorn?" Eli called, taking the head of a spawn with a back swing, and another one's arms with the follow-through. "What's going on?" When I didn't answer, he said, "I want you between my legs, but not like this. Get up!"

My glove-covered knuckles brushed the smooth floor of the passageway. Suddenly I glimpsed a secret truth, saw it fully formed in the way of my people—a mage-truth. Barak, Baraqyal, had been the lover of Daria, the first mage to mate with a seraph, the first mage to produce a litter of kylen. I had questioned it before. Now it was all a horrifying kind of certainty—if Lolo was also Daria. "Yes," I said. Beside me, a spawn fell, a leg half severed, its mouth working, sharp predator teeth rimed with blood. Almost mechanically, I brought the tanto down, beheading it. The blade jarred twice, on the thing's spine, and on the stone beneath. A second one fell across the first, burned and smoking.

If Lolo had known he was here, then had she set all this up? My birth? Thadd's birth? Machinations and devious, conniving schemes, set in place so we could—what? Rescue her lover? Take his place? Had she allowed so many to die, just so she could free Barak? Could Lolo have done this? And worse, if she had done all that, was I being fool-ish to assign only one motive to the wily old woman? Either way, could I leave him here, being tortured?

"Thorn?" Eli shouted.

Mage-fast, I spun from between his legs to my feet. "This way!"

Blades blurring, my flesh shining with speed and battle-lust, I ducked into a constricted cleft and out the other side. Raced along a narrow corridor. The tunnel was empty. No guards, no spawn. Holding swords low for defense, I looked into a cell.

Behind me, I heard a cry of pain and the grinding sound that flesh makes against rock. Eli squeezed into the tunnel and raced to me. "The others are too big to make it through. They're holding the pass. What are we— Holy moly. It's a seraph," he said.

An exceptionally notorious seraph. "Meet Barak, also known as Baraqyal, the father of the kylen," I said, hearing my bitter tone. "A Watcher. One of the Fallen Allied."

"Dang, woman," Eli breathed, leaning in toward the bars. Even shorn of his wings, the seraph was utterly beautiful.

Silver hair slid over his perfect body, a veil that glistened. He glamoured a kilt to cover himself to his knees, and the kilt shone like his hair, like kyanite stone. "You are not in heat," Barak said. "You have engaged in battle dire, then, to reach me here."

"Yeah. We did." Two Flames buzzed into the corridor, lighting it with a brilliance that blistered my vision into a white glare. They soared through the demon-iron bars and danced along Baraqyal's body, singing a piccolo of notes, high-pitched and pure, a beautiful song. He laughed and held out his hands; they lit on his palms and he crooned to them, sounds like bells, in a language no mortal could speak.

As if Barak had given them orders, they darted to the bars and sliced through them like plasma torches. Red-hot demon-iron fell to the corridor chiming minor tones, ugly sounds, off-key and dull, leaving the cell open. Lips parted with wonder, Baraqyal stepped into the hall and threw out his chest as if unfurling his wings, breathing the foul air as if it were clean. The movement cracked open the wounds on his back and the Flames darted to him, droning urgently. They did something to his back and he laughed. It was a beautiful sound.

Screams and clashing steel sounded through the cleft to the outer hallway. Gunshots echoed and cordite overrode the smell of brimstone, followed by the scent of human blood and excrement. Human death. From a doorway down the hall, Durbarge crashed, trailed by Joseph, carrying Tomas. They had found another way in. The EIH operative was badly injured, an avulsion on his thigh gouting blood. The thigh muscles had been sliced away from the bone and hung forward. The Flames darted into the wound, instantly sealing torn vessels. The seraph followed their motions, his eyes wide. I could have sworn that Barak had never seen them heal.

"The succubi nest," Durbarge said to Barak. "Where is it?"

"Ahh," Barak said, turning from the healing Flames as Tomas took a weak breath. "Succubi. That is the scent that caused me—" He stopped and looked into my eyes. His were silver and guileless, and I distrusted such forthrightness. It was too easy to see his beauty and forget that seraphs couldn't be trusted to speak the complete truth, only the parts the Most High deemed important. Worse, the Most High no longer spoke to Watchers. Did they have to speak truth at all? "You are too late," he said. "The eggs have hatched. The larvae were moved through the tunnels and away, south."

Too late? The thought shattered through my defenses. "Moved?" I asked.

"Their scent grew stronger for hours. At its apex, there was great movement in the tunnels to the south, movement that was both Darkness and Light, human and mage. Then all the scents were gone." He breathed deeply, testing the air. "But for the pitiful creature across the passageway and a few spawn, most are no longer here."

"What about Zadkiel and Amethyst?" I asked. Barak's eyes flickered the slightest bit. If I hadn't still been seeing with mage-sight, I would never have noted it.

"They are far below. I am wounded, without weapons, unable to transmogrify, unable to fight Darkness." Quick translation, "I'm not going down with you." Big shock there.

"I won't ask you to go down with me. But give me a boon." When he didn't turn away, I said, "Give me a seraph feather." The words were as much a surprise to me as to him. His eyes narrowed, and this time he didn't try to control the reaction. Seraph feathers, freely given, were strong weapons in the hands of a battle-mage, powering her other gifts. I might be only a half-trained stone mage, but I knew the power of a seraph feather.

Barak hesitated. "Though I am not among those Powers

and Principalities who rebelled and fought against the
High Host in the Battle of Heaven, as a fallen Watcher I
have long been away from the Most High. I have been
trapped here, in the lair of the beast, for decades. The gift
might be weak. Or . . . polluted." When I stared at him,
silent, he bent to the feathers on the cell floor and reluctantly lifted one. The wing moved with a lifelike shudder as
he plucked and said, "Stone and fire, water and air, defense
and flight prevail. Wings and shield, dagger and sword,
blood and shelter prevail."

A sudden spike of instruction came from my amulet
necklace, from the visa, and I bowed deeply, saying, "Stone
and fire, water and air, blood and kin prevail. Wings and
shield, dagger and sword, blood and kin prevail." The com-
pulsion from the visa ceased. *What the heck did I just do?* I
accepted the feather and bowed again over the gift.

Almost three feet long, it was a primary flight feather,
lighter than air, and power trembled through it. A current
of air lifted it. Barak could have chosen a small, insignificant feather. Instead he had given me his best. It was a lus-
trous, deep green that threw back the plasma light of the
Flames in burgundy and silver and ocean blue. I was
ashamed of my earlier distrust, and touched the feather to
my forehead once before sliding it through my dobok belt.
I met his beautiful eyes and said simply, "Thank you."

A surprised look crossed his face. "Much welcome, neomage. Fight true."

I walked to a clear place and dug in the bag over my
shoulder, pulling out a stone jar of clean salt, never used.
The supply was limited, and so the circle I made was small,
barely large enough to hold me, sitting yogi-style. Prepared
to draw on the stone beneath me for power, I placed an
amulet in front of me, outside the circle, settled myself, and
closed the salt ring, shivering with the energy that quivered
up my spine.

I looked at Eli and Durbarge. "Don't kill the daywalker." At Durbarge's fierce glance, I added, "I, uh, I
sorta bound one of those to me too." He reached for his
sigil, before his fingers grudgingly clenched. I figured he
wanted to arrest me, but thought he had better wait for a

more propitious occasion. Like, if we survived the night in a hellhole.

Taking a calming breath, I opened the stone jar holding the scrap of cloth saturated with the walker's dried blood. I began to chant, "Malashe-el. Malashe-el. Attend to me. Malashe-el, attend and obey." Long minutes passed. Demon-fast, the walker appeared before me. The rune of forgetting blazed on its chest and it carried a sword of demon-iron. It swept the blade back with a swish of sound; I held up the cloth. "Hold," I said, praying the word would stay the blade. I hadn't opened a shield of protection. Demon-iron held power of its own and would surely disrupt the energies I had drawn around me.

The blade stopped at the apex of its arc, quivering slightly. "Drop the blade," I said. The walker's arms trembled with resistance until I repeated the command. Its fingers slowly opened. The sword dropped to the floor with a clang.

This was not a boy. Now it looked like a man, fully grown, in its late twenties, perhaps. Deep black hair was still long and braided, but a stubble of beard marked its chin. It wore black, a short-waisted jacket of silk velvet over a black charmeuse shirt with lace cuffs and nubby silk pants. Its eyes were red and labradorite in equal measure.

Untouched by sunlight, tainted by the dark energies in the place, my mage-sight saw it as it really was. A mesh of power the reddish-black shade of old blood passed through its body, as though the webbing of a spider wrapped it. The mesh twisted along the walker's legs, into its intestines, through its loins. The other threads were interlocking rings of blue Light, a conjure that swathed it, plunging into its body, entwining its heart and lungs.

I understood immediately that any exorcism I had done on the surface was useless here, close to the power sink of the resident evil. But I wasn't powerless. I could try to bolster the power of Light that held it. From my place on the floor I looked into its face and said, "By the power of your Mistress, see the Light." I had clearly said the correct words because the red in its eyes vanished like a mist dissipating over a sea at dawn, leaving its labradorite eyes clear and sparkling with relief, a blue-gray-green. "Bring me my blood."

"By the power of my Mistress," it whispered, and tears glistened in its eyes.

I pointed to the amulet. "Take that. When you have my blood, bring it to me."

Faster than my eyes could follow, the walker snatched up the small peridot nugget and was gone. *That was easy,* I thought. *Too easy?* Settling myself again, I tried to follow the amulet's progress through the tunnels. It led deep, demon-fast, to a place I had seen before.

I closed my eyes, envisioning the cell trapping Mistress Amethyst. I had linked the trails of the warren into a map and stored it in a stone. I gripped it now and compared the map to the walker's position. Its path led into the foulest parts of the lair, a pall of unbreathable smoke occluding many of the tunnels. Or the smoke could be a Dark trap. In a quick mind-skim, I sniffed; it was the stench of burning spawn flesh, not conjures. Suddenly, I lost the walker's trail. *Seraph stones.* All in one motion, I broke the circle and stood.

Suddenly Malashe-el was standing right in front of me, its lovely eyes blazing with Light and filled with tears. "My Mistress says this to you. My master has your blood. He is approaching the Mistress' prison. He goes to drain unto emptiness the Holy Ones he trapped, and he carries a chain coated with Mole Man's blood."

"Crap," Eli said, understanding. Silently, I echoed the miner's mild obscenity.

We were three levels down in a pit, and the primary mission was compromised. Well, defunct actually, because the larvae were gone. But I wasn't leaving without my blood. That meant I had to battle a Major Darkness and free the Mistress and her consort while I was down here. Careful not to speak Forcas' name, I said, "The Power of the Trine trapped a seraph and his cherub about a thousand feet deeper."

Durbarge touched the patch over his eye. Clearly, he re-membered that one seraph had never reappeared after our last encounter on the Trine. "A cherub?" he asked. I hadn't told him about Amethyst. I hadn't told much of anyone. He dropped his hand and a look of wonder crossed his face. "They're real? As the scriptures claim?"

"Yeah. They're real," I said. "That ship that exploded out of the Trine and mowed down Darkness not long ago? That also just happened to vaporize the ice cap? That was the cherub's wheels. I'm going down to battle the Darkness. And to see if I can free the seraph and the cherub." Fear and horror clotted my throat, but battle-lust allowed me to push through it. I looked at Malashe-el. "Show me the way." His mouth set in a thin, unhappy line.

"Count me in," Eli said.

Durbarge and Joseph glanced at one another and then at me. "Us too."

Five was not a propitious number and six was even worse, but I didn't say it. To the Watcher, I said, "What about you?" Before he could reply, I spun the short sword out of my spine sheath and extended it, hilt first. The hilt was heavily plated with silver set with garnets. Taking a chance, I said, "Daria, the priestess, gave this to me when I was a child. I think she sent me to free you." He looked at the sword and his fingers clenched involuntarily. "I can't do anything about your wings," I said, "but you wouldn't be weaponless." Prompted by the visa, I said, "Your presence would be a thing of joy."

At my words, the Flames whirled and darted behind the Watcher. Barak hissed and fell to his knees, exposing his back. The Minor Flames blazed with abandon, racing up and down the allied seraph's spine. From his torn flesh, nubs and ripples appeared, hillocks that quickly grew to fist-sized prominences. The humeri ripped through his flesh. Wings began to form. The Watcher screamed. Reaching up, he took the hilt of the blade from my hand. He curled his body around the sword, cradling it. He screamed again, body wrenching. Barak blazed like a small sun, driving us out of the room, covering our faces.

"That went well," Eli said. "Have you noticed that you live an interesting life?"

"Pre-Ap Chinese blessing interesting? Yeah. I noticed."

I pulled my blades and thumbed the amulet with the map of the Trine, copying it to the bloodstone hilt of my longsword. Looking at Malashe-el, I said, "By your Mistress' power, take me to your master."

From the cleftlike opening in the tunnel wall, a chitinous clacking and snapping sounded. A dragonet skittered into the passageway, bouncing up and down on segmented legs. Its exoskeleton was scarlet and orange stripes, its carapace humped and spiked with black barbs. Another dragonet followed. And another.

Demon-fast, Malashe-el took off in the opposite direction. More dragonets poured through the opening. As one, they attacked. Eli blasted one batch with flames, and Joseph tossed a hand grenade. We all ducked. The explosion rocked the cavern. Dust and debris, some of it slimy, rained down on us.

"No!" Eli shouted over the ringing in my ears. "Grenades'll bring the roof down!"

I offered the original amulet for the map and the one for the moving shield to Durbarge. "You can use these?" I asked, not really hearing my voice. He hesitated only an instant before taking the stones. I thought he mouthed the words, "Go with God the Victorious," but I wasn't sure.

As fast as I could, I followed Malashe-el down, into the Dark.

Chapter 27

Opening mage-sight to its fullest, I sighted Malashe-el's heel as he rounded a corner and took a downward ramp. I raced after. Smoke billowed up, and the ramp turned again, deeper into the thick fumes. I could scarcely breathe. I thumbed open the map in the bloodstone hilt and followed the daywalker down, and down, spotting our route on the three-dimensional interpretation in my mind. We were descending much faster than I had thought possible.

"Save us," the remembered voice belled in my mind. *"Save us!"*

"Yeah," I said, my breath harsh in the contaminated air as my hearing returned. "I'm working at it." I rounded the next hallway and stopped short.

Forcas stood in my path, a tall being, over six feet in physical form. In mage-sight it bulked twelve feet tall, powerful in this place and beautiful as a seraph of Light. In one hand it clutched Malashe-el by the throat. The walker's feet thrashed; its face was mottled, its tongue protruding through swollen lips. Without thought, I dropped and rolled across the cold stone floor, sheathing the longsword, drawing the blades along my calves and throwing. As they spun, I shouted, "Jehovah sabaoth!" The knives slammed into Forcas' chest to either side of the walker. The Darkness released its hold and Malashe-el fell in a boneless heap. Its hand opened, revealing a small vial that glowed in my sight like gathered diamond dust. The walker had done it. It had my blood. *Blood that can be used against me. Or blood I can sacrifice. Blood I can use as a weapon.*

I scuttled across the intervening space, directly under the feet of the Darkness, and grabbed the vial. Elation pulsed through me. Almost in slow motion Forcas withdrew my blades, tossed them, and reached for me. Its seraph face, the beautiful face that once was, rippled and changed as a glamour fell away. A cat head, puma or lion, its flesh leathery and burned, took shape in its stead, all that was left of its once holy mien. This was much more formidable than a Watcher allied with Darkness. This was a true Fallen, one of the Powers who rebelled against the Most High and was swept out of heaven in the war that was only hinted at in holy scriptures. A crimson metal chain, the color of fresh blood, was around its neck. The spur amulet was in its hand.

Forcas laughed and grabbed me about the waist with one hand, as it had once before. No. Twice before. It held the spur before me and raised me to its face. Holding me close, it rammed the spur into my side. Pain, exquisite and elegant as a shaft of poetry, lanced through me. "Time, time, and a third time I have held you thus. Time, time, and a third time has your flesh been pierced with the conjure of binding. The full flower is now mine," he said.

Tied to my stomach, the visa flashed with ruby light, and I knew I couldn't let it say the line three times. The vial of my blood felt warm even through the battle glove. "The full flower is now mine," it said a second time.

Pain froze my muscles, paralyzing me, the blood arrested in my veins. I heard myself gurgle as the conjure in the spur stopped my breath. I crushed the vial in my palm and slid the tanto's edge in the blood-soaked glove. With a single thrust, I took the beast through the throat. His grip eased and I inhaled, chanting, "Mage in battle, mage in dire, seraphs, come with holy fire."

Forcas dropped me and I landed on Malashe-el, even as I ripped the spur amulet from my side, tucked it into my boot, and drew my sword. Smoke billowed up around me.

Over my head, Forcas roared, a lion's roar. I rolled across the tunnel, leaving splatters of blood from the wound in my side, pulling the walker into a crevice with me as I called mage in dire again. Still nothing happened. "Like being held in the grip of a Major Darkness isn't dire enough?" I croaked to the heavens. I looked at my side, but that wound wasn't sacrifice; it was battle. I picked a scar that looked like it might open easily.

"Inadequate," a familiar voice belled, closer now, audible. I blinked away the smoke, turned, and saw the Mistress far below me in a cavern, her seraph trapped above her, on top of the scarlet cage that imprisoned her. Zadkiel, only feet below me, was burned to the bone, his legs wrapped in chains, dragonets attached at his waist, sucking and engorged. The seraph held neither sword nor shield, a thing I had never heard of. When in battle, the weapons were said to be part of them, as much an appendage as a leg or hand. Amethyst's seraph face was turned to me. "To reach us you must offer much blood. Much blood."

"So I'm the sucker after all," I said. When it came to the High Host, other supernats always had been. Behind me, Forcas stepped closer, its footsteps vibrating the rocky ground. I dropped the daywalker and darted along a ledge above the Mistress' cell, holding my elbow against the wound in my side. I checked the map in the hilt and saw that while there were numerous channels leading to the deepest prison, this doorway was the only way in. I had no way out. *I won't live through this anyway.*

Lifting my left wrist, I sliced the sleeve of the dobok. With a deeper slash, I opened the artery at my elbow. Mage-blood gushed, drenching Zadkiel. One dragonet lifted its teeth away and spit at me, a snake hiss through bloody fangs.

I jumped toward the trap, falling to my knees in the sticky red adhesive that buried the seraph's feet. "I sacrifice myself for Zadkiel and the Mistress," I said. "I sacrifice myself for Zadkiel and the Mistress." I had lost blood from the wound in my side and my throat injury, and my blood pressure dropped fast. I fell forward, my face sticking in the red snare. The trap smelled of old blood. Like Mole

Man's blood. Like Lucas. The huge clawed feet of another beast landed beside me. "I sacrifice myself for Zadkiel and the Mistress," I murmured, my lips touching the trap made of blood. "Mage in battle, mage in dire, seraphs, come with holy fire," I whispered. "Mage in dire. Raziel. . . ."

Far below, I met the Mistress' eyes. "Help him," she commanded. If I'd had breath, I might have laughed. Instead I managed to turn my face.

Zadkiel was locked in mortal combat with Forcas, now a lion-headed beast bulging with muscle and radiating Darkness, its body strong, scaled, and crested with horns. Winged dragonets were wrapped around the seraph's leg. Forcas reared back and drove its lion fangs into Zadkiel's throat, the bloody chain on its neck clinking.

Tears of Taharial. All this for nothing. I was dying, and no help had come for my sacrifice. But then, I was soulless. What more could I expect? With my last breath, I smelled Lucas' blood, blood that had been used in the creation of the beasts, the cell, and the chain Forcas wore. My vision telescoped into tiny holes.

The scarlet, spherical cage beneath me undulated, as if hit by a great force. A foot stepped near my head, sinking into the red adhesive. Strands leaped up and wrapped around the crimson battle boots. "I hear, little mage," Raziel's voice called, ringing like bronze bells. "I am here, as I promised, in life and battle and love." His hand rested for a moment on my spine, fingers hot against my chilling skin. At his touch, strength flowed into me. My body shuddered hard. My lungs found a breath and vision expanded. I could see. His hand lifted, and I heard the crash of fighting over my body, swords clashing. Raziel screamed his battle cry. Hot, acidic blood splattered over my body, burning through my cloak and dobok. I smelled sulfur and brimstone, and chocolate and blood. Lust and battle-lust twined and rose up in me.

"Now," the Mistress belled, *"now."* Her lavender eyes caressed me, the soft purple eyes of the cobra that had come to me; that had drowned me. "Use the *otherness.* Use it as you used my wheels. As you did once before."

There wasn't time to tell her I didn't know how. I

opened mage-sight and a mind-skim, the blended scan. The world took on strange hues and scents and textures. The *otherness* was there as well. Hooking a metaphysical finger in it, I slid sideways, outside of my body, my world moving with a whoosh of sensation. I rose to my knees and inspected my physical remains, which still hurt on a distant level, but the pain was growing more remote. I looked at my elbow in this not-here body. It wasn't cut, but my feet were still trapped in the red ooze. Interesting. I felt my heart beat, then nothing for a long moment. Even with Raziel's touch, I was dying. *Blood loss. The spur.*

A beat. If I cut myself free of the glue, would I fall off of the sphere or restick?

I was dead anyway, I reminded myself. Which really sucked big-time. But at the same time, I was still alive. Sorta. Since I didn't have a soul, I figured that meant I had about a minute to help Zadkiel and Raziel before my consciousness vanished, yet I had a feeling that nothing was the same in this odd reality, not even time. My otherness body still held two swords. Using the shortsword, blinking to reconcile the two divergent worldviews, I cut through the strands that held my feet, and then through the strands imprisoning Raziel. He saw me in both places and blinked once, as if startled.

Screaming his battle cry, he spun away. With a scent of ozone, lightning bolts flashed from his hands and thundered into the foul trap. The rank smell of Darkness burning and the smell of singed seraph flesh filled my nostrils. Below me, my body lay prone in the mire. Still dying. I had a moment to feel sorry for myself; I hadn't wanted to end this way.

Swords swinging, I raced to the seraphs. Raziel fought dragonets: one with its fangs buried in his hip, its legs clawing in my seraph's thigh and calf; another with its fangs in the juncture of his shoulder and neck. Seraph blood ran in rivers, and the dragonets absorbed each drop. Zadkiel fought Forcas, taking sword blows to his forearms, still secured by dragonets and the red trap. With three slashes, I cut through a beast on Zadkiel's leg; clean swipes that missed seraph flesh yet cleaved the Darkness in quarters. Instantly, it repaired itself.

"Use blood," the Mistress murmured. "The sacrifice of blood and life defeats evil."

"I'm soulless. What good is the blood of a mage?" When she didn't answer, I flipped the shortsword and repierced the wound that wasn't there over my left elbow. On the surface below my feet, *my heart beat*. In the otherness, blood that was more than blood spurted from my arm into the air. I directed it over my blade, flipped it, and cut through the Darkness in a long arc, the crimson blade glowing with mage-life. I whirled the sword and cut again, slicing through the dragonet. Screaming, it fell away. I took the others as quickly, their bodies flopping on the red web.

Startled, Zadkiel looked at me. His face was burned, wings leathery and crusted over with scabs, leaking from the nevus, drained nearly powerless. But his eyes still glowed with holy light. Forcas embraced him, fangs in Zadkiel's spine, its body huge, dwarfing the seraph. With my bloody blade, I stabbed the beast's calf. Forcas reared back, pulling its fangs free. Its mane of horns fluttered in an unseen breeze. I twisted my blade from it. Blood spurted over me and through me.

I aimed my bleeding arm up between the fangs, into its white maw. On the surface of the trap, *my heart beat,* a thump of life and power. My lifeblood pulsed into Forcas' pale, bloodless maw, a gush of sacrifice. Raziel screamed my name. The Darkness pulled the chain from its neck and swiped it through Zadkiel's blood.

Zadkiel hit Forcas' mouth closed with his elbow. I flicked the tanto into his palm, and he drove the blade up from its jaw through the top of its head. In a single liquid motion, Zadkiel bent and retrieved the sword and shield at his feet, seraph-steel swinging. Wrist sure and strong, he cleaved Forcas in two. In the place of otherness, the pieces fell, thrashing like snakes.

The sword cut through it again. Screams echoed in the cavern. The beast looped and spiraled, a writhing coil, trying to reknit. Trying to heal. One snakelike segment flipped high, red chain links catching the light as it landed on Raziel and slithered down his body.

With a flip of his wrist, Zadkiel sent its other parts spiraling away into the dark in different directions. He whirled, seeing the sphere, the Mistress chained within, and me. When I looked for the section of Forcas that wore the linked chain, it was gone.

That was bad. I knew that. But more dragonets were coming, a swarm of the snaky, insectoid beasts. Raziel was wrapped with dragonets, a dozen or more latched to his body, his flesh burned and scored, smoking. Zadkiel hacked at others.

My sight was dimming again, growing tighter, spear points of images. "Raziel," I whispered, and held out my arm to him. "Blood of sacrifice." For a fractured moment, his eyes met mine, filled with fear and battle-lust and a strange kind of tenderness. He extended his blade and I dribbled blood on it. With the death-blessed blade, he attacked the dragonets, killing one, then another, calling his battle cry.

I turned to the Mistress. *"Dying sucks, you know that?"* I thought at her. *My heart beat* a final thump, a soft, rubbing sound, tissue against tissue, nearly bloodless. Slowly, I fell back toward my body, seeing the otherness world in slow motion, with crystal clarity. Seeing the river of lava flowing below the otherness, scintillating with lights. In both realities, Forcas was gone. In one reality, two dragonets still attacked.

Sword hacking, Zadkiel tossed the attackers away and tore through the red adhesive bars of the cage. "Amethyst," he crooned. A long arm scooped her up, the other slicing through the chains binding her. They dropped with a clang of cold demon-iron. "Amethyst, my cherub," he breathed, cradling her. As she touched him, his flesh reknit, flowing across his bones with a patina of blue and lavender light. Feathers that had been burned away budded and spiraled out, the white feathers of a kylen child. The deeply scored chain marks across her body radiated gently, healing. I caught myself on my arms, balancing over my physical body. In both realities—the otherness, as well as in the human world—Forcas was still gone. Dead? Had we truly defeated him? If so, maybe my death was worth it.

"My mate," the cherub whispered. "My flame." Her wings unfurled, several sets of them aligned along her body, each smaller than the seraph's. Her many eyes stared at Zadkiel. "The Dragon comes. We must away."

The Dragon. . . . Ahh. I remembered the links of chain smeared with the blood of two seraphs. Three including Barak. *Does a Watcher count?* Vibrations thrummed through the crimson net like footsteps. Like a heartbeat.

Zadkiel spread his wings. They were covered with pale down, white at the root, soft violet at the tips. Though only partially healed, he was beautiful. The two together would be my last sight—only pinpoints of vision left. My elbows began to give way. "Bring her," the Mistress said, turning several eyes to me.

"No *time*. She gave herself for you," Zadkiel said. "She will be remembered."

The red threads beneath me thrummed faster. My sight was dimming. Numbing cold spread through me and I settled into my body. I was cold. So cold. In some small part of my faltering mind, I thought, *This is a bad way to die.*

"Save her!" Raziel screamed, his beautiful voice raw.

"Quickly, my love. Bring her," Amethyst agreed. "*Time* is enough."

Zadkiel shouted with frustration, scooped me up in his other arm, and threw me over his shoulder. A tendril of . . . something . . . grabbed my ankle and whipped away, smeared with my dying blood. If I hadn't been dead, I'd have laughed.

Chapter 28

⚸

I came to on the surface, surrounded by the smell of blood. I was lying on ice, cradled in my filthy, bloody cloak, shivering. On the night wind I smelled seraphs, mage-blood, decaying devil-spawn, daywalker blood, and the overriding reek of the blood of a Major Darkness. And, oh, yes, *seraphs*. Heat wisped through me. I stuttered a laugh and dragged air into my lungs. They made an awful sucking sound, like wet rubber being pulled apart. I was alive. I was pretty sure of it. Hurt too bad to be dead. I coughed hard, the sound like leather ripping, causing a shocking pain through my ribs.

"She laughs. I like her laughter," Amethyst tinkled.

The moon winked over the shoulder of a seraph. Zadkiel lifted his head from my stomach. His lips had been touching me. Healing me. Mage-heat strengthened, delicate fire in my veins. He placed my amulets on my bare stomach, and the heat dimmed. "Can you control it?" he asked.

I considered his question, but before I could answer, another did, his voice like baritone bells. "Yes. I believe so."

Zadkiel laughed, heat burning in his eyes. "I hope so, Raziel. I have no *time* to satisfy the cravings of a mage in heat."

The unexpected laugh and the odd emphasis on the word *time* resonated in my mind for a moment before sliding away in exhaustion. Zadkiel's face filled my vision. "Be safe, little mage. I thank you for the return of my mate, the

Mistress, Holy Amethyst. Complete her healing, Raziel, and take her to her home. Wait there for us. We will come soon. The Dragon is striking. Battle has commenced as he seeks freedom."

"Mate?" I croaked, the first thing I ask after being brought back to life. Weird.

"Not as you think of mates," the cherub said, her voice like tiny bells in a night breeze off the Gulf, amusement in the thought. "But purposes met and satisfied, even when one of us is away from the Most High, alone in the river of *time,* on earth."

I remembered the river of lava in the otherness. That river?

Zadkiel placed a warm stone on my stomach where his lips had been. "For your prayer, your incantations, your blood, and your sacrifice; for all these, I thank you. And for your willingness to gift us your life, though it was not needed in the end. I thank you."

I didn't think it politic to mention that he had been willing to leave me to die in the pit while some big papa Dragon came looking for supper.

"Thanks be to the wisdom and compassion of Amethyst. You are healed," he finished. "Be blessed. Be at peace." He swiveled his head to his mate and said, "Call your wheels." Amethyst looked to the heavens with all her eyes and sang one perfect note of calling, a tone so beautiful nothing could resist it. I tried to rise from the ground where I lay to reach her. Pain arched through me, paralyzing. *This was healed?*

With Amethyst cradled against his chest, Zadkiel, the Right Hand of the ArchSeraph Michael, spread his patchily feathered, burned wings and gave a single mighty thrust. Wind like a tornado, scented with mint and pepper, swirled around me. And they were gone. I was left, cold and drained, on the frozen and cracked ice at the lip of the pit of the hellhole. Blackness closed in around me.

Pain woke me. Two balls of flame, plasma-bright, zipped from my stomach with a sizzle of energy and danced in the air, blinding me. I closed my eyes against the glare.

Warmth trickled into my bones from the stone on my
torso. I'd been touched by two seraphs in the same night.
Three if one counted Barak. *Did* one count a Watcher? Yet
I still felt no mage-heat. A green flight feather poked my
thigh. I had forgotten about the gift. At my waist, my
amulets glowed, giving me strength. On my belly was a seraph stone. *I'll never be able to swear that way again, not
without a chuckle.*

Slowly I sat up, stiff muscles creaking. My injured arm
was healed, another ugly scar marking my skin. The wound
in my side was no longer bleeding, but the pain when I
moved was electric, stealing my breath. The scent of battle
clung to me, incubating in the warmth of my body. The
stenches of smoke, old blood, and death roiled out of my
clothing, nauseating me. I reeked. I found a bottle of water
in my cloak pocket and finished it, before attaching the
seraph stone to my necklace. I thought it might be a black
agate, and it felt hot against my fingers.

Overhead, a sickle-shaped moon rested its lower point
on a distant mountain. The sun was a golden glow in the
east. Morning. I had survived the night, underground.

"Hours have passed as you healed," Raziel said. "There
is great battle in the heavens."

In mage-sight I found him, a faint glow perched in the
limbs of a tall spruce, green branches framing his scarlet
radiance. His crimson wings were tightly furled, wrist tips
high over his head. His cloak hung loose, moving in the
slight breeze. He was a bright ruby hue of energy, eyes like
gems. I felt his gaze all the way to my toes. "Amethyst is
wounded. She is failing. You must relinquish her wheels."
He tilted his head, a half smile hovering on his lips and I
could have sworn he was curious. Seraphs are never curious. Never.

"I don't have her wheels to give up." I shifted on the
frozen ground. In a single heartbeat, everything changed.

A roar shivered the air. Forcas crashed from the mouth
of the pit. The beast had been in pieces last time I saw it.
What did it take to kill a Major Darkness?

Forcas was carrying Eli in one clawed hand, Durbarge in
the other, and Malashe-el was hooked over its shoulder,

impaled on a horn. Neither man looked so good. The daywalker looked dead.

Light blazed. Raziel opened his wings and stepped off
the limb, hands throwing. Lightning hit the ground in a
brilliant blast. Thunder boomed, eardrum-cracking, deafening. Raziel rocketed toward the Darkness, wings outspread, gathering the lightning. Thunderheads built
overhead. The wind roared, buffeting me where I lay.

Light illuminated the cleared area, shining from Raziel's
battle armor. Armor and sword hadn't been there only a
moment before. Electricity crackled along the red-gold
plate. His face was set in stern lines, his eyes glowing with
battle-lust. Instinctively, I rolled under the overhang of a
boulder. Too weak to rise, I curled tight, making myself
small.

The seraph and Forcas met in the mouth of the hellhole
with a crash. The humans fell and rolled close to me, Eli
facedown, Durbarge looking at the sky. His eye was open
and didn't blink. His patch was gone, the empty socket
black in the night. Malashe-el rolled down the incline and
landed below me in a heap of tangled limbs. The Dark and
the Light fought sword to sword, blades ringing.

Checking my weapons, I found the walking stick sword
restored to its sheath beside the tanto that I had last seen
in Forcas' jaw. Two throwing blades had been left in the
corridor outside the Mistress' prison. The silver-hilted
sword I had worn over my spine now belonged to Barak. I
had only my two blades and a single throwing knife,
amulets, and a feather, which I may or may not be able to
use. Ducky.

I tested the amulets on the necklace tied to my waist and
I found them half empty, or worse, drained to uselessness.
The seraph stone felt like a null, a stone with potential
power, but sealed, locked away. Beyond the ledge, lightning flashed and hit the ground near me. Dissipating energies flayed my body. Eli yelped nearby. If I'd been human
I would have been hurt too. Instead, power flowed into my
amulets, restoring them. But not enough.

Through the mountain beneath me, I felt familiar
tremors, regular and evenly spaced, like footsteps. I re-

membered the Dragon who had been imprisoned by Mole Man's sacrifice and blood, remembered the chain drenched with seraph blood, the links made with the blood of Mole Man's progeny. Made with Lucas' blood. Raziel had mentioned a war in the heavens. My muzzy brain put it together. *Crack the Stone of Ages. Forcas' boss, the Dragon, is loose.*

The last time it was free, it took dozens of seraphs and the self-sacrifice of a human to chain it. I closed my eyes. The Dragon was loose, the Mistress was wounded, and someone seemed to think I had her wheels. *I can't do this. I don't know how.* But I had to.

I gathered myself, seeking my center, that calm place of nothingness in my mind. And I reached down, below me, into the rock heart of the mountain. Ancient energies reached back to me; the might of stone, cold and hard and without remorse. I pulled them in, fast, storing them in my blood, my muscles, my nerves, and bones.

Drawing on the strength of the Trine, I opened the blended scan, feeling a sickening lurch as the *otherness* caught me up, the world and my stomach surging drunkenly. Through my torn and acid-pocked dobok, light flared, yellow and dark blue. I pushed away the tattered cloth and pulled the pear-shaped citrine nugget and the sapphire owl out, the wild-mage-stones glowing. Through the otherness, they scintillated like small suns. I touched the owl and felt the otherness settle as power trickled into me from the sapphire.

I had a moment, a moment in *time,* to study the sensation. Finger on the amulet, I saw movement, the river of energy, of Light. It flowed beneath me, through me, picking me up and floating me along the current. It meandered through its flat plain: the river of time, I was pretty sure. Whatever that meant.

In the world, lightning hit the ground again, a huge burst. I felt my body jerk as the power crackled through me. But it wasn't important. Almost as an afterthought, I directed the energies into the amulets at my waist. I felt Barak's feather shimmer with power.

Swords clashed, seraph-steel and demon-iron. I smelled

fresh seraph blood. The footsteps of the Dragon were
growing nearer as his might pounded the mountain I was
drawing upon. The earth quaked. Dust rained down from
the boulder, covering me. Beside me, the river flowed. In
it were stones and boulders and eddies—incidents and
people?

From the otherness, I studied the entrance to the hellhole; sickly yellow-orange-reddish light emanated from
the rocks and from the ground. The stone of the mountain
itself had been polluted, a malevolence much more powerful than the first time I saw it, as if my ability to see it was
growing. Or as if it was gaining power. *Tears of Taharial,
I'm pulling that into me.* With a wrench, I cut off the draw
of power. Something was coming. Something big. Fear
tightened my body.

Relinquish her wheels, Raziel had said. I recalled the
huge purple cobra that had entered my conjuring circle,
the snake made of eyes, the snake that had filled my lungs.
A snake that was part of Amethyst's wheels, I was sure of
it. I concentrated on the purple eyes that had nearly
drowned me, remembering their concentrated stare.
"Come," I said.

Overhead, in the otherness, thunder boomed, a concus-
sion that knocked Raziel and Forcas to their knees. Hanging above us was a massive, interconnected ring of
lavender stones, faceted amethyst hoops the size of a football field pulsing. It looked like a gyroscope turned on its
side, concentric wheels within wheels, each turning its own
way, each releasing mists of blue plasma. And on one end,
a golden nosecone, its navcone, bursting with Light. It was
Amethyst's wheels, her vast crystalline ship, healed and
whole.

The stone sang, a single note of joy and hope and life.
And it opened its eyes, eyes on every square inch of its
lavender structure, dark purple eyes, hundreds of them,
thousands of them, all looking at me. The song of the wheel
changed key and hummed a softer tune, an audible caress.

"Crap," a voice murmured nearby.

Instantly, I was back on the Trine. Smoke, fire, and a
ghastly reek of death whipped in the icy wind. A golden

rim of sun glanced over the mountains to the east and cast long rays onto the world below. Shadows still gripped the valleys, streambeds, and Mineral City. Below me was a ledge of rock; above me was another. I was still sandwiched between them. I blinked and remembered to breathe, surprised that I still could.

Eli held me, our bodies wedged beneath the boulder edge. In his fist shone the healing amulet I had given him. And in this reality too, hanging in the air before us, was Amethyst's wheels. As one, the eyes blinked, crooning. "Saints' balls," Eli whispered. I laughed brokenly. His arms tightened about me.

In the dawn sky far overhead, lightning flashed, thunder rumbled. A battle was taking place there, in the upper layers of the earth's atmosphere, in the here–not here. In the small, nearly level space, Raziel and Forcas were locked in combat, bodies writhing and straining as they wrestled. Below us, the earth shook. The big, bad Dragon was dangerously close.

Chapter 29

☦

Two Flames zipped under the ledge and did their little dance along our bodies, whizzing and burning their way through us and back out. "That hurts like heck, but it's better than being dead," Eli growled. "Ouch, quit that." The Flames obeyed and converged together, hovering before me, as if awaiting orders. It hurt my eyes to look at them.

"If I ask you questions, can you answer in English?" I asked them.

"Yessss," they said, their voices a strange sound, as if bells were being rung by a current of electricity.

"Who fights overhead, and who's winning?"

"Zzzadkiel and Holy Amethyssst battle the Dragon who wasss chained. Without her wheel, Darknessss winsss." As they spoke, the sky darkened. Clouds boiled, huge thunderclouds reaching for the heavens.

"The same Dragon I feel coming up from the deeps?" I asked. I looked up at the wheels, and gripped the sapphire owl. Taking a chance that the owl allowed increased communication to the wheels, I said, "Save the Mistress." And they were gone. The air concussed, rushing to fill the vacuum. A feeling like icicles bored into me. Eli tensed with shared pain. Careful not to look at the remaining Flames straight on, I said, "I don't guess you could find some more of you guys?" Flames popped away. The icicles in my blood shattered and I shivered hard. Once could be coincidence. Not twice.

"Crap in a bucket," Eli said into my ear, his voice hoarse with exhaustion and pain. "What the hell are you? Never mind. That can wait. This big evil sucker I can feel coming up from the pit—it can be in two places at once?"

Not knowing how to explain what I didn't understand, and still dealing with my reactions to having the wheels and the Flames do what I wanted—at least I assumed they were doing it—I said, "I think so. Yeah."

"Then let's you and me just sit tight here under this rock until the war is over." He pulled me closer to his body, jarring my side. I hissed with pain. "What?" he asked.

I eased his arm away from me and wriggled over, pulling up the edge of the dobok top and peering at my side. I expected to see scar tissue or a healing wound. Instead, I found a blackened puncture site, deep enough to bury my finger to the second knuckle. The edges around the cavity were raised and red, and pus trickled from a spot that had broken open.

"That's gotta hurt," Eli said. Master of understatement.

"Yeah. It does." Not far from us, Forcas and Raziel rolled on the ground. I didn't know what would happen if Forcas completed binding me to him. I looked at the miner, his face so close I was cross-eyed to focus. "Can you get his eyes with your flamethrower?"

Eli ducked his head to see under the ledge, watching the fight, considering. "And you'll be doing what?"

"Slitting his throat to keep him from completing a binding." That is, if I can find the energy. But I didn't say it.

"Binding? You?" He glanced at my wound and I nodded. "How close is it to making you his?"

You are mine. "Three words."

"Girl, is there any kind of trouble you can't find?" Sighing, Eli said, "Let's go then." I forced my body into motion and together we crawled out from under the ledge. I was so tired, so drained, I had to pull on the Trine for the energy to move, for the energy to breathe. I had to. But I felt the pollution of its power. The mountain was changing. Using it could change me, as using the amethyst power had changed me. Or it could simply kill me. But I couldn't

make it on my own, and my seraph was too busy to help
me right now.

Eli spun his flamethrower forward, checked the appara-
tus with a critical eye, cocked it, and made eye contact with
me. "Come in behind me." In concert, we ran, me barely
able to keep up with the human. Eli moved like the wind
through trees, like the Gulf over the beach when the tide
came in, like sunlight over stone. I pulled my blades and
stumbled behind.

Yet, even tired, we fought together as if it were a
dance—move forward, spray with flame, back away,
move forward, strike, back away—ganging up on the
Darkness. Raziel was locked in combat with it; we hit it
from behind and the side as the two Powers wrestled on
the ground. In two feints, Eli had blinded Forcas, the
Darkness roaring his fury and pain, his claws scoring Raziel's sides, rocking back his head. I raced in mage-fast
and slit the beast's throat, silencing his screams. *I'm safe.*
Tears flooded my eyes, leaving me limp with relief.

Overhead, the wheels reappeared with the same concus-
sive force, the boom throwing Eli and me to the ground.
For the first time in long hours, I felt a spark of hope, instantly shattered. Forcas threw off Raziel and rolled at me,
demon-fast. Blind, he still knew where I was.

From the side, a hand gripped my leg, bowling me to
safety. I landed hard against the sloped rock ground. Before me, my silver-hilted sword glittering in a two-handed
grip, his wings partially healed, was Barak. Behind him, in
the mouth of the hellhole, stood Joseph Barefoot, breathing hard, Tomas slung over his shoulder fireman-fashion.
He eased his friend to the earth and joined the Allied
One in hacking at Forcas. Raziel swept back into the fray
from overhead, wings buffeting dust into abrading spirals,
his blood sprinkling the ground.

Eli pulled me back to safety and left, to reappear pulling
Durbarge by both arms. The assey was still breathing, fast
and shallow. Blood trickled from his mouth to the ground.

Over the clearing, the wheels rocked gently, humming,
its many eyes on me. In the center, the ship secured around

her, sat the cherub, her four faces blazing with anger. She pointed at me with one demi-wing. "You have stolen my wheels. Return them to me!"

"You stole something from that big purple mama?" Eli asked.

I dragged myself to my knees, my blades clinking on the cold stone. An icy wind was blowing from the thunderclouds, turbulent with battle and seraph wings. "I think I bound her wheels to me. And I don't know how to unbind them."

"Bound a cherub's wheels?" he said incredulously. When I didn't answer, Eli gripped my shoulders and shook me. "You know what that makes you?"

I met his amber eyes, too tired to read what I saw there. "It makes me dead, if I don't figure out how to unbind them."

Eli laughed, the sound coarse and disbelieving. "The EIH has been looking for a mage like you for decades. You're an omega mage."

"I'm not." Not that I knew what an omega mage was.

"Tell the wheels to kill Forcas," he said. "Tell them!"

I looked at the eyes overhead and said, "Kill Forcas." When nothing happened, I pinched the owl, repeating the command. Again nothing. I looked at the owl, to find it totally drained, an inert, poor-quality semiprecious stone. Despair stole over me. "I don't know what I'm doing," I whispered. I was a half-trained neomage with pretty baubles.

"The Flames did what you wanted."

I shrugged. That was different. Wasn't it? Fatigue caught up with me in a single moment and I collapsed to the ground in a boneless sprawl. Even with the Trine to draw on, I was worn out. On my waist, the amulets shone weakly, nearly depleted, wasting their last energies keeping me alive. From my side, pain radiated, Dark tendrils caressing my heart. Nearby, Forcas hid behind a small shield, its limbs exposed to the blades of attackers, but its throat healing. It met my eyes and . . . *pulled* . . . at me. My energies flagged again.

Suddenly I knew; if Forcas died, I would die too. He was

draining my energies through the wound in my side, using
my life force to fight Raziel. I chuckled softly at the irony.
After all this, my life was forfeit to a Darkness. Knowing I
had no choice, knowing I was about to die, I touched the
citrine and the sapphire to the visa and my prime amulet,
transferring power between the amulets.

Once again, I fell into the otherness. The world slid
sidewise sickeningly. I rolled to the side and retched,
throwing up the water I had drunk. In the otherness vision, the wheels overhead pulsed with life. I looked up at
them, seeing Amethyst in the center, her lion face staring
at me, her mouth wide with shock and fury. "Give me
back my wheels," she roared.

In the place of the otherness, the river of lava flowed beneath me, so close I could feel its heat. In the otherness, I
saw the stream of energy flowing from me to the beast,
draining me. I reached up with my finger and *twisted*. "Oh
wheels," I sang softly. "Kill Forcas," I told them. "And seal
the hellhole."

"Yes," the wheels sang. "We will drain him to nothingness until the Last Day."

"No!" Amethyst shouted.

A shaft of rainbow light shot from the wheels. Only as it
fired did I understand the cherub's cry. She too was linked
to the beast through a torrent of stolen energy. She too
would be drained, following Forcas into nothingness unto
the Last Day. "Stop!" I shouted to the wheels as purple
light speared down. But the eyes were turned away and
didn't respond.

From the mouth of the lair came a bloodthirsty roar.

Chapter 30

༡

The river of energy and Light flowed beneath me, through me, floating me along the current. In the world of humans, lightning hit the ground again, a huge burst. My body jerked as the power lashed through me. Eli yelped. Almost as an afterthought, I directed the energies passing through the stone beneath me into the amulets at my waist.

"You use the omega-sight." Amethyst, her eagle face cold, watched me in the otherness. "I have done this. I showed you how. I will be punished." She bowed her head.

Below her, swords clashed, seraph-steel and demon-iron. Forcas, blinded and bloodied, thrust up through the violet light of the wheels' weapon and stabbed Raziel. Bright blood gushed. Raziel placed a hand over his wound. Slowly he dropped into the river, landing on his knees, the water-lava chest high. The weapon firing at Forcas ceased. The footsteps of the Dragon shook the ground with an earthquake. Dust rained down, pattering on me, and cracks opened in the earth. But beside me, the river flowed. The river of *time*? I didn't care what he called it, Raziel was dying. "You can save them," the wheels said plaintively. "You can save them all. Join with Raziel."

Amethyst shrieked in fear. "Punished. I will be punished."

"Blasphemy. Mages cannot do this," Raziel said, his voice weak.

"Not blasphemy," the wheels sang. "Hope. If a seraph and a mage join their prime amulets, they become one spirit, as the seraph and my cherub became one."

"We mate, I die," I said.

"Not mate body to body. That you may not do," the wheels said. "But merge."

From the entrance to the hellhole, from the rocks and the ground, emanated a suffocating yellow-orange light, the heart of the mountain itself, polluted, malevolent. *Death and plagues.* Whatever was coming was something big. Fear tightened my body.

"Throw off your amulets," the wheels cajoled.

I looked at myself in the otherness. Every bone ached. Every muscle, every sinew, every half-healed wound. Even my blood ached, what there was of it. The wound in my side was a swarm of writhing worms and my life force flowed out through it to Forcas.

"We can try," Raziel said. Floating in the river of time, he gripped an amulet, one that looked much like a prime, and tore it from a thong around his neck. I ripped my prime amulet off, flipped it around, and pressed it into his palm.

Both worlds fell away. Light, sound, smells, textures blasted at me, smothered me, flailed me like barbed chains, rolled me like water, and trapped me there, dying.

I fell. And fell. A thought flashed in my awareness. What had Forcas said when he held me in his claw? Something about the *whole flower.* Rose? My twin?

The otherness crashed around me. Raziel pulled me beneath his wing, against his side. Surprised, he murmured into my ear, "A third place, but not a place. A here–not here."

I had no idea what he meant. I was too tired to care.

Raziel was a crimson flame in the lava of everything and nothing. Standing, he drew his sword, shouting a battle cry, a note of true sound, a gong of challenge in a language I couldn't understand. I saw the tones as they left his throat, floated a moment, and entered the river. Turning my head, I saw Forcas in the real world. It bent its body in a violent arc, and buried its fangs in Raziel's neck, clinging to him.

In this third reality, a netting of conjure emanated from
Forcas through the air to me, like the web of a spider. A
vein of the web traveled up to the Mistress, holding the
ship and cherub in a conjured snare. I understood what the
new sight was revealing. I had called them all to me. I was
killing them all.

In the otherness, flowing down the river toward me,
came another Darkness. A monstrous thing, so huge it
blotted out a third of the nothingness-sky. Around its neck
was a glowing chain and, where the links touched, blue
light flared, but instead of harming the beast, it gave the
Darkness power, pulling power from Raziel, from
Amethyst, from Zadkiel. From Barak. It drew power from
me. The chain smelled of Lucas, of the blood of Mole Man.
It smelled of Uncle Lem, my foster father, of Gramma, and
of three seraphs.

Raziel hissed a breath and we understood together,
mind-to-mind, *knowing*, what was happening. The Dragon
wore the chain Forcas had forged, the chain made with the
blood of Mole Man's progeny and smeared with all of our
blood. Forcas had given it to his Master, the antichain to
the one that had bound the Dragon in Mole Man's battle.
With this weapon the Dragon was freeing itself.

From somewhere, I heard Eli whisper, "Oh, crap, crap,
crap."

The wild mage-stones on my chest vibrated, humming
with the flowing energies. Before me, from the surface of
the river, a finger of lavender energy rose from the water-
lava-energy flow. A long, sinuous snake of power with purple eyes, many eyes, hundreds of them. A snake body
composed of eyes. I understood. It was a vision of the life
force of the wheels. Amethyst's wheels. They were alive.
Sentient. Separate from the cherub. "Yes. Your wheels," it
sang. "Yours. Call us."

Around the wheels Flames whirled, flashing. Seraphs
came toward us, moving fast through the river. Zadkiel and
Cheriour. One—Barak?—was silver. Another was emerald green, one was golden, another was black as jet. Inside
the wheels, Amethyst lay covered with her wings, her eyes
all closed. Malashe-el lay on her chest, crying, his fists

clenched in her feathers. In the place–no place of the otherness, I touched the snake with my sword and pointed at
the mouth of the hellhole. From it a bright orange light is-
sued, light filled with shadows and Dark things that
writhed. "Seal it up," I said.

"This beast has great power," the wheels sang to me. "I
cannot do this thing alone." The seraphs all watched me,
waiting.

"Seal it up," I said to them, not really sure what I was
asking.

As one, they all drew swords and flew into the hellhole.

"Breathe, Thorn," I heard Eli say. "Saints' balls. The seraph is dying too."

In front of me, Minor Flames danced. I watched them
from the aspect of death, lying on the stone of the Trine.
Behind me, Forcas was dying, and he was taking Mistress
Amethyst, Raziel, and me with him. I recognized the trap
as a version of the one that had imprisoned the cherub for
a century. I figured I had one chance in a thousand that it
could be broken by Minor Flames. Maybe one in a million.
Or the anticonjure might kill us. Or I could die before I got
done. Or hell would freeze over and I'd do it right by
chance.

"Can you see the conjure that binds the cherub, the
wheels, the seraph, and me to Forcas?" I asked the Flames.

They bobbed up and down. "Yesss," they hissed, the
clean, pure hiss of fire.

"Can you . . ." I envisioned a saw composed of blue
flames, diamond-bladed, cutting the threads of the Dark
conjure. "Can you do this?"

"Yoursss to command," they said together.

"Do it," I said. The Flames divided into three batches of
five—surely not an auspicious number—and attacked the
incantation.

On Earth, Eli cradled me against his chest. Nearby, Durbarge rolled slowly to his knees, his face ashen with blood
loss. I had meant to kill him, I remembered, to save Thaddeus Bartholomew. Too late. We were all dead anyway. He
stumbled across the broken ground to the rocket launcher
that Rickie had dropped what seemed eons ago.

To Joseph Barefoot the assey said, "If we can fire these shoulder-mounted rockets into the hellhole, the nuclear warheads might seal it up."

"Nukes?" Joseph said. "Mighta been nice to know we were carrying some real firepower."

"Yeah," Durbarge said, his voice so tired it whistled on his breath. "Yeah. Well. Last-ditch weapons to stop that thing from getting free."

Joseph wiped a hand across his face and it came away bloody. "The Indian always gets it in the end. Just don't expect me to yell Geronimo."

"No," I tried to say. My lips moved, papery against one another.

Durbarge looked at Eli. "Stay down. Get Thorn back down the mountain in one piece. I don't know exactly what she is, but she's something important. Call the person on this card." He handed the miner a business card. "She'll be taken care of."

Overhead, the wheels lurched drunkenly and pulled back from the earth. On the ground, Forcas released Raziel and the seraph dragged himself away. The wheels began firing into the body of the Darkness. I saw Eli turn from the light show and take Durbarge's card, tucking it into a pocket. The assey and Joseph Barefoot, the leader of the EIH, turned and headed toward the lair. From within it, light flashed, and rumbles echoed through the heart of the Trine.

The scents of seraphs filled the air with all things alive and good. I sobbed, the sound smothered by the concussions belowground. My last sight was Durbarge and Joseph, silhouetted by blinding light as they entered the mouth of hell.

Epilogue

✦

I woke in my bed, my entire body aching. This was getting to be a bad habit, waking in bed after nearly dying in battle. But I was pretty sure I was alive.

Audric was stretched beside me, my head on his shoulder. Cradling me, Rupert snored softly, one arm thrown over my waist. A pale sun lighted the loft as dawn brightened the sky. I stretched slowly, trying not to wake them. Rupert rolled over, his back against my thigh. Audric simply opened his eyes and studied me. There were fresh scars across his shoulder and along his neck, scars that matched the claws on the hands of the succubus queen.

"We survived," I said, my voice wispy. "How long was I out this time?"

He gave me the ghost of a smile. "Good thing you got yourself some decent champards. We've guarded you for two days."

Over his damaged shoulder, my seraph appeared. Raziel was in human guise, his face emotionless. But his scent flowed across me like a bakery and flowers. Like a sleeping cat, mage-heat stirred within me. His ruby eyes studied me, considering. "You charged Minor Flames to do your bidding. You commanded seraphs and the wheels of the cherub. You broke the binding of a Major Darkness, saving the cherub Holy Amethyst. Omega Mage," he said formally, the words spoken in caps, like a title. "You are in great danger."

"Of course I am," I said tiredly, rising up on my elbows. "What else."

Beside me Rupert sat up. The covers fell away and I saw that I was wearing an unfamiliar long-sleeved silk nightgown. Its scooped neck had small, buttoned straps that secured my amulet necklace in place. I took a moment to wonder where it came from before Rupert said to Audric and the seraph, "Tell her."

Audric sighed and sat up as well, plumping my pillows behind his back. His dark-skinned chest gleamed in the dull light, crisscrossed with new scars. "Omega Mages have the power to command seraphs in battle. There have been others. None have survived for long."

"Absolute power tends to corrupt absolutely?" I quoted, not liking this at all.

"They were tempted to use the seraphs of the Most High for their own purposes," Raziel said. "They were destroyed. I can save you from such a fate if you desire it." He extended an amulet, a wing-shaped ruby the size of my fist. To humans it would have been priceless. I was afraid of what it meant to a seraph. "You accepted merging with me in the river of time to save us. If you accept a binding with me as well, you will be safe. The seraphs you commanded on the Trine will not touch you." I waited, and he went on. "They will not destroy you, for you will not be allowed to overstep your bounds."

"You'll be bound like me," Audric said. His voice was carefully toneless, but his eyes held a note of warning. "You'll be a slave to the seraph Raziel. As such, the revealer of the rock will have all the power of an Omega Mage."

Which would move him up in seraphic hierarchy. Gotcha. "And if I refuse?" I asked.

"You will be watched."

That didn't sound so bad. Long as I was a good little mage, Big Brother would leave me alone. I thought about my options as the seraph considered me. "Before I decide, will you answer a question about my sister Rose?"

"Yes," the seraph said, his ruby irises glowing softly.

"Is she alive?"

Raziel thought a moment, his face pensive. Slowly he dropped the hand holding the amulet to his side. "She is." He added, "Rose is yet a captive."

Shock whispered through my system at his words. My eyes locked to his, I said carefully, "I refuse the offer of binding and protection at this *time*."

He bowed slightly and said, "I am yours to call, now and always, as I promised, in life and battle and love." Light flashed and he was gone.

Far south, in the New Orleans Enclave, the priestess Lolo raised her head from her conjuring bowl, eyes alight. With a lifted finger, she broke the circle and stilled the musicians. The drum and flute fell silent. The old, old mage took a breath, filling her lungs with the warm, moist heat of the Louisiana air. "Ahhh," she breathed out.

From outside her window, massive wings beat the air, creating sultry eddies. Mage-heat drenched her, her heart fluttering painfully with the surge of want. Pressure, heavier than the weight of decades, constricted her chest. Outside, excited voices raced nearer, but they would not enter without her permission.

Gasping, breathless, suddenly too weak to rise, she watched the doorway as shadows shifted. Her left arm too heavy to lift, she raised her right fingers, holding a branch of lilacs.

Silver hair caught the sunrise as the seraph entered the room and knelt at her side. One hand stroking her forehead, his wings draped over her and to either side for privacy. "My love," he said. "She came. She freed me."

Lolo's eyes widened. Her breath caught. "No," she whispered. She clutched her throat, the lilac falling away.

"Yes," he said, and stood, his smile revealing small, pointed fangs. As the morning sun came through the window, his eyes glowed red.

About the Author

A native of Louisiana, **Faith Hunter** spent her early years on the bayou and rivers, learning survival skills and the womanly arts. She liked horses, dogs, fishing and crabbing much better than girly things. She still does.

In grade school, she fell in love with fantasy and science fiction, reading five books a week and wishing she "could write that great stuff." Faith now shares her life with her Renaissance Man and their dogs in an enclave of their own.

She is currently working on two projects—the Skinwalker series, a current-day, alternate-reality world peopled by vampires, witches, and by Jane Yellowrock, a Cherokee Skinwalker, and the roleplaying game Rogue Mage, based on the world of Thorn St. Croix.

To find out more about Faith, go to www.faithhunter.net.